THE EVER AFTERS

of ENEMIES AND ENDINGS

SHELBY BACH

Simon & Schuster Books for Young Readers
NEW YORK   LONDON   TORONTO   SYDNEY   NEW DELHI

SIMON & SCHUSTER BOOKS FOR YOUNG READERS
An imprint of Simon & Schuster Children's Publishing Division
1230 Avenue of the Americas, New York, New York 10020
This book is a work of fiction. Any references to historical events, real people, or real places are used fictitiously. Other names, characters, places, and events are products of the author's imagination, and any resemblance to actual events or places or persons, living or dead, is entirely coincidental.
Text copyright © 2015 by Shelby Randol Trenkelbach
Cover illustrations copyright © 2015 by Cory Loftis
All rights reserved, including the right of reproduction in whole or in part in any form.
SIMON & SCHUSTER BOOKS FOR YOUNG READERS
is a trademark of Simon & Schuster, Inc.
For information about special discounts for bulk purchases, please contact Simon & Schuster Special Sales at 1-866-506-1949 or business@simonandschuster.com.
The Simon & Schuster Speakers Bureau can bring authors to your live event. For more information or to book an event, contact the Simon & Schuster Speakers Bureau at 1-866-248-3049 or visit our website at www.simonspeakers.com.
Also available in a Simon & Schuster Books for Young Readers hardcover edition
Book design by Chloë Foglia
The text for this book was set in Usherwood.
Manufactured in the United States of America
0516 OFF
First Simon & Schuster Books for Young Readers paperback edition June 2016
2 4 6 8 10 9 7 5 3 1
The Library of Congress has cataloged the hardcover edition as follows:
Bach, Shelby, author.
Of enemies and endings / Shelby Bach.—First edition.
pages cm.—(The Ever Afters ; 4)
Summary: "Rory Landon and her friends are determined to stop the Snow Queen once and for all in this final book in The Ever Afters series!"—Provided by publisher.
ISBN 978-1-4424-9787-0 (hardback)
ISBN 978-1-4424-9788-7 (pbk)
ISBN 978-1-4424-9789-4 (eBook)
[1. Characters in literature—Fiction. 2. Magic—Fiction. 3. Fairy tales—Fiction.
4. Adventure and adventurers—Fiction.] I. Title.
PZ7.B1319Od 2015
[Fic]—dc23
2014040851

To the readers:
One of you named this book;
all of you fueled this story.

And in special memory of Leila,
who died of leukemia this February.
For you, I wish I could have written faster.

The morning before my fourteenth birthday, the witches ambushed us before Mom had a chance to finish her coffee. We were arguing about the usual things.

"The triplets will be here any minute," I said, shoving my cell-phone and my M3 into my carryall's front pocket. Those guys were always a couple minutes late for guard duty. Sometimes they slept through their alarm. It *was* summer. That happened. "Then we can get out of here." I slung on my raincoat. Big heavy drops pattered on the window.

Mom set down her mug and folded her hands carefully. I knew what that meant: I wasn't going to like what she said next. "I've been meaning to talk to you about that, Rory."

Amy didn't even try to break it to me nicely. "No. They're not coming with us today. We're meeting with the play's producers."

"You *need* protection." I reached for my magic combs and reminded myself that it wouldn't do any good to get irritated. They just didn't really understand—not yet.

"They're teenagers." Amy crossed her arms. "It *looks* like we're babysitting them, not the other way around."

"It is beginning to look strange, Rory," Mom said. "Normally, I'm fine with them tagging along with us. I know that it makes you feel better, but today's meeting is important—"

"Makes me *feel* better?" I wrestled with my temper and lost. "The Snow Queen attacks a new Character almost *every day*."

Mom took a very deep breath, like she usually does when she thinks I'm exaggerating but doesn't want to call me on it. "We've taken all these precautions, but we haven't been in any danger since that wolf attacked us in the grocery store."

She *always* brought that up in arguments, and it was getting old. "You didn't want to move to Ever After School, even though it's the safest place for us," I reminded her, "and I said okay, but only if you accepted bodyguards. That was the deal. You promised me."

Mom winced. She'd obviously hoped I'd forgotten about that. "They're just kids, Rory. Just like you."

"You could come with us," Amy said. "That wouldn't look as weird."

"I have responsibilities too." I had class in Hansel's training courts in an hour, and I was on call for rescue duty until dinnertime. I'd explained this to them at least a hundred times.

"Besides, your mother made that promise more than three and a half months ago," Amy said. "Maybe the Snow Queen forgot about you."

"She hasn't." I was about to turn fourteen. According to my Tale, I would hold the fate of magic in my hands some time this month. The Snow Queen had to move now, but I'd been saying that since before Independence Day. They still weren't convinced.

I wished the triplets would hurry up and get here. Company always cut our arguments short.

Something pounded against the roof. No matter what they said about the Snow Queen losing interest, Mom and Amy both jumped just as high as I did. Outside the window, white spheres bounced across the back porch. "Just hail," I said. We didn't usually see it in San Francisco.

"Great." Amy dug through her purse for her keys. "I better check on the car."

Movement flickered in the yard. It had to be one of the dirt servants. Lena had rigged them to patrol the yard's perimeter—our own magical security system. And this one was shuffling toward us, as fast as its stubby dirt legs could carry him. It was hard to tell in the crummy weather, but it looked like it was missing a foot.

My heart stuttered. I reached for one of my combs.

It could be another false alarm.

The dirt servant jolted to a stop in the middle of the backyard, its mangled limbs bleached to gray. It toppled over. Turned to stone.

"Found them!" Amy stepped toward the exit, her keys jangling from her hand.

"No!" I tossed the comb in front of the back door. It fell with a clunk, and bars as wide as my wrist sprang up from the floor.

"Not again!" Amy said. Bars crunched against the ceiling. "Rory, you damage the house every time you overreact. We'll never get our security deposit back."

Mom tried to be more soothing, but she was obviously a tiny bit peeved too. "It's probably just the neighbor's dog again. The dirt things always think he's a wolf."

I picked up the other combs. The Snow Queen's allies were coming, just like I knew they would.

The front door banged open. Someone—*several* someones—stampeded into the living room. We couldn't see them, but we could definitely hear them squawking and cawing through the drumming hail.

I threw the second comb across the entryway to the living

3

room. In two breaths, it knitted up the door frame with a chain-link fence. I tossed a third comb between the island and the kitchen table, and metal bars sprouted from the wooden floor.

Amy shrank back. "Oh my God."

Four green-skinned, black-haired witches trampled in from the dining room, the only entrance to the kitchen the combs hadn't sealed off yet. They wore toothy grins under their warty noses and raised long wands in their gnarled hands.

So, the Snow Queen had kept her word after all: the Wolfsbane clan would get their chance to kill me. They had even gotten first dibs.

One witch fired off a spell. I grabbed Mom's elbow and yanked her aside. The enchantment landed on the fridge, turning it to stone. Mom would have to pay for that too when we left this rental.

"Get behind the island," I said, snagging my carryall and dodging another shot. The top was marble. It would protect us from most spells. "Where are those rings I gave you?"

The week after I'd gotten back from the Arctic Circle, I'd made them *swear* to keep the rings on them at all times. When school was still in session, I refused to get in the car unless they both showed me the rings, but I hadn't done a check in a while. I definitely should have.

"My nightstand," Amy confessed.

Mom's mouth thinned and twisted, the face she always made when she realized she'd messed up. "It's over there." She pointed to where her red purse sat on a side table—on the other side of the chain-link fence.

I pulled my own ring out of my jeans' pocket and stared at it. One ring for three people.

"Well, you know what you have to do," Mom said. Calm as

anything, she placed a hand on my arm. "You go to EAS. Get help. Come back and rescue us. The bars will keep us safe." ·

There were a million things wrong with that plan. I hadn't heard the third comb's bars hit the ceiling yet. Mom and Amy knew nothing about fighting, even less about magic. But I didn't bother arguing.

I squeezed her fingers reassuringly. With my other hand, I gripped the ring.

"I love you, sweetie," Mom said. The only way she could have been more obvious was if she actually *said* she never thought she would see me again.

"I love you too." Then I slid the ring on her finger.

She didn't have time to look surprised. She was just gone.

"She's not going to like that," Amy said quietly. "She wanted you safe first."

"If they captured her, they would use her against me." I'd explained this a hundred times too. I didn't mention that the witches would do the same with Amy.

"I never said I didn't understand your *reasons*." Amy scooted up just enough to peek over the counter at the witches. "Is that supposed to happen?"

I poked my head around the island, just for a sec. A spell whistled past my hair and blasted the dishes drying beside the sink. A mug—the one I'd painted and given to Mom for her birthday a couple years ago—exploded, and its clay shards cascaded to the floor.

I ducked back to safety, but I'd seen what I needed to see.

Three of the four witches had leveled their wands at the third comb. The bars were still growing toward the ceiling, but slowly. Maybe just an inch a second. I'd never seen this spell.

"No, it's never happened before." The Snow Queen's forces were adapting. They had trained just to stop these combs—just to fight *me*.

"I thought so." Amy crawled over to the last cabinet, where we kept most of our canned goods. She opened the door, plucked out some green beans and some cream of mushroom soup, and launched them over the island.

The first one struck a witch's elbow. She shrieked and dropped her wand. The soup can caught the second witch in the face. She crumpled, her nose gushing blood.

"Wow," I said, impressed. Only two witches were still performing the spell that countered the enchantment. The bars rose faster—two inches a second.

"I was the pitcher on my college softball team, remember?" Amy reached for another can. The witches outside must have sensed trouble. Their footsteps thudded across the patio, louder than the hail. "You do your thing. I got this."

I reached into my carryall and pulled out my sword. I felt calmer, having it in my hand. Then I grabbed my M3. "Chase?" I shouldn't have tried him first. I *knew* he wouldn't answer. "Lena?"

The mirror stayed blank. I frowned. Lena never left her M3 lying around.

Two more witches stamped in. Their spells hit the marble island with wet sizzles. Amy launched a counterassault of diced tomatoes, but these witches were ready for her. They raised their wands. The cans exploded, and red chunks rained down on our heads.

The bars grew, inch by inch.

Only one witch was left on comb-enchantment duty. She had gray hair and a huge gap between her crooked teeth. I didn't understand why the other three witches had stopped helping her. "Now!" she shouted to someone behind her. "It must be now!"

"You don't need to tell me," said another voice.

A witch stepped out from behind the rack where we hung our raincoats and umbrellas. The edge of her long cloak was stitched with silver, and a string of moonstones was braided into her dull black hair. Her lashes were long, and her eyes tilted up at the corners like a cat. If witches hadn't been cursed with ugliness, this one might have been beautiful.

The three witches turned their wands on the newcomer. An invisible current crackled through the air. The moonstone witch rose, her cape flickering around her ankles. She bent her legs and hugged her knees, and the three witches floated her toward the comb cage. More specifically to the three-foot gap between the bars and the ceiling.

I could guess where they were going with this.

I grabbed a can of chicken soup in front of Amy, and I launched it at the witch in charge of slowing down the comb. It went wide and clattered on the table. That was why I usually stuck with weapons you didn't have to throw.

"Please don't waste my ammo." Amy threw three cans in rapid succession. One hit a witch on the shoulder, another in the arm, and the last in her huge warty chin, and all three casters levitating their sister witch stumbled back.

But it was too late.

The moonstone witch had floated past the bars, and when the spell dropped her, she landed hard on the kitchen floor. Plates and glasses clinked inside the cabinets.

"She's inside with us, isn't she?" Amy asked me.

I swallowed. "Yep."

The gray-haired witch lowered her wand. The bars zoomed up and buried themselves in the ceiling, cracking the plaster. "It is all up to you now, Istalina," she said.

The moonstone witch drew herself up taller. So she was Istalina. "Come out, Aurora Landon, or I shall flush you out."

"Stay where you are," Amy hissed, grabbing another can. "I'm sure I can get her."

But Amy had no idea what we were dealing with. The last time I'd had to fight some witches, I jumped off a moving train to get away from them. I couldn't throw the fourth comb. I couldn't risk her using that slowing spell again. I couldn't risk her *capturing* it.

I wished that Chase and Lena were here instead of Amy. They would know what to do.

It doesn't matter if you've never fought a witch before, Chase would probably say. *Magic users usually stick to spells. Most of them have no close combat skills.*

I poked my head out. Istalina was waiting for me. She raised her arm and fired, only ten feet away. I jerked back just in time— the spell took a big chunk out of the island's cabinets and blasted the pot Mom had used to make macaroni the night before.

I knew what Lena would say too. *Wait! You need something to intercept her magic.* I forced myself to stop, to look at the materials around me the way she would look at it.

We had the fourth comb. We had all this kitchen stuff. I opened the cabinet next to me. Pans and their lids. I started shifting through them, careful not to touch the one Istalina's spell had hit. It burned a glowing orange.

"What are you doing?" Amy asked.

I ignored her.

"I doesn't matter what you try, Aurora Landon," said the witch. "It won't work. We have you trapped."

I ignored her too.

I found the lid I wanted. It was bigger than most and pretty heavy, but it had an extra strip of metal, almost two inches wide, that ran all the way around the rim. I dropped the comb inside it.

Please let this work, I thought. *Please please please please*.

It did. Slender metal rods sprouted from the pot's lid. Tentatively, they wove themselves together, like the comb wasn't totally sure about my plan either.

"Stay here, Amy." I concentrated on protecting her and stood up, my lid-shield in one hand, my sword in the other.

Istalina threw off her cloak. It puddled around her feet. Her cheeks were even greener than the rest of her face, like she was flushed or something.

Beyond the cage, seven green-skinned witches lined up, their beady eyes watching us, like crows circling a picnic. A fight with an audience, just like dueling with Torlauth at the Snow Queen's palace.

Before I could shudder, Istalina launched a spell. My sword's magic flowed into me, and my left hand shifted slightly. I caught the spell on the pot lid right in front of my belly. Good. My sword had adapted to the new shield, just like it had with my ring.

The moonstone witch's eyes widened above her warty nose. She launched a few more. I couldn't see the little zings, but I heard them sizzling toward me. The runner's high seeped through my body. I danced to one side and then the other, dodging three more blasts. I caught a fourth, right in front of my face.

Okay, defense was solid. Time for some offense.

I sprinted forward. Istalina tried to fire off another shot, but

I was already in range. I bashed my shield down on her wrist, knocking the wand off course. I flipped my sword over and swung the hilt toward her temple.

A dagger blocked the blow. Istalina's weapon was black, its blade made of shiny stone instead of metal. The witch twisted her dagger around my hilt. I was so surprised that she almost managed to wrench my sword out of my hand.

The Wolfsbane clan had sent the witch who could actually fight.

The witch's heel shot out, trying to smack me in the chest. I caught it with my left hand.

But it was a feint. She squeezed off another shot from her wand. I ducked, crouching low to the ground so that it sailed over my head.

"Rory!" Amy cried. I whirled around, checking to see if she was all right, but it turned out to be just one of those *be careful* kind of yells.

Mistake. I shouldn't have looked away.

The witch's second kick caught me in the shoulder before I could stand. I went sprawling. My head cracked against the hardwood floor. The witches outside the bars cawed, like a green-and-black flock celebrating. Istalina preened. She raised both her dagger and her wand, like she wasn't sure which one she wanted to use on me first.

Half-dazed, I waited for her to decide. Another wrong move could cost me.

"Watch out!" one of the witches shouted.

Istalina took a step back, and a can of tomato sauce sailed past her face, inches from her long nose.

"Don't worry, Rory," Amy said. I couldn't see her, but I could picture her on the other side of the island, her arm cocked back, another can at the ready.

Istalina lifted her wand toward Amy's hiding place with such a sinister smile. In the Arctic Circle, the Snow Queen had raised her hand, just like that, right before the ice shards flew from her fingertips, seconds before Hadriane died.

"No!" I sprang to my feet and tried to push Istalina's wand arm out of range with my blade and my shield. She caught my sword with her dagger easily, but the shield . . . well, the tip of her wand slid through the metal weaving and exploded. Tiny splinters flew in all directions.

The pot lid saved me from the worst of it. I only felt one big sliver impale itself in my left shoulder.

Istalina wasn't so lucky. Shards stuck out from her forearm. The witch's green blood spilled down her elbow, over her fingers, and dripped off the end of her wand, which was considerably shorter than before.

Hopefully, that meant she couldn't use it.

The Wolfsbane clan stopped squawking. They stared at Istalina's wand, horrified.

"You still have your blades!" one of them shouted.

If that was all she had left, I could handle her. *I* still had a magic sword.

She slashed her dagger at my face.

I blocked it with my shield arm, hitting her fingers with the lid's edge so hard that she shrieked. Her dagger clattered to the floor. She struck with her other hand, swinging a second knife. I hadn't seen it. She must have dropped her ruined wand and grabbed the hidden blade.

With my luck, she probably had extra knives stashed in her boots. Well, if disarming her didn't work . . .

I kicked out, three times in quick succession just like Chase and I practiced—once to bash the weapon out of her hand, once in her stomach to knock the wind out of her, once in the face to stun her. She choked, gasping for air. Her face twisted with rage, her lip bleeding. With a fresh knife, she tried to stab my belly, but the movement was much slower than before. I whacked her blade aside with my shield, stepped inside her guard, and smashed my hilt into her temple. She dropped into a heap, her arm twisted under her in a really uncomfortable-looking way.

She probably wasn't faking.

"Behind you, Rory!" Amy yelled.

I glanced back. A third knife sailed though the air, aimed directly at my head. I jumped out of the way, but then a throwing star shaped like a snowflake flew into my path. I deflected it with my shield.

The witches of the Wolfsbane clan had lined up along the comb cage. I gulped. The bars only stopped *magical* attacks. A regular blade or arrow could make it through. The Wolfsbane witches had come prepared for this, armed with knives and snowflake-shaped throwing stars in every green hand.

"We gave Istalina the honor of first blood, if she could get it," said a short, squat one. "But make no mistake, Aurora Landon. We bring your death with us today."

They all threw at once. Amy screamed, but the witches' aim was less than awesome. A few barbed snowflakes knocked into the bars and fell to the floor. A small knife bounced off my shield. Only one grazed my jeans and sliced open the fabric near my shin.

No blood, but too close for comfort. These weapons could be poisoned.

It would have been smart to tie up Istalina to make sure she couldn't attack us again, but I made an executive decision to just get out of the way. I dove behind the island.

Amy slid closer. "Are you all right?" I nodded, slightly out of breath.

"Again!" barked one.

Another barbed snowflake clattered into the sink. They could throw all they wanted. Their aim had gotten even worse now that they couldn't see me.

The same thought must have occurred to someone else. "Stop. Do not waste your weapons." It sounded like the gray-haired witch. She was probably their leader.

"Why?" whined another witch. "We can always call for more. *They're* not going anywhere."

She was right. We were safe for now, but we were definitely trapped.

Amy's eyes bugged out a little more. "What are we going to do?"

I grabbed the M3 I'd left on the floor. We needed help. We needed my friends.

I flipped open the velvet cover. I looked how I always did in mirrors these days—eyebrows pinched, hair messy, purple smudges under my eyes.

No answer from Lena. Okay. Still not a big deal. She'd been scattered recently. The Director had assigned her too much to do in the workshop. But tons of people had M3's now. "Hey, come in. We have a code Gingerbread here. Requesting at least two squadrons for backup immediately."

Only my reflection stared back at me.

A witch cackled. "Call your Character friends all you like. Her Majesty has devised new enchantments to confound your tiny mirrors."

I froze. If the Snow Queen had figured out a spell to block the M3's, we really *were* trapped until reinforcements came.

The triplets should still be on their way. Plus, Mom was back at EAS now. She must have raised the alarm when she arrived. She would track down Lena—or even Chase, if she could find them. She would make sure they brought back-up.

One of the witches guessed what I was thinking. "It wouldn't matter if your message got through anyway. The warding hex we've cast blocks *all* enemy enchantments. None of your allies can travel here by magical means."

No wonder the triplets were almost half an hour late. Their temporary-transport spell probably hadn't worked. My friends couldn't rescue us if they couldn't *get* here.

"Hush," said the gray-haired witch in charge. "We aren't supposed to speak of the hex."

"They're captured by their own combs!" protested her ally. "It doesn't matter what we tell them now."

"Does that mean the ring of return didn't work?" Amy asked. "Did your mom get through?"

I stopped breathing. I didn't know. I'd never heard of a warding hex. I had no idea what they did. Lena wasn't here to explain.

But Mom *had* disappeared. If she hadn't gotten through, where had she gone?

I'd been so sure I was keeping her safe.

"Call the archers," said the gray-haired leader. "Tell them to bring their flaming arrows."

The door creaked open. Oh no. The archers' aim didn't have to be good anymore. All they needed to do was light the kitchen on fire. The smoke would kill us if the flames didn't.

"That's right, Aurora Landon," said the witch who liked taunting me. "We will flush you out as we would a Dapplegrim from its herd. We have brought your death with us."

I wished they would stop saying that. It was starting to sound true.

"And the death of the woman you seek to protect," said the gray-haired witch.

I looked at Amy. She held a can in each hand, and her scowl clearly said, *Well, I'm going down fighting.*

"But it doesn't have to be that way," said the gray-haired witch. "Release the combs, and surrender to us. We will let the woman go free. It is your death we seek, after all."

It was a trick. It had to be.

But maybe it wasn't.

My Tale had begun two years ago. The beginning lines hadn't changed that much: *Once upon a time, there was a girl named Rory Landon. Though she did not know it, the fate of magic would fall into her hands during the month she turned fourteen. With it, she would meet winter, death, and despair.*

Maybe the hail counted as winter. Maybe despair was finding myself down to two choices: my death by surrender or my death *and* Amy's by fire.

No. I could ask them for a Binding Oath. I could make them swear on their lives that Amy would go free, and it would all be over.

My expression must have given me away, because Amy began shaking her head. "No. Rory, don't you dare—"

The door creaked open again. More feet thundered in. The witches' archers had arrived.

We were trapped. Help wasn't coming. I knew my choice.

hen a new voice said, "The EASers are here."

My heart leapt. I hadn't even needed to *ask* for help. My friends had come anyway, warding hex or no warding hex.

"Then we must do our work quickly!" said the gray-haired witch. The witches launched their weapons. The air filled with silver snowflakes, their sharp barbs sparkling.

Amy screamed again. I yanked up the shield, over our heads. Two throwing stars clattered against the lid. Half a dozen more fell on the floor inches from our feet.

Too many more assaults like that, and something was going to hit us.

"This isn't how it works," Amy muttered. "I'm the adult. I'm supposed to protect *you*."

"What are you waiting for, archers?" said the gray-haired witch. Oh great. I couldn't see the new arrivals, but I bet they all had bows. They were probably trained to fight, just like Istalina. I braced myself.

Then the glass window above the kitchen table shattered. I half stood, risking a peek over the island to see what was going on. Two arrows sailed in, tiny little packets tied to their shafts. They landed, releasing great puffs of a green-and-gold powder. It glittered and stank of sulfur.

The witches coughed and choked. "Powdered dragon scales?" croaked the gray-haired one. "Why?"

Another arrow flew in. I stood on my tiptoes to get a better look. The arrow had landed right in the middle of all the witches. Someone had tied some sticks to it. The string they'd used looked weird, like a braid of brown hair with a blue bead at the end.

Lena's hair.

I knew what it was. I'd seen Lena experimenting on long-range spells like this one, modeled after the transmitter General Searcaster had fashioned in the city of the Living Stone Dwarves. The powdered scales in the air made it impossible to dodge the enchantment.

She *had* them.

Then my friend's clear, high voice rang out, shouting in Fey. I didn't have my gumdrop translator in, so I only understand one word: "beep."

"Did it work?" It sounded like Lena was at the bottom of the porch stairs.

The witches stared at each other in horror, waiting to turn to stone or sea foam, waiting to writhe in agony.

"What was it supposed to do?" I called back.

"Lena, you forgot the buzzer," said someone else outside. Kyle.

"We will not be defeated by a bunch of Character children." The gray-haired witch took a step toward the bars, toward *us*.

"Oh, yeah," Lena said. An alarm beeped, almost identical to a kitchen timer.

All at once, the witches' eyes rolled back in their heads. Then they dropped, collapsing all over each other. Weapons scattered across the wooden floor. I hoped none of them had fallen on their blade. Then I immediately felt stupid for worrying. They'd just tried to kill me. They'd tried to kill Mom and Amy.

Lena burst through the back door. Glass crunched under her feet. She half tripped over one of the witches' bows. *"RORY?"*

I leapt out from behind the island. "Here, Lena." Behind me, Amy stood more slowly.

"Oh, thank gumdrops." Lena ran forward, jumped over the motionless body of the gray-haired witch, grabbed the second-to-last bar of the comb cage, and muttered the counterspell. When the bars shrank down to a comb, she threw her arms around me, hugging so tight that her bony elbows pinched my ribs.

We both took a deep breath. As I exhaled, I let go of that awful trapped feeling of no escape and no choices.

It had been a close call, definitely, but it was almost business as usual. We had been through all of this before. Not here, specifically. Not at *my* house. But at other Characters' houses. Daisy's house, just a few weeks ago. Ben's house, just a few *days* ago.

"What did you *do* to them?" Amy said, staring at Lena like my friend could rain sulfur-smelling death down on us all.

"Long-range sleeping spell," Lena said, clearly proud of herself. "I knew you had put up the comb cage. Magic can't get through the bars, so even if the powdered dragon scales reached you, the spell would only be able to activate outside the bars. I figured if the whole clan was in one room, we had better knock them all out at once."

She always talked this fast when she was explaining an invention she was excited about. I found it supremely comforting. "How did you know to come?"

"The triplets couldn't get through," Lena said. "They came to me, thinking the enchantment was broken, and when I was trying to sort out the temporary-transport spell, we ran into your mom."

The rest of the panic ebbed out of my chest. So the ring of

return *had* gotten her there safely. I tried not to think about how angry she was going to be.

Kyle walked in and smiled at Amy. "Good morning, Miss Stevens." We could usually count on him to be polite.

Conner and Kevin crowded in behind him, knocking their spears against the doorway. "Backyard's clear," said Kevin. Daisy stomped in from the entryway, her bow out but not drawn.

"Tina and Vicky are sweeping the street," added Conner.

"Anyway, we realized that something was blocking the transport spell," said Lena. "So we went through the Door Trek door to San Fran and took a cab over. We got here as fast as we could."

"Thank you." I wanted to tell her how much it meant to me, but a lump started to clog my throat. I couldn't risk it. "Any idea how long the sleeping spell lasts?" Forever would be fine with me.

She made a face, and Kyle answered, "When she tested it on me, I was out for a couple hours."

"But you're a human. I don't know how witches react to the spell," Lena said. "Could be longer. Could be shorter."

"We better call in reinforcements," Kyle said. "Ben's squadron can handle confiscating wands, putting them in manacles, and hauling them off to the dungeon."

"Where's Chase? Is he with the stepsisters?" I knew he probably hadn't come, but my eyes strayed back to the door anyway.

Lena's face fell. "We couldn't find him."

I'd expected it, but still the small bubble of hope died. Something closed up inside me, knotted and cold. I pressed my lips together, trying to keep myself from saying anything I might regret later.

"We didn't look very hard," Kyle added. "We didn't have time."

"Maybe he's *getting coffee*." Daisy's voice dripped with sarcasm. She was still angry. She had a right to be. She was the only other person in our grade whose home had been attacked. When the Director had announced the mission, the rest of us had taken a temporary-transport spell to her front door and held off the invading trolls long enough for Daisy's family to escape. Everyone came. Everyone *helped* . . . except for Chase and Adelaide. Afterward, they came back to EAS carrying iced coffees. They said they'd gone to a café for a little peace and quiet. Daisy still hadn't forgiven them.

"Maybe they're getting ice cream," said Kevin. He wasn't quite as sarcastic as Daisy, but he was pretty fed-up. We all were.

"You guys might have it all wrong," said Conner. "It's a hot day at EAS. Maybe they're swimming."

I pushed my anger aside. "The Director *might* have sent him somewhere. That's what happened last week when you were all ragging on him for missing our rescue of the Goose Girl."

That shut them up. Chase *was* going on just as many missions as the rest of us. He was just going on them with Ben's grade, and George's, and Miriam's, and every once in a while, with his dad, Jack. He was working just as hard as we were to stop the Snow Queen. He just wasn't fighting with us.

That was enough for the triplets. Not Daisy.

"Whatever," she said. I didn't blame her. A troll had speared her father in the belly. The Water of Life brought him back, but he would keep the scar forever. If anyone I'd cared about had gotten hurt like that, I would have a hard time even pretending to be nice.

Silence followed. It might have gotten awkward, but then Lena spotted the lid-shield in my hand. "Ooo, did you make this? Can I see? I can't believe I didn't think of this before."

The stepsisters tramped in with four bundles of hazel sticks, dripping with mud. "Look what we found," said Vicky, dumping an armful on the kitchen counter, her lip curling with disgust.

The source of the warding hex. It had to be.

"One in each corner of the yard." Tina dropped her bundles too, and she went straight to the sink to wash her hands, completely ignoring the shattered dishes under the faucet.

"You dismantled it?" Lena said, horrified. "Oh no, I should have told you! I needed to examine it. If I can't look at their hex, I can't figure out how they blocked the temporary-transport spell!"

Vicky frowned at her. "What happened to us needing to call Ben right away? Didn't we need to break the enchantment to use our M3's?"

"Does that mean you don't need us?" Ben stumbled up the porch steps and yawned in the doorway. "Because before the M3 woke me up, this was supposed to be our morning off." He got a good look at my kitchen, and all the green-skinned sleepers lying on the floor. "Oh. So, *which* task did you want us to perform?" Then he laughed.

"Ugh, Ben," Darcy said, right on his heels. She stepped inside, flipped a sleeping witch on her stomach, and started tying the new prisoner's hands behind her back.

Kenneth almost slipped on the hail melting on the porch and cursed. Then he saw the witches inside and cursed again. "No way. I'm not carrying them. You woke me up saying we would get to fight some witches, not clean up after these guys."

We slid back into our usual habits so easily. It always amazed me, when I had time to think about it. Sure, the Wolfsbane clan had almost managed to kill me this morning. They'd even used some very scary spells, but we couldn't dwell on it. We had too much to do.

Only one person in the room hadn't chimed in. Amy hadn't

told me off for putting myself in danger. She hadn't even protested about the muddy sticks on the clean kitchen counter. She just stared straight, her eyes unfocused.

"Amy?" I was suddenly worried she was going to faint.

Her eyes met mine. Slowly, her slack mouth formed a wry smile. "I'm just shocked that you haven't said 'I told you so' yet. I would deserve it. It's definitely time to move. Do you think we could recruit any of these kids to carry boxes, or are they too busy bagging and tagging witches?"

I smiled back, not fooled. She was pretending she wasn't scared, making wisecracks like nothing was wrong. She was following our lead.

Conner craned his neck into the dining room. The table had almost disappeared under a pile of cardboard boxes. "You mean these?"

Kyle leaned his spear against the wall and picked one up. "We can handle it, Miss Stevens."

For a second Amy half-smiled, like she'd realized how nice it was to have a squadron of athletic teenagers around on moving day. Then she said, not bothering to joke, "Your mother knows the emergency's over, right?"

Mom was probably still terrified for me, and I just stood around chatting with my friends. "Lena—?" I said, my voice weirdly shrill.

Lena handed me two shining blue rings of return. "Go. We'll take care of the rest."

I took one and slipped it on.

It always throws you—to blink in a kitchen and open your eyes in the EAS courtyard. It was even worse this summer. It looked more like a loud, crowded village than an afterschool these days. You couldn't see any of the colored doors lining the walls. Too many houses blocked the view. At least a hundred families had seen Lena's home in the middle of the courtyard, and they'd decided to skip the rooms the Canon had offered and just move their whole *house* to EAS instead. So, we had a weird sort of neighborhood, buildings of all different sizes, all different styles. Lena's spell had plopped them down at random, so they weren't even lined up in anything resembling a street. Dirt paths wove through them instead. So many people were living here this summer that we'd worn down the once thick grass.

"Wow. You guys redecorated," Amy said, suddenly appearing at my side with Lena's second ring of return on her finger. Amy hadn't visited EAS since sixth grade when Chase, Lena, and I were in a skit together. "I'm not sure I like it."

I wasn't sure either. At least the Tree of Hope was the same though, its thick branches dipping down to the ground and swerving back up to the sky. It dwarfed the brick house with white columns that had been relocated just beside it. Under the Tree's canopy, the Table of Never Ending Instant Refills was still covered with its silver trays of food. Right now, strangers in suits surrounded it and balanced their plates on their briefcases. Some older Characters and some parents were grabbing breakfast before work. Even the shabby mismatched furniture hadn't changed. Heavily armed Characters on call sat waiting for mission assignments, eating and brushing crumbs off their breastplates.

I knew my mother. If she wanted answers, she would go talk to the person in charge—the same way she would interview the principal every time I changed schools. I tried not to imagine what kind of scene they would make if Mildred actually opened the door. I walked toward the Director's office. "This way," I told Amy. The fastest route was through all the people.

Dozens of eyes flashed toward me. Hands hid mouths. Hissing whispers reached my ears.

". . . Unwritten Tale . . ."

". . . dueled Torlauth di Morgian. She beat him in less than . . ."

". . .Triumvirate with Lena LaMarelle and Chase Turnleaf. The last Triumvirate . . ."

I squared my shoulders and held my head high. I schooled my face to stone, determined not to show how concerned I was about Mom. Knowing the EAS rumor mill, they would assume something worse was happening.

On the other side of the Table where she assumed I couldn't hear her, one of the seventh graders was practically shouting the story of what had happened just last week. Her friends were pretending they hadn't heard it a dozen times before. ". . . the Snow Queen's trap. The villains, they drove her to the top of the sky-scraper all by herself."

I hadn't been alone because I'd *wanted* to be.

I walked faster, like I could outrun the story and the memories that came with it. I sincerely hoped that Amy was too shaken up to pay attention to what these kids were saying.

Unfortunately, the seventh grader was just getting warmed up. Her back was to us. She didn't see me and Amy getting closer. "And you know what was waiting for her? A roof full of enemies. A hundred ice griffins and wolves. They attacked, but they couldn't even touch her. She was too fast. Then Ripper showed up, thinking he could finish Rory off. Rory couldn't kill him, because he was—you know—a pillar. But she hurt him really bad. The Big Bad Wolf was out of commission for three whole days. And the best part?"

It wasn't the best part. It was the worst part, the part that still made me want to puke.

"She couldn't fight her way back to the stairs, so she tried something else," said the seventh grader. "She jumped off the roof and had the West Wind catch—"

We drew even with the little storyteller. She spotted me and went as scarlet as Red Riding Hood's headwear.

But mixed in with the embarrassment was happiness. Her face brightened with admiration. It was terrible to see it there. I had to figure out a way to live up to being her hero.

She couldn't know how much I wanted my mother. I wanted Mom to hug me the way she had when I was small—I wanted her to take away all my fear by kissing my forehead and asking me who her favorite daughter was.

I nodded at the seventh grader, and she beamed back.

The rest of her friends gaped at me.

We rounded the tiny bungalow that belonged to the Princess and the Pea representative. This section of the courtyard was much quieter. A group of seniors sat on the steps of a Tudor mansion, sharpening some spearheads and arrows. Miriam waved to me.

Amy had definitely heard. "So, those rumors . . . They exaggerate, right?"

I didn't say anything, which I guess kind of answered the question.

"You didn't tell us," Amy said. That accusing tone felt way too familiar.

"I did." I didn't lie to them anymore. "I told you that two students here, Kelly and Priya, got their Tales, and the Snow Queen set a trap for me when I went to help them."

"You left a lot out," Amy said. She sounded more like herself now that she was scolding me. "The *wind* caught you?"

"The West Wind," I said. "He owed me some boons. I only

have one left now, and I won't use it the same way, I promise."

"Good. Because I thought you were afraid of heights," Amy said.

"I am. I threw up before I jumped." I tried so hard not to think about it, but the memory was pressing in on me, so strong I tasted bile the same way I'd tasted it then.

"Your mom deserves the whole story, every time, after—"

"Amy, please." I squeezed my eyes shut. Not a great idea. The whole terrifying scene bloomed behind my lids. The army waiting for me. All the teeth and talons trying to rip me apart. The blood pumping out of Ripper and pooling across the roof. My feet leaving solid ground, and air whipping my clothes flat and my lungs empty. That horrible instant where I was absolutely 100 percent positive that West wouldn't reach me in time, and the instant after that, even worse, when I wondered if it would be better if he didn't catch me.

This was why I couldn't talk about it. I pressed my hand against my mouth, sure I would vomit again.

"Okay," Amy said, sounding genuinely freaked out. Then, more gently, she added, "Okay. Let's just find your mom."

I nodded and opened my eyes. We headed around the log cabin where Darcy and Bryan's family lived.

The amethyst door to the Director's office came into view, and right there, banging on it, was my mother. Her hair was wild, her eyes rimmed with red.

My chest clenched. I'd wanted to move here, but not like this.

"Mom!" I called, starting to jog toward her, but she didn't hear me. She was too busy arguing with my dad.

Just like old times.

"Mom!" I pushed my way through a herd of elementary

schoolers, trying to get closer. They were too busy fighting to hear me. Totally the joyous reunion I was hoping for.

Brie, my stepmom, spotted us first. "Rory! We were so worried." I hadn't seen her, all tucked away in the shadows of a tall and skinny Victorian home. She had an arm around me a second later. Just one. The other had a passenger.

"Hey, Brie." We were careful not to crush the baby she was cradling. Stepping back, I put on a hand on the infant's back and kissed the crown of red fuzz on her head. Her hair was new. It had just started growing in this month. "Hey, Dani," I told the baby. Dad and Brie had picked out her real name, Danica, but I'd come up with her nickname.

I'd tried to stay away from my little sister. Really, I had. The last bearer of an Unwritten Tale had driven *her* sister kind of insane. But I might not even live till the end of the summer. I couldn't do that much damage in such a short amount of time, especially when she was so small. And so helpless. I couldn't help wanting to check up on my tiny sister. Pretty much *all* the time.

"Maggie told us about the attack," Brie patted the baby between her little shoulder blades. I took a bigger step back—I knew that move, and burping Dani usually ended in baby puke. "Witches? Seriously? I'm beginning to think Eric and I got off easy with trolls."

A squadron of trolls had ambushed my dad and stepmom in Los Angeles right after school let out for the summer. The stress had convinced Dani it was time to be born, and Brie had gone into labor a month early. All three of them had moved straight from the hospital to their new EAS apartment.

My parents finally noticed me.

Mom held me so tightly, I was too breathless to tell her how sorry I was. Dad stopped just short of making it a group hug: He came up behind me and gripped both my shoulders. I closed my eyes. For a second, I felt almost as small as Dani again—young and protected, like I did in the days when my parents could solve all my problems.

It was a nice moment. It didn't last long.

Mom let go. It was hard to hug and yell at me at the same time, I guess. "Never *ever* do that again. If there's a choice between me or you being safe, it should *always* be you. I don't want to be safe if you're still in danger. Do you understand?"

I nodded. Of course I understood. I felt exactly the same way, but I was a lot better at protecting her than she was at protecting me. I didn't see that changing any time soon. I knew better than to say that, though.

"*I* am your mother," Mom went on.

"Lay off, Maggie." Now Dad got his chance for a real hug, almost lifting me off the ground. "We haven't even asked her if she's been injured or not."

"I'm fine," I said.

"You have a giant bruise on your forehead, Rory," Dad pointed out.

"She came home with that yesterday," Amy explained. "After rescuing a fourth grader in Tennessee."

"Dragon tail." I didn't mention the bigger bruise on my back, where the dragon's tail had actually hit me. I'd flown half the length of the yard and knocked my head on a swing set.

Everyone except Amy winced. Dad and Brie exchanged a glance. They were obviously wondering if it was worth telling me to be careful. I sighed. It was a lot easier to have adventures when my parents just thought my injuries were from being accident-prone.

"Mom already told me off about it," I told Dad and Brie, hoping this wouldn't become a four-person lecture.

"You've been lucky so far," Mom protested. "Right now, you just have cuts and bruises, but if you keep putting yourself in danger . . ."

This would be the perfect time for Amy to repeat the story she'd just heard, but she didn't. Maybe she wanted to tell her in private.

When I didn't say anything, Dad tried to defend me. "Maggie, technically, the witches came to you."

"But that's the exception, isn't it?" Mom said. "Every time you go on one of these 'missions,' you push your luck a little more. If this keeps up, you'll come home much worse off."

A group of tenth graders glanced at us sidelong. Great, as if people weren't talking about me enough already. Now my family had to go and have a huge public fight in one of the busiest parts of the Courtyard. "Mom, can we please talk about this somewhere else?"

"Finally," said a clipped voice at my feet. Puss had taken to wearing some chainmail over her dress. It clinked faintly as she lashed her tail. "This courtyard is a nightmare to cross these days. The Director should have sent Ellie or Sarah Thumb instead of me."

I couldn't remember if I'd ever introduced Mom and Amy to this particular member of the Canon. Judging by the way their eyes bugged out, I guessed not. "Mom, Amy, this is Puss-in-Dress. Puss, this is—"

"Yes, I know." The cat was in a bad mood. Someone must have

stepped on her tail again. "Amy Stevens and Maggie Wright, the Director bids me to welcome you to Ever After School. I'm here to bring you to your new home. The young Characters are carrying in your boxes. This way."

Sometimes the Director *was* helpful. "Mom, can we talk this afternoon?"

"What? You're not coming with us?" Mom asked. The *you plan to leave me alone with a talking cat on my first day here?* part was implied.

"Rory has class in less than five minutes." Puss's tail flicked again.

"I'm sure they can do without her for *one day*," Mom said. "I'll write a note to her teachers."

Puss, Dad, and Brie all paused and looked from Mom to me.

"Oh," I said, kind of sheepishly. With everything I'd needed to tell them, I'd *known* that something had slipped through the cracks. At least, this explained why Mom never understood why I needed to be at the training courts so often.

"Rory *is* one of the teachers," Puss said.

"An assistant," I corrected quickly when disbelief crossed Mom's face.

"Rory, I'm also supposed to tell you that a Canon meeting has been scheduled at noon," Puss said. "All student representatives need to be there."

"Got it," I said, trying not to notice the *why didn't you tell me?* frown coming from Mom and the *why did I have to hear it from a talking cat?* scowl coming from Amy. I started walking away, backward so that I could wave good-bye. "Mom, seriously, we can talk about it when I get home, okay?"

She was going to protest. Her mouth opened, probably to tell me that I *better* not go to some random meeting without seeing her first. I didn't give her a chance. I turned and ran to the training courts.

Chase's group usually met five minutes before the official classes. They liked to get their pick of metal dummies. But they wouldn't be having a lesson if Chase was still away on a mission.

I hoped with all my heart he *had* been on a mission this morning. I wished I didn't. It wasn't right to prefer the option where his life might be in danger.

No. I refused to actually worry about him. Chase and George were the only warriors who could single-handedly slay squadrons of trolls or ice griffins as soon as they woke up. I knew, because Chase had been bragging about doing just that at breakfast twice in the past week.

But if he was just out doing something stupid . . .

I swung around a one-story house and saw the Tree of Hope ahead of me. Under it, at our usual table, was Chase. His sword lay next to his plate, but he didn't look like he'd been in a fight. He was stuffing his face with pastries, right beside his girlfriend, Adelaide.

He hadn't been out on a mission, not today.

That hard, cold knot settled back into my chest. I stood over the table and crossed my arms.

Adelaide immediately started glaring at me. Nothing new there.

Chase didn't even notice. He shoved a croissant into his mouth. Flaky crumbs fell on the M3 he was watching. I recognized the mirrorcording—he'd filmed it when we rescued a seventh grader and her family from ice griffins in Denver. He stopped the image and rewound it to replay the snippet of me slashing and bashing my way through four ice griffins. He'd isolated dozens of combinations like this one. Then he broke them down into steps and taught them to the group that would be meeting in a few minutes.

I knew all this. I knew how important learning my magic sword's attacks had become to him. But every second I stood there, staring at the top of his head, the knot got colder and tighter.

He should have *been* there this morning.

He should have been fighting beside me, like Lena. Same as he should have been fighting on the rooftop with me a week ago, and fighting the dragons at that tenth grader's house the week before that, and fighting those trolls at Daisy's house last month.

Actually, he and his girlfriend hadn't fought beside the rest of the grade since the skirmish recorded in Chase's M3. In *May*.

Finally, Adelaide cleared her throat.

Chase didn't look up. He reached for another pastry. "I told you, I'm working."

"Then *stop*," I said.

His face broke into a grin, one that took up half his face, framed by all his dimples. I didn't understand how my stomach could flip even when I was so angry with him. I didn't understand how he could look so happy to see me when he'd been ignoring our whole grade for months. "Hey! Look at this one. It's a lot like the move we worked out three weeks ago, but different here." He rewound the mirrorcorder again, completely oblivious.

Sometimes, he and Adelaide acted like we weren't in the middle of a war.

"Where were you?" I hated how my voice shook.

"I took him to this cute little bakery around the corner from my old house," Adelaide said, with a touch of triumph. "They have the best croissants ever."

I stared at Chase, who just looked confused. The knot in my chest was so tight that it hurt to breathe.

Rory, if you're in trouble, I'll always come for you, he'd said during Miriam's quest. Just three months ago. I had expected Chase's "always" to last longer than that.

"Was I right?" called a voice behind us. Daisy stalked down the row between the houses, carrying a cardboard box toward the door to the student apartments. Conner and Kyle flanked her, carrying boxes of their own. "Were they getting coffee again?"

Guilt flashed across Adelaide's face. She had missed just as many fights as Chase had, but I was pretty sure she only felt bad about Daisy's family. "Someone else is moving?" she asked, obviously hoping her friend would start talking to her again.

Daisy just glowered at Adelaide.

Chase slowly realized what happened. All the blood drained from his face, and he went bone white. "Who got attacked?"

"Me," I said. "The Wolfsbane clan."

"Oh," Adelaide said with relief. "I thought it was Candice."

"Candice moved two weeks ago," said Conner, like he couldn't believe Adelaide was so out of the loop.

"Yeah. We're the only ones in our grade who haven't moved here yet," Kyle said.

That wasn't completely true. Alvin Collins—the Character who had just joined our grade at Christmas—had moved to Hong Kong with his family and transferred to the Asian chapter of Ever After School.

We never mentioned him though, or any of the other families who fled as far as they could to avoid the Snow Queen.

"Maybe Dad will finally change his mind and let us move," Conner said hopefully.

"Why didn't anyone tell me?" Chase said, like he was ticked off. He had no right.

"How? No one could *find* you." I couldn't keep the anger out of my voice this time. I could feel Kyle, Conner, and Daisy staring at me. So much for convincing them that I wasn't upset.

Chase's face paled even more. I didn't know that was possible. "I left my M3 in my room. I just ran up to get it."

I wanted to lay into him. I wanted to tell him that he'd been as flaky and self-centered as his girlfriend. I wanted to say that we were depending on him and that he kept letting us down.

The others would back me up. That was the problem. The rest of the rising ninth graders were losing patience with these two. If

I let loose on them, the others would do the same. It would break our whole grade apart, and we couldn't afford that.

Chase was part of the Triumvirate. He, Lena, and I were stronger together, just like Rikard, Madame Benne, and Maerwynne—the first Triumvirate, the one that had founded the Canon—had been.

We needed him, or otherwise, the Snow Queen really would win.

I took a deep breath. The knot in my chest didn't loosen, but I forced my voice to be as neutral as possible. "Well, at least no one was hurt. Your group has a session soon, right? Did you still want to go through that drill before then?"

That was all I needed to say. Conner and Kyle moved off with their boxes, but before Daisy followed them, she shot me an irritated glare, like I'd disappointed *her* by letting Chase off the hook.

I didn't wait for Chase to answer. "I'm going to the training courts to set up," I said. I walked away, pretending I didn't care if he followed me or not.

Behind me, I could hear him struggling to his feet, cursing in Fey like he only does when he's really rattled.

"Chase, it's fine," Adelaide said. "At least finish your breakfast."

Heavy footfalls thumped toward me. Then Chase's hand fell on my arm. It was probably wrong to feel glad that he'd come after me, but I did. I looked up. He'd grown more than a couple inches since spring. It still made me feel like my best friend had been replaced with a stranger.

He was standing too close, his eyes as green as they had been when we were dancing at Queen Titania's pavilion. "Are you really okay?"

"Yeah." I resisted the urge to add, *No thanks to you*. Kenneth and Bryan were passing, carrying an unconscious, bound witch on a stretcher toward the dungeon.

Some fifth graders had clustered outside the iron-studded door to the training courts, waiting for their lessons and chatting with huge, eager smiles. The younger kids treated these classes just like summer camp. "Excuse me, please," I told them. They skittered away, watching us, wide-eyed and awed. I broke out of Chase's grasp, opened the door, and went inside.

He followed me down the hall that separated the courtyard and the training courts. I slammed through the second door.

The training courts had grown, just as the courtyard had. The entire army of metal dummies stood guard along the walls. The Director wanted them out at all times, in case of an attack.

Frowning, Chase beckoned three ice griffins forward. Lena had made them for EAS's standing army. They couldn't fly or freeze water with their breath, but their claws and beaks were plenty sharp—last week, they'd ruined my favorite blue top.

I barely even glanced at them.

Chase had his time with his girlfriend, and he had his time with me. I'd accepted that, but I couldn't stand the way it had changed him.

This used to be my favorite part of the day. Once, it had been easy to pretend that nothing had changed. Except for the dummies, it could still be spring. We could still be training for the Tournament. I could forget about my Tale and my destiny and Miriam's Tale—

I stopped myself. I refused to think too hard about the quest in the Arctic Circle, especially when Chase was around.

"Rory." Chase planted himself right in front of me, but I didn't want to look at him. "On a scale of one to ten, how mad are you?"

I didn't answer. "Mad" didn't cover what I felt, but I didn't know what you called it when you were standing right beside your best friend and still felt like you'd lost him. I didn't know how to explain that I fully expected the Snow Queen to send people after me again, and I fully expected him not to be there.

"Rory, I didn't *know* you were in trouble." His mouth twisted, frustrated and unsure. "I'm sorry. I wish I'd been there."

He meant it. I knew he did. But he'd also meant what he'd said in the Arctic Circle, and that hadn't stopped today from happening.

"Outside, you said no one had been hurt . . ." Chase said slowly. "But we had to jump off a train to get away from the Wolfsbane clan last time. How close was it, really?"

"I thought I wouldn't be able to get Amy out of there." My hands began to shake. "I thought I was going to have to surrender to keep her safe. I almost did."

"Rory . . ." He took a step closer to me, arms outstretched, like he was going to hug me. That set off little warning bells in my head.

I wasn't sure what I would have done if he'd actually put his arms around me, if I would have pushed him away or just started crying on his chest. I never got to find out.

The door on the far side of the room creaked open. "You two ready?" Hansel asked, and for the first time all morning, I smiled.

If you had told me this spring that I would be happier to see the sword master than I was to see Chase, I wouldn't have believed you. Funny how things change.

Making me an assistant teacher had been Hansel's idea.

He'd called me into his office back in April. I'd never been there before, so naturally, I assumed I was in trouble. Hansel's office was a third of the size of the weapon's closet, but I only spotted one weapon in the whole room—his sword, leaning against his knee. Books and papers covered the rest of the shelves. Volumes on troll cultures, encyclopedias on ice griffins and dragons, histories on old Fey wars, guides to learning medieval fighting techniques, and even instructions on teaching. He'd moved some lesson plans off the only other chair in the room. "Take a seat, Rory."

I'd sat, bracing myself for some monstrously unfair punishment. I'd already started composing the rant I would unload on Lena and Chase later about how Hansel *always* picked on me. I mean, he'd started messing with me during my very first sword class.

Hansel had propped his elbows on his knees, his eyes hard on my face.

Way too intense. My gaze drifted to the shelf behind his head and the framed picture resting on top of it. In the photo, Hansel had a real smile and a lot less gray in his hair. His arm was around a pretty, laughing woman. Three little girls—blonde and tanned like their mother—were piled like puppies in front of them.

Hansel had a family. Who knew?

"Rory, I need to ask you a favor. A big one," Hansel said. *That* got my attention. "You can say no if you aren't comfortable, but I want you to really think about it."

I nodded so he knew I was listening. I'd never heard him sound so serious without also sounding kind of . . . mean. Or at least stern. It made me even more nervous.

"Tomorrow, the Director will announce mandatory weapons training for everyone inside our walls, not just Characters," Hansel had explained. "We're creating more classes. I want your help with a class that teaches defensive techniques with a staff."

I stared at him. The rant I'd been composing fell to pieces.

"Me?" Two years ago, I'd been his worst student.

"There's one kid in particular I know you'll help," Hansel said. "The Character we discovered among the kidnapped children from Portland."

I knew exactly who he was talking about. I remembered her scowl and the cartoon unicorns on her nightgown perfectly. I'd asked Ellie what the new Character's name was. "Priya?"

"I put her in the staff class. A weapon with a longer reach will keep her safe, but she doesn't want to learn," Hansel told me. "She says EAS already has enough fighters without her."

That sounded like her. She did have an attitude.

"I've never been any good at motivating kids like Priya and Lena," Hansel continued. "Kids like Chase are easy. A couple well-timed insults and a few scary stories about villains, and they pay attention. Now, girls—well, you're one of the few girls that worked on. Kids like Priya and Lena attend the required classes and just go through the motions. I'm not saying that they wait around to be rescued, but most of them assume that they won't save themselves with a weapon."

I continued to stare. I knew the scary stories had been on purpose, but the *insults* . . . "You *don't* think girls can't fight?"

Hansel snorted. "I spar with Gretel every morning. She beats me seven times out of ten. It's her metal foot. She lands one good kick, and it's all over for me."

Well, my mind was blown. "Why don't you ask her to be your assistant instead of me?"

"She is going to be teaching a class," Hansel said, "but she's not patient. Especially not with students who don't want to learn."

"You could ask Chase."

"Chase is a fine teacher for a boy of his age," Hansel said. "He taught you, an easy, talented pupil, but *you* taught Lena. She used to let you and Chase cover for her. Now she's a competent fighter on her own."

He'd been paying attention. All this time.

I never expected to say yes. I'd asked for some time to think about it and then scurried straight to the infirmary, where Rapunzel spent most of her time as Gretel's assistant nurse. I'd found her in the back, past the curtain that hid her from the sleeping patients and their visitors.

The whole story gushed out of me before she'd even had a chance to say hello. Excuses tumbled out too: The staff wasn't even my best weapon. I'd just taught Lena for a few weeks. She'd only gone along with it because she was my best friend.

Rapunzel listened, rolling bandage after bandage and stacking them in the cabinet. We needed them now. The Director had restricted the use of the Water of Life only to fatal or critical injuries. Nothing convinces you to start rationing a magical life-saving cure-all like a war. When I was done, Rapunzel offered no advice. She just lifted her gaze over my left shoulder.

Gretel stood there, scowling. I felt instantly awkward. I'd been talking about her brother right beside her. "Has Hansel ever told you why he became sword master?" she asked.

"Knowing would make little difference for some young Characters," Rapunzel told Gretel quietly, "but Rory should understand why Hansel chose his position."

"Know *what*?" I could already tell it wouldn't be a happy story.

Gretel's face was stone. "Hansel's daughters weren't warriors. They weren't even interested. He didn't push it. My nieces always joked that they had their father to fight for them. He liked that. Then, during the last war, the previous Hansel and Gretel were killed, and the two of us joined the Canon. During our first meeting as official Tale representatives, the Snow Queen sent Ripper to Hansel's home. There were no survivors."

The damage the Snow Queen caused should have stopped surprising me. Most Characters carried around griefs like secrets, the same way Chase did.

Sadness etched deep lines around Gretel's mouth and under her eyes. "Hansel asked the Canon to let him develop Ever After School's mandatory training program only a few months later. It's the only thing he still wants, the only thing that gets him out of bed in the morning. Teaching kids how to keep themselves safe."

Because his family hadn't been. I wondered how old his daughters would be if they were still alive.

"He would not ask you to teach if he didn't truly believe you would be the best help for the students," Rapunzel added.

So I agreed.

Hansel ducked into the weapons closet and returned, rolling a rack of staffs in front of him. "Two minutes before your group arrives, Chase."

"Are we going to practice or not?" I asked, extremely pleased that my voice was cool and unemotional.

Chase sighed and gestured the dummies forward. He must have given them detailed instructions before we'd come in. They knew exactly how to attack.

The griffin on the far right tried to bite Chase, but Chase rolled forward and popped up again further down the line. The middle ice griffin lashed out—he dodged that swipe too, and the talons aimed at his face scraped across the metal feathers of the griffin on the left. That one reared, beak open, like it was shrieking in pain, and Chase thrust his sword at its metal heart. The blade didn't pierce the metal hide, but the griffin on the left dropped anyway. Chase planted his foot on the dead one's shoulder and sprang up, way too high for a human, his blade flashing in a huge, fancy circle. When he came down, he struck a blow on the middle of the griffin's neck—it would have beheaded the statue if it weren't metal. That ice griffin fell on the last one, trapping it. It squirmed piteously as Chase slid his blade in its eye, like he was stabbing its metal brain.

Even at half speed, it all happened in less than a minute.

"Don't jump so high. You're showing them what to imitate. You're not trying to impress them," Hansel said. "And cut that flourish you do while you're in the air."

"That's exactly how Rory does it in the recording," Chase said, a little resentfully.

"She has a Fey sword. They're needlessly showy, and a smart opponent could get inside your guard," Hansel said. "Cut it before you teach it. Let's see you, Rory."

I stepped forward, ready to go. After all, the lesson plan came from the moves of *my* magic sword. Most of the drills were already in my muscle memory. All I needed was for my mind to catch up.

The metal griffins stood back up on their four feet. I unsheathed my weapon. They attacked at full speed. I rolled. I ducked. I stabbed. I leapt off one's shoulder, beheaded the other without the flourish, and then swiftly dispatched the one that got pinned.

"Good," Hansel said. "Chase, you see how Rory was just a fraction faster? That's exactly what I mean. These maneuvers need to be as efficient as possible."

The door opened, and the first members of Chase's group started to trickle in. For a second, Chase looked deeply annoyed that his students were watching his lesson get tweaked right before the start of class. Then he smacked his hands together. The clap rang out in the huge chamber. "Ready? This new technique is *awesome*."

Kenneth rolled his eyes. "According to you, they're all awesome." He was slightly out of breath. He must have had to run from witch duty.

"That's because they all are," Chase said. "But this one is especially epic."

Chase's group gathered in front of the dummies. It wasn't a real class, but it could have been. They'd all found out that Chase was teaching himself how to fight a bunch of opponents at once, and they'd asked to learn too. George had been the first. He took his usual spot in front, between his two best friends, Thomas and Keon. Three guys in Miriam's grade hung out awkwardly in the back, but their female classmate stood near the front too. I was pretty sure she had a crush on one of the older Characters. They came in, shoving each other and laughing. They'd graduated EAS before I got there, and they said they were studying with Chase to brush up on their skills before they actually went into battle. Strolling in quietly, like they were pretending they had better things to do, were the two youngest members of the Canon, the Aladdin representative and the Boy Who Cried Wolf representative. They had refused to let any of their classmates call them by their real names. Ben ran in last, panting as hard as Kenneth had a few minutes before.

These were just the regulars. Our whole grade had joined in the day Chase held a giant-slaying seminar.

Was Chase ridiculously proud that all of his students were older than he was? Absolutely. But that wasn't what he bragged about.

He'd been the one who'd figured out that my sword's magic specialized in defeating multiple enemies at the same time. "We're outnumbered, right?" he'd told me. "With a little practice, this squadron could take out a force ten times its size."

He raised his hands, ready to begin. Older or not, his students listened. No one else could do what Chase could do. I'd seen those guys in Miriam's grade watching the mirrorcordings, trying to understand the way my sword worked, but none of them could break it down into steps.

I used to feel proud of him at the beginning of every lesson. I used to feel extremely awkward with all these warriors scrutinizing *my* every move.

Now, I mostly wanted to get class over with.

Chase had me demonstrate at half speed, then at full speed. He pointed out how many times you needed to roll, how many feet away from ice griffins you should be when you pop up, how long to wait before you dodged, where to step on the ice griffin's shoulder when you leapt for the killing bow, where to slice, and where to land.

"Any questions?" Chase asked when I was done.

The students shook their heads. They picked up every combination almost as quickly as I did, and they didn't even have the muscle memory advantage.

"Good," Chase said. "Thanks, Rory." Normally, I would smile and wave before I went to join Hansel, but I couldn't muster the energy. If Chase noticed, he didn't let on. "The rest of you, time to practice." The twenty fighters lined up. Kenneth was first. He ducked into a roll before the first ice griffin tried to strike.

Now I had to get ready for the second round of students.

I put my sword away and rolled another rack of staffs out of the weapons closet. Hansel was picking out the dummies he wanted to use. He always did this before Gretel came in for her sword class, and Gretel often complained that he always took the good ones. "Once a bratty little brother, *always* a bratty little brother," she'd muttered back in April. Chase and I had exchanged a look, and then we'd laughed for five minutes straight. That felt like a long time ago, now.

"Hansel, I forgot to tell you," I said, stopping beside him. "Priya wants to try the spear."

He snorted. "Of course she does. Getting her Tale has made her even cockier."

Priya was the new Little Red Riding Hood. The Tale had begun while she and Kelly were visiting Priya's grandmother in Seattle for a sleepover. I'd played the part of the heroic woodsman who comes and slays the wolf, like the Snow Queen knew I would. That had been how I ended up on the roof fighting Ripper and a hundred other creatures. Before I got there, though, Priya had taken out a bunch of wolves on her own.

It had given her star status. Hansel disapproved. "I'll talk to her about the spear thing," he said, very ominously.

"I already did," I said, instantly nervous. "I told her it was a great idea, but not the right time. Is that okay?" On top of the rest of my morning, the last thing I needed was to get in trouble for overstepping my boundaries as Hansel's assistant.

He smiled. "Probably better than I would have done." Oh. I'd overreacted. I'd gotten so used to being in trouble with Hansel over the years that I kept forgetting he had asked for *my* help. "I heard about this morning. Are you all right to teach for today?"

His kindness threw me too. Weirdly, it made me feel *less* okay, more shaky, and I tried to stave off the emotion swelling within me. "I have to. My other option is to go see my mother and listen to her yell at me about the fight."

Hansel looked up from the row of Fey dummies he was moving into position. "The Director wants all newcomers to attend the first weapon class after their arrival. It's mandatory."

I'd forgotten. The training courts weren't the escape I'd hoped it had been.

"Rory!"

I turned. My mother strode toward me, her smile cheerful but her gaze steely. She was about to say something I wouldn't like, especially not in front of the younger staff students walking in behind her.

"There you are." Mom pretended she didn't notice heads turning. Some of the other students had recognized the famous actress in their midst. You'd think they would be used to celebrities. Dad and Brie had been living here for months.

"Are you *in* this class?" I couldn't keep the horror out of my voice.

"No, I just wanted to ask you something—" Mom started.

"Ms. Wright, you're going to be having class with Gretel," Hansel said, pointing to his sister. Gretel had just clunked in, and now she stood at the front of her class, taking attendance. "You're welcome to talk with Rory, but I have to warn you: All latecomers are welcomed with gingerbread jacks."

That was *definitely* a rescue.

Mom hesitated but then made her way over to Gretel's class. She was always a stickler about following the rules in public. Even here, she worried that people would say she thought Hollywood stars deserved special treatment.

"I *am* in your class," Amy said, walking up to me with her arms crossed over her chest. She clearly didn't want to be there.

Man, this was shaping up to be an especially challenging day.

It would be almost as uncomfortable having Amy in the staff class as having Mom. "You don't want to try archery?" I whispered. That was where Brie was.

"Rory, I'm nearsighted," Amy said in the exact same tone she used to remind me that I'd promised to clean my room.

"Let me show you where the staffs are." Hansel led her away. He was still running interference, and I was grateful. "Rory, check if we're missing anyone."

I glanced around the room. We were all here.

Half of my students had gathered in rows in front of me, facing the witch and dragon dummies along the wall; they were young Characters, too small to be good sword fighters. The other half included some high school Characters who had goofed off instead of paying attention during their first year of weapons classes, adult Characters who had attended EAS before the Director made classes mandatory, and parents who had never been Characters but had kids who were.

In other words, the most inexperienced fighters. The most unlikely ones.

But their unlikeliness was an advantage. Our enemies would underestimate them. During a battle, my students would be placed as a final line of defense at some key point on the field. We were training them to hold off a bigger and stronger force until offensive squads could come—like Chase's sword fighters or the archers training outside.

Two students stood in the front, as close as they could get to me without actually standing on my toes. They were ridiculously excited to see me, considering I'd seen them the afternoon before.

"Rory, you were in a fight this morning, weren't you?" cried

Kelly. I was glad to see her so eager. She'd been a little subdued since she'd gotten her second Tale. "The Feather Bird" was gruesome, but she and Puss had put Priya and her grandmother back together again. "What was it this time? Dragons?"

"No way. She would smell more like sulfur," said Priya, right beside her. "I'd say . . . ice griffins! No, trolls!"

They loved to guess what I'd been fighting. I didn't understand where they got their guts. They were going into sixth grade. When I was their age, I would have never been brave enough to ask random questions of someone going into *ninth* grade.

"Witches," I said, a little bit surprised that they had to ask. I mean, Ben's grade *had* just carried unconscious green-skinned prisoners through the courtyard.

That got *everyone's* attention.

"Witches!" Kelly and Priya said together.

"Has anybody fought witches yet?" Priya asked Kelly.

"Aladdin," replied Kelly. "But he got captured. Jack had to go rescue him."

Their excitement made me want to warn them exactly how deadly witches could be, but it made me want to change the subject, too. They would learn about the dangers soon enough. "We're all here," I told Hansel.

Amy had taken a spot in the far back, on the opposite side from where I was standing.

"That's enough," said Hansel, and our students fell silent. He scared them nearly as much as he'd freaked me out when I was younger. "It's time for class. Are you ready, Priya?"

Priya stepped up, her jaw set. She tossed her long dark hair back. She had definitely gotten cockier since her Tale. "Ready for anything you can throw at me."

She reminded me of Chase when she said stuff like that. She'd never been able to handle what I'd sprung on her. It had started during my very first class. She had seen me come in with Hansel and refused to learn from anyone she could defeat by kicking them in the shins.

But she hadn't beaten me in the Snow Queen's prisons. I'd just been trying to restrain her. Hansel could have told her that the Director had ordered him to send anyone who refused classes to a dungeon cell, to give them a taste of what the Snow Queen had in store for them if they were captured.

But he hadn't. He'd just looked at me, waiting to see how I'd deal with it.

So I'd said that if she could beat one of the dummies, then she could leave class.

She took me up on it. The evil Fey dummy disarmed her in less than a second. Since that embarrassing defeat, she'd worked *hard* in class. She was now one of the best students.

Okay, maybe she reminded me a little of myself, too.

"As long as you're ready," I said. I gestured to one of the wolf dummies at the edge of the room. It sprang forward and, in two bounds, reached Priya. It jumped and knocked the girl to the ground. She shrieked and threw up her arms.

Amy shot me a shocked look, obviously wondering what kind of classroom this was. She took a step forward like she would help.

Then Priya laughed, and the rest of the class laughed with her. "No fair. It attacked from behind."

"That will happen in a battle," Hansel said.

"Okay, class," I said, "who would like to tell Priya what she could have done to counter the attack?"

A dozen hands went up. I pointed at Kelly, who'd been a fraction ahead of everyone else. "She could have dodged. You don't need a weapon for that."

"That *might* work," Hansel said. "The Snow Queen's wolves change direction slower than a human does, but not as slowly as a troll or a dragon. How would you counter a wolf's charge if you had a staff?"

Kelly had an answer for this one too. "Thrust the end at its chest. That should halt the wolf in its tracks *and* knock the wind out of it."

"Excellent, Kelly," I said, and she beamed.

"Not good enough," said Hansel, who still didn't believe in positive reinforcement. "You need to neutralize a wolf opponent while it's struggling for air. How?"

A boy to my left spoke up. He was one of the youngest warriors, only eight, but he made up for it in enthusiasm. "Hit it on the head—to knock it out! And then on the legs—to make sure it can't stand!"

Hansel grunted, but he didn't correct Melvin, which meant it was the answer he'd wanted. I grabbed my staff, the same one I'd used to teach Lena, and waited for Hansel to gesture the dummy forward.

But apparently, he wasn't done making the class nervous. "You lot aren't taking this seriously enough." His voice boomed out across the training court. "You think a villain will give you time to laugh if he sees you down? You've never seen their speed. I'm sure you've heard of Iron Hans, an ancient Character with metal skin. He's the Snow Queen's deadliest warrior. When he last entered a battle, he cut down fifty Characters in twelve minutes."

Melvin and most of the younger students looked decidedly uneasy. Kelly and Priya—the only ones in the class who *had* faced villains—were as ashen as they'd been during their Tale, and I couldn't stand seeing them that way. "No one has seen him in years," I whispered to them.

It was a lie. Actually, I'd fought him once, years ago, and Chase had made him swear a Binding Oath to become our secret ally. Iron Hans had actually helped us on more than one quest since then.

Across the room, Chase caught my eye and grinned. The icy knot in my chest began to thaw. We'd been through so much together, the two of us, and as Hansel gestured for the metal dummies to move forward, my anger drained away.

The bell rang two and a half hours later. Our students racked their staffs. Hansel had ordered me never to tell the whole class that they'd done well, but they had.

Priya and Kelly left, chatting like they always did. I ignored it until Priya asked, "Which one do you think is better? Rory or Chase?"

Oh geez. I felt my cheeks burn.

"That's not even a question," Kenneth said, walking out behind them and obviously eavesdropping. "*Chase*. He taught Rory everything she knows."

I couldn't argue with that.

Priya shot Kenneth a withering stare, which was pretty impressive, considering she was five grades below him. "I don't believe you. I think Rory could beat Chase, if she really wanted to."

I'd never even gotten *close* to beating Chase in our sparring sessions. Before I could say anything, Chase piped up. "A duel! Awesome! Let's schedule one. Maybe Sunday."

Priya and Kelly actually cheered.

I turned to Hansel, fully expecting him to put a stop to this, but he nodded. "It would make a good lesson."

My jaw actually dropped open. I didn't look forward to Chase kicking my butt in front of all our students, but I was outranked.

"We're going to go tell everyone!" Kelly said.

"So you can't change your mind," Priya added, and then they ran out. Half of EAS would know about it by the time lunch ended.

"You weren't super helpful," I told Hansel accusingly.

He grinned, and I could see why Gretel still thought of him as her annoying little brother. "I'd like to see that fight. My money's on you."

"Hey," Chase said, clearly unaware that Hansel was just trying to rile him up.

"Rory, are you coming?" Mom called from near the door. Her voice was full of forced cheerfulness again. "I'm not sure I remember how to get to our new home."

I opened my mouth. We'd gone over this already. I didn't want to fight in public, even if the training courts were nearly empty.

"We have a Canon meeting," said Chase, who obviously still wanted to make up for this morning.

"I'm afraid it's required," Hansel said. "Each grade sends a representative. Rory will be going for the rising ninth graders."

Mom gave me a look that clearly said we would be discussing my responsibilities later. But at least she wouldn't follow me *this* time.

Chase jumped up on an empty bench and jumped again until his hands closed over the branches that formed the ceiling of the Canon's meeting room. He pushed his head through the leaves and then dropped back to his seat, grinning at me. "Just checking. No eavesdroppers."

He did this before almost every meeting. It usually made me

smile, but this time, I only remembered my first visit here when I'd spied with Chase, watching the Canon vote on whether or not to tell me about my own Tale. He had been close to Adelaide then too, and I hadn't liked him much at the time. I hated that it was starting to be true again.

Today wasn't the first time he'd "left" his M3 in his room. Unfortunately, that was only one of his excuses.

Twice, after failing to show with the rest of the grade for planned missions, he'd said, "Oh, that was today? I totally forgot." Another was, "I lost track of time." Once, when he missed rescuing an eleventh grade Character from some invading trolls, he'd said, "I just had so many mirrorcordings to watch." That excuse was so lame that the stepsisters almost stopped talking to him.

When he took a seat, he didn't seem to have any clue as to what I was thinking, and that bothered me even more.

Lena dropped heavily onto the bench beside us. "The Director ordered way too many M3's. She must think that I can make each one in five minutes. I wonder if it would be worth it to explain the cooling process to her—"

"Shhhh," hissed the representative for the Princess and the Pea, a finger over her lipstick-covered mouth.

The Director stood in front of her chair, the one covered with roses. Her long blond hair was braided, and she wore a shirt of golden chain mail over her blue silk dress. "Be seated. We have much ground to cover." She turned to me. "Aurora Landon, you were attacked at home by the Wolfsbane clan. They used unknown magics against you. Please report."

I forced myself to stand, flushing. I hadn't expected to open the meeting, but they needed the information. When I explained how the witches had stopped the comb cage from rising to the ceiling, Chase squirmed in his seat, clearly feeling even guiltier now that he knew more about the fight. When I told them how swiftly Lena's sleeping spell had taken out the Wolfsbane clan, Stu the Shoemaker and Rumpelstiltskin smiled at our favorite inventor. Lena was too busy shooting me a worried look to notice. Chase glanced pointedly at my hands. They were shaking again, so I put them behind my back.

The first response came from the Character whose chair was taller than all the others. Rapunzel's long silver braid hung over the side and trailed across the floor. "For every spell, there is a counterspell, but every weapon is revealed in its own time—a time determined by my sister."

The other Characters glanced at each other, clearly confused. It wasn't *that* hard to figure out what she was saying. "She's right. They *prepared* to fight me," I said. "They may have known how to stop the combs and block M3's for a while, but they didn't use those spells until today. They wanted to take us by surprise."

"But they have lost that advantage today. We will question the Wolfsbane clan about these new methods," the Director said. "Lena, where are you with those improved Bats of Destruction we spoke of? I asked to see a prototype last month."

Lena gulped. "I've just been really busy. I've been trying to focus on the M3's and rings of return first. And Rory's magic shield was a great idea. I'd like to run it past—"

"Shields won't stop the pillars, Lena," the Director said. "You have had almost three months for this. I expect to see a prototype in the next ten days, and I want to see the M3's and rings of return in five. Have I made myself clear?"

I narrowed my eyes. We wouldn't even *have* half these items if not for Lena.

Lena didn't try to argue again. "Yes, ma'am. I understand."

The Director swung her gaze over to the Canon's champion, Chase's dad. She didn't even bother welcoming him back from his week-long mission to Atlantis. "Jack, what is the news from the Unseelie Court?"

Chase perked up, instantly interested. His mother, Lady Ayalla Aspenwind, lived there.

"King Mattanair hasn't changed his mind," Jack said heavily. "He refuses to move against the Snow Queen as long as his son and heir is her prisoner."

I shifted uncomfortably. I didn't like Fael, the Unseelie crown prince. He'd bullied Chase back when Chase still lived with his mom. But I kind of felt responsible for the Snow Queen getting her hands on him. When we were in her palace last spring, we'd watched Likon, the ice giant, carry him and the Seelie prince inside—I'd been so focused on rescuing my friends, and the kids the Pied Piper had kidnapped, that I hadn't even thought about rescuing *him*.

Snow White spoke up from her glass-backed chair. She'd abandoned her recruiting duties to serve as the Director's ambassador. "Queen Titania and King Oberon still refuse to even see me. But the other Seelie Fey say the same. They cannot fight until their prince is returned."

We all knew what that meant. The only reason we'd defeated the Snow Queen's forces in the first war was because the Fey had joined our side. Without them, our chances of winning weren't so great.

Battles are about tactics, Forrel had said, *but wars, they're won with numbers and weapons.* We were short on allies.

"I did visit the other EAS chapters, like you asked. Again," said Sarah Thumb. Her chair and her husband's sat on a pedestal so that they could give dirty looks from a decent height, just like

Sarah was doing now. "I think they're getting tired of seeing me, but they say that their position remains unchanged."

The interchapter delegates had come to my first Canon meeting as a grade representative, soon after the attacks had begun. The man with silvering hair had given a long-winded speech, which I hadn't understood at all. The other delegate, his wife, a beautiful blond woman, had summed it up, saying, "The other chapters of Ever After School suggest that you search for a peaceful resolution with the Snow Queen, as they have. They regret they cannot enter this conflict."

In other words, we couldn't even rely on the Ever After Schools on other continents for support. We were all alone in this.

After that meeting, I'd found out that the interchapter delegates were Adelaide's parents, and then I wasn't surprised that I hadn't liked them.

They had apartments at every chapter, but they mostly operated out of the oldest chapter, in Europe. That was the first and last time I'd ever seen them.

Chase and Adelaide dating made a certain amount of sense. They both had parents in the Canon. They were two of the few kids who had *always* lived here, not just when the Snow Queen threatened them. Their parents left them both alone most of the time. Their relationship shouldn't still feel like a puzzle I needed to figure out.

"The goblin priestesses?" the Director asked, moving down her list. "The mother of the four Winds?"

"Still in hiding," said Gretel, "and even if they weren't, I suspect they would say they have done enough."

The Snow Queen had found out about the letter the goblin priestesses had sent her allies, the one that told them not to underestimate me. She had sent almost as many troops after them as she had against us.

Probably safe to count them out too. They had other problems.

"The elves of Muirland will probably say no," said Jack reluctantly. "Solange's wolves kidnapped their king. I heard some Fey discussing it in Atlantis."

"This is unacceptable," the Director said, like all these reports were the *Canon's* fault. "To date, the only alliance we've secured is with the MerKing."

Chatty had convinced her dad. The mermaids had a bunch of skilled warriors, but they could only fight from the water. It wasn't a huge help.

"We've fought the war on our own so far," Sarah Thumb protested. "We've done okay."

Hansel shot her a pitying look. He was our general. "You wouldn't say that if you had survived the last one. This war hasn't taken hold yet. These are just skirmishes, not battles."

Rapunzel glanced at me, her eyes sorrowful. "It's a hunt now, not a war. She hunts our numbers and our courage."

Sometimes, news is so bad your body reacts before your mind can catch up. I reeled so hard I almost lost my balance, forgetting the bench didn't have a back. Chase turned my way, and Lena grabbed my arm, steadying me.

It was going to get worse. That was what Rapunzel was saying. It was going to get worse, and I felt like I was barely holding on as it was.

"What of the Living Stone Dwarves?" the Director asked Henry, the Frog Prince.

I didn't want to get my hopes up about it, but I did want to see Forrel again. We hadn't heard from the Living Stone Dwarves since April, when Miriam, Lena, Chase, and I had helped save their young prince and princess, Iggy and Ima.

The Frog Prince sighed. "The ice city of Kiivinsh is still abandoned. They haven't relocated to any place they'd lived before the Snow Queen gave them a new home."

Canon members started suggesting areas the dwarves might be hiding.

I barely listened. I didn't blame the Living Stone Dwarves for not wanting to fight. They were still in mourning for Princess Hadriane. She had stood up to the Snow Queen in front of all her allies, telling them what a tyrant Solange was. Hadriane hadn't flinched when Solange raised her hand and threw those ice darts. I hoped I could be that brave.

Sarah Thumb's voice rose above the rest. "Too bad we can't help them resettle in their homeland in Arizona. We would at least know where to find them. If they had their petrified wood back, they would never budge."

It had been a weak joke. Only a few people smiled.

"Why can't we?" It took me a second to realize I'd said it out loud, but judging by the number of Characters who turned to stare at me, I definitely had.

The Director had made it *very* clear that we young Characters were only there to give reports and receive orders. We were *not* supposed to talk. I tried to pretend that I had just been muttering something to Lena, but that didn't work.

"Do you have something to say, Aurora Landon?" said the Director shortly.

I froze.

Maybe I should have kept my mouth shut. Maybe I should have pretended that I let the grown-up Characters do all my thinking for me. Maybe I would have—if they had been talking about anyone besides the Living Dwarves.

I *knew* Hadriane. I remembered the longing in her voice when she spoke of her people's homeland. So I said, "Why can't we help them resettle in the Petrified Forest National Park? We should be able to talk to the ranger people. The dwarves would need to hide during the day, but . . ."

I drifted off. The whole Canon was still staring at me. Most of them looked kind of scandalized. I guess it was a stupid idea to suggest during a war. We had enough to deal with.

Chase sat forward. "They might come to us if they hear we have something to offer."

Then Lena piped up. "I could probably cast a cloaking spell over their settlement, so no humans could see it unless they were inside."

"They really want their homeland back," added Miriam, the representative for the rising twelfth graders. She and Hadriane had spent most of the quest side-by-side. Miriam had even started a new fashion among the high schoolers—four-strand dwarvish braids, just like the princess had taught her. "That's the only reason they allied with the Snow Queen, but we could probably help them more than she could. I mean, we still *live* in the human lands. We know more stuff."

"Actually, this is pretty random," said Ben, who was the representative for the grade above us, "but I have a cousin married to a park ranger who works there."

For three whole seconds, it seemed kind of *possible*.

A few members of the Canon were warming up to the idea. Red Riding Hood scratched her chin under her red baseball cap. Henry stared at me with the same shock I'd felt the day the sword master invited me to be his assistant—like I'd never seen him properly before. But Hansel and Rapunzel both smiled.

The Director's look was cool. "The dwarf king will be truly eager to accept our help, I'm sure. The last time his people allied with ours only resulted in the death of his eldest daughter."

Everyone but Ben flinched. We had invited Hadriane on the quest with us. I wasn't the only one who felt responsible for her death.

"Mildred." Rapunzel's voice was soft, but the reproach was obvious. "One child was taken from him, but his twins and heirs were returned safely. The king would not forget."

"It's a fair point," said Gretel. The guilt lodged in my stomach barely budged.

"The king does owe us," Hansel agreed, "and his people may want revenge for the death of their princess."

"So, this should be our new policy, then?" said the Director. "To lure allies to us the same way Solange does? Offering them lands we do not have?"

Ugh. In every meeting, the Director found a way to remind everyone how similar the Snow Queen and I were. We weren't just the only two Characters in history with Unwritten Tales. Sometimes, we thought the same way too.

She didn't need to tell me. I'd been doing my research. I knew I could turn evil just like Solange.

"Not necessarily," said Henry. "There's a world of difference between promising something you never deliver and offering to help them do something immediately."

The Director stared at me instead of Henry. I shrank back between Chase and Lena.

Then the door banged open. It was Rufus, one of the elves who manned the emergency phones and M3 lines these days. He was too out of breath to speak at first, but he would only interrupt the meeting for one reason. Someone had called in another attack.

"Who?" the Director asked Rufus.

"Marty Mason's farm in Idaho. He graduated more than ten years ago," Rufus said, "so he thought he was safe. But dragons have burned down his house. His family is fleeing to the nearest Door Trek door, but he called on his cell phone for backup."

"How many dragons?" Hansel asked.

"Marty saw at least four. He also said that he spotted smoke farther out," Rufus said.

I struggled to my feet. My legs were still wobbly, but I *was* on duty until dinner.

"Sit down, Aurora," added the Director. "As talented as the rising ninth graders may be, you had your own battle just a few hours ago."

Chase stood up. "I'll go."

The Director nodded. "You and Ben go, and take as many students from Ben's grade as you can find in the next few minutes."

Chase followed Ben out the door. He didn't look back. I could hear him yelling that he had to grab his sword and a sandwich from the Table—he couldn't fight on an empty stomach.

Then we all were dismissed.

Lena buried her face in her palms, muttering about stupid rings and stupid bats and stupid Directors. If rescuing me hadn't put her behind schedule, then getting an ultimatum from the Canon definitely did. "Did the exploding bats just put you over the edge?" I whispered to Lena, only kind of joking.

She dropped her hands. "I don't *want* to make them," she whispered. Her fingers curled around the edge of the bench, like she was anchoring herself to her seat. "I keep thinking about what happened in the Snow Queen's palace. I mean, the Bats of Destruction were great at first, but when General Searcaster got control of them . . ."

She had been blaming herself for our capture for months. Honestly though, it would have probably happened even if General Searcaster *hadn't* turned the bats against us. "It's not your fault, Lena."

She nodded, but the frown didn't leave her face. "That's what Gran says too. But, Rory, we were just lucky that time. What if I make some of the exploding kind and she gets them, too?"

They could kill hundreds of Characters in minutes. "You've told that to the Director?"

"She says that we just won't use the bats in direct battles with the Snow Queen and General Searcaster," Lena said, keeping her voice low so none of the others could overhear. "They're the only magic users strong enough to take over another weapon."

If Lena still felt this guilty over the regular bats, I didn't want to find out how she would feel if the exploding bats fell in the wrong hands. "There's a lot wrong with that plan," I said cautiously.

"What choice do I have?" Lena said. "She's the *Director*."

"You just have to give her *something,* not necessarily what she wants," I said.

Lena's head popped up again. That idea had clearly never occurred to her. "The Director shot down the shield idea . . . ," she said, thinking aloud.

"An offensive weapon, then," I said, relieved. "Something that helps her feel like we're not so outnumbered."

Then I saw what I'd been hoping for—that flash in Lena's eyes, the one that meant an idea for a new invention had snapped into place. "Rory, you're a genius!"

She pushed through the crowd, hurrying toward the workshop.

I stayed where I was, smiling after her. I didn't have anywhere to be except my new apartment, and I wasn't exactly looking forward to seeing Mom again.

Across the room, sitting quietly on her extra-tall chair, Rapunzel met my eyes, waiting too. Good. I'd thought up a new question the night before.

I made my way over as the rest of the Canon and the grade representatives finished filing out. The Director noticed. She sighed in a terrifically disapproving way, but she didn't have time to actually stop and find out what we were up to. She was too busy. So far, that was the only good thing about the war.

The last member of the Canon, the Goose Girl, shuffled

through the doorway, feathers stuck all the way down her back-side. Then Rapunzel turned to me, her dark eyes worried. "Are you all right?"

I nodded. She must not have foreseen the Wolfsbane clan. It used to be rare that an attack took her by surprise, but EAS had so many of them now. Her visions couldn't keep up. "I wanted to ask you something," I said.

Rapunzel pressed her lips together so hard they looked white. That was the only way you could tell how much she hated me asking questions about her sister.

I couldn't help it. I had convinced the Director to let me borrow all the books the reference room had on Solange when I found out how my Tale was connected to hers. I even had a copy of Solange's Tale, transcribed by the librarian at EAS's European chapter. But texts didn't answer all my questions about the Snow Queen.

Only her sister could know certain things.

"Why snow?" I asked.

Rapunzel was quiet a moment. It took her a while to gather her thoughts sometimes, especially when she wanted to make sense. I appreciated her effort. Once, I had asked her why Solange had kidnapped a boy named Kai in her early days, and Rapunzel's only explanation was, *What would you do if power flowed through your veins instead of blood?* Not super helpful.

Then Rapunzel looked at me, dark eyes narrowed. That usu-ally meant she'd figured out how to explain something. "Do you remember what I told you of her mother?"

"Yes," I said, although I kind of regretted asking that question. Solange's mother had been a noblewoman during the French Revolution. She hadn't survived. Solange had been hiding in the mob that executed her mom.

"It snowed the morning after her mother died," Rapunzel said. "She found such comfort in the way the white wiped the landscape clean of the previous day's terror. She said it was like a blank canvas on which she might paint a world of her own devising. So she always enjoyed creating snowflakes with her sorcery, even before she became heartless."

Yep. This was another question I wished I hadn't asked.

It is supremely annoying to pity the person trying to kill you. It didn't even help me stop her.

"The idea you put forth before the Canon. It was a good one," said Rapunzel.

I half smiled. She had definitely changed the subject, and she hadn't even *tried* to be subtle about it. "Thanks." The Director hadn't liked it, though. So nothing would probably come from it.

Then Rapunzel said something that made the dread return a hundredfold.

"You will not like what your mother asks of you this evening," she murmured, "but do not fault her for wanting it. She doesn't understand yet, not as the others do. You will refuse her, but do so with kindness."

Our new apartment was in the same hall as the rest of my grade. Well, except for the triplets, but they had picked out rooms just in case their father ever let them move.

I'd picked *our* new home almost as soon as I'd come back from Miriam's quest. Well, technically, Chase had found it for me, but I'd given him very specific requirements: three bedrooms, and mine needed to have a closet, so I could use a temporary-transport spell to escape even if Mom tried to lock me in my bedroom. I wondered what Mom and Amy thought of the place. It was so much smaller than anywhere else we had lived in the past few years.

I almost managed to get past the apartment where my dad, Brie, and the baby had been living for the last few months, but before I'd gone two steps down the hall, the door opened. Brie popped out, dressed in a pretty sundress and high heels. Her standard uniform for business meetings back in L.A. "Hello again, Rory! Your dad and I have a dinner thing back at home. You're welcome to come. We can do something afterward. Maybe an early birthday celebration."

"You can even bring your sword." Dad stepped out too. His hair was still wet from the shower, and Dani was strapped to his chest. She was awake now. I knew she was supposed to be too young to recognize people besides her parents, but she was looking right at me. She knew we were sisters. I stretched out a finger, right next to her tiny palm, and she gripped it, blinking.

"Right!" Yes, Brie always sounded that enthusiastic. I'd gotten used to it. "Eric has decided to introduce our bodyguards as the kind of extras he wants for his next project. He even reserved them their own table. He'll come across as somewhere between over-the-top and eccentric, but—"

"But I've decided that I'm okay with that as long as my girls don't mind an over-the-top, eccentric father." Dad wrapped an arm around my shoulder and squeezed. I smiled. "What do you say?"

"You haven't heard about this project yet!" Brie said.

Since Dad hadn't been able to take on another film without endangering his life, he'd announced he was on paternity leave for the rest of the year. But before my workaholic father could go into withdrawal, Brie had suggested he try to write a screenplay. Dad had always wanted to take a stab at being a writer-director. Now he finally had the time.

He'd never mentioned what it was about. But if he thought fully armed teens could be great extras, then my guess was an action flick.

Dad shoved his hand through his wet hair. It was going to dry like that, going in a thousand directions. "I'd love to run the story past you. I can tell your mother I invited you to come weeks ago, if you want."

I gave him a look. I couldn't do that to her. After this morning, ditching her for Dad and his new wife would just add insult to injury. "Maybe next time."

So Dad and Brie gave me great big hugs and kisses, and they promised to call me if they ran into any trouble. They had their cell phones if their M3 got blocked. Then they were gone, and I was at the door of my new home.

I couldn't procrastinate any more. I turned the doorknob and stepped inside.

Mom smiled broadly when she saw me. "There you are!" She'd tied a bandanna over her hair. She held a folded rag, and the tiny living room smelled like the orange oil soap Amy always used to wipe counters and mop floors. "Can you believe how dirty this place is? But it's small—that means it's easy to clean."

I knew what this was. Mom called them "nesting afternoons"— if we moved in that morning, we always spent the rest of the day getting settled in. She was trying to pretend this was just a normal move.

The hard conversation would come later, but I was grateful. I knew how to deal with this. I unbuckled my sword belt and slung it over the back of a chair. Moving to one of the boxes, I pulled out Mom's sheets. "Which set do you want? The blue flowers or the green stripes?"

We put on some music—one of the soundtracks to a sixties period film Mom had starred in. We knew the lyrics to every song, and we belted them out as we tackled our usual chores. I made up all the beds and vacuumed the carpet. Mom scrubbed the sink, hung her favorite pictures on the walls, and set up framed photos of us on the side tables. Amy unpacked the kitchen and mopped the floors. We drew straws on who had to clean the bathroom. Amy lost.

While she got started, Mom and I sat on the couch. "Home isn't where all your stuff is," she said, like she always did when a rental started to feel like ours. She threw her arms around me and squeezed hard. "It's where your favorite people are."

I hugged her back, but I'd already lost my smile. If this was a normal move, we would declare our first evening a movie night and fill the new place with the smells of popcorn and brownies, which might not actually be edible. But this apartment didn't have a microwave. It didn't even have a TV. And as much as we tried to pretend, it was hard to ignore the fact that all the light in the room came from extra-bright, smoke-free torches.

I sighed. "I know you're still mad at me, Mom."

"No, not mad," Mom said, but I didn't believe her. Steeliness had snuck back into her voice. "Rory, I don't think you realize how difficult this morning was for me."

"I *am* sorry." I couldn't remember if I'd said that to her yet. "But if they had captured you—"

"They would have used me to draw you out. You would still be in danger. Yes, Amy told me," Mom said. Wow. I couldn't remember the last time Amy had taken my side. "I don't pretend to understand what all this means—you having this Unwritten Tale, and being part of a Triumvirate, and having a destiny to stop the

Snow Queen. But today's attack was probably my fault. We would have been safe if I'd agreed to move here when your father did."

Hearing her admit that was nice. It would have been great if she stopped there.

Mom spoke slowly and carefully. She must have rehearsed this. "Some of these dangers *are* unavoidable. I have to make peace with that. But some of them aren't. I'd like you to promise me that you won't risk yourself when it's not strictly necessary. Those weapon lessons are fine, but no more missions, no more rushing off for daring rescues, no *seeking* danger."

Rapunzel was right. I didn't like it. I was mad at Mom for even asking this. She made it sound like I was doing everything for *fun*. "I can't, Mom."

"Yes, I know—the Director assigns you many of these mission things," Mom said, still not getting it. "I'll talk to her. It's not fair to ask you kids to do so much."

"Mom, I'm one of the best fighters EAS *has*," I said. "If I refuse to fight, people will die. More people, I mean."

Her voice rose. "Rory, you and your friends are *so young*—"

She wasn't the only one having a hard time controlling her temper. "We don't have a choice. If the Snow Queen wins, we'll have to live under her rule just like everyone else."

"You might not get the chance if—" She stopped. Her eyes grew bright, but she must have decided she wouldn't cry in front of me. She stared straight ahead, taking deep breaths until she got herself under control.

This *was* hard for her. I should have given more than a few months to get used to the idea that magic was real. It might have been easier for all of us if I'd told her the truth after my first day at EAS.

But I couldn't hide in my room while everyone I knew went out to fight. Even if the Director agreed to let me sit out missions, I couldn't handle the guilt of wondering if I could have kept people safe.

So, as gently as I could, I said, "Mom, I'm really sorry, but I can't make you that promise."

Mom's eyebrows pinched together. She ripped off the gloves she'd been using to clean the sink. "I'm not *asking*, Rory."

"I know." I didn't have to tell her that she couldn't stop me. I stood up. I would probably need that secret exit in my room sooner rather than later. "I'm going to take a shower."

She sputtered a little bit. I'd never refused her outright before.

I kissed her cheek and walked away.

I was used to dreaming of the ancient black door by now. I saw the frost tracing the grain of the wood and my breath clouding the air almost every night, and I felt the cold in my bones and knew with absolute certainty that the fate of the world depended on what was on the other side.

But that night, I dreamed of Chase.

He slept on a cot in a small room. Old-fashioned furniture was scattered around him, across a worn stone floor, the legs of stools tangled with the spokes of some wooden wheels. A window was cut into the pale wall. Far below, a river glittered in the sunlight, and birds chirped outside.

Chase's sleeve was spotted with blood but, besides that, he didn't have a mark on him. It was so peaceful, and he was only napping. I didn't understand why, in the dream, I was so worried that he wouldn't wake up.

In the morning, even before I opened my eyes, I remembered two things: It was my birthday, and the Snow Queen wouldn't let it be a happy one.

Something terrible was going to happen. I just knew it.

I rolled out of bed, pulled on battle-ready clothes, double-knotted my sneakers, and strapped on my sword. When I opened the door, a big pile of wrapped presents waited on the side table. This was the first year *ever* that I wasn't even a little curious about what was inside the gifts. I wondered if this was what grown-ups felt like on their birthdays.

Mom sat drinking her coffee at the counter, just like she would have if we were still in San Francisco. "Happy birthday," she said with a tight smile. Her flat tone gave me the feeling that if it *hadn't* been my birthday, she would have brought up that promise again.

"Thanks," I said, smiling back. It felt unnatural on my face, and it probably looked that way too.

"Breakfast?" Amy asked, scrambling eggs on the stove.

I really hoped that they were for Mom, not me. Just the smell was making my stomach churn. "No. Thank you."

"We get it," Amy said. "You probably have plans with your friends first thing, and I'm guessing your dad reserved lunch. We'll be at work anyway—that's fine. But dinner belongs to Maggie."

"Just like every year," I said, even though it felt nothing like other years.

Mom didn't tease me with hints about what presents she'd gotten me. She stood up and poured herself more coffee, saying nothing. Things had gotten pretty bad between us if she couldn't even pretend nothing was wrong.

"Six o'clock sharp," added Amy. I could hear a note of desperation in her cheerfulness. "You can *try* to be later, but that stack of presents might get a tiny bit shorter."

No way could I tell them that I didn't feel like celebrating at all.

"Got it. Dinner is reserved. I'll see you later." Then I hurried out of the apartment. Rapunzel was just outside the door. The churning in my stomach turned into a whirlpool of anxiety and bile. I thought I might actually throw up. She usually only waited for me when I was about to go on a quest.

"Is this the part where you tell me today is *the* day I stop the Snow Queen?" Because as scary as that sounded, I kind of relished the idea. At least then, we could get my Tale over with.

Rapunzel's mouth twisted. "No."

"Then is today the day you tell me what I need to know to defeat her?" That was the other reason she usually sought me out.

"Time, for me, is messy, and timing delicate," she said, like she'd said at least a thousand times this summer when I'd asked her something she didn't want to answer. I resisted the urge to roll my eyes. "No, this is the part where I give you presents. Do not tell me," she added when I started to protest, "that you don't want to celebrate this birthday. I am not trying to cheer you up. You must understand, at a certain age, your birthday gives others an excuse to celebrate *you* and show their affection. Your birthday is a gift to us."

"You're on fire with the guilt-tripping," I told her, but I was a tiny bit pleased in spite of the roiling in my stomach. She'd never given me a birthday present before.

"After all these years, I have learned something from Mildred." She put something cool and round in my hands.

A glass vial. Silver had been wrapped up and down the outside, and a chain hung from its end. The light I had used when I'd fought a litter of dragons in Jimmy Searcaster's house. "I can't take this." It was precious to Rapunzel. She'd never let Lena examine it no matter how much my friend had begged.

"It needs to be yours." Rapunzel walked down the corridor. "Come. The next gift cannot be held in your hand. The Director does not know that I found it, or that I moved it."

We walked down a few more halls. Scratch what I said about not being curious about presents. "You must know the easiest way to reach it," she said, turning a corner. "Start at the base of my tower. Take the door that once led to the kitchens. Take the third right four times, then your immediate left. That will bring you straight here."

She stopped. The door in front of us was plain white except for the red trim around the frame. "See the way it shimmers, but only when you look at it on a slant?"

I nodded. Out of the corner of my eye, I could see light playing under the red, like Rapunzel had painted over mother-of-pearl.

"It reveals this door's true nature: it is a one-key safe." Rapunzel sounded almost smug. "My sister taught me the spell. It requires much planning. For this one to be ready in time, I had to start years ago, before you arrived at Ever After School."

I looked at her. She'd said this wasn't a lesson in how to defeat the Snow Queen, but I didn't believe her anymore. Rapunzel never mentioned her sister casually.

"To finish the casting, I had to steal some Water of Life. I know where Mildred hides it," she said, which meant the one-key safe was powerful *and* complicated. "The spell is sound. Look." She reached for the doorknob but, an inch from the metal, her hand stopped midair, straining against an invisible barrier. "This door can only be opened by one person, and this fact cannot be changed after the spell is cast. I have linked this one to a certain quality of yours."

"Which one?" I said, wondering if it was normal to feel a little apprehensive when a seer gave you a birthday present.

Rapunzel smiled, in a sly way that clearly said, *I'm not telling*. "Not your status as a bearer of an Unwritten Tale. If I had specified

that, Solange would be able to enter. Your present is safe inside."
She stepped out of my way.

My hand closed over the doorknob. It turned easily.

The room beyond was closet-size and empty except for two
objects: one was a statue of a soldier in an old-fashioned uniform
with a yellowing tag tied around his wrist. I knew what it said. I'd
read it the first time I'd seen this guy: *Wolfgang Sebastian Bruhm,
1788–1804*. The third member of the previous Triumvirate.

This time, I knew what had turned him to stone. Arica the sorceress had cast a spell on him. He'd been protecting the same
object he was stored with—a battered, metal saltshaker, sitting in
dented glory on top of a pedestal. The Pounce Pot. The last I heard,
the Director had used it to make sure that Chase, Lena, and I didn't
find out that my Tale had begun.

It was so powerful it could make a person swallow their tongue
if they tried to share the secret. I'd seen that happen. It wasn't
pretty.

I took a deep breath. I focused on not puking.

Rapunzel leaned against the wall beside the door frame. With
all that triumph in her face, she looked almost exactly like Solange.
"Someday soon, you might need to hide a secret."

The second I stepped out into the courtyard, Lena, the triplets,
the stepsisters, and Paul Stockton immediately started singing,
"Happy birthday to you." That wouldn't have been so bad, except
the courtyard was crowded with people eating breakfast. Half of
them turned to look. Some of them *joined in.*

I flushed, but some of the tension in my stomach eased.
"Payback will come."

"Our birthdays are *months* away," Lena said happily. Balanced over her hands was a tray of cupcakes. She must have gotten it from the Table of Never Ending Instant Refills. I wondered how she convinced it to take requests. At this time of day, all it wanted to produce were muffins, pancakes, and cereal. "Chocolate for breakfast."

I scanned their smiling faces again. I didn't even realize who I was looking for until Tina said, very gently, "We invited Chase."

"No show," Vicky said, less gently.

It was worse than Mom barely talking to me this morning. Birthdays were important to Chase. He wouldn't miss mine unless . . . well, unless our friendship had fallen *really* low on his list of priorities. "Maybe he's still on the mission at that farm in Idaho."

"Overnight?" Kevin scoffed, but worse than that was the silence from the others. Their pitying looks.

"Ben's back," Kyle said reluctantly. "He said he's glad Chase is busy and lessons are cancelled for the day. He was going back to sleep."

Chase's group wasn't like Hansel's classes. They didn't meet every other day besides Saturdays on a strict gingerbread jack–enforced schedule. They just met whenever Chase was free.

If he wasn't celebrating with us and he wasn't on a mission, then he must be on another date with Adelaide.

I *was* that low on his list of priorities.

I should have defended him again. I should have made a joke about how we would have all slept in like Ben and Chase were doing if we'd been up past midnight hunting dragons and helping Marty Mason move.

But I couldn't make myself. I was too hurt.

Because the problem had never been him and Adelaide disappearing so often. It was that this summer felt like our final days, and both of them were choosing to spend those days away from us.

I tried to ignore the cold thread of fury worming through my veins and focus on the friends who were here. "Thank you," I said, and meant it. I picked up a promising-looking cupcake—chocolate with smooth chocolate frosting and cookie crumbles on top. "Please tell me you don't expect me to eat all of these by myself," I added.

"Definitely not." Paul reached for a cupcake.

Tina grabbed one next. "It's a shame we can't *really* celebrate. We're all too busy, but maybe afterward."

"The war will have to end soon, right?" said Vicky. "I mean, it *is* your birthday, and July's almost over."

The triplets goggled at the stepsisters, and Lena actually glared, like bringing up the beginning of my Tale should be off limits. I'd told the rest of our grade about it just once, the day after Daisy's home had been attacked. I thought it was only fair for them to know why the Snow Queen always tried to take out Characters close to me. After that, we never mentioned my Tale, definitely not in public. They knew I didn't want to discuss it.

But bringing it up now made the dread back off a little.

She had given us all an *after*.

I smiled. "That would be really nice."

After the cupcakes were gone, we split up. The stepsisters went to archery class. The triplets and Paul went with them, hoping to beg a target off of Hansel for their own practice. Lena ran to the dungeons to collect more scales from the dragon we kept down there for an ever-refreshing supply.

I didn't have class. I wished I did. I needed a bigger distraction than cupcakes.

Something terrible *was* going to happen, and Chase wouldn't be around for it. *Again.*

I did what I usually did on mornings when the staff class didn't meet, everyone else was busy, and no one needed saving. I slipped inside the workshop and went over my research.

The workshop was empty—the shoemaker and the elves were manning the phones and M3's in a room closer to the Director's office. But Lena's section was abandoned too, with dragon scales and baseball bats scattered all across the worktable. Melodie, Lena's golden harp and assistant inventor, must have gone out for extra ingredients as well.

I walked over to a shelf Lena had cleared for me back in April. A stack of dusty, leatherbound volumes waited there, most of the lettering rubbed off their spines. I'd read one more than the others: *The Livves & Tymes of Sorcerers & Sorceresses*. I had it out on semipermanent loan from the reference room, because when Rapunzel had seen me with it, she'd said, "In my tower, my sister had a book of that title. She read it to me as bedtime stories, but usually not the endings. Too gruesome."

I pulled out the papers underneath it. My notes covered the first dozen pages—I wrote down anything I could find out about the Snow Queen's immortality or her sorcery or her Tale. I flipped to the last page and quickly scribbled down the answer to the *Why snow?* question Rapunzel had told me yesterday. Not that I thought I would forget.

Rapunzel had answered my questions all summer, like what body part Solange had lost during her Tale to make her a sorceress the first time (two toes to frostbite—she was eleven) and how powerful that made her (not very—she could cover a room with frost or hold a glamour for seven minutes) and why the European chapter of EAS had kicked her out (they found out she had kidnapped and enchanted a boy named Kai; she gave back the golden apple and didn't age a bit).

When I'd had a question about Unwritten Tales, Rapunzel had sent me straight to Sarah Thumb, who turned out to be the Canon's expert. I only had to bring up the subject, and then I'd lost almost an hour listening to how many Tales Solange had sparked and how many she'd changed. Most of it was crazy magical theory that went over my head. I'd only copied down one thing she said: *If you could see the magic around a person having a Tale—it follows the Characters, clings to them like a giant bubble of pure energy—you would see that it fills an entire room. For an Unwritten Tale, like yours and Solange's, it fills up the entire courtyard.*

"You mean, like a football field?" I'd asked, startled.

"No. Not the way the courtyard used to be," Sarah Thumb said, her eyes gleaming the way they always did when she talked about magic. "The way it is now. As big as a village." I must have looked kind of creeped out, because she added, "It won't stay like this. After your Tale ends, the magic mostly disappears. I mean we think the magic revisits the Tale bearer even after the Unwritten Tale ends. We think—well, *I* think—that's how Solange got so powerful. She learned how to control all that magic."

I didn't want to control it. I didn't want to even think about how magic from my Tale was filling up EAS, sparking and chang-ing other people's Tales. It made me feel like Kelly and Priya's Tales were my fault.

I abandoned the book and my notes, and turned to "The Tale of Solange de Chateies" and the earliest known version of "The Snow Queen." Rumpelstiltskin had asked the librarian at the European chapter to make a copy for me—a magical copy, so the illustrations were as crisp and clear as they would have been if they'd sent me the volumes instead.

This version of "The Snow Queen" was a let down. It was almost exactly the same as Hans Christian Andersen's, which you could check out in the reference room. But the illustrations weren't. The first Kai, in his portrait, looked almost exactly like Rapunzel: white-blond hair, dark eyes under light eyebrows in a heart-shaped face. But when I asked Rapunzel, she said she and Solange had no known relatives in Scandinavia.

"The Tale of Solange de Chateies" had a lot more to process.

I pulled my notes toward me and stared at the chart I'd written after reading Solange's Tale.

Solange's Tale	Mine
Found and destroyed the Seelie scepter before King Navaire could get control of both Fey courts.	Lena's Tale—Melodie.
Mildred struck with a curse that turns her slowly to glass; Solange and Sebastian go on quest for the antidote and trick a witch into making it for them.	Ben's Tale—cockatrice poisoning/ Lena/Water of Life.
King Navaire starts capturing and killing all Characters questing through Atlantis; Solange decides, on her own, that he must be stopped. Meets Arica. Loses Sebastian.	Miriam's Tale—kidnapped Portlanders/Hadriane.

The second Triumvirate lost Mildred less than two weeks after losing Sebastian. A witch's arrow, dipped in a sleeping enchantment, grazed her arm. It was enough to jumpstart her Tale—"Sleeping Beauty." She wasn't quite as lost as Sebastian had been, but Solange was still alone.

She went to the Unseelie Court anyway. She glamoured herself as a Fey, and in the seven minutes she had until the illusion wore out, she added cockatrice poison to King Navaire's dinner. He was dead before he took two bites.

When I first read this, I'd worried just about keeping Chase and Lena safe, but this summer, a new worry had replaced it, one that grew every time I went over these notes.

Years ago, Rapunzel had told me, "She knows the value of heroes, as she was one once." Solange had saved so many people the day she'd taken down King Navaire.

Everybody agreed that the old Unseelie king had been seriously evil. He'd conquered all of Atlantis with the help of the Pentangle, and he'd started to conquer the other hidden continents. For more than two decades, everyone had been terrified of this guy, and now . . .

Well, now he was mostly known as the guy Solange de Chateies defeated during her Tale. At the time, it had probably seemed impossible that another villain could grow even more evil and famous than King Navaire, but it had happened. And the same could happen with the Snow Queen, too.

I had the potential to become the next villain.

At first, that thought had been hard to swallow—that I could *ever* be as much of a threat as the Snow Queen was. I was just me. But Chase insisted again and again that I was better than I thought I was. This summer, I was finally starting to believe it. All by myself, I'd held off a hundred wolves and ice griffins. I'd wounded one of the pillars. I'd survived jumping off a sky-scraper. I'd defeated Istalina, the Wolfsbane clan's champion, and Torlauth di Morgian, the Snow Queen's champion.

I'd been at EAS for less than three years. I didn't want to think about what I could do if I lived in the magical world as long as Solange.

Maybe it was selfish to survive. The Snow Queen scarred us enough. The world couldn't survive another villain like her.

I pulled out the one page of notes in Lena's handwriting. She'd tried to hide it from me at the beginning of the summer, but she'd given up when I'd started *Livves & Tymes*.

Deaths of Sorcerers & Sorceresses

• *Death from Natural Causes: their magic drifts back to wherever it came from, plus their spells fade gradually.*

• *Death from Unnatural Causes (spell/blade): "A rip in the fabric of magic, creating a vacuum where that power should stand in the world." Magic the sorcerer had within their body explodes. The magic and the sorcerer vanish from the world forever.*

Exploding didn't sound good. The more powerful the sorcerer, the bigger the blast. It tended to kill whoever was nearby.

I'd read about hundreds of slain sorcerers. So far, only four of the people doing the slaying had survived, and it didn't help me: In 1601, a group of Characters had turned a new sorcerer back into a regular guy by replacing his magic ear with a human one.

Taking out the Snow Queen was pretty much the same as deciding to let her take *me* out.

The workshop's steel doors slid open. I whirled around.

"Oh, gumdrops," Lena said.

"Who?" My hand fell on my sword. I was sure I was about to find out what terrible thing had happened. "Who got attacked?"

"What?" Lena said, bewildered. "No one. At least, not recently. I just forgot the Wolfsbane clan was in the dungeon, that's all."

The witches would probably be pretty ticked off to hear that. Lena had put them in prison. "They didn't attack you, did they?" I asked.

"They *can't*," said Lena. "The dungeon has the same protection on it as your combs. No magic can pass through the bars. Probably a good thing too. They're all trying to call their wands to them."

"I didn't know they could do that." My research had made me an expert on sorceresses. Witches were still a mystery.

"It won't work unless someone else opens the cell door for them." Then she shuffled the dragon scales in her hands like cards and looked at me, biting her lip.

"They told you something," I said. One of the witches had liked to talk. Her clan mates hadn't been able to shut her up.

Lena nodded slowly.

The terrible thing didn't have to be another attack. It could be finding out something the Snow Queen had already done, something she'd kept secret from all of us until now, something a lot worse than the warding hex. "We need to go tell the Director."

"I don't think the Director will care. They told me why they needed the Dapplegrim—the one they put on the luggage car in Atlantis." Lena darted a glance at me and then back to the dragon scales in her hands.

I understood. Lena didn't think the Director would care, but she thought I definitely would. "Tell me," I whispered.

"Istalina's mother was clan leader. She got cursed," Lena said slowly. "One of those curses that act like slow poison. Fresh Dapplegrim blood was part of the antidote."

Istalina's mother must have died. If she'd lived, Lena would have told me, to make me feel better.

I still didn't regret what I'd done during Ben's Tale. The witches would have killed that Dapplegrim, who didn't deserve it, and that Dapplegrim had helped me save Lena.

But no wonder they hated me. What they'd said on the Fey train didn't feel like an overreaction now. I didn't just have the potential to be a villain. I'd already become one—at least if you asked the Wolfsbane clan.

"Too bad they couldn't have come with us. The Water of Life probably would have saved her, too." I glanced at the door and then away again. If Chase had been here, he would have reminded me how many people we saved with the Water—hundreds of Characters rescued for one witch's life. I would have reminded him that wasn't much comfort to Istalina.

Lena guessed why I'd looked toward the door. "I'm sorry that Chase didn't make it," she said softly, and I didn't know if she meant this morning or the fight with the Wolfsbane clan the day before.

"If he's at a bakery again like yesterday, or at a skating rink like that time we rescued that fifth grader from those wolves in Dallas, or at the Eiffel Tower, like that time Snow White needed backup—" My voice rose higher and higher. I could keep going. I had a whole summer's worth of stuff Chase had missed.

"If he—" I started again, but this time, my voice cracked.

Lena dropped her dragon scales on her worktable and looked at me. "You know why you're really angry, don't you?"

The rant died in my throat.

Yes, I knew.

I remembered Queen Titania's pavilion. I remembered dancing with Chase—how green his eyes were, how close his face had been to mine, and how he'd talked me through the enchantment without once teasing me for being scared. Sometimes, alone with Chase, that feeling came back—a sort of specialness, like we were the only two people in the room, even when we weren't, like the air between us was electric and too wide.

Sometimes, around Chase, all I wanted to do was hold my breath and see what happened next. Even with Adelaide around, I felt that, but usually, it was laced with guilt.

I'd even thought Chase had felt it first. *Rory, if you're in trouble, I'll always come for you*, he'd said, and the *way* he'd said it . . .

But all summer, he hadn't come. He hadn't been there when I'd needed him.

My heart turned to a molten lump of rock in my chest, like it always did when I tried to figure out what had gone wrong. No matter how much I wondered, my thoughts always ran along the same lines.

On the day we'd fought off the trolls in my dad's office, we'd come back to EAS, and Adelaide had been waiting. "What have you been doing with my boyfriend?" she'd asked. I'd laughed, waiting for Chase to deny it. He'd just *smiled* at her. He hadn't even looked surprised.

Maybe I'd misread him. Maybe that specialness was all in my head. I couldn't be sure. We'd never *talked* about it.

The closest we'd come had been in Arica's house, right after she glamoured herself to look like me. She had grabbed his hand and gotten kind of lovey-dovey with him, and Chase had looked a little bit happy about it. When I'd brought it up afterward, he'd whirled around, our faces inches apart, and said, *I will tell you if you really want to know, but I don't think you do. I think all you want is to get to the palace, rescue those kids, and deal with everything else afterward.*

And I'd frozen. I couldn't say anything. I'd been an idiot. Maybe, just *maybe,* that was the moment he'd decided that he might be better off dating Adelaide. At least *she* could admit that she liked him.

It couldn't have been easy for Chase on the quest to the Arctic Circle, to like me and then have to deal with my cluelessness and then my hesitation. It must have hurt. It must have made him *stop* liking me, if he ever had at all.

Maybe I didn't have anyone to blame but myself. Maybe I'd lost my chance.

"I miss him too," Lena said softly. "Not the way you do, but I still miss him."

That was her way of inviting me to talk about it. I couldn't. If I let it all out into the open, I wasn't sure I could fake *not* being mad out there. I wasn't sure I could stop our grade from tearing into Chase if I admitted out loud how angry I was with him.

We were the Triumvirate. We needed Chase to help defeat the Snow Queen, no matter how flaky he'd gotten.

"Okay," Lena said decisively, moving to the other side of the table. Old wooden axes were laid out, waiting to be sanded. "I know I'm not him, but I'll pull a Chase and change the subject."

That made me laugh, and Lena beamed. She wasn't used to being the funny one.

"If you're done with your research, want to help me with these bats?" she asked.

Trying to recruit me for free inventing labor didn't totally count as changing the subject. "Depends. What are those?" I nodded at a pile of what looked like computer chips.

Lena glanced up. "Oh. Voice recognition software. We're trying to merge science and spells. Melodie is strongly *opposed* to the idea, so Kyle and I work on it when she's not around. Want to see how many we can get through before she gets back?" she asked, smiling.

I was coughing on sawdust by the time I took a break for lunch.

Father-daughter meals had become a tradition. I think it was Brie's idea. Every Friday, Dad, Dani, and I met up and grabbed something at the Table of Never Ending Instant Refills. Well, Dani slept more than ate, but it was still nice to see her.

We even had a usual table, tucked up close to the Tree of Hope's trunk. Low branches draped their leaves over half the surface and two of the chairs, hiding it from most of the courtyard.

Dad was already there, his sandwich and Dani's fancy white baby carrier thing on the table, holding our spot. He grinned when he spotted me heading over from the workshop. "How's the birthday girl?" he asked, pulling me into a hug as soon as I was close enough.

His hair was going in a hundred different directions again. Usually, this was a sign that he'd been working on his screenplay all morning.

"Fine." I definitely felt better than I had earlier. It had helped, having something to do with my hands. I almost thought I'd been overreacting to my birthday. The Snow Queen might *not* do anything. Considering what had happened back in San Francisco, she might have planned her big evil surprises for the day *before* my birthday.

"Fourteen! I can remember when you were as small as Dani," Dad said. "Actually, it doesn't seem that long ago."

I couldn't think of a response. The month before, I'd let it slip at home that every time I saw Dad, he had the baby strapped to him. Mom actually laughed, a bitter-sounding laugh that made my skin crawl. "I don't believe it. Rory, when you were little, I don't think he ever changed a diaper," she'd said.

She'd apologized for it afterward. She'd said she was exaggerating, but I knew it was kind of true.

I picked a chair next to my sister and sat down with my pizza. Danica was wearing the red-and-white-striped baby suit I'd given Brie at the baby shower a few months ago. She was still too young to roll over all the way, but her eyes swiveled all around until she found me. I smiled and stuck a finger under her hand. "Hello, Dani." My sister squeezed hello back.

I wasn't jealous, exactly. I wouldn't let myself be like Solange. When she'd found out *her* father had started a new family, Solange had decided to steal her little sister and groom her to be the next Rapunzel.

But I did feel like Dad's least favorite daughter.

Sure, Dad and I had spent a lot of time together recently, but Brie had arranged all of it. I was pretty sure that he didn't think about me when I wasn't around—except maybe to remember he wouldn't have moved to EAS if it hadn't been for my Tale.

A long, flat box sat next to her fancy baby carrier. It was about the same size as the gift box you usually get in clothing stores and wrapped with black paper printed with hot pink bubble letters that said HAPPY HAPPY HAPPY BDAY over and over again. "Is that for me?"

"Yes," Dad said slowly. I didn't know why he suddenly looked nervous. I mean, I could already tell he hadn't picked it out.

Only Brie would use that paper, and only Brie would tie a pink bow that big. She'd probably chosen the gift inside, too. She had non-embarrassing taste, but considering it might be the last birthday I ever had, I would have liked it if Dad had put in a *little* effort.

Then again, Dani was still so small. Both of them had their hands full. It was nice of them to take the time to give me a present at all.

"You might like it," Dad said. "You really might . . . *not*."

"Okay . . ." Maybe it *wasn't* another shirt.

"In fact, it may be more a present to *me* than a present to you." Dad was babbling slightly. If he hadn't seemed so antsy, I might have gotten slightly upset that Dad was giving *himself* a present on my maybe-last birthday ever. "Actually, we got you something else. Something bigger. We ordered it online, but the post guy couldn't deliver it to the address the Director gave us, so—"

Whoa. *Seriously* babbling. "Dad, what *is* it?" I asked, staring at the box with alarm. Not trapped-on-a-rooftop-with-monsters-trying-to-kill-me alarmed, but you know, *concerned*.

"It's—" Dad's face darkened. "That kid's not coming, is he? I don't want him to interrupt us."

I wished I hadn't known exactly who Dad was taking about. "That kid's name is Chase, and he's one of my best friends." It was annoying to have to defend him when all I really wanted to do was yell at him a little.

"I don't like him," Dad said.

I resisted the urge to roll my eyes, but only barely. "I know. And trust me, he knows too." Last time Chase had crashed father-daughter lunch, Dad had glared at him the whole time, determined not to like my friend. It was almost as disturbing as seeing how polite and friendly Chase could be when he was trying to win Dad over.

Dad hesitated, and you could practically see him thinking, *Should I tell her this on her birthday?* He must have decided to go for it, because all of a sudden, he straightened up, very serious. I braced myself. Serious Dad almost never appeared, but when he did, I *never* liked what he had to say.

"He likes you. And not just as a friend," Dad said. "I can tell, and it's not right that he likes you while he's dating someone else."

I hated that he felt like he could say any of this. He had no right to pass judgment on the people in my life. Except for this summer, I'd seen a lot more of Chase in the past few years than I'd seen of Dad. Also, for the record, when you've just turned fourteen and your father tells you some boy likes you, you're almost obligated not to believe him.

I refused to encourage this conversation. I took a bite of pizza.

"I don't know who is supposed to tell you that, but someone has to," Dad said. "Even if you don't have feelings for him, he's not being a good friend to *you*. That's what really bothers me."

He looked too earnest. I was afraid that if I looked him in the eye, I would admit that he was right.

I'd been telling myself that one flaky, emotionally confusing summer couldn't destroy two years of friendship. But if we weren't part of the newest Triumvirate, I probably wouldn't have pretended as hard as I did.

"Happy birthday, Rory!" said a loud, cheerful voice.

"Not again," Dad said.

But it wasn't Chase who pushed the leaves aside and plopped into a seat. Ben reached a hand out to Dad. A new scar crossed his palm, where he'd lost his shield and had to block a troll's spear bare-handed. "Pleasure to meet you, Mr. Landon. I'm Ben Taylor. My mom and I loved *Hallow End*."

Dad looked slightly less upset about being interrupted, now that Ben had complimented one of his movies.

"Fourteen! I remember turning fourteen like it was just yes-terday," Ben said. "Probably because an ice griffin dropped me in Lake Michigan two days later. An experience like that tends to make a *splash*."

I groaned. Dad looked from Ben to Dani, like he hadn't known kidnapping by ice griffin was a possibility and he was worried about the daughter too young to defend herself. Chase would have told Ben that there was a line between good corny and bad corny, and he had just crossed it.

"No, come on. That was a good one! I've been saving it up for a special occasion," Ben said, which meant that he'd said it mostly to cheer me up. Then he ruined it. "Do you know where Chase is?"

Of course I didn't. I tried to keep my voice even. "No. Did you ask Adelaide?"

"Yeah. She says that she hasn't seen him since he rushed off to Marty Mason's farm," Ben said.

"He didn't come back with you?" That would explain so much. Already, I could feel guilt creeping in. The Director hated to send us on back-to-back missions, but sometimes it couldn't be helped.

"No. *You* called him, didn't you?" Ben said. "You called him at midnight when we were moving all of Mr. Mason's stuff, and Chase dropped everything and painted a temporary-transport spell right there in the garage."

I stared at Ben. The terrible thing that was going to happen today—this was it.

Ben was beginning to catch on. "It wasn't you."

I shook my head.

"I thought it was weird that he was speaking in Fey," Ben said. "I just assumed you both had those gumdrops in."

I fumbled through my carryall. My fingers brushed the velvety cover of my M3. I pulled it out. "Chase? *Chase?*" No answer. My heart thumped hard. "Ben, he brought his mirror with him, right?"

"Yeah. You really don't know where he is?" Ben said, starting to sound worried. "Rapunzel was with Adelaide when I talked to her earlier. She—I mean, Rapunzel—said, 'Rory should know.' Those were her exact words."

"She was telling you to let *me* know he was missing. Not that I knew where he'd gone." I stood up so fast I knocked my chair over.

Dad clamped his hand around my wrist. "Rory, what's *wrong*?"

Maybe nothing.

Chase did sneak off to Atlantis sometimes. He liked to visit his mom and Iron Hans, though only Lena and I knew about the ancient character. But Chase wouldn't abandon a mission for a regular visit.

It was one o'clock in the afternoon. If he'd left before midnight, then he'd been missing for more than twelve hours. A lot could happen in half a day.

My dream thundered back to me. It didn't seem so harmless now. He could be knocked unconscious in a tower somewhere. The Snow Queen could have already captured him. That would explain why he wasn't answering his M3.

"I have to find Rapunzel," I said.

"The girl with the long hair? She's over there." Dad pointed across the courtyard.

Rapunzel stepped out of the door to the infirmary, Gretel behind her. On Mr. Swallow's back, Sarah Thumb swooped and fluttered around them.

I took off running. Ben was on my heels.

Across the courtyard, Rapunzel noticed us first. She shook her head at me. "I know only that he is on Atlantis. I am blind to his location upon it." Gretel shot her a look that clearly said, *Do you think you're making sense?*

But she was. I wished she weren't. "No one knows where he is?"

"Who? Chase? No." Sarah Thumb reached me, and Mr. Swallow landed on my shoulder. His pale feathery chest heaved. The

Thumbelina representative's face twisted with distress. "We're calling an emergency Canon meeting," she said.

"Why?" I asked. Gretel's face was so pale.

"Need the grade representatives?" Ben asked.

"I don't think so. Missions won't help," Sarah said. "There's nothing we can do. The Snow Queen attacked the Seelie Court this morning. Queen Titania has been captured. King Oberon and his nobles have fled."

"My sister is no longer satisfied with a mere hunt," Rapunzel told me sadly.

My heart hammered against my ribs, like it was desperate to escape my chest and start searching for Chase on its own. So, the Snow Queen had been waiting until my birthday to jumpstart the war, and she'd begun by destroying any chance we Characters had of allying with the Seelie again. They couldn't rally their armies if their king was on the run, but right then, they weren't the Fey I cared about. "What about the Unseelie?" I asked.

If the Director had been here, she probably would have refused to tell me anything more, but Sarah's tiny face softened. "We haven't gotten a response from the Unseelie. The Director sent Jack to see what he could find out."

It would be crazy to attack two powerful courts on the same day. It would take genius planning and perfect timing and lots of guts, but the Snow Queen could do it if she had the element of surprise. She *would* do it too.

"You think Chase went there?" Ben said. "To one of the Fey courts?"

Yes. Lady Aspenwind must have called Chase on the M3. Chase would have dropped everything to go save his mother.

And judging by their grim faces, the grown-ups thought the same thing.

I bolted for the Atlantis door. It was just on the other side of the Tree of Hope, and I tore dozens of leaves off it as I bashed my way past a low-hanging branch. Then I skidded to a halt. One of the Canon members guarded the door. Hansel's arms were folded, his stance wide. "You can't go to Atlantis, Rory," he said.

"He's in trouble, Hansel," I said. "Of course I'm going."

"If you knew where he was, I wouldn't stop you," Hansel said. "I might even go too. But you haven't got a clue. Besides, if he did meet up with the Unseelie, they're probably en route in the air."

"I have a boon left from the West Wind," I said.

"Doesn't matter," Hansel said. "Atlantis is the largest hidden continent, too big to search in a week, let alone an afternoon."

"I don't care." It didn't matter how long it took. I had to find my best friend. He *needed* me.

Hansel ran a hand over his face and sighed. "Rory, we can't risk losing you to a mission that can't succeed. We can't afford to lose *two* of our best fighters. We need you here."

For the first time in a long while, I hated Hansel. Not because I thought he was picking on me, but because he was right. And he knew exactly what to say to stop me from fighting my way past him and into Atlantis. "You just want me to wait?" I whispered raggedly. That was the worst torture I could imagine.

"It won't be easy," Hansel admitted, sounding relieved, "but wait for news. If we find out where he is, we'll send you there, I swear it."

It didn't seem like enough, but it was the best we had. Hansel went to the emergency Canon meeting. I found a nice cushy couch positioned underneath the Tree of Hope facing the Door Trek door to Atlantis. Ben reappeared a few minutes later with Lena in tow. They settled in right beside me.

It seemed so strange. The rest of the courtyard continued on like nothing was wrong. Moms and kids lined up at the Table of Never Ending Instant Refills. Parents thronged through the doors from the East Coast, happy to be home from work. The adult archery class met at its normal time, and the air filled with the thwacks of bowstrings and the thunks of arrows hitting targets, as it always did.

And yet, word about the Snow Queen's attack and Chase's disappearance must have spread. When someone near me sneezed, I glanced sideways and was shocked to see others. Kyle had claimed the spot to Lena's right. Adelaide had taken over a leather love seat beside our sofa. Candice had squeezed in beside her, but Adelaide was the only one who *looked* as worried as I felt. That comforted me a little, knowing someone else felt as scared as I did, even if she didn't understand why Chase had gone to help the Unseelie. I couldn't decide whether knowing made the wait easier or worse.

Kevin and Conner joined us after that, then Daisy, Paul, and the stepsisters. Darcy stopped by to see if we had any news, and when we didn't, she ended up staying. Chatty—I mean, Sherah— called Ben at least a dozen times on his M3 to find out if Chase had contacted us yet. Kenneth walked by every ten minutes or so. He didn't want to sit down—I guess it would be bad for his image— but I could tell he was worried too.

Any one of us could have pointed out that it didn't make sense for us all to wait for him there. He might not even use the Atlantis door to return.

He might have taken one of Lena's new rings of return. He might use a temporary-transport to get home. He had a supply of them that went to the weapons closet in the training courts instead of the courtyard. Hansel had told Chase off for asking Lena to make them. "There's only supposed to be one way in or out of that room. The training courts double as our safe house. It's useless if it's not secure." Lena had grumbled too. Figuring out how to make a temporary-transport spell that went somewhere *inside* without any dirt had taken up a huge chunk of time, which she could have used to complete the Director's order of M3's.

Even if you didn't count Chase failing to show up for our battles, he still drove *everybody* insane sometimes, but we would miss him so much if he didn't come back.

Later, my family came to check on me.

Dad's warm hand slid around my shoulder. "Hansel told me what happened. Chase is still missing?" he asked, like he was worried too. That surprised me, considering what he'd been saying earlier.

I nodded.

With Danica cradled against her shoulder, Brie passed around a plate piled high with sandwich halves. "Well, we're here for you, sweetie. We support you in your vigil thing, but we don't support you skipping meals, especially on your birthday. You've all been out here for hours already."

I took a sandwich half and passed the plate down the couch. Brie smoothed my hair away from my face. I didn't know if I wanted them to go or if I wanted them to give me my space, but I felt a rush of warmth, knowing they were there if I needed them. Dad kissed the top of my head and told me to call him and Brie if we heard anything.

We waited. The sun hung so low that not even the Tree's leaves could shade us from its glare. No one came through the Atlantis door.

Around dinnertime, Mr. Swallow flitted down and landed on the arm of the sofa beside my elbow. Sarah Thumb actually dismounted and walked closer to me. The news must have been serious. "The Canon meeting's over."

Silence spread across the sofas. I didn't even notice the others had been talking until they stopped.

"Jack checked in," said Sarah. "He didn't find Chase. The Unseelie Court's palace has been abandoned. Burning and empty. The Fey have fled."

I'd visited the Unseelie palace a little more than a year ago. It was colossal and ancient, magically made from trees woven into walls, towers, turrets, arches, and staircases. It was hard to imagine it in ruins. The Fey who had lived there had seemed so powerful.

"Jack stayed in Atlantis," Sarah Thumb added. "He's trying to track them."

Sure, Jack got to track them, but I couldn't leave.

Sarah Thumb gathered Mr. Swallow's reins and leapt back into the saddle. "I'll let you know if Jack finds anything. Hang in there, kids."

After that, none of us talked. I barely breathed.

The next thing I knew, Mom and Amy were hovering over the couch, smiles on their faces. They must have just come home from work. Behind them, the setting sun stained the sky red. "Are you ready for some celebrating?" Mom asked. She looked like she'd never been angry with me.

"We picked up a surprise." Amy lifted a bakery box, cake–size.

They had no idea. They had missed so much. I couldn't believe it was still my birthday, and I couldn't imagine trying to celebrate it. It was worse than if Mom had just launched straight into lecturing mode. I knew I had to tell them about Chase's disappearance and the fall of the Unseelie Court. I knew I wouldn't even get through telling her about the first part without breaking down.

But I didn't need to speak. Mom's expression shifted from birthday excitement to fury when I didn't move from my spot on the couch. "Rory, we talked about this. The evening is family only."

She could yell at me as much as she needed to. I couldn't go *home*. I would just stay where I was, where I could see the Atlantis door. "I can't."

Mom didn't soften.

I braced myself, waiting for her to lay it on me, in front of Lena and everyone.

But before Mom could say anything, Amy said, "Rory, what's *wrong*?"

"Maggie!" Across the courtyard, Dad jogged toward us. "Rory, it's okay. I'll explain."

I was suddenly sure I had the best father in the world, and for the first time ever, I was glad my parents lived in the same place again.

"Please," I told Mom. "Just let me wait a little longer."

Mom looked like she might argue, but when Amy tugged her away to go talk to Dad, Mom let her.

The sun sank behind the western buildings. Gloom descended on the courtyard. The door stayed shut.

I wondered if it was dark in Atlantis yet. I could never keep the time differences straight.

I wondered if I should tell Sarah Thumb about my dream. I wondered if Jack was searching all the Unseelie towers. Chase could be in one right now, one beside a river. He could be knocked unconscious and captured and need us to rescue him. He could be—

I'd been pushing that thought away ever since I found out Chase was missing.

I couldn't remember seeing him breathe in the dream. He might not be *sleeping*.

I drew a big, shaky breath. Beside me, Lena looked up, already listening, ready to hear my terrible theory.

Then the Atlantis door cracked open. A bunch of winged figures stumbled in. The Unseelie Fey, their weapons drawn, their clothing torn, their faces haggard.

One winged guy held open the Door Trek door and directed a stream of angry-sounding Fey at a woman with pale pink wings and dots lining her face.

Chase.

He didn't stand like he was hurt, but his T-shirt was full of stains, tears, and singes. He was missing an entire sleeve. His mother was a mess too. Absentmindedly, she wiped her bloodied blade on her tattered skirt.

I glanced back over to the couches. The other kids just looked dumbfounded. Even Lena hadn't recognized Chase yet. Maybe we could still keep it a secret. Maybe if I distracted them. "We should go get the grown-ups," I said.

Candice gasped and pointed. *Not* at Chase, thankfully. At the Door Trek door to Atlantis. A young Fey woman and her child eased through the entrance to EAS. One of her emerald-green wings had a hole in it, but Candice wasn't looking at them. She was looking at the person helping them to safety.

The sun hadn't set on the Atlantis side of the door. Light bounced off the figure's pewter skin. The red edging his double-headed ax was easy to spot. Two more Fey children stumbled through, clinging to each other. The pewter figure straightened, and his eyes met mine.

"Iron Hans," Lena breathed. She was one of the few people who knew he was on our side, but she hadn't actually ever seen him before.

Chase must have recruited his help.

The old Character reached his hand through the door. Half the kids on the couch shrank back. As far as they knew, Iron Hans was still the Snow Queen's deadliest warrior.

I stood up, ready to throw myself between them.

But Iron Hans just reached over, grabbed the handle, and closed the Door Trek door. Well, with that distraction gone, the others were going to get a good look at Chase before his wings disappeared. I had to act fast. "We *need* grown-ups. We need a nurse. *Gretel*—" I started.

"I am here, Rory." Rapunzel stood beside the couch, holding a silver tube. The ointment of the witch whose power was in her hair. It was almost as good as the Water of Life, and better yet, you didn't need the Director's permission to use some.

Adelaide didn't pay any attention to us. "Chase!"

He and Lady Aspenwind both turned to see who was interrupting their argument, their wings fluttering with irritation. The secret was out then: No one could deny the family resemblance.

All of our friends froze. You would have thought an enchantment had turned them into stone.

Chase drew himself up to his full height and scowled, defiant, but he didn't fool me. He stilled his wings with visible effort—a last-ditch attempt to make them disappear.

Rapunzel glided around the couch and the dropped jaws of all the kids sitting there. She paused just long enough to shoot me a look that clearly said, *Are you coming?* Then she began to cross the fifty yards that divided us from the Fey.

I went with her, even though I didn't exactly remember telling my legs to move.

The Fey soldiers noticed. The one in green armor gave a shout. The rest of his comrades fell into line beside him. Behind them, some older nobles were leaning against the wall, half-collapsed with exhaustion. The knights couldn't seriously think we were going to attack. Maybe they remembered me from that time I chewed out Prince Fael.

"Welcome to Ever After School, Fey of the Unseelie Court." Rapunzel swept out her skirts in a swift but unmistakable curtsy. "We offer you sanctuary."

Then she glanced at me. I gave it a try. My curtsy was wobbly and awkward, but it *was* the first curtsy I'd ever tried. "Welcome," I echoed, glancing at Chase.

His eyes locked with mine. He hasn't lost that trapped, defiant look or his wings. All I really wanted was to tell him how glad I was that he was all right and how much he'd scared us. I wouldn't mind a hug, either, but that would have to wait until we were sure nobody would try to fight anyone else.

The newcomers weren't expecting curtsys. The knight in green armor narrowed his eyes. I think he suspected a trick. A noble in the back straightened up. He was the oldest Fey I'd ever seen—with steel gray hair and tiny lines around his eyes. He nodded deeply to Rapunzel.

"We thank you," he said, "and we accept."

Some of the tension went out of the Fey, Rapunzel, and especially Chase.

Rapunzel held up the ointment. "I am one of the nurses. Which one of you bears the worst wound?"

The old Fey gestured to someone on his right, and Rapunzel hurried over. The knight in green armor didn't look super happy about it.

I stepped toward Chase.

The relief of seeing him safe spread through me slowly. It was too hard to believe he'd come out fine. The Snow Queen's attack on the Fey courts had been almost twenty-four hours ago. Hours of worry had built up inside me, but they empited out as I looked him over. His left forearm was one big bruise. Besides that, he was okay. He was alive. He was *safe*.

I couldn't speak for a second, and I think he knew.

"Hey," he said, very gently.

Lady Aspenwind curtsied to me. Her hands left dark smears on her skirts. "A pleasure to see you again. My son tells me it is your birthday. Please give your mother my congratulations."

I never got a chance to answer that.

"You lying idiot!" Kenneth shouted behind us. "You told me anyone could jump as high as you. You never told me you had *wings*."

The triplets whooped.

We only had a few seconds. Our friends were going to mob us, demanding answers.

I leaned in. "They're orange. Reddish in the middle, tangerine at the edges. Kind of like leaves in fall. It's a good look for you, actually."

"Right. Because *that's* what I'm worried about." But his mouth twitched, and he flapped his wings once slowly, keeping them around. That was good enough for me.

Ben reached us first. "I knew you liked to make an entrance, but you've just taken it to new *heights*."

"Dude, all the flying jokes you could crack, and you went for that? I must have really shocked you." Chase's grin grew even wider when the triplets caught up.

"You *can* fly, right?" said Conner.

"Duh," said Kevin. "Wings aren't just for show."

"But you can do magic, too, can't you?" Kyle asked.

I knew Adelaide was happy to see him, but she didn't look like it. She shook her long hair back and scowled, arms crossed. "*Rory* knew, and I *didn't*?"

She probably wasn't the only one who'd had that thought. I looked around for Lena.

The last member of our Triumvirate was all the way across the courtyard in front of the Director's amethyst door. She must have followed my advice and went for help. When the Director charged toward us, Lena trailed behind her slowly, hanging back.

She wasn't okay.

"I need to go check on Lena," I told Chase.

He followed my gaze and spotted her, then the Director. "I'll catch up when I can."

I slithered through the crowd, letting the Director pass me, and reached Lena. "Want to go talk somewhere?" I asked. I waited for the accusations to start, but Lena just nodded. She had that intense, determined look she got when she was trying to figure out a tricky invention.

We went to her house. She handed me her keys so I could unlock the door, and we shuffled inside. I waved hello to George and Miriam watching a movie on the couch. Lena just headed up the stairs to her room.

By the time I got there, she was sitting on her bed. She'd worked most of it out.

"*Chase* is the Turnleaf," she said. "Not Jack's father or Jack's grandfather?"

I nodded, pulling her desk chair beside the window and settling into it. Before this, Chase had let her believe he was descended from a Turnleaf. Inheriting the title was one thing. Becoming one was much rarer, and even if the rest of our grade was still clueless, she knew what it meant. She knew that Turnleaf was what the Fey called someone who rejected the chance to live among them forever and decided to join the human world instead.

"When? It's not in the history books," Lena said.

"He was five." I didn't mention how many years he'd been five.

Lena was aghast. "And his parents just decided that for him?"

I shook my head. "It was Chase's idea."

Lena was silent for almost a whole minute, her eyes wide behind her glasses. I knew what she was doing. I'd done it too. She was examining her memories of Chase—of the loud, bragging show-off who liked to boss us around whenever we had a battle. She was trying to match up those memories with the Chase I knew—the kid who had changed the course of his life when the rest of us were in kindergarten.

"How long have you known?" Lena asked.

I told her. I told her the answer to every question she asked me, and she asked tons: Why hadn't the Canon told us? How had Chase gotten a whole room of important grown-ups to swear a Binding Oath? How long could Chase use his wings before they stopped being invisible? Was that woman outside his sister or his mother? My tongue never stumbled over a response. Now that the secret was out, the Binding Oath I'd sworn didn't bother me.

Eventually, she asked, "How old is Chase *exactly*?" She clearly knew more about how Fey children aged than I had.

"She doesn't know," said a voice at the open window. "Neither do I, actually."

Lena and I both jumped. Any other time Chase would have laughed at us, but he just waited outside, his wings a blur behind his shoulders, his face drawn and weary. "Can I come in? We were fighting most of the night and flying most of the day. If I have to fly much longer, you're getting a front-row seat to my first crash landing."

Lena waved him in. She looked a little wary.

"Thanks." Chase swung himself inside and leaned against the windowsill. The tips of his wings nearly brushed the low ceiling. "It took me forever to get away. You guys missed a four-way fight between me, Amya, the Director, and Rapunzel. Basically, the Director's okay with them staying here, but not with Rapunzel offering sanctuary before it was approved. Then King Mattanair said he would accept our help, but he couldn't let the Unseelie fight while the Snow Queen still has Prince Fael. Well, unless it's self-defense like it was today. It nearly morphed into a five-way fight then." I was about to ask which one of the nobles was Fael's dad, but then he turned to Lena. "Don't be mad at Rory. She tried to convince me to tell you at least five thousand times. It got annoying, actually."

Oh. *That* was why he'd rushed over.

"I'm not mad," Lena said slowly, but she did sound kind of freaked out.

"Oh. Good," Chase said. I waited for him to start giving us a play-by-play of rescuing his mom, but he started rubbing his face—hard, then harder.

"Chase, you're okay, right?" I asked.

"No," he said shakily. He could fill a room with his long limbs and huge gestures. It was hard to watch him curl up like that, nearly doubled over beside Lena's window, like he was trying to make himself small. "Amya called me on my M3 at the end of that mission in Idaho—"

"Your mom has a M3?" Lena asked. I shot her a look—now was not the time to interrupt.

"I gave her one. For emergencies." He didn't look at us. He was *shuddering*. "She called me and told me the Snow Queen had come. She said that she was going to see Cal. She only called to say good-bye."

It felt like the time the trolls beat him up on the Snow Queen's balcony—all I wanted was to stop him from hurting, but all I could do was watch. "She shouldn't have said that," I whispered.

Chase shook his head. I couldn't tell if he was agreeing, disagreeing, or just trying to think. "I told her I refused to let the Snow Queen kill her *and* Cal. I said she couldn't put me through that. I said she had to hang on till I got there."

He'd convinced Lady Aspenwind to keep fighting. He was probably the only person who could have, but he shouldn't have had to.

"I couldn't get her out alone," Chase said. "You would have been my first choice as backup, Rory, but I was afraid the Director would try to stop me if I contacted anyone at EAS before I got to the Unseelie Court. So I used one of my temporary-transport spells to Iron Hans's place."

"I'm kind of shocked he let you use your boon and went with you," I said.

"Didn't he say he refused to fight with us in the war?" Lena said.

Chase hesitated. "Actually, he said no. I couldn't convince him to come until I swore on my life that I'd help him turn human again."

Lena and I glanced at each other. I had the feeling she was thinking exactly what I was thinking: Chase hadn't *used* one of his boons. He'd *given* one.

And he wasn't bragging about it.

"You know how I got that dirt to make temporary-transport spells to Atlantis?" he asked me. I nodded. He'd started making temporary-transport spells to visit his mom almost immediately after Lena invented them. "Well, I made sure to get the dirt about a half mile away from the court. I didn't want the Unseelie to see me coming. But I don't know what would have happened if I'd gotten dirt any closer. The enchantment that blocks stuff—what do you call it?"

"The warding hex?" Lena and I said together.

"That. They'd cast one by the time we got there," he said. "Iron Hans and I fought our way in. The temporary-transport spells and my M3 were useless. Well, not *completely*," he said, with a hint of his usual grin. "I threw the mirror at a troll's face. I'll need a new one. Sorry, Lena."

"Done," she said, although on any other day she would have reminded him that the mirrors didn't grow on the Tree of Hope.

"We found Amya in the throne room," he went on. His voice was gravelly with exhaustion, and the more he spoke, the hoarser he sounded. "These goblins were coming at King Mattanair pretty hard, and Amya was helping the royal guard protect him. It took us at least half an hour to push the goblins back and seal the door."

"But how did you get them all out?" I said, scooting Lena's chair closer to him. The throne room was in the heart of the palace.

"Well, we almost didn't," Chase admitted. "I thought about just grabbing Amya and leaving the rest. Especially Himorsal Liior. He didn't want to retreat, and he definitely didn't want to split up to do it, no matter how many times I told him that small groups were our best bet. If all of us wore a glamour, nobody but us would know who was the king."

"Did Iron Hans convince them?" asked Lena.

"No way," Chase said. "They still hate Iron Hans. He volunteered to smuggle out the fliers who couldn't keep up. You know, those kids and Lady Eyira—you saw her wing, right? I think he volunteered just so he wouldn't have to deal with the rest of them. King Mattanair made the rest leave. He issued a direct order, and he put himself in my group. We fought our way up to the roof. It was still dark then, and cloudy. I thought we'd lose them, but there were so many ice griffins up there. They practically covered the sky. Do you have any idea how much harder they are to slay from the air?"

Lena and I shook our heads, but I don't think he even noticed.

"Iron Hans had made it to that stairway—you remember it,

Rory?" Chase asked. I did. It was carved on a steep cliff and led down to the beach. The only way I'd ever managed to climb it was on a Dapplegrim's back. "He borrowed one of the royal guards' bows and *all* of their arrows. He took out half the flock," Chase said, his broken voice full of awe. "Then Likon would have gotten us, but Amya got him first. The tendons behind his knees. He left a crater in the beach where he landed."

Wow. Chase clearly didn't get *all* his fighting talent from his dad.

"The Door Trek door back to EAS was clear on the other side of the continent. We met up with the other fliers. We probably could have gotten here faster, but some of us were injured." Chase stretched, like he'd just remembered how stiff he was. "I haven't flown that long in forever. My wings are completely out of shape. The kids never would have managed. Good thing they went with Iron Hans." He hunched over again, his eyes on the floor. "We made it," he whispered.

"Your mom's safe." I hugged him, hard. "You didn't lose both of them."

Chase leaned into me, his head resting on my collarbone. My heart gave a happy little flutter, and it annoyed me. I shouldn't have been thinking about him like that earlier. It was too hard to stuff the feelings back where I normally hid them afterward.

I didn't let him go. Not while he needed me.

He was quiet for a long moment and way too still. His shoulders jerked, and he kind of hiccuped.

I'd never seen Chase cry. I wouldn't blame him if he did.

Lena sat on the bed, hugging her knees, worried.

Finally, Chase straightened up, and I stepped away. His eyes were dry, but a little bloodshot. His grin was shaky, but it was there. "Lena, stop talking so much," he teased.

"She couldn't exactly get a word in edgewise," I said.

"I was just thinking about how nice this is," Lena said softly.

I stared at her, stunned. Chase snorted.

"Sorry! That came out wrong!" Lena said, mortified. "Not the part where you almost died! Or the part where you basically had a secret life! But this—the three of us. I'm trying to remember the last time we all got to hang out together, without your students or Melodie or Adelaide or someone from the Canon around."

At Adelaide's name, my stomach plummeted to my toes. I dropped back into Lena's desk chair and repositioned it by her bed.

Chase just looked thoughtful. "You know, in the last war . . ." Out of the corner of my eye, I saw Lena quietly balk. He hadn't told her yet that he was old enough to remember the last war. "All I wanted to do was help, to be involved like Cal was. I am now, I guess, and I thought I would feel like Cal, all heroic and stuff. But mostly, I feel tired. Please tell me you guys are tired too. If you feel tired, that means Cal probably felt tired, and I was just too young to notice."

The answer was easy. "Exhausted." Not as tired as I might have been if I'd been flying all day, but worrying had left me spent.

"I would give an arm to sleep in tomorrow. I spend so much time alone in the workshop that I'm starting to feel like Rapunzel in her tower." But Lena wasn't smiling. "Who's Cal?"

Oh. Maybe I should have covered this part before Chase arrived.

"My brother. Well, half brother." The grin had dried up on his face. "He was betrothed to Dyani, crown princess of the Unseelie Court. That's how I know the king."

Lena realized in an instant. Her eyes filled with tears. "Chase, I told the story about their deaths right in *front* of you."

"It's really okay," Chase said cheerfully, trying to head off the crying. I wondered if she knew he was faking it for her. I wondered if she had realized yet how many times he'd done that. "Lena, come *on.* We were having a moment. We haven't hung out in forever. We're not going to spend the whole time talking about me. Rory, tell me the truth. Did I ruin your birthday?"

"No." Well, waiting for him had sucked, but Lena was right. This was pretty nice. "If you had died, *that* would have ruined it."

Chase's smile turned real. Warmth bubbled up in my stomach, and I told it, very firmly, to stop.

"We had a cupcake breakfast," Lena said smugly. It must have been her idea. "*And* we sang."

"Ugh. I can't believe I missed it," Chase said. "I can't believe I missed the fight yesterday. Rory, I'm so sorry. Adelaide—"

"It's okay," I said swiftly. I would let anything be okay as long as I didn't have to hear Chase talk about Adelaide.

"It's not," he said. "You could have *died.*"

Of course I could have. But that was true for everyone, including Chase. He'd left big chunks out of his story. His first home had been invaded. He'd gotten his mom out, but how many people had he left behind? How many people had been killed—people he'd known all his life?

I tried to make a joke. "I can't die yet. According to my Tale, I'm supposed to hold the fate of magic first."

That backfired in a big way.

My best friends reacted like I'd slapped them with my ring hand. They jerked back. Chase nearly toppled out the window.

"Don't *say* that." Lena's voice wobbled.

"*Never* say it again," Chase snapped.

"I'm sorry. It sounded funnier in my head," I said, and I meant it. But suddenly, I realized why Chase's mother had said what she did about Cal. Sometimes, you need to say the thing you can't stop thinking about, especially if it's terrible.

Waiting to talk to Mom was a mistake. Back in our apartment, she was totally out of celebration mode. I wasn't even sure she remembered it was my birthday. All she wanted to discuss was the promise I refused to make. The day was catching up with me. I kept yawning, wishing I could sneak off to bed like Amy had.

"Rory, these Fey people are so powerful, and *they* didn't stand a chance. I'm glad your friend came back safely, but you guys are so *young*." Mom was gearing up for another rant—something about how I was just a kid, how it wasn't my responsibility, how I shouldn't put myself in danger, etc. I had almost all her speeches memorized.

I was sick of getting yelled at for doing the best I could. Mom opened her mouth again. I didn't care. "I didn't do anything wrong. I *didn't* lie to you. Now you're just punishing me for not telling you what you want to hear."

She stared at me for a second, completely shocked. Then I ran into my room and slammed the door behind me. It was the only way I could have the last word.

The dream came back again that night—the stone tower, the river glittering far below the window, the furniture scattered all around the room, the cot set up in the middle. I ignored it all and focused on Chase. He *was* breathing. He didn't snore, not even a cute little purring snore like Lena, but every once in a while, something—a weird sort of noise somewhere between a sigh and a hiccup—would interrupt his long, even breathing. His eyebrows would pinch together and then smooth back into place, like he was in pain.

I woke up worrying, just like I'd done the morning before. *It's nothing*, I told myself, even though I'd dreamed the same scene twice. *You just had a lot of worry left over from waiting. Chase is safe now*.

I almost believed it.

Mom was already gone by the time I worked up the courage to leave my room, so I couldn't even apologize. I just left to go have breakfast with Lena. I found her in one of the armchairs beside the Table of Never Ending Instant Refills. She was staring into her M3 and ripping her pastry into flaky buttery pieces instead of eating it.

Something was bothering her. I made a guess at what. "Are you still upset about Chase?" We had been keeping a major secret from her. No matter what she'd told him, that had to bother her a little.

"What?" Lena turned the M3 facedown instead of letting me see it, which made me think she'd been freaked out by something completely different, something she wanted to hide from me. "The Canon snuck in another meeting this morning—one *without* the student representatives. I convinced Rumpelstiltskin to tell me what they talked about."

"Bad news?"

"The Snow Queen's allies were impressed with her attack on the Fey courts," Lena said reluctantly. "King Licivvil pledged his goblins to her. The East Wind convinced his brother, North, to join her. Likon recruited the last of the ice trolls to help—you know, the abominable snowmen? And—"

"And basically, everyone who was in the Snow Queen's palace when we rescued those kids the Pied Piper kidnapped. Got it." I'd been there. I'd seen that enormous room filled with her allies. I didn't need to go down the entire list. "Did anyone *not* join the Snow Queen overnight?"

"Yes!" Lena said, brightening. "The Trolls of the Hidden Court."

I looked at her, not sure why she thought this would cheer me up. I mean, I'd fought pretty much all the Hidden Court Trolls when

I was twelve. They weren't too hard to defeat. They were only three feet tall.

"They sent the Snow Queen a letter," Lena went on. "They said they had no quarrel with Rory Landon. Sure, she came and stole their scepter, but she didn't hurt anyone when she was there. See? Not killing people paid off! You should tell Chase."

I hadn't seen him yet. Considering how much rest he'd gotten since he'd rescued his mom, I fully expected him to be asleep. "Chase would say they *wouldn't* have stood up to Solange if we'd told anyone how to *get* to the Hidden Troll Court."

Lena sighed, like she'd been hoping I wouldn't bring this up. "The Snow Queen offered the rank of general to any ally who slays the troll king. That's what Rumpelsiltskin said."

The Trolls of the Hidden Court were only safe to rebel because the Snow Queen didn't know where they were. Kind of like EAS. Now that the Fey courts had fallen, we were probably one of the few safe places left. "Let me guess. The grown-ups are freaking out about allies."

"The Director wanted us to try and recruit Iron Hans," Lena said. "The rest of the Canon isn't sure we can trust him, though. That was why Rumpelstiltskin stopped by to see what I knew."

She stopped and bit her lip. There was something else. I waited to find out what it was.

"Arica, the sorceress, is dead," she said. "The Snow Queen and General Searcaster *both* went after her."

Then Lena flipped over her mirror and slid it over to me, her lips pressed together tight, like she wanted to keep them from trembling.

She had scryed the battlefield.

The fight had ravaged the landscape. Arica's ramshackle house was completely destroyed. So was her garden. Instead, a crater scarred the earth, gouging layers of ice and snow down to the gray rock beneath. Canyonlike cracks spread out to the horizon, melted water gushing down them, emptying into the crater and disappearing into the dark abyss.

So *that* was what happened when you killed a powerful sorceress. I couldn't imagine anyone walking away from an implosion like that. I would have to make sure Chase and Lena didn't get caught in the crossfire when I fought Solange.

"Well," I said, because I kind of felt like I should say *something*, "I really don't think she would have helped us again."

Lena looked at me in surprise. I guess it had sounded kind of like something Solange might say. Still, Arica hadn't ever been nice to me. I shouldn't feel sorry for her death. Chase would be the first person to tell me that.

"Chase! The Fey!" someone shouted.

I shot to my feet. My hand clamped on my sword hilt, even before I spotted the kid who'd shouted.

It was Kevin, his hands cupped around his mouth so that his voice carried farther. "The training courts! HURRY!"

Half the courtyard got up and drifted toward the iron-studded door, their faces sleepy and curious. I barreled past them, elbowed a few out of my way, and caught up to Kevin in the hall. "What is it? Did they attack him?" I asked, slightly out of breath.

"Definitely," said Kevin, and he sounded ridiculously happy.

Everyone had ringed around the warriors going at it in the middle of the training courts. Metal clanged on metal, and the spectators chanted, "Fight! Fight! Fight!"

I slipped to the front of the crowd and found a spot in between Ben, Kyle, and Conner.

The fighters flew at each other, clashing swords, and exploded apart too fast for me to recognize anyone, but you could tell there were more than four people. Then the Fey with green armor from yesterday face-planted onto the mats in front of me. His sword landed a few feet away. He snatched up his weapon and cursed so harshly in Fey that I almost took my gumdrop translator out. Then he flapped his wings and threw himself back into the action.

I didn't let go of my sword. "What is going on?"

"I wish I could tell you." Ben had his M3 tilted toward the fight, so either Chase had asked him to record it, or he had called Chatty so she could watch. "The Fey were doing their drills when we came in for practice. Chase wanted to make up for missing yesterday. He started demonstrating today's lesson for us. I guess that really put a bee in the knights' bonnets."

"He means they got angry and attacked him," said a voice from the M3. Definitely Chatty on the line.

Another shorter Fey with gold wings landed hard on his butt on the other side of the circle. With a dazed scowl, he scrambled to his feet, and then he leapt back into the fray.

"Wait. Chase is in there by *himself*?" I couldn't believe no one was helping him. "How many Fey is he fighting?"

"At least six," Kevin said gleefully. I couldn't believe he had just announced it to the entire courtyard so more people could come watch.

"No, seven," said Kyle, even more impressed.

Unbelievable. I drew my sword and stepped forward. A blur of orange wings filled my vision. Chase, soaked with sweat. "No, Rory. I got this," he called.

Another Fey, rail-thin with slender wings with spiraling tips, chopped an overhand blow to my friend's head while his back was turned. I squeaked, but Chase blocked it easily. Then he twisted hard. A second later, Chase was holding both swords.

"Sorry," Chase told the Fey. His grin took up half his face. "I'm just gonna borrow this for a second. Ask nicely, and I might even give it back."

A stocky man, wearing armor coated in dust, shouldered his way to the front. His grin was very white on his dirty face, and his dimples were in exactly the same place as Chase's. It was his dad, Jack, back from Atlantis.

"Hey, Chase! I hear you're having a great week," he said, clearly as proud of his son as Chase had ever wanted him to be.

"Week? I'm having a great *life*." But Chase didn't have time to be cocky.

He stepped toward his father, like he was going to clap Jack on the back, but the other six Fey descended on him. Chase ducked and wove through them all.

Wow. Chase was *enjoying* this. I guessed I would let him have his moment. If there was anything that could cheer Chase up from the close call he'd had yesterday, it was totally whooping seven Fey knights in front of his dad.

"For the record, we offered to lend a hand too," Ben said, "but Chase told us he could *handle* it."

I groaned, but I was smiling. "Ben, you're getting worse."

"No," said Chatty, through Ben's M3, "he's getting *better*."

Well, at least *she* liked his jokes.

Adelaide elbowed her way to the front and glared at us all, but me especially. "How can you joke about this? He rescued them yesterday, and they're *attacking* him."

I didn't bother explaining. Even if I tried telling her, she wouldn't listen to me.

A door slammed open behind us. An angry voice rang out, "What is happening here?"

The triplets and Adelaide looked confused. Knowing I had my gumdrop translator in, Ben turned my way, but I didn't see how I could explain without being totally obvious. All the Unseelie knights fell to one knee, panting. Even Chase swept a beautiful, unhurried bow, his shoulders rising and falling in quick breaths.

Across the room, Jack shrank back and let the rest of the crowd conceal him. Everybody at EAS knew he wasn't a huge fan of the Fey, but something about his reaction made me wonder if certain Fey just didn't like *him*.

The circle opened up to let someone through. It was the old Fey from the night before, all cleaned up. Gray hair hung in long waves and brushed his shoulders, but his body was limber and strong under his black silk clothes. So *he* was the Unseelie king. He had the same inky black wings as his son, Prince Fael, and he strode across the room like he owned it. His dark eyes blazed with anger.

Behind him was Lady Aspenwind. Well, I guess we knew who had told the king what was happening. She didn't even glance at Jack.

King Mattanair stood in front of the fighters. Our evil Fey dummies were lined up against the wall, ready for our lesson. I sincerely hoped he wouldn't notice them. "I am waiting for your answer," said the king.

"The Turnleaf has been teaching our secrets to the humans," said the one in green armor.

"He teaches them Itari," said the one who'd lost his sword.

The translator gave me the definition a beat afterward—"branch battle." It ranked right up there with "Pounce Pot" on my list of all-time most ridiculous magical names. I'd never heard of it, but the others obviously had.

Silence reigned across the room. The king cocked his head to the side, with a cool, assessing stare. Even Chase shot them a frown that clearly said, *Someone left their brain back in Atlantis*.

But Jack, who had been creeping toward the door, stopped and turned around, suddenly interested.

"You believe that Chase Turnleaf has rediscovered the techniques that allow one Fey to fight like ten?" The king laid the skepticism on thick. "I haven't seen such techniques since my youth, more than a millennia ago."

Wow. He *was* old.

Adelaide stepped closer to Chase, in full-on loyal girlfriend mode. "He—" she started in English. She obviously *wasn't* wearing a gumdrop translator.

"Not now, Adelaide," I said. "Let him deal with it."

"What do you say in answer, Chase Turnleaf?" asked King Mattanair.

"I know nothing of the Itari," said Chase, his face suddenly as smooth and respectful as a perfect Fey courtier, "but I did know that I was teaching movements guided by a Fey-forged blade."

"Where is this weapon?" asked the king.

You would have to know him really well to notice, but Chase stiffened. He didn't as much as glance in my direction. If he was in trouble, he wanted to make sure I didn't go down with him.

Very sweet, but it was going to come out eventually. Besides, he really *hadn't* done anything wrong. "I have it, Your Majesty," I said.

The Fey all swiveled. They stared at me so blankly that I worried that Lena's gumdrop translator had malfunctioned.

"Who the hiccups are *you*?" asked one of the kneeling knights. Except he didn't say "hiccups."

I couldn't read the king's face. "This is Rory Landon, bearer of the Unwritten Tale," he said.

Great. If he knew who I was, then he probably also knew that

I'd kind of forced his son to do my bidding the last time I'd hung out with the Unseelie Court. He knew I'd left Fael in Likon's clutches when I escaped the Snow Queen's palace. This king had no reason to like me.

So I said the first thing that came to mind. "Nice to meet you."

Either Chase choked on his own spit, or he started coughing to hide a laugh.

Luckily, King Mattanair just looked amused. Chase had said that the Unseelie king liked him. I guess that was true. "May I see the sword?"

I had kind of expected this. I also kind of expected never to get the sword back. I tried not to look upset. I drew my sword, balanced the blade flat on both palms, and presented it to him.

He took it. He squinted at the Fey lettering etched on the flat of the blade. "This sword is older than I am. Did you know that?"

I shook my head.

"Where did you discover it?" the king asked. I opened my mouth, but he answered his own question. "The dragon's lair in Yellowstone."

It never failed to shock me when important people knew so much about my life. I wondered if this had happened to Solange too, a couple of centuries ago, when the first Unwritten Tale had started.

"Under Solange's very nose, hidden in her beast's hoard . . . ," said the king, like he'd forgotten we were there. The Fey knights' eyes had glazed over, which kind of made me wonder if the king went off on tangents like this a lot.

"Sire, you are keeping our curiosity at its peak," Lady Ayalla said, half exasperated, half teasing. They must have actually been good friends if she could use that much sarcasm with him.

King Mattanair passed the sword to me. I was so surprised he actually returned it that it nearly tumbled out of my hands. "That is a sword of legend, a relic from an age when the Fey's very name recalled ancient greatness. It is a training sword used by the newly sworn squires of the Itari. All of their make were thought to be destroyed when the knights were overcome, their fortress conquered, centuries ago. It is likely the last one left."

"Oh." Now I really couldn't believe that I'd gotten it back.

The knights looked like they felt *exactly* the same way. Their eyes lingered on the blade, and even Jack cast a longing look over it. Before, Chase was the only other person interested in my magic sword. Now I wondered if one of the Fey might try to fight me for it.

I think Lady Aspenwind noticed. "Rory, the writing on the sword—do you know what it says?" She glanced back at her king, worry pinching her face into a frown.

I shook my head. Chase couldn't read it, and Lena had said it was a language lost to most of the magical world. Even her gumdrop translator was stumped.

"It is a training sword," said King Mattanair. "It was not meant to be kept by one person all their life. In fact, many of these weapons were cursed to discourage one warrior from keeping it too long."

The jealous looks instantly melted into smugness.

That explained why he'd returned it. *Here. Keep one of our ancient legendary swords. By the way, it's cursed.*

King Mattanair flicked the blade, and a tiny ping ran out in the still room. "'With this edge, I shall protect you.'" He did the same on the other side with a sly sort of triumph. Yep, definitely Fael's dad. "'With this edge, I shall destroy you.' Hold on to this weapon for much longer, and it will turn against you."

He probably expected me to *give* it to him. Maybe not today, but after the Snow Queen was defeated. I was almost sure that was what he wanted.

Ugh. As if my life wasn't complicated enough. I wondered if anyone had noticed I was holding the sword slightly away from my body now.

"We said it was of the Itari tradition," said the gold-winged knight, clearly afraid the king had forgotten why they were upset. "We said he was teaching our oldest secrets. It is no less than we should expect from a Turnleaf."

Chase flinched, his shoulders hunched slightly, and if Adelaide hadn't shifted closer to him, I would have. I bit my tongue and looked at Lady Aspenwind and Jack, waiting for one of them to defend their son.

"No less?" repeated the king quietly. No one could see magic, but sometimes you could feel it—a slow crackle that built, like an electrical charge, until the hairs stood up all along your arms. As the king spoke, we could all feel it.

The knights bowed their heads.

"It is true. Chase Turnleaf has chosen not to be of the Unseelie," said the king. "However, he has chosen to be a friend to our people, and it was well for us that he did so. We would be dead otherwise. Or worse, captured. My knights did not lead me to my freedom."

Chase managed not to smirk, but joy shone out of his eyes like a beacon.

The knight in green armor was resolute. "Even so, he has no right to share the secrets of our people—"

"Have you not been listening, Himorsal Liior?" the king said impatiently. So the dude with green armor was the one who had been annoying Chase so much. Not surprised. "Chase Turnleaf teaches the lost art of Itari. It would still be lost without him. The secrets are his more than ours, and he is free to share them as he sees fit."

The king might have felt differently if Chase hadn't saved his life the day before, but this was pretty obviously a victory for Turnleafs everywhere.

Chase didn't have the sense to stay humble about it either. "There's room in my class, if you want."

Three knights sprang into the air, ready to avenge their honor or whatever, but what the king said next stopped them mid-flight. "A generous offer, Chase Turnleaf. I look forward to hearing of their progress."

Then he swept from the room before anyone could argue with him. The Itari teacher and his new students stared at each other in horror.

"He cannot be serious," muttered the knight with gold wings. "Will we spar against statues of our own likeness?" He gestured to the evil Fey dummies in the back wall.

Yikes. So they *had* noticed.

"I refuse to learn alongside humans," the shortest knight sputtered.

Chase's teacher mode settled over him like armor. He sounded so bossy and indifferent that Hansel would have been proud. "Then you are out of luck. I only have time for one session."

"Okay, so *what* just happened?" Ben said. It wasn't just him and the triplets looking at me expectantly. It was half the room. Even Kenneth had crept up behind us.

Chatty must have understood Fey; I could hear her cackling through the M3. I wasn't sure if I could explain without laughing too.

"Your study group just got a lot bigger," I said, gesturing to the Fey glaring at Chase.

Ben looked even less excited than the knights. "You mean, we have to learn with that Himorsal guy?"

"Himorsal is the stupidest name I've ever heard," Kenneth said.

"That's because it's not a name," Chatty said through the M3. She hadn't warmed up to Kenneth since Ben's Tale. "It means 'Captain.'"

I probably should have told him that. Chase's old students and his new students were never going to get along if they couldn't understand each other. "Maybe I should go see if Lena has any spare translators. She—"

"Where are the Zipes triplets?" Hansel's voice managed to cut across even the loudly protesting Fey and the excited chatters of the other Characters in the training courts.

Kevin's face grew half-worried, half-defensive. Kyle looked like he wanted to get popcorn and watch Chase's first lesson with the Fey. Tentatively, Conner raised his hand.

Hansel charged over, spotting the Canon's champion on the way. "Jack, the Director wants you." Jack looked extremely relieved to have an excuse to leave, but Hansel didn't spare him a second glance. He turned back to the triplets. "Have you packed? You're relocating to EAS today. I just finished confirming the details with your father."

Oh wow. A *lot* of people were moving to EAS this week.

Kyle shoved Conner's shoulder. "Told you. Destroying Fey courts is enough to freak out even Dad."

"That was a factor," Hansel said, "but the Director offered him space in the stables for his livestock."

"For *what*?" said Ben and Kenneth together.

"We live on a working ranch," Kyle said, like he didn't understand why this concept was hard for the rest of us to understand.

"Enough," Hansel said. "Have you packed or not?"

"*We* packed," Kyle said. "Months ago. Mom and Dad haven't."

"Then you can wait here," Hansel said. "The move begins as soon as your father confirms that his last herd has been relocated."

"Got it," said Kyle, sounding a little relieved. I was too. Tonight our whole grade would be safe at EAS.

"Who's on call?" Kevin asked.

"The rising ninth graders," Hansel said, surprised that this was even a question.

Our first mission since the Snow Queen's invasion of the Fey courts. Since my *birthday*. Since the Snow Queen had stopped her hunt and started waging war.

Something sharp and cold pricked deep inside my chest, like an icicle had lodged itself there.

I didn't know how the Snow Queen would find out about this mission, but it seemed impossible that the move would go smoothly. It seemed way more likely that something worse than the Wolfsbane clan would show up.

I wasn't the only one worried. Everyone went quiet. Everyone but Adelaide. "But we can't. Chase and I have dinner reservations with my parents."

At the look Hansel gave her—at the look we *all* gave her, somewhere between revulsion and disbelief—I'm pretty sure even Adelaide wanted to sink into the ground and disappear. Her cheeks flushed a little but she pressed on. "We've been planning this for weeks. My parents haven't even *met* Chase yet, and—"

Kyle cut her off. This was the first time I'd ever heard him sound angry. "Chase! We're moving today. You interested in helping?"

The shard of ice in my chest morphed into a clamp, squeezing the air from my lungs. I hoped the doubt didn't show on my face.

Chase looked up from the wolf dummies he'd been moving into position. "Kevin, didn't you say that you had a horse as cool as a Dapplegrim? That I gotta see. I'm in."

Hansel did something rare. He bestowed an approving smile.

"But—" Adelaide started.

"I'm going," Chase said, and he turned back to his class. Then he caught a glimpse of Himorsal Liior's scowl, which clearly said, *Our king orders us to learn Itari and you abandon us during our first lesson for a horse?* Chase turned back reluctantly. "Well, as long as

125

the call comes an hour from now. I want to get them started on a few drills first."

"Take your time," said Kevin. "Dad will probably try to drag this out."

Hansel humphed, which basically meant, *Not if I have anything to do with it.* "Meet me outside. I want you suited up in fifteen. Turnleaf can join later." Then he turned and stormed out, probably to go track down our archers.

Chase looked at me, and my face must have been doing *something*. His grin faded. "I'll be there."

I wanted to believe him. I wanted to believe that something had changed since yesterday. I wanted to pretend that Chase had never let me down.

But he had, all summer.

"Great," said Kyle, but all the triplets were eyeing Adelaide, her pout and crossed arms. I knew they expected to be disappointed too, just like I did.

evin had called it right. His dad was definitely dragging out the move, and we'd been waiting for *hours*. Eventually, standing around sweating through our armor gave way to stealing some of the couches from under the Tree of Hope and moving them over to the Door Trek door to the Zipes's place, painted a dusty sort of hunter green. Paul and Vicky took over a love seat for themselves, staring into each other's eyes and sitting entirely too close for people wearing chain mail. Tina asked them what time it was every few minutes, but I think it was mostly to keep reminding them that they were surrounded by people and not allowed to make out. The triplets had helped Lena and I move one of the tables over to the door too. Lena and Melodie kept themselves busy—attaching a stack of shiny new M3's to easy-to-carry covers.

She'd started sharing theories on my maybe-cursed sword. "We can't know *when* the curse will kick in," Lena said. "You probably have a few more years, considering how slowly the Fey age. It was probably just supposed to prevent squires from depending on the magic too much. They were supposed to learn the techniques, not just depend on the enchanted sword."

No matter what she said, I still felt betrayed by one of my first allies.

I couldn't sit still like Lena. I didn't even think I could practice any drills like the triplets. The ice shard in my chest had been joined by three or four more, and I couldn't stop craning my neck around a tiny little blue house, trying to check the orange door that led to the Canon members' apartments.

"Another day," Daisy said, tossing one of her arrows in the air, watching it flip end over end, and catching it by the wooden shaft. At first, it had been impressive. Now it was only annoying. "Another evening, waiting for Chase."

"That was different and you know it," I said, more sharply than I meant to. "Besides, he was waiting with us just a little while ago."

I wasn't sure what had shocked us the most: the fact that he showed up or the fact that he brought the Fey with him. He'd spent most of the afternoon demonstrating how the Itari moves worked while flying. It had been nice to watch while it lasted. The Fey knights picked up the maneuvers even faster than I did. They had the potential to be great Itari warriors before the summer ended, but only if they started focusing on their lessons instead of plotting against their teacher.

"That was two hours ago," Daisy shot back, and I couldn't argue. She was right.

When the Fey *finally* showed signs of tiring, Chase had sent them back to wherever the Director had set them up. Soaked with sweat, he'd walked over to make sure we hadn't scheduled a departure time, and then he'd looked at the triplets, at *me*. "Just let me go get my armor," he'd said.

Then he'd disappeared beyond the door, and hadn't returned.

"It's dinnertime in New York," said Kevin irritably.

"Almost past dinnertime," added Conner, squinting at the sun, which was now touching the wall at the end of the courtyard. His voice was tinged with hope, like Chase might finish up and come back in time to join us.

"We never talk about Adelaide," said Tina thoughtfully. "Have you ever noticed that? But she's gone as much as Chase is."

"Chase is our best fighter," Kevin said. "Adelaide's a good shot, but she's no Rory."

That was a compliment, kind of, but mostly I felt like a poor substitute for Chase.

He wasn't just our best fighter. He was . . . *Chase*. He could joke his way through any pre-mission stress. If he were here, he would have asked the triplets if there were any embarrassing items they wanted to tell us about *before* we reached their ranch. Or maybe he would have told stories about growing up in the Unseelie Court—something to keep us all entertained.

Hansel poked his head out of the hunter green door to Texas. He'd crossed over hours ago, trying to hurry Mr. Zipes along. "It's time," Hansel said wearily. "Turnleaf isn't here?" he asked me, like *I* was supposed to know. I shrugged, careful not to meet his eyes. If I did, he would be able to tell how ticked off I was.

Lena was already tucking Melodie into a bag and pulling the straps over her shoulders.

Sighing, our sword instructor opened the Door Trek door wider. "Well, we've wasted too much time already. He'll know where to find us." Great. Even Hansel didn't expect much from Chase anymore.

I followed first, tight-lipped, and led the others down a corridor with worn wooden walls and old-fashioned lanterns. I hated that I'd thought anything had changed.

"They're both getting on my nerves," said Vicky.

"I wrote Adelaide off a long time ago," added Tina. "I expected better from Chase, though."

I shot them a dark look. "We're here for the triplets. Let's just concentrate on the mission for now."

Hansel didn't have much patience for it either. "If you're too distracted, I can send you back and request the tenth grade archers in your place."

He would do it, no matter how long we'd been waiting. He was that strict.

The stepsisters immediately straightened up, and the whole grade's mood went from pretty irritated to mildly concerned.

"Hansel, are you threatening to take away our mission and give it to the grade above us again?" I said, determined to break the tension. "I thought those days were behind us."

The triplets gaped at me. I couldn't help but notice that it did sound like something that would come out of Chase's mouth.

Hansel pretended to consider it. "To tell the truth, the tenth graders could use the extra practice more than you lot."

I opened the door at the end of the corridor. "But the triplets could use *us* as their bodyguards. We'll fight harder. We like them more."

Hansel laughed. "Nice to see that old grade rivalries haven't completely disappeared. We'll fight harder. We like them more."

The rest of the grade exchanged glances. I wasn't sure any of them had heard that sound come out of the sword master before. Then we stepped outside into Texas, hot and dry even in the twilight.

The ranch had a bunch of buildings, all charcoal gray in the dim light. Two barns, something that was shaped like a barn but was small enough to be a storage shed, and at least five *actual* storage sheds. Our Door Trek door was attached to the closest structure, a large white house with red shutters and a huge porch.

It was funny. I'd spent years fighting alongside the triplets, but I'd never imagined where they came from.

"Kyle, Conner, Kevin, we need to rendezvous with your parents," Hansel said. He nodded at the man on the porch and the dark-haired woman beside him. The triplets broke off and followed him. "Search the buildings and sweep the perimeter for any threats. Then we're going to help them with their boxes."

The rest of the grade turned to me, grumbling. They were clearly more interested in guarding than carrying stuff, but it took me a second to realize they were waiting for assignments. If you had told me a few months ago that I would miss Chase giving me orders, I wouldn't have believed you, but I did. Most of the archers wanted to see the animals, so I sent them to search the barns. The spearmen were interested in the heavy machinery—they went to check the storage sheds. Lena took another good runner, Tina, to sweep the perimeter on the opposite side of the compound. Then I jogged around our side with Paul and Vicky. They tried to hold hands as they ran, which instantly irritated me for no reason at all.

We didn't see any trolls or dragons. We didn't hear any wolves or ice griffins.

We didn't hear or see much of anything. Away from the buildings and their lights, the sky felt bigger. The stars were beginning to come out—brilliant bursts peeking through a growing darkness. I'd never seen so many stars in my life, not even when Mom had a film in Wyoming, and *that* town had seemed plenty small and isolated. We ran past some crooked shapes clustered up on the hill. We ran a little closer, weapons out, but the shapes just turned out to be low cypress trees.

Still, a creepy feeling crawled up my spine, like we were being watched.

"Stop procrastinating," Hansel called from the main house. "If you don't see anything, come back and help the others."

With heavy sighs, Paul and Vicky turned and started obediently jogging back. I paused, squinting hard at the next rise. Its shape blotted out the stars, too narrow and lumpy to be a hill, but somehow familiar too.

Probably just a rock column. Everything seemed creepier in the dark.

I put my hand on my sword hilt, so it wouldn't knock against my side as I ran. Then something did happen, something big.

The rock column shifted closer. It was roughly four stories tall.

I'd *known* the Snow Queen wouldn't let this be easy for us. "Giant!" I shouted.

The giant heard. It took another step, and its enormous foot fell with a bone-rattling thump. I couldn't let it get close enough to grab me.

"Regroup!" Hansel called.

I whipped around and sprinted back to the main house, unsheathing my blade on the way. I peeked over my shoulder, hoping I wouldn't see General Searcaster.

I didn't. It was her son.

On my very first quest, I'd overheard Jimmy Searcaster moaning about having to feed the Snow Queen's pet dragons. I'd heard him snoring. I'd read the love poems his wife had written him. He shouldn't have been terrifying, but he *was*. He'd become a pillar, one of the giant bodyguards who couldn't be killed except by another pillar.

Jimmy stepped into the light coming from the buildings, and then I could see his glinting teeth and green face. "Did I hear that you had a birthday yesterday, Rory Landon? I've been meaning to give you a present, since last time we met, you gave me something to remember you by."

He raised his arms. Even in the dimness, the new scars were easy to spot—raised bumps and healed gashes that ran from his wrists to his elbows. Lena's exploding bats had really torn him up.

I gulped and ducked into the open area between the house and the barn, where some of the others were clustered together.

I skidded to a stop beside Lena. Her hands fumbled inside her carryall.

"Did we call for help?" I asked.

Melodie had popped her head out of Lena's bag to see what was going on. When Lena looked too shaken to answer, the harp spoke up. "Hansel did."

So, Solange's minions hadn't put a warding hex up. Maybe the ranch was too big for the spell to work.

Then Tina screamed and hid her face. She hadn't done that since the day we first met her, when a dragon she hadn't known existed had cornered her in a tennis court.

Kevin tripped over his own feet, trying to back away.

I turned to see what had freaked them out. It couldn't possibly be worse than one of the four pillars.

I was wrong.

Goblins. Ranks upon ranks of the creepily skinny creatures marched down the driveway. We had just enough light to spot bat-like ears, bald heads, and sneers. At least a hundred and fifty of them.

Two desires ripped through me: One was to make a break for the Door Trek door that would take us back to EAS, to safety. The other was to sprint toward the goblins, sword raised, to throw myself at their ranks and take down as many as possible. I probably wouldn't survive, but I might distract the Snow Queen's forces long enough to let everyone *else* reach the Door Trek door. I wanted to do both things so badly I couldn't think of anything else. So I just froze.

Melodie rubbed Lena's arm soothingly. "Mistress, what is it? This isn't like you."

It wasn't like *any* of us. We didn't lose our heads in battle. We'd *trained* for this.

"Something's wrong," I said. "We shouldn't be this scared."

"I'm going to protect my *family*," I heard Mr. Zipes yell. And then suddenly he was running down the house steps, toward the goblins.

"Come back!" Mrs. Zipes rushed down the driveway, intent on stopping her husband.

It was like they had both become too emotional to think clearly.

"Mom! Dad!" Conner started after them, and Kyle and Kevin raised their spears, ready to follow.

"Wait." Hansel had joined us. He must have been trying to stop Mr. Zipes, because even though our enemies hadn't reached us yet, he already looked like he'd been in a fight, torn clothes and a swollen lip. "The goblins are using their magic against us."

Right. I had dealt with this before. Goblins have a special brand of magic: They can learn your deepest desires and turn those desires against you. They can manipulate you to feel the way they want you to feel—until you make the decision they want you to make.

That magic must have hit Mr. and Mrs. Zipes first, sending them both sprinting down the driveway, exactly where the goblins wanted them. A swarm broke away from the ranks and dashed forward, in full-on capture mode.

"Well," Paul said drily, "they locked onto my desire to *not die* pretty strongly."

"Take a second," Hansel said. "Calm down. You're useless if the goblins are controlling you."

Lena pulled out her retractable spear and dropped it, sobbing so hard she couldn't see where it landed. I'm not even sure she noticed her harp yanking on her sleeve.

"Mistress, these are just foot soldiers," Melodie said. "They don't have the control the goblin priestesses have. They're exaggerating *all* your desires, not just the one where you want to save yourself."

Melodie was right. We could still choose which feeling got amplified.

"Focus on saving them," I told Conner, who looked like he might faint. I turned to the rest of the grade. "Focus on helping the triplets and their family." That was what we all wanted. That was what we'd spent hours waiting to do in the first place.

Slowly, Lena stood tall. She wiped the tears off her cheeks and opened her retractable staff to its full length. The stepsisters' eyes cleared. The spearmen fell into line, and the triplets glanced at Hansel for orders.

"We need one team here, defending the Door Trek door. Our exit is useless if their forces cut us off," Hansel said. "Another team will go rescue the Zipes before the goblins can get them back to whatever portal *they* came through. Rory and I will deal with the giants."

Giants? As in *more than one*?

I whirled around.

Jimmy's wife, Matilda, stood in front of the garage. She tugged her chain-mail tunic into place and winced like it pinched her. It probably did. It was made of refrigerator doors and steel cables.

In her huge hands, she wrung something green-gold and floppy, like a huge glittery handkerchief. Then she thrust it away from her and shouted in Fey, *"Give us ice, let it rain, turn slick and white this terrain."*

I knew a spell when I heard one. The thing in Matilda's hands disintegrated.

She'd been carrying a *whole* dragon skin. I didn't want to think about how they'd peeled it off a *Draconus melodius* so that Matilda could use its scales. "How many giant magicians are there?" I asked Lena.

"Right now?" The wind picked up and ripped Lena's voice away. She had to shout so I could hear her. "Only one!"

And she was my opponent. Lucky me. Hopefully, Matilda hadn't brought any more dragon skins to the battle.

The temperature plunged, way too cold for the T-shirts and shorts we wore under our armor. The dark sky spat sleet—just a few tiny stings at first, and then sharp rice-size ice pellets assaulted my whole face. I squinted, trying to see.

"What is with you guys?" snapped Vicky, shielding her face and sounding a lot more like her usual self. "We get it. She's the *Snow Queen*, but I don't think you like fighting in this stuff any more than we do."

"It's a present," said Jimmy with a smile. "A gift from Her Majesty to Rory Landon."

This was *winter*. Solange was trying to trigger the first lines of my Tale. My stomach knotted.

Three goblins had already pinned the triplets' father. Four more chased Mrs. Zipes.

"Kyle, Conner, Kevin, Paul, Tina, Lena, and Daisy, you're the rescue team." They started running before Hansel finished speaking, so he called after them. "If you can't fight your way back, hold them off until we get reinforcements! The rest of you, defend the

Door Trek door, or the reinforcements can't reach us."

Jimmy had finally caught up. The motion-activated floodlights on the Zipes house burst on and illuminated his green knees. The giant glanced from my group to the kids dashing down the driveway, like he was trying to figure out who to attack first.

Hansel didn't give him a chance to decide. He slid his broadsword out of its sheath. The metal shinked as he pulled it free and sleet pinged against the blade. "I'll handle Jimmy. I want to test out how far we can push the Snow Queen's protection spell."

Jimmy smashed his fist down so hard that the ground shook and Vicky lost her balance. I didn't see Hansel move out of the way. I only saw the new slice as long as the barn on Jimmy's arm. The giant stumbled back, cursing.

I'd heard a rumor once that the Canon had asked *Hansel* to be their champion before they asked Jack. Now I thought it was probably true.

Matilda dusted off her hands and put them on her hips. "Well, what are you waiting for, *Rachel*?"

I had told Matilda my name was Rachel when I first met her, during Lena's Tale. She'd known we were Characters, and she still let us inside her house. She'd hidden us in the bread box while her husband and mother-in-law, General Searcaster, ate dinner, and after that, she'd let us go.

And in exchange, we'd lied to her. We'd broken into her house. We'd stolen from her.

From Matilda's perspective, *we* were the villains, and I didn't blame her any more than I blamed the Wolfsbane clan.

The giantess glanced at the Door Trek door behind me. I strongly suspected she had orders to destroy it before more Characters arrived.

I liked Matilda, but that didn't mean I was going to let her lay a finger on our way home.

I yanked all four combs out of my back pocket. I tossed them to Vicky. The comb cage bars rose half a minute later. They met in a peaked roof and sealed together with a clang. Inside, Vicky and Candice notched arrows to their bowstrings, aiming for Matilda's eyes, the only place where a two-foot-long arrow could do any damage to a four-story-tall giantess.

I raised my sword and felt its Itari magic flow into me, determined to protect the others.

"What are you *doing*, Maddy?" Jimmy said. I remembered how much I hated the way he talked to his wife. "Finish this fast, or there will be more of them."

A foot the size of a sailboat swung toward me.

I was quicker. It was easy to dart to the side, straight to Matilda's other foot.

Maybe Chase wasn't there, but he'd given us his Giant-Slaying 101 seminar. You go for the feet. You trip them, wound them, whatever you have to do to get them on the ground, and then . . . well, Matilda wasn't a pillar. *She* could be killed.

I changed my grip and raised my sword like a dagger, preparing to pierce Matilda's flimsy canvas shoe.

She noticed. She skipped backward, light on her feet for a giant. I went for her left foot, and she danced past the house. I charged her right Achilles tendon. She slipped out of range again, flattening some shrubs. When I stabbed at her knee, she moved out even further, all the way to the barn. She was drawing me away from all the other fights in the compound. I wondered if she was up to something.

The answer was *definitely*.

She ripped up a cypress tree. Soil showered from the roots onto my head. The tree looked tiny in her hand. But it didn't *feel* tiny when Matilda smashed it into me. One branch walloped me in the stomach. A smaller one split my lip open—I was lucky not to lose any teeth. I didn't realize I'd gone flying until my body crashed into an old storage shed.

The battle would have been all over for me if the shed's wood hadn't been soft and rotting.

Smart, I thought fuzzily, wiggling my toes to check if any leg bones were broken. She was using a weapon that kept me at a distance—too far away for my sword to reach her. I wondered if she had taken a Character-killing tutorial.

A shadow flickered above me. Matilda raised her tree again, her mouth grim.

I dove through the opening. The tree mallet left a car-size crater in the ground.

Sleet had melted in my hair. A few muddy strands were plastered to my mouth. I shoved them back impatiently. I barely noticed the cold anymore.

"Her Majesty was right." Matilda picked a wooden shutter out of her tree-mallet's branches and flicked it at me. I dodged it easily. "You *are* hard to kill, like a cockroach."

I couldn't see any trace of the woman who had been so nervous about fixing dinner for her mother-in-law, who had tried so hard to please the cranky, demanding Searcasters. It had been stupid to think about her that way. We were just two warriors meeting on the battlefield, and one of us had more battle experience.

She couldn't jump away as easily out here. All these trees would trip her.

I sprang forward and stabbed down at her left foot. She lifted it out of range hurriedly, her eyes on my sword. She didn't see me draw my left arm back and slam my fist into her leg.

The ring of the West Wing could destroy tree trunks and send wolves flying thirty feet back. It could easily break a giant's ankle.

Matilda bellowed and toppled. She threw one arm out to break her fall. The other arm curled around her stomach, and then the rest of her hit the ground, crushing a dozen trees and splattering me with mud.

I sprinted up the length of her body and stopped near her head, beside her exposed neck. A human-size blade can't behead a giant, but Chase had taught me where the arteries were. I'd only killed wolves before. This blow would flood the ground with red.

"Please." Even her whisper was frantic. She couldn't see me. I was too close, tucked right under her chin, but I'm sure she could feel the prick of my sword.

I wished I hadn't seen her arm go instinctively to her middle.

Brie had fallen just like that a week before Dani was born. We'd been walking home from dinner, and she'd tripped over a crack in the pavement. She'd gotten a huge bruise down the left side of her face, because both arms had wrapped around her belly, protecting my little sister.

I backed away, careful to keep my weapon poised under her chin. I had to see the giantess's face. "Matilda, are you *pregnant*?"

Her bravery crumpled. Gallon-size tears dribbled from her eyes, and steam rose as they hit the sleet-covered ground.

"Jimmy doesn't know," she whispered.

No.

She was lying. She had to be. It had to be a trick.

But sobs choked the giantess's throat. I was so close. The sound thundered in my ears. She wasn't afraid for herself.

If I still felt bad about the wolves, murdering Matilda would haunt me forever.

I sighed. At least no one else was around to see me do something so insanely stupid in the middle of a war.

I stepped back, resting the flat of my blade against my shoulder. "Go home. Take your husband with you. But I will kill you if you hurt any of my friends on your way out."

She rolled up onto her hands and knees. Her broken ankle wouldn't let her stand, so she began to crawl away, snapping up trees and scooping great grooves out of the soil. She hurried, obviously terrified I would change my mind.

Somewhere to my right, Lena screamed. I had better things to do than bully an injured giantess.

I sprinted through the woods and up the next rise, following the sounds of the skirmish. Metal clanged on metal. Bowstrings twanged. Goblins bellowed their battle cries, and the triplets hollered right back.

The other EASers had clustered around another old, ramshackle storage shed. Tina and Daisy stood on both sides of the shed's open door, their bows aimed at the goblins. Lena had taken up a position right in front of them. Blood oozed from a slice on her shoulder and dripped down her elbow, but besides that, she seemed to have the situation under control. She blocked the serrated sword of the goblin on the left and smashed the butt of her staff into the temple of the one on her right.

Our spear squadron had taken on the troop of goblins a hundred feet away. In the middle of the skirmish, Mr. and Mrs. Zipes struggled against the goblins holding them, but they couldn't get free. We were too outnumbered.

Well, I could help there.

I swerved around the shed and headed over to back up the spearmen. The goblins must have seen me.

An old one stepped up front. I recognized him and his rusty circlet from the Snow Queen's palace. He was King Licivvil. He pulled a dagger from his waist and placed it right over Mrs. Zipes's heart. She went still. We *all* went still, but it wasn't just the threat that stopped me in my tracks. It was the calm deliberate way he did it, and the confident patient way he spoke. For a second, it was so quiet that the only sound was the shouts and thumps of Jimmy and Hansel's battle drifting through the trees. Then the goblin king said, "You're going to let us pass."

"*After* you let them go. According to my mirror, this is your portal home," said Lena. So that was why she and the archers were guarding the shed. She must have used the M3's scrying function. "I'll destroy it if you hurt her. You'll be stuck here when our reinforcements arrive."

King Licivvil actually smirked. "This isn't one of your temporary-transport spells. It's much harder to destroy a portal. You'll have to bring down the whole building to break the magic. All I need is one stab." He twirled the blade.

"You sure about that?" Lena said. "Up, ax! *Chop!*"

Something flew out of her carryall and smashed against the doorway behind the archers. The shabby building couldn't take it. The whole structure shuddered. Dust shivered from the beams.

"What is *that*?" asked the goblin king.

It was a new invention, an ax, flashing in the sun and chopping away at the old boards. Chunks of wood rained down, and all the goblins started shouting at once, mostly at their king, like he should do something.

Lena stepped closer to Tina and whispered something. Tina nodded.

King Licivvil raised the dagger and stepped away from Mr. Zipes. "All right, all right."

Right then, emotion rose in a wave, and those same two desires tore my concentration apart: I could run back to safety at EAS; it would be so easy, if I didn't have to worry about anything but myself. Or I could turn myself over to King Licivvil in exchange for Mr. and Mrs. Zipes. I could let him have the glory of taking me to the Snow Queen. At least then it would all be over.

I shouldn't have thought that last part. I hadn't realized that I wanted it all to end so badly, not until my stomach lurched with excitement. I squeezed my eyes shut, trying to ride out the goblin magic.

I heard the arrow thwack before I saw it sticking out of King Licivvil's neck. He fell backward. Spears flew from the triplets and Paul Stockton, pinning the goblins who held Mr. Zipes. Tina loosed an arrow. It hit the goblin restraining Mrs. Zipes in the heart.

Totally disorganized without their leader, the rest of the goblins retreated, leaving us. I stared shakily at the blood staining the sleet. The Searcasters' blood was green, and trolls' blood was orange. I hadn't expected goblin blood to be the exact same shade as a human's.

I hadn't expected the others not to *need* me.

Mrs. Zipes scrambled toward her husband and kissed him, which made the triplets groan. Daisy was congratulating Tina on her shot, and Lena was calling her axes off.

My friends were acting like we'd already won, and I still couldn't catch my breath. Something terrible would happen. Terrible things *always* happened.

I wondered what Matilda was doing. I wondered why the crashing sounds from Hansel and Jimmy's fight had stopped. I sprinted back to the main house. "We need to get to the Door Trek door!"

Then I came out of the trees and saw them.

The two giants stood between the house and the barn. Jimmy had thrust a hand high in the air. Matilda balanced on one foot, trying to reach the white cuff on her husband's wrist. The snowflake charm dangling from it was as big as a shield.

Our reinforcements had crowded around them. The comb cage had been taken down, and two hundred high-school fighters lined up in front of the portal. Their ranks bristled with raised swords, spears, and bows, but they didn't attack.

A second later, I spotted the reason.

Our sword master was in Jimmy's other fist. Blood poured from a cut over his eye, down his cheek and off his jaw, and he squirmed in the giant's grip, trying to fight fingers longer than he was tall.

"Hansel!" I charged at the giants, furious at our fighters for not helping him. He didn't even have his broadsword.

Hansel looked straight at me. He threw a hand up, telling me to stop.

So he had a plan. Maybe he had a knife in his boot. Maybe he wanted to use it to prick Jimmy and get him to loosen his grip. Maybe he thought it was too embarrassing to let his students rescue him, especially when so many of us were here.

"I told you, Maddy." Jimmy Searcaster thrust his wife back, holding her at arm's length. "We have our orders. We can't retreat."

Then Jimmy squeezed, like he was wringing out a sponge, and all the life went out of Hansel. The giant tossed him to the ground.

I didn't notice the screaming at first. Not when Lena caught up to me, not when she and Kyle held me back. Not when Jimmy smiled and dropped his arms, and Matilda's pale, shocked face turned our way. Not when the giantess plucked the snowflake charm from her husband's wrist, and both Searcasters disappeared, leaving four huge footprints and Hansel's body.

It wasn't until Lena grabbed my face with both hands that I heard the wail. The sound was coming from *me*. I stopped. My throat felt raw.

All of me felt raw.

The house lights glittered on Hansel's armor, and his chain mail dipped into his rib cage—a crater the same width as Jimmy Searcaster's thumb. I was shaking, so Lena took my sword away and passed it to one of the stepsisters. I tried not to cry. This kind of crying would horrify Chase. Then I remembered that Chase wasn't here.

"It's okay," I heard Lena saying, as she started to guide me toward the Door Trek door. "The reinforcements will round up the goblins in the trees. Let's just get you home."

Someone brought a horse blanket from the barn and covered Hansel—an eleventh grader who was sobbing so hard she was hiccuping. "I'm sorry," I told her as we passed. "I'm so sorry."

"It's not your fault, Rory." Lena opened the dusty green door. "He told you to stop. He told everyone to stop." Then she pushed me through the portal.

I stumbled into the EAS courtyard, exhausted and numb, and totally unprepared to see Chase kissing Adelaide a few feet away.

He'd buckled on his sword belt, and she had her quiver slung over a flouncy silk dress. They had been on their way. They had no idea they were too late. They didn't even know we were there.

Their lips were locked, and their eyes were closed, and he was stroking her pretty blond hair.

I had refused to think about this. I'd been determined to go on believing that Chase hadn't had his first kiss, the same way I'd never had mine.

I opened my mouth to yell, to tell them to *stop*, but my throat—still aching from my scream—closed up tight. All I managed was a tiny squeak.

The rest of my grade didn't have that problem. "How was *dinner*?" snapped Daisy behind me.

Chase and Adelaide burst apart.

Her gaze slid to me. Triumph rolled off her in waves, but I didn't look back. This wasn't about her.

Chase blinked at us. He'd looked less dazed the time a troll's club had knocked him flat. "You're back *already*? I thought Mr. Zipes wouldn't be ready until at least midnight."

We were the Triumvirate. I thought the three of us were fated to help each other. I thought I could rely on them—on *him*.

But I didn't even *know* him anymore. Triumvirate or not, I didn't *want* to know him. I swallowed hard, and my voice came back, cracked and ragged. "You should have *been* there."

"You said we would only be fifteen minutes late, tops," Chase told his girlfriend.

"Fifteen minutes is a long time in a battle." Even Lena—my careful, neutral friend—sounded livid.

Chase focused on me, and then, like he was finally seeing us, he said, "Something happened." He reached out.

I flinched away from his hand. I hated him for making me break the news. "Hansel's *dead*, Chase. Jimmy killed him, and if you'd been there, like you *promised*, he wouldn't have had to take on a pillar alone. He—"

I stopped myself. If I kept going, I would have to explain how I could have stopped it too. I should have gone to help Hansel with Jimmy instead of helping the others with the goblins. No, I shouldn't have let Matilda go. I should have taken *her* as a four-story-tall hostage. I should have threatened her to control Jimmy. It was the last thing Hansel had asked me to do.

At the news, Adelaide reeled back, hands covering her mouth, stunned and guilty, but Chase just stood there, like he hadn't understood what I'd just said.

He glanced toward Adelaide and back to me again. "Listen, Rory—"

"I don't *want* to listen." He couldn't give me an excuse today—not for this.

Characters began to push through the Door Trek door behind us. Eventually, some of them would be carrying Hansel's body back through the portal, and I didn't want to be here when that happened.

So I ran.

I didn't even try to go home. I knew what Mom would say. *You see? Even experienced adults like Hansel aren't safe. You can't expect to make a difference.*

But I was *supposed* to make a difference. Everyone was counting on me.

I went to Dad's apartment, but through the door, I could hear Danica wailing. It didn't seem fair to make Dad and Brie deal with *two* daughters having a meltdown.

Kelly and Priya came down the hall, chatting excitedly. They didn't know yet. I couldn't bear it if they asked me what monsters I'd fought today. I couldn't listen to them ooh and ahh over battling giants and goblins. They hadn't been there. They hadn't seen their teacher die. They didn't know how horrible that instant was—the second between realizing what Jimmy was about to do and him actually doing it, the fraction of an instant when I saw Hansel's death coming and knew I was powerless to stop it. Kids shouldn't have to deal with stuff like this. *I* shouldn't have to carry those memories in my head, of Hansel and Hadriane. I turned and walked in the opposite direction. I turned around every time I spotted a Character I knew.

The thing about EAS is that it seems endless. It seems like you could explore it for days and always find an unknown corridor, a new door, fresh mysteries to puzzle out. But after living there, you realize the labyrinth folds back on itself. It doesn't keep going and going. It always takes you to the same places, and sometimes, it takes you exactly where you need to go.

Rapunzel was waiting for me at the base of her tower. Her long silver braid trailed across the bottom three steps, like she had just come down from her room.

"I know the news of Hansel." The sympathy on Rapunzel's face made me feel all shaky again. She touched my arm, very gently. "And I know of Matilda, too."

I burst into tears.

It was all so messed up. The Snow Queen would keep killing people, and I would keep trying to stop her and totally failing. And eventually, it would be *me* she killed, and I didn't want to die. But I didn't want to live, either, if I would end up just like the Snow Queen. I didn't want to hurt all the people I loved.

Rapunzel lifted some folded handkerchiefs from the bottom of the banister; she was always prepared.

I cried my way through half the stack. Rapunzel didn't hug me, like I kind of wanted. But she didn't ask anything of me either. She didn't try to calm me down or tell me everything was going to be okay or strategize on ways I might live through this.

Somehow, that was exactly what I needed.

Finally I took a shaky breath and blew my nose. I knew how this scene was supposed to play out. "You're going to tell me that it's not my fault Hansel is dead. Just like with Hadriane."

"This death is different than Hadriane's," Rapunzel said. "Yes, it was unfair. Yes, his was a purposeful sacrifice, but Hansel was much older than he looked. He was at the end of his life. Some can live centuries, and still not be ready for death, but Hansel was."

I stared hard at the crumpled mound of handkerchiefs next to me. "But I could have *stopped* it."

"If you had threatened Matilda, you may have convinced Jimmy Searcaster to release Hansel," Rapunzel said, "but Hansel's fate was sealed the moment Solange gave Jimmy his orders. She wanted to create in you a terrible grief. She wanted to distract you."

A terrible grief. Those words seemed too small for what I was feeling. "But we could have gotten him out of there." No one should have died.

"A pillar could not be slain on that field. So the next safest solution would be to *give* Jimmy the life he wanted to take. Otherwise, the giant may have taken a student's life, and Hansel would have done anything to prevent that."

Rapunzel dropped a hand on my head. She waited until I looked up. Her dark eyes glistened, bright with tears, and I remembered: She had known the sword master longer than I had. She was even older than Hansel was. She had probably watched him grow up. "Every instructor here would make the same sacrifice Hansel did. Our time is almost past, and you children are the future we fight for. We would *prefer* to die to protect you than to witness your deaths, your futures snuffed out. It is natural for the old to die before the young. You gave that gift to Hansel, even if you can't give it to your mother."

I shot her a look. That was a low blow, especially right then. Mom and I argued about that constantly. We would probably fight over it the next time I saw her. Finding out that Rapunzel took her side didn't help.

Rapunzel must have known she was pushing it. She pulled a Chase and changed the subject. "Rory, have you thought about who you might become after the war ends?"

I almost snorted. I couldn't think past the death, winter, and despair the Snow Queen kept throwing my way. When I thought about the future, I thought about dealing with the fate of magic and defeating the Snow Queen. Reaching high school seemed a little less possible every day.

"I don't believe anyone ever asked my sister such a question," Rapunzel said softly. "She focused only on King Navaire's destruction."

So. There it was—one more thing Solange and I had in common.

"It may be better if . . ." I was relieved that my hoarse voice only trembled a little bit. ". . . if I didn't see the end of the war. The world doesn't need a second Snow Queen."

I hadn't told this to anyone. No one else would listen. Mom wouldn't have let me finish my sentence. Amy would have given me her thin-lipped glare of doom. Dad and Brie had their hands full with the baby. Lena would just cry, and Chase would say, in his cocky way, *You're not going to die, Rory*. And the Director, well, she might agree with me.

Rapunzel's expression didn't change, like maybe she'd known I'd felt this way all along. "You are seeing only two options—Hadriane's end and Solange's change. It is not like you to lack imagination. Usually, you see a dozen choices where others see only a few. Your own life should be no exception."

"So you still don't see my future?" I asked. I'd gotten used to her knowing what would happen.

"I do see it," said Rapunzel. "But not with my foresight."

I felt gazes on me as I walked back to our apartment. Even though I'm sure they could all see that I'd been crying, I kept my head up high and my face blank. I could still play the brave and steady Rory Landon they wanted me to be.

I reached the hallway of apartments. Students and older Characters clustered together, full of sad murmurs and half-hidden tears. The only activity in the corridor came from the triplets' new place. The Zipes, the LaMarelles, and Paul Stockton streamed in and out with boxes. One of them—I couldn't have told you which one—passed on the news: Only Gretel and her family would attend Hansel's funeral, but the memorial was for everyone. We would hold it at dawn.

It was a welcome excuse to go to bed early. After crying that hard, all I wanted was my pillow.

The only person I saw inside my apartment was Amy, and she launched a barrage of questions as soon as she saw me: "Rory? Are you okay? Your mom is taking a shower—do you want me to get her? Your friend Chase stopped by. Then Lena did. Did they ever find you—?"

I started shaking my head before she'd finished her first sentence. I walked over to my room during the interrogation. I grasped the doorknob, and then I looked at her.

She bit off her last question, looking stricken. Then uncertain. She glanced at the bathroom door.

"I just need to sleep," I said, my voice almost gone. So I did.

When the dream came back, I hated it. I hated the dusty tower room, the abandoned furniture crowding me, and the tiny cot that looked even tinier with Chase's lanky body sprawled across it. I hated Chase's stupid, sleeping face and the pain that sliced through my chest as I listened to his slow, deep breathing. I hated the worry crashing through me and the terror that he wouldn't wake up, that I was going to lose him forever.

By the time my alarm went off, fury had licked away the concern. I didn't care that I'd now dreamed it three times, which usually meant that it would come true. After all, I'd already lost Chase. Tiptoeing through the quiet apartment, careful not to wake Mom and Amy, I couldn't imagine why I would worry so much. After everything we'd survived this summer, sleeping didn't strike me as especially dangerous.

Outside, the courtyard was dark. Already a line of hundreds of people snaked out from an old-fashioned wooden door, hung with black ribbons, waiting for their turn to pay their respects at the Wall of Failed Tales. The wind rustled the Tree's branches.

By the time I found the others in my grade, all I felt was hollow. Sadness had carved a great, echoing emptiness inside me.

It didn't seem fair to add Hansel's name to this memorial. His Tale had ended years ago. He hadn't failed anything.

Maybe after this war was over, we could lobby to name it something else. The Wall of Fallen Characters was closer. The Wall of Fallen Heroes was even better.

When red-orange light crept over the buildings, and the door to the wall finally opened, the Canon members went in first, but Sarah Thumb had made sure that we—the kids in my grade who had gone on Hansel's last mission, the ones he'd died to protect—got the turn right after them.

Chase and Adelaide hadn't showed. None of us were surprised.

When we entered the memorial, Snow White held the chisel and mallet. She passed them to Kyle. Instead of going out the door, she moved deeper into the room, further down the wall. She reached up to trace a name: *Don White.* Her husband, I thought. Judging by the date engraved there, he must have died in the last war.

I'd always feared this place, but the idea of having my own name on the wall didn't seem so terrible anymore. Adding a friend's name up there was much worse. It was the names of the dead that left the worst scars, and the longer you stayed at EAS, the more grief you learned to carry. This wall held so much pain.

One swing of the mallet, and Kyle finished his turn. The chisel and mallet hung loosely in his hands. He stared at the spot where someone had already penciled the name, *Hansel Keifmeier.* The *H* was already complete.

Then Kyle handed the tools to me. He stepped back, shoulder to shoulder with Lena. She was too miserable to even look happy about standing next to her crush. "The tools are enchanted," he said. "I'm pretty sure. So we know what to do."

The chisel was heavier than I expected it to be, the mallet unwieldy, and they filled me with a much milder version of the runner's high my sword gave me. I raised the chisel to the curve of the first *A*. The tool corrected the angle slightly. I struck. The mallet regulated the blow—precise and firm, not nearly as hard as I wanted to smash things.

A tiny chip fell from the wall and joined a pile at my feet.

I passed the mallet and the chisel to Kevin.

Lena looped her arm through mine. When everyone had their turn, we walked together to the end of the hall.

Gretel and the Director waited there. Tears glinted on Gretel's cheeks in the torchlight along the memorial, but she didn't seem to notice them. Snow White told her how sorry she was, and Gretel nodded her thanks, expressionless. In a black dress that looked way too grand for grieving, the Director gripped Gretel's shoulder.

We slowed when we saw them. None of us were sure what to say. Chase was always the one who knew what to do when someone was hurting like this.

Once an annoying little brother, always an annoying little brother, Gretel had once said. But now Hansel would never complain about her using her metal foot to win a sparring match again. He would never steal all the good metal dummies before she got to the training courts for class.

Remembering made me want to hurry past. I didn't think any of the grown-ups would mind if we just left. They never expected much from the young Characters.

But Hansel had died to protect *us*. If I didn't say anything, I would hate myself. "Gretel, I'm so sorry about Hansel," I said, and then I knew why the Director held Gretel's shoulder. Words seemed pale and stupid next to what I was feeling. I wanted her to know how much I wished I could make it better.

Maybe she understood anyway, because Gretel looked at us. She hadn't looked at Snow White. "Thank you."

We left. Outside the back door, the sun was rising. Indigo-gray clouds were painted across the orange-gold sky, blocking out the light. Flames in a tall brazier licked the air, too hot for summer but pretty in the dimness. Ellie was in front of it. Beside her was a basket of life-size paper models of Hansel's broadsword. Ellie passed one out to each of us. It felt strange to hold something that looked like a weapon but felt so light and flimsy.

She waited until everyone in our grade assembled in front of her. "On our wall, we engrave his name. On our hearts, we carve his memory. By these flames, we let him go."

Mr. Swallow landed on my shoulder. From his back, Sarah Thumb said, "Hand her one for me, will you, Ellie?"

Ellie passed a second paper broadsword to me. Sarah Thumb and her mount rode on my shoulder to the bonfire. We pitched the paper weapons in and the flames devoured the swords in seconds. Sarah Thumb's face was impassive. "Usually, we burn paper gingerbreads for Hansel representatives, but I think he would have liked this better."

I didn't know. This was the first time we had added a dead Character to the Wall since I'd come to EAS. Hansel would have said we were just lucky, but maybe we'd been protected. By the Snow Queen's shortage of allies. By *Hansel*, who was gone now.

"He never laughed at me," Sarah Thumb added softly. "When I told him I wanted to learn to fight, he taught me. He never said I was too small. He showed me how to coat my needle in poison."

It wouldn't end with Hansel. We would burn more bonfires before the war ended.

I wished I knew how to stop it.

Sarah Thumb and Mr. Swallow flapped off. The other kids in my grade drifted toward the overstuffed armchairs. Both stepsisters were crying. Candice and Conner too, but they were trying to hide it.

I almost went with them.

Then I spotted someone standing alone in the line snaking out from the Wall's front door. The shock of seeing him there, looking weary and shaken, drove everything else away from my mind.

"Dad?" I said.

He raised his head and spotted me. He opened his arms and I ran into them.

"You *came*," I whispered. He'd come when I thought I would have to face this without my family. He'd come even though I'd skirted around all of them on purpose, trying not to involve them in what wasn't their fight. I thought if anyone came to check on me, it would be Brie, my mom, or maybe Amy.

"Of course. He was my teacher too." Dad fished a tissue out of his pocket—crumpled but clean. That was the nice thing about my father. He never minded when I cried. "And the way I heard it, he saved my daughter's life."

I swallowed hard. Hansel had saved us *all*. People crowded up behind us as the line moved forward.

When I didn't answer, Dad added, "You really cared about him, didn't you?"

I nodded. I didn't realize how much. Not until he was gone. "I was helping him with his class."

"He made it sound like it was *your* class," Dad said. "He said you were a natural teacher. He'd never seen someone learn so fast or work so hard. He was proud of you."

Hansel had never told me. Until this year, I'd never thought he noticed.

"I used to *hate* him," I whispered. "Or I thought I did."

Dad nodded. "Funny how people can surprise you. You learn a little more about them, and it changes everything."

I stayed with Dad until he reached the wall. Then I headed over to the overstuffed armchairs where the others had gone. Some of them had grabbed breakfast from the table, but no one was eating. The stepsisters, Daisy, and Paul sipped coffee. Lena and Kyle sat beside each other, their hands not quite touching, their fingers only an inch apart.

They felt hollow too. I saw it on their faces. It was a small comfort, but it was still comfort. Together, we watched the line move.

The sun climbed, and clouds closed overhead.

When the line began to dwindle, I remembered it was Sunday. My students had staff class.

Chase found us approximately two seconds after that. "You have to let me explain."

"We really don't." It was shocking—the sheer amount of anger that could fill me in the space of a breath. It squeezed out every other emotion. It made me miss the hollowness.

I glanced around, searching for Adelaide. I spotted her across the courtyard. It looked like she was arguing with Rapunzel. Good. I hoped Rapunzel was telling her off.

No one else spoke. The stepsisters were glaring at Chase. Paul just stared. The triplets weren't even acknowledging him. They scowled ahead, arms folded. Lena turned to me, totally unsure.

"I'm telling you," Chase said. His face was getting red, like it does when he's really mad. "I left my room, all suited up, and then *bam!* I'm in this restaurant. The mission completely fell out of my mind."

He forgot? *That* was his excuse? I didn't think my anger could grow, but it did. I wondered if the words "I'm sorry" had even crossed his mind. "You don't get it. We don't owe you *anything*." Dad had been right. Chase hadn't been a good friend to me, not for months, and I couldn't even stand the sound of his voice right then.

"I was sick of you and Adelaide before this, but now I'm just . . ." Tina drifted off, trying to think of a strong enough word.

"Done," said Vicky.

"I can't believe you're not going to say anything about Hansel," said Candice, wiping her tears away with the back of her hand. "Isn't today about *him*?"

"You should have just said you weren't coming," said Kevin, "if *dinner* was more important to you."

"It's not just Hansel," Kyle said, his voice low and furious. "Even without Jimmy, it was bad. Goblins almost captured our parents."

Lena didn't say anything, but she didn't stick up for him either. Neither did I.

"Something is wrong." Chase forced the words out, like his tongue had forgotten how to deliver an apology. "With *me*."

I couldn't believe that was all he had to say. "No one's arguing with you there."

"Listen, Rory—" Chase started again.

"No!" I stomped over and glared up at him, letting him see how angry I was. I gestured to our friends, who had just told him exactly what he needed to hear. "You're the one who should be listening. It's the *least* you could do."

He tried to say something else. His jaw worked, like he had something stuck in his teeth, and his scowl deepened. If that was all he could offer us, I was done with him too.

I walked away, toward Hansel's training courts. "I have to go to class."

Then I remembered: they weren't Hansel's courts anymore. He'd never enter them again. He'd never teach another student.

No way could it be like a normal class. No way would anyone even show up, but I still had to go. Their teacher was dead, and I was the only thing they had left.

A hand closed over my elbow, and I jumped, my breath hissing over my teeth. I knew who it was even before I turned to look.

"Class is going to be hard *enough* today," I told Chase. "Leave me alone."

Sympathy flickered across his face. His mouth pulled down at the corners, the same stupid lips that had been kissing Adelaide while Hansel was dying. Finally, a sign that he felt crappy about it too.

"I can't." With a trace of his usual self—the guy who could joke about anything—Chase added, "You're stuck with me."

I stared at him, breathless. Ice invaded my insides again. My lungs had frozen over, my heart speared through.

He'd said something like that before. Just once, after Iron Hans had explained what a Triumvirate was and how Chase, Lena, and I made up the newest one. It had comforted me then, knowing that whatever we faced, we could face it together.

But it was like he *knew* what I'd been telling myself all summer. He knew why I kept giving him second chances—he knew that I needed him to defeat the Snow Queen. We were stuck in this together, and so he thought he could treat me however he wanted.

For the first time, I *hated* being part of the Triumvirate.

"At least I'm not stuck with you for much longer," I snapped. "By the end of the month, we won't need a Triumvirate anymore." By the end of the month, my Tale would be over—one way or another.

I yanked my arm out of his grip and slammed through the iron-studded door to the training courts.

I hadn't expected so many people, and I hadn't expected some of them at all. The Aladdin representative, for instance. He wasn't standing with the rest of Chase's group. He stood in front of Gretel's sword class, speaking to them with a grave look on his face. I didn't expect to see my mother, either. I definitely didn't expect to see her paying attention. She was so focused on what Aladdin was saying that she hadn't noticed me yet.

"Hansel named replacement teachers in his will." Chase had entered behind me. "It took most of last night and some of this morning, but I convinced the Director to keep the classes going like normal, even today. It helps people after, to keep their regular schedule. It's what Hansel would have wanted."

This was why it was so hard to stay mad at Chase. He could let me down spectacularly, but he was always doing *something*. I'd been—what? Wallowing outside with the rest of our grade. Meanwhile, he'd been making sure all Hansel's students had someplace to come after the funeral.

"The Aladdin representative is just filling in until Gretel feels ready to come back," Chase continued. "Hansel would have given you the staff class outright, but he knew the Director wouldn't go for that. If you suggest anyone, the Director's supposed to consider it, but for now, he picked Amya to teach your class."

I spotted Lady Aspenwind. She was standing beside a row of metal wolves. She wore boots and a chain-mail tunic. A staff rested against her shoulder.

That didn't explain why all her new students had formed a ring in the middle of the training courts or why Chase's group had joined them or why they were both careful to leave an empty space in the middle. Even the Fey looked like they were waiting for something interesting.

I didn't see Amy; at least *she* was sleeping in.

"There you are," said Kenneth.

"We thought you forgot," Kelly said. I was surprised to see real hope on her face, and on Priya's. "You did, didn't you?"

"Of course not," Chase said, so smoothly that I knew he was lying. "The demonstration duel."

It had completely slipped my mind.

Lady Aspenwind shrugged. "I don't think they could focus on anything else this morning."

"Then it's settled." Chase drew his sword.

A halfhearted cheer went up from the younger staff students.

It was *not* settled. "No way. Not today."

"It's just sparring," Chase told me. "We spar all the time. Plus, this way, I'll still be close enough to talk to you."

He *still* wasn't listening to anyone. "If you want a demonstration, we should use dummies. Someone could get hurt."

"They want to see *us* fight. Even Hansel wanted to see it. One of the last requests he ever made," Chase said.

He had no right to bring that up, no right to twist my grief just so he could get his way.

Chase didn't exactly meet my eyes. He knew he'd crossed a line but he pushed anyway. "So I'll just go easy on you."

He didn't understand. All my anger wanted to destroy something, and he was such a tempting target. "I'm not worried about *you* hurting *me*," I said.

To his group, Chase added, "We're going to start right now." Then, in the space of a breath, his sword flashed toward my face. My response was automatic: I ducked under the blow, stepped close, and swung out with my left fist.

I barely stopped in time. I could feel Chase's breath on my fingers, my knuckles just an inch from his mouth. You wouldn't have known he was shocked unless you knew to look for the way he rocked back on his heels. "Ready to change your mind about the dummies?" I asked, shaking with fury.

He thought it over. "You don't need to be calm. You just need to hear me out."

Unbelievable.

"Ring off, please," said Lady Aspenwind, who apparently had a lot more sense than her son. "As a safety measure only, to appease Chase's worrying mother."

She didn't need to tell me twice. I ripped it off and thrust it into Priya's hands. "Take care of this for me," I said. She and Kelly looked positively delighted at the idea.

"Beginners learn only the techniques," said Lady Aspenwind. "Past that stage, a fighter develops a unique style. Chase trained Rory for years, but notice how different their styles are. Rory, for instance, uses her fists and feet more often than Chase."

She was making up a lesson out of the fact that I'd almost smashed a West Wind–powered punch into her son's jaw. So *that* was where Chase got his poker face from.

"Again, please," said Lady Aspenwind.

Chase came at me again. Two high strikes I could dodge and then a low one aimed at my legs—I had to use my sword to deflect that one. "The whole thing is so screwed up," he said. "I don't remember how I got to that dinner. I don't even remember *how we started dating*. I sure as *dioslik* didn't ask Adelaide out," he said, cursing in Fey. "Something is *wrong* with me."

All that buildup about needing to talk to me, and he wanted advice on how to deal with *Adelaide*?

It was his mess. He could clean it up on his own.

I struck out with a snap kick. It would have caught him in the stomach if he hadn't used his wings to leap clear.

The Fey in green armor glanced from Chase to my weapon. "The sword is helping her. Not a fair fight."

Lady Aspenwind shook her head. "The magic doesn't work like that."

I didn't need some idiot thinking I was basically cheating on top of everything else. I turned to George and pointed at the sword in his hand. He handed it over wordlessly and took mine. He looked kind of disturbed.

The balance was different, the blade thicker and longer than I was used to, but my sword had been too big for me in the beginning too. Chase let me have a few experimental swings before he swooped down at me. His next blow was a Fey move, full of flourishes and ridiculously easy to block. Without the ring, it was slightly harder to grab Chase's ankle and swing his flying momentum off course. He tumbled across the mats and popped back onto his feet, breathing hard.

My younger students began to chant, "Rory! Rory! Rory!"

Some of the older kids pumped their fists in the air. "Chase! Chase!"

"Chase prefers much movement, much offense," Lady Aspenwind said, still teaching. "Rory will defend herself while waiting for an opening."

Chase came close again, and before I could dodge, he locked swords with me. He was stronger and heavier. All he had to do was press, and I started bending, back toward the mats. It *hurt*.

"I don't remember . . . a lot," he said very slowly, like every syllable took concentration. "It's like Adelaide has this power over me. When she's around, my mind goes kind of fuzzy. Sometimes, everything else just slips away."

Something slammed shut inside me. I did *not* want to hear how Adelaide made him feel.

"It's not like me. It's not—" Chase continued.

"Stop! I refuse to listen to this right now." I dropped George's sword and rolled to the side. Chase had leaned too far. He staggered. I scooped up my blade.

"However, in her own way, Rory favors risk. It is bold to drop your weapon in the middle of a battle," Lady Aspenwind pointed out to the class. If she hadn't been Chase's mom, I might have told her to cut the commentary.

"I spotted another difference: Rory talks less when she's fighting," Priya said.

"Yeah, that's usually true," Chase admitted. "Unless she's yelling at me."

I would have yelled at him a lot more if our students weren't watching. I wondered how many of them knew something had gone wrong between us. Not too many, because the crowd went back to whooping and chanting.

Then Chase whispered, "I thought we had so much time. I thought it would be easier for us, being friends—"

We had so much time? But dating Adelaide, it was better to *rush*?

He was wrong. I'd been running out of time all summer, and Chase had barely spent any of it with me.

That was the answer to Lena's question. That was why I was really mad.

Chase stabbed toward my left shoulder. It was a feint. He *always* feinted left before he tried to slash at someone's feet.

"We're *not* friends right now," I said.

He swung low, and I stamped down on his blade, ripping the hilt from his hands.

He could have tackled me to get his sword back. He could have knocked my legs out from under me. He didn't try to do either, so I rested my blade against his throat.

The whole room had gone silent.

My fury drained away. I wanted to send them all out of the room—I didn't want anyone witnessing Chase like this.

I'd never seen that look on his face, not even when he found out how his brother had died in the Snow Queen's dungeons. I'd never seen him look so pale and defeated.

I still cared, no matter how angry I got. I knew, because I hated myself for hurting him.

"Then what are we, Rory?" he whispered. "You know me better than anyone else in the world. If we're not friends, what are we?"

I wanted to take back what I'd said, but my voice was trapped in my throat.

A muscle worked in Chase's jaw. His whole expression darkened, like now he couldn't stand me either. He picked up his sword and walked away. The crowd scurried out of his path, and the door slammed behind him.

I'd never won a match against Chase before. I wished I still hadn't.

When Lady Aspenwind spoke again, it sounded like she was accusing me too. "While Chase's strength lies in being able to battle many opponents at once, Rory is a born duelist. She can read an opponent, no matter how skilled, and target his weaknesses without fail."

Even though I wasn't sure that it was true, I said, "He threw the fight."

Lady Aspenwind didn't agree or disagree. As Chase's group drifted away toward some dummies and prepared to practice without him, the new staff instructor turned to her class. "Now, tell me what maneuver you wish to learn, and I shall adapt it for a staff wielder."

Chase never came back to the training courts.

Snow White needed an escort for her trip to meet the gnomes in Avalon, and Jack—the guy in charge of the mission—had picked Chase and a few others to come with them. I found out, because Jack sent Rufus to pull George and Ben out of class.

I tried so hard not to feel bad. I tried to believe that Chase had deserved what I'd told him.

But it nagged at me. I knew I'd gone too far. I wondered how long it would be until I could apologize. After class finally ended, Lady Aspenwind didn't discuss it with me like Hansel might have. She didn't even look at me. She flipped open her wings and flitted to the doorway, flying over the crowd so that she could be the first one out. I was pretty sure that was the Fey version of a cold shoulder, and at first I was angry. I'd *said* the duel wasn't a good idea. Chase and his mom had forced me to go through with it anyway.

Then I spotted Priya and Kelly's faces as they put away their staffs, their frozen, helpless looks. I knew how they felt. When my parents had fought, I used to feel like a huge part of my life was going to pieces and I'd caused it somehow. Priya and Kelly probably thought it was their fault that Chase had stormed out, because they'd suggested the fight.

Shame rolled in and threatened to sink me. Chase was right. Everything had gotten so messed up.

"Are you okay?" Mom stood behind me, close enough to touch my shoulder, but she didn't.

I wondered if she'd seen the duel.

"I heard about Hansel," she said tentatively, like she didn't want to start another argument. "I checked on you while you were sleeping, and I didn't want to wake you. I could tell you needed the rest."

Maybe I should have protested, considering Mom had just told me she checked on me at night, like I was still a little kid. I mean, some of the staff students were still in earshot. But instead it was kind of nice to know she was looking out for me.

"So you're all right?" she said.

I started to nod, but that felt like a lie. "I'm not hurt."

Mom peered into my face for a long minute. Then she said, almost like nothing was wrong, "Is it teatime?"

"Sure," I said. I'd been planning to go to the workshop and do more research, but I couldn't stand fighting with *two* of the most important people in my life. We cut through some corridors toward the apartment, because neither of us wanted to face the courtyard full of people mourning Hansel.

On the way, I tried to persuade her to see my side of the situation. "I know we've had a bunch of close calls. But you have to understand—that trap at the Zipes's ranch was set for *me*. I couldn't just let my friends go alone."

"But, Rory, you're so *young*."

This time, I just took a deep breath. I refused to let myself get mad. "You and I see being young very differently. For me, it means we have more time left in the world than the grown-ups. It means we have *more* responsibility to make things better."

Mom looked at me with a tiny little crease between her eyes, but she didn't automatically disagree. That was new. We turned left, down another corridor.

Angry voices drifted toward us.

"The effort was never going to work like you wanted. You can't sustain it for more than a few months."

"Like I said, I don't know what you're *talking* about."

"Please. Time is wearing thin. Give it to me. Otherwise you shall make a villain of yourself."

Mom and I cautiously eased around the corner so we could see who was talking: Adelaide's face was screwed up in a snarl, her fists clenched. She leaned toward Rapunzel. "For the last time, I DON'T KNOW WHAT YOU'RE TALKING ABOUT, YOU CRAZY OLD—" Well, I won't repeat the last thing she said.

Rapunzel's response shocked me even more. "Yes! But you are a shortsighted infant! You'll regret this before today's sunset!"

Mom and I glanced at each other. For the first time all summer, I could tell we were thinking exactly the same thing: *I'm glad we don't argue like this*.

Then Adelaide marched out the door at the end of the corridor. She slammed it behind her, so hard that Mom gasped.

"Um . . . ," I said, wondering how to break it to Rapunzel that she'd had an audience.

"It's all right, Rory," Rapunzel said wearily. She wrapped both arms around herself, cradling her elbows. "I know that you're there. May I speak to you?"

Mom shot Rapunzel a skeptical look, like she really wanted to ask my friend what kind of example she was setting. But even my mother knew that our teatime was postponed. I could use any advice Rapunzel had to offer. "We'll discuss this later," Mom said, kissing my cheek, and it didn't seem so ominous this time. "This door, right?" She pointed at the door Adelaide had just smashed through, the one that led to the back of the student apartments. I nodded. She waved and left.

Rapunzel stared at the ground. I didn't think I'd ever seen her so rattled. This time, I was pretty sure it didn't have anything to do with Hansel's death. "Is there something I should know about Adelaide?" *You shall make a villain of yourself* sounded pretty serious.

"Not yet. Time, for me, is messy," she said, staring at the ground.

"And timing delicate. Got it." I didn't want to push her. Or to keep talking about Adelaide.

"I need a favor from you," Rapunzel said.

"Okay," I said, kind of freaked. Rapunzel had never asked me for anything before. She hadn't even asked me to trust her the day I found out Solange was her sister. Of course I would do it.

"You will go on a quest with Adelaide soon," Rapunzel said. "Watch over her, please."

Rapunzel wanted me to look after the girl who'd just screamed in her face? "*Adelaide?* There's no way we would go on a quest together." We would have to be Companions on the same Tale, and there was absolutely *no* overlap between the people who would choose her for a Companion and the people who would choose me. "Rapunzel, I would never travel with such a spoiled, selfish—"

Her silver head jerked up. Her dark gaze was fierce. "Don't speak that thought in my presence. Family is the one part of my life I haven't made my peace with."

I stared at her, completely confused about what family had to do with Adelaide.

Then Rapunzel said, "On her mother's side. My great-grand-children emigrated to the United States at the turn of the century before last. I followed them, and Solange followed me. I have watched over my descendants as best I could. Adelaide is the youngest, and I am failing her."

No. Not Adelaide. She had more in common with the Snow Queen than with Rapunzel.

Rapunzel must have seen the disbelief on my face. The fierceness left her, and she hurried toward me and dropped her hand onto my crossed arms. "*Please*, Rory. Friendship can survive anger, but only if you choose the person over the rage. We must part as friends."

She sounded so desperate. "Of course we'll part as friends—" I started. Oh. So she'd already heard about what I'd said during the duel. "The thing with Chase is *different*," I said. "We're in the Triumvirate together."

"Even the tightest bonds don't make you inseparable. Even Maerwynne, Rikard, and Madame Benne were not together all the time." Rapunzel was one of the few people who often compared us to the first Triumvirate, not just the one Solange had been in. This time, I wished she wouldn't. "They were united in purpose even when their paths diverged. They trusted that they would return to each other in time."

That wasn't the point, and she knew it. She had to know why protecting Adelaide was asking a lot. "Don't you think I have a right to be angry?" I asked.

Rapunzel's tone was careful. She clearly didn't want to set me off again. "You have a right to all your emotions, but it is best not to let them control you."

I would have told Chase off even if I was calm. I started to say so, but she interrupted.

"Rory, it is *too* easy to pass pain on when pain is all you feel," she said. "This will not be your hardest day. The shock numbs you now. It will not last."

So it was going to get worse too. Lately, that felt like the only thing Rapunzel ever told me, and I kind of wanted to say so, and not in a nice way. But that was the same thing as hurting Chase just because I was hurting.

So I took a deep breath and said, "Does Adelaide know she's related to you?"

"No. She must not know. She believes I only seek to stop her," Rapunzel said. "Protection has not crossed her mind."

And to protect her, Rapunzel was recruiting me, even though she knew how Adelaide and I felt about each other. I kind of wished I hadn't already agreed, but after all Rapunzel had done for me, I guess I could do this. "Anything else I should know? About 'watching over' Adelaide?"

Rapunzel sighed. "She will speak harshly with you. She will be distracted, and the stair will strike."

Ugh. I didn't know what news was worse: that Adelaide would yell at me right before I saved her, or that stairs would be involved. Stairs usually mean heights.

"We must go," Rapunzel said, leading me down a short hall to the door that opened into the courtyard. "I tried to buy us as much time as I could. I thought we would have more. I hope it will be enough."

I wondered why everyone was suddenly trying to tell me that they thought we'd have more time. I thought I would have more time too. I thought I would live to be older than fourteen. Then it hit me.

"It's happening, isn't it?" I whispered. "The Snow Queen is *really* starting to move. Not just to get more allies, but for real."

"Yes, and I will do what I have always done," Rapunzel said. "I will try to minimize the damage."

She opened the door.

George and Kyle were right outside, nearly frantic. Ben was a little farther down, hammering on the amethyst door of the Director's office. They looked up when Rapunzel and I came out, and I could tell from their faces: Something was wrong with Chase. They should have all still been in Avalon, helping Jack and Snow White with the gnomes.

"We didn't see it coming," Kyle said, his face white.

"Chase has been enchanted," George explained. "The ring of return didn't work on him."

"We had to leave him," Ben said, like he would never forgive himself for doing it.

"Stone?" I croaked, remembering Sebastian.

I wouldn't think about what Arica had said. I wouldn't think about how horribly she'd died.

Kyle shook his head. "A sleeping spell."

My *dream*.

"Tell her about the message," said Rapunzel. She'd seen this.

"As soon as we got there, the gnomes said they had seen some of the Seelie Court refugees. They said some of the younger Fey had been arguing about whether or not to seek refuge at EAS, or some other stupid sh—" George bit off the curse, like his gran would be walking by any second.

"The gnomes thought they were in one of their old forts, just a couple miles away," Ben said. "Jack called in the tip to the Director, and she ordered us to go check it out."

"And now she won't even *see* us," said Kyle. "She says she's in a meeting."

"What happened in the *fort*?" said an annoyed voice behind me. I hadn't realized Adelaide was there, and she stared intently at the guys, clearly pretending that Rapunzel and I hadn't showed up.

"Nothing happened," George said. "That was the problem. We walked right into the tower, expecting them to attack. You know, to test us and see if the Itari thing was true. But it was abandoned."

"We went all the way upstairs. There was a room. Totally empty except for all this furniture—tables and chairs and weird spinning wheels," added Kyle. Goose bumps sprouted on my arms. "Then Chase pretty much lost it."

"He'd gotten his hopes up. He thought we'd come back with Fey allies in tow." George shrugged. "It wasn't that big of a deal. He took it out on the furniture."

"Until something scratched him. One of the tables was metal. That could have done it," Ben said.

"When we saw the blood on his arm, Ben stopped him," said Kyle. "Then Chase's eyes rolled back in his head and he fell over."

"I thought Chase fainted," George said. Chase would've flipped if he'd heard his name and "faint" in the same sentence. "But then we couldn't wake him up. We shook him. We poured water over him. We waited for a while."

"Then we got worried he'd hit his head. He fell *hard*," Ben said. "So we tried to get him back to EAS. We thought he needed medical attention."

"His ring of return didn't work." George sounded completely stunned that one of his sister's inventions had failed him.

"Ours did," Kyle said. "It wasn't one of those warding hex things."

"So you left him there? *Hurt?*" Adelaide asked shrilly. Rapunzel cast a tender look over her, but her descendant didn't even notice.

"They needed help," I pointed out. "Did you guys get dirt from outside the fort?"

George lifted a glass vial filled with dark soil flecked with bright, healthy grass. "Lena sent me prepared."

"But there's something else," Ben said. "When we left the tower for the dirt, something started growing."

Kyle nodded. "Right outside the door."

If I was going to rescue Chase, they would both have to be more specific. "What do you mean, 'something'?"

A bell began to ring, the one that always announced the beginning of a new Tale. The door to the library opened. Sarah Thumb swept out on Mr. Swallow, winging straight toward us, and Rumpelstiltskin hurried after, carrying an enormous book bound in blue leather—the current volume of Tales.

Great. This was exactly what we needed.

I wasn't the only one who thought so. Before Sarah Thumb could cut in line, Adelaide stepped between Mr. Swallow and the door to the Director's office. "We're next to see the Director. It's an emergency. Chase needs rescuing."

"I know! It's *Chase's* Tale!" Sarah Thumb said.

No way. He'd given up on his Tale. He thought he'd never get one, only being half human.

"What is it?" Adelaide asked, way more excited than she had any right to be.

"Sleeping Beauty," said Sarah Thumb.

Then I did something worse than telling Chase we weren't friends, something he would never forgive me for. I laughed.

 felt terrible about laughing as soon as I realized that Sarah Thumb wasn't kidding. "Wait, really?"

Lena sprinted up. She'd obviously left the workshop in a hurry. Her shorts were covered in dragon-scale dust, and she hadn't zipped up either of the carryalls in her arms. "The elves told me. When do we leave?"

"Leave?" repeated Rumpelstiltskin.

"To rescue him," Lena said, like this was obvious.

"As soon as we get approval from the Director," said George.

I took the carryall Lena handed me. "Do we really *need* approval?"

"Would it kill you to wait for the grown-ups for once?" Sarah Thumb said, annoyed. "Give me a second to talk to the Director, and we'll help you." The tiny woman urged Mr. Swallow up higher. She knocked on the top of the door twice with both hands and then thumped it with her fist. The door cracked open, and she flew inside. Our librarian hurried through afterward. Rapunzel too.

George gave me and Lena a stern look. I thought the bossy older sibling gene had skipped him, but he was giving Jenny a run for her money. "You're waiting."

Lena sighed. "At least it's an enchantment we know how to break."

Gross. Seeing Chase and Adelaide kiss once had been one time too many.

"What makes you think *you're* going?" said Adelaide. "I'm the one he needs."

I stifled a groan. That was a good point, and rescuing Chase was probably the only reason Adelaide and I would go on a quest together.

"Right," I said. "Lena and I will get you up to the tower."

"What about us?" asked George. "We're the only ones who have already been there. We have to go."

"Same team, everyone," Ben said.

"If *they're* coming, then I'm bringing Candice." Adelaide turned to look at her friend, who was waiting under the Tree of Hope with her bow and quiver. Archery class was supposed to start any minute. Adelaide ran toward her, screaming. *"Candice!"*

This was getting ridiculous. "We can't *all* go."

"You want to tell *her* that?" Ben asked, nodding at the center of the courtyard.

Chase's mother soared across the grass. The other kids drew back a little. The Lady Aspenwind they knew was the aloof Fey noblewoman who instructed in the training courts, every bit as intimidating as Gretel. They had never seen her out of her mind with worry for the only son she had left. They'd never seen her cry.

I braced myself.

"I am to blame." Lady Aspenwind didn't bother landing. She just clamped her hands around my forearm, all the coolness from before forgotten. "I thought with my blood in his veins, he was safe from Tales! But it was *our* tradition. Upon his christening, I allowed Chase's godmothers to bestow their gifts upon him."

I'd met some of Chase's godmothers—the same day I first met

Lady Aspenwind. They'd argued over what gifts they'd given Chase as a baby—his curls, I think, and his singing voice. Chase had been so embarrassed, I'd never mentioned it again. I had no idea why she was bringing that up now.

But apparently, Lena did. She must have read about this. "Giving someone a magical gift is pretty much the same as creating an outlet for more spells to come in and take hold," she explained, sounding a little horrified. "For most Fey, it's not an issue, because they have enough magic of their own to fight off enchantment. But Chase is only half—he doesn't have that much power."

"He has a really strong will," I said. "I've seen him fight enchantments."

"Sleeping curses are different," Lena said. "It's hard to fight something your body does naturally."

"He pricked his finger, as most Sleeping Beauty Tale bearers do, but the sleeping enchantment in the spindle is only the trigger." Lady Aspenwind's wings beat hard. The grass around us rippled. "A sorceress must touch him to administer the actual curse. The Snow Queen could have cast it over him, but I don't know when. . . ."

The boys just stared at her. They clearly thought Solange personally enchanting Chase was farfetched.

I didn't. My stomach sank down to my knees. "It happened at the Snow Queen's palace. After she caught us, she put her hand on his face." I thought she'd been doing it to intimidate me. But no, she'd been planning ahead in case we escaped. She'd cursed him with a sleeping spell she could activate whenever she wanted.

Adelaide had finally noticed Lady Aspenwind. She ran back, dragging Candice behind her. "Don't worry! We're going to rescue him."

Lady Aspenwind looked even more alarmed. A mean, petty part of me was glad that Adelaide wasn't inspiring a lot of confidence. "But— He needs—"

"We'll get Chase back," Lena told her. "All of us."

That calmed Lady Aspenwind down. She landed on the grass, taking deep breaths.

"Well, not *me*," Candice said, twisting her wrist free of Adelaide's grip. "I told you earlier. You can borrow my bow if you want, but I'm not about to risk my neck for you or Chase. Not after you ditched us."

Wow. I would have expected that kind of response from Daisy, but Candice hadn't seemed upset until today.

For a second, guilt flashed across Adelaide's face, but when she noticed me watching, her expression settled into a glare.

Before any of us could respond, the door swung open, and Mr. Swallow flitted out. "Oh, good—you waited," Sarah Thumb said.

The Director stood in the doorway behind her. This had been her Tale. I don't know what I expected. Maybe a wisecrack about how the level of beauty this Tale required had gone way down in the twenty-first century. But her skin was paper-white, and she whispered, "If she was going to manipulate the conditions of a Tale again, I thought it might be this one."

I should have thought of that. I should have guessed that the Snow Queen would try to take a member of our Triumvirate the same way she'd lost *her* best friend.

Well, I wouldn't let her.

The rules for this quest were clear. If a Character's Tale took them out of commission, then the leader of the Canon or the current representative of that Tale would choose the Companions. In other words, the Director had a decision to make.

Suddenly, I wished I'd been nicer to her over the past couple years.

"Just so it's clear, I'm volunteering to rescue Chase," Ben said.

"Me too," added George, Kyle, Lena, Adelaide, and me together.

Adelaide glared at me and Lena. "Not them."

The Director took our side. Probably for the first time in history. "You don't have a say in this matter, Adelaide. It's not your Tale."

"But—" Adelaide said. It wasn't a good sign that she was *already* getting on my nerves.

"The Director has double authority here," Sarah Thumb told her fiercely.

"Ben, you have a meeting with the MerKing in a couple of hours. I'm afraid I must ask you to stay," the Director said. Ben made a face, but he didn't argue—ever since he'd started dating Chatty, he'd kind of become EAS's unofficial ambassador to the mermaids. "The questers will keep you updated on their progress, I'm sure. George, how's your leg?"

"Fine." But George was lying. He had a shallow gash right above his knee, and blood had streamed down his shin and stained his sock red. Lena gasped when she saw it. I couldn't believe the Director noticed it before the rest of us. "I don't even feel it. Honestly."

"You should find a nurse to examine you," the Director said. George headed off toward the infirmary, limping slightly and swearing. "The rest of you *will* go. Four Companions or more during wartime—we shall make that standard procedure."

She was sending me and Lena after all. I hadn't expected it to be so easy.

The Director turned back and called into her office. "Rumpelstiltskin, please give these students as much information

Shelby Bach

as you can glean from the current volume. They are eager to be on their way."

"I am *trying*," snapped our librarian.

Rapunzel emerged with the huge blue tome. She held it open, just out of the dwarf's reach, staring at the illustration of the old fort. It was made of warm yellow stone, and a blue river wound through the background.

"This place is known to me," she whispered. "I lived there once. Solange moved me from tower to tower often when I was small."

After she heard that, the Director looked positively ashen.

"Wait, you mean, the tower where Chase is trapped is the tower from your Tale?" said Kyle.

"*One* of them," Rapunzel corrected. "One of the first. There will be traps on the stairs."

"We didn't run into any," Kyle said.

"Then they have most certainly been activated now," said the Director.

"Take caution," Rapunzel said. "My sister sets traps within traps."

Great. Adelaide, heights, *and* an obstacle course on the stairs. Chase was really going to owe me.

"Is there anything else the kids should know?" Sarah Thumb asked.

Rapunzel passed the librarian his book. He humphed and made a big show of flipping through the pages. Almost everyone was watching him, so they didn't see Rapunzel tap Lena's shoulder and whisper something in her ear. Lena's eyes widened and darted toward Kyle.

Like we needed one more thing to worry about.

With a brief smile at me, Rapunzel melted into the shadows of the Director's office. I guess that meant she wasn't seeing us off.

"The Seelie Fey that the gnomes saw was an illusion the Snow Queen cast herself," said the dwarf finally. "Besides that, there is nothing here that Kyle cannot tell you."

"Really helpful. So glad we waited," Adelaide said acidly. "Can we go now?"

I thought the grown-ups might tell her off for being so sarcastic, but the Director just started leading us across the courtyard toward the door to Avalon. Sarah and Lady Aspenwind swooped ahead. Rumpelstiltskin trailed behind, trying to read and walk. I halfway expected them to swear us in as Companions, but there didn't seem to be a point. Plus, we didn't exactly have an audience. The bell that announced the new Tale hadn't drawn a crowd.

We probably could have used any old door, but we stopped in front of the one to Avalon. It glittered with gold underneath the emerald paint. Some people thought it was the prettiest door in the Courtyard. Personally, it had always reminded me of dragon scales.

Lena hurriedly started the temporary-transport spell.

"I wish I could accompany you," Lady Aspenwind said, a little choked up, "but Chase would never forgive me."

She was right. Chase was already going to hate his Tale. He would be beyond mortified if his mom came to rescue him.

"Don't worry, ma'am," Kyle said. "We'll get him back."

Muttering the spell in Fey, Lena held open the door. Trees grew just beyond the frame, and I heard running water. Lena opened her hand. In her palm, five rings shone slightly blue. "Everyone take one. I have an extra for Chase after we grab him."

Adelaide hurried forward. I let her go in first. It seemed important to her.

But I went second, my sword drawn and my guard up. Rapunzel *had* mentioned traps within traps.

Once I stepped through, it was easy to see why the Avalon door was painted the way it was. Each tree was almost as big as the one we'd left behind in the courtyard. The bark in this forest was golden, and moss grew on every trunk and almost every branch— such a vivid green that it practically glowed. The river I'd seen in my dream wound through the trees, mottled with reflections of blue sky and green leaves.

It was beautiful. Clearly, Solange had wanted her sister to have a tower with a view. I doubted Chase had gotten a chance to enjoy it.

"George said that Avalon is the hidden continent that *looks* the most like a fairy tale," Lena said, coming up to stand beside me. "He was right."

"Where's the tower?" Adelaide said, clearly still prepared to act like this was her Tale and she was the boss of it. That wasn't what happened during rescues like this. After the Director picked Companions, all the questers were supposed to work together.

"Under that." Lena pointed.

You could see the tower, but barely. Even though it was the height of two Matilda Searcasters, only a few sections of yellow stone peeked out. The rest had been conquered by vines.

I'd been expecting some sort of vegetation like the beanstalk, green and thick and covered in flexible spikes, but these vines were slender. They'd grown shaped more like spiderwebs than climbing roses. Plus, they were white, and they sparkled in the sunlight.

It seemed wrong to find something so pale and colorless in such a vivid, green world.

Only the vines' thorns were a silvery sort of blue. It made them easy to spot.

"That was *not* here when we left," Kyle said.

I squinted upward, to the top of the tower, where Chase had been sleeping. Fear crept inside me, the same kind I'd felt in my dream.

He might not wake up. We might not even be able to reach him.

Lena approached the tangle of vines. Careful not to touch them, she stuck her face close to one crystal-white tendril. When she blew over it, her breath fogged. "I thought they were made out of ice at first, but maybe not. They kind of look like those trees of diamond in Queen Titania's court, but cold."

"I can think of something that could handle them," Kyle told Lena, and I couldn't figure out why he was smiling.

"Me too." Lena slid a hand into her carryall and pulled out an ax, the same one she'd used on the goblins' portal. She raised the weapon and swung down hard.

Adelaide leapt back, like the magic from the vines might spill out and grab her. The rest of us pretended not to notice. She *did* have the least quest experience.

"Yep," Lena said, inspecting the severed ends. Even the vines' insides sparkled with ice crystals. "It cuts like regular plants, not diamond. That's reassuring."

"Great." I raised my sword. If there weren't any enemies for me to fight, at least I could take out my frustration on the plant life.

"Hold it," Kyle said. "I think we should avoid touching them, just to be sure."

"I'm not afraid. Hand me the ax," Adelaide said, holding her hand out.

I shot her a look. First of all, she needed to stop acting like it was *her* Tale. Second of all, we weren't her servants. We were her fellow questers.

"Good idea." Lena slapped the ax's handle into Adelaide's palm, but she didn't let go. "Do me a favor and read this out loud for me?"

Shock to end all shocks, Adelaide just glared at Lena. She didn't even glance at the paper my friend was holding up at face level.

"Lena won't let you borrow her invention unless you read that, Adelaide," Kyle said.

Adelaide huffed, but then she read, "Up, ax. Chop." Then she looked a little nervous. Even she had heard about the Bats of Destruction.

But the ax just stayed where it was, motionless in Adelaide's hands.

"Looks like it's a dud," she said, annoyed.

Lena actually did a little happy dance, and I realized what this was really about. Our favorite inventor was testing her voice recognition software. "Up, ax! Chop!"

Now the ax ripped free of Adelaide's grip and started hacking away at the vines with so much gusto that a path started to form— two feet wide and littered with frosted clippings.

"I guess it likes Lena better than you," Kyle said.

"Wait. Was I just your guinea pig?" Adelaide asked, outraged.

"Join the club. She does it to me all the time," I said.

"Me too," Kyle said, "but I usually volunteer."

Lena charged forward. The ax had already cleared about seven feet of trail. Vines fell steadily under its blade, clicking as they landed, like a pile of icicles. "Come on. Try not to touch the sides."

Adelaide plowed ahead. I went next. Kyle fell into step behind me, careful not to poke anyone with his spear.

We marched single file. The tangle rose about a yard above our heads. Soon, all we could see to our left and right was white vegetation and our breath fogging out in big white puffs.

I felt kind of lightheaded. I was so focused on *not* remembering my dream that I kept forgetting to breathe.

"Rory, are you okay?" Kyle asked.

Maybe I'd been swaying. I concentrated on walking straight. "Fine."

"Chase was all torn up during the mission too," Kyle said. "He mentioned you two had a bad fight."

We aren't friends. That was the last thing I had told him. It might be the last thing I *ever* told him.

I really hoped Adelaide hadn't heard what Kyle said, but she must have. Lena did. All the way in front, she glanced over her shoulder. "I don't think it has sunk in—" She spotted something farther back. "Oh, my gumdrops."

We whirled around. The vines had grown across the opening behind us, not as thick as they'd been before, but I had the feeling that if I looked away, the tangle would unfurl across the gap, closing in.

"We need to go faster," Adelaide said.

And I thought *I* was the master of the obvious.

Kyle gripped his spear. "Rory, don't freak, but you've got one growing right by your ear."

I stood stock still, afraid to turn and look, afraid to reach for my own sword.

"Relax." Kyle slashed once, so close to my head that I heard the blade whistle through the air. "Done. Oh, crap." His spear was too long for the narrow trail. He had gotten it snagged in some vines. "Lena, I'm beginning to think I need a spear that's retractable, like your staff."

He yanked it free—too hard. The fist gripping the spear crashed into a knot of vines behind him.

Adelaide and Lena gasped. I actually shouted, sure that he was doomed to whatever fate the Snow Queen had in store for us.

"I'm okay. No worries," he said, a lot calmer than I would have been. He just leaned his spear against his shoulder so he could inspect both hands. "It might even be a happy accident. We *can* touch the vines. I even got pricked. See?"

He held his hand out, to show us the tiny bead of red where the thorn had stuck him.

Kyle hadn't looked closely enough. That tiny drop of blood had frozen. The flesh on his hand had turned transparent, and it glistened with a wet sheen, exactly like an ice sculpture.

he enchantment doesn't get us if the vines touch us," Lena whispered, aghast. "It gets us if the vines draw blood."

Kyle looked at his hand again. The ice had spread up to his wrist, and he watched it creep up his elbow. He looked at us. "Tell my brothers not to panic," he said. "Enchantments aren't always binding."

The ice reached his chest before he had a chance to take another breath. Kyle could barely whisper. "You'll have to come back for . . ."

No, no, no. This couldn't happen.

I was so close to him. I was looking straight into his eyes. I could see the resignation in them, and the determination. I blinked, and the brown irises, the dark lashes, everything, was pale, colorless, *life*less ice.

We should have known this was another trap. We should have been more *careful*. We should have prepared more for this mission.

"He's right," Lena said in a tiny voice. "We can change him back. The Water of Life can do it."

We should have brought some of that Water with us.

Something splashed beside my feet. It took me a second to

realize it had dripped from the ice statue. Horror rose in me, and I tasted bile in my mouth. "Lena, he's *melting*."

Even the Water of Life couldn't bring him back from a puddle.

We would lose Kyle. Just like Hadriane. Just like Hansel.

Lena unzipped her backpack and grabbed a handful of round things. They looked exactly like rubber bouncy balls with gold-and-green glitter swirling around inside. "Let me try something." She pitched one of the balls at Kyle. It went wide, sailing past his shoulder.

"Is this the time for target practice?" Adelaide pointed at the vines. They'd risen over our heads, long tendrils snaking up and swaying a little, like dragons getting ready to strike. "We need to save ourselves."

"Oh, who *cares*? The voice recognition works," Lena said, and I really hoped she was talking to herself, not me and Adelaide. She ripped open the back pocket of her carryall as wide as it could go. "Up, axes and swords and sabers. Chop! All the way to the tower, as fast as you can!"

I'd thought she'd gone overboard this April when I saw how many Bats of Destruction she'd brought to the Arctic Circle, but that was nothing. A whole *armory* sailed out of Lena's bag. The axes hacked their way to the tower. The sabers held off the vines, cutting any that grew over the path the axes had just cleared. The swords scythed through the tendrils that had been threatening us. Frosty clippings rained down around us, so close that I felt one brush the bare skin of my arm.

Lena threw another bouncy ball. It connected with Kyle's shoulder and splattered across the ice of his T-shirt. "There. Now, run!" She pointed at the tower. The axes had almost reached the front door.

No one needed to tell Adelaide twice. She sprinted, too fast. Some of the frozen bits slid under her sneaker, and she almost lost her footing and got a face full of thorns. But with a shriek, she caught herself and kept running.

I hesitated. "But Kyle . . . We can't just . . ." I looked back. He was gone.

"I took care of it." Lena grabbed my arm and dragged me along. "Well, my inventions did. That's a throwable-transport spell. I wasn't sure it would work. I was planning to test it on Chase, but Rapunzel told me, 'Don't worry. Send him back. I'll wait with the Water of Life as long as I can.'"

So that was what Rapunzel had whispered to Lena in the courtyard. "How did you know she meant Kyle, not Chase?" I was definitely out of breath.

"We don't need the Water of Life to break Chase's enchantment," Lena said, pulling ahead.

Adelaide reached the base of the tower first. "We have a problem," she said, pointing. The door was made of thick wood and crossed with big iron strips. It looked heavy, and the lock under the handle was as big as my hand.

Lena skidded to a stop. "Move, Adelaide! Axes—"

Seeing the weapons turn and stand to attention, Adelaide dove behind us.

"—together!" Lena continued. The axes rose up in unison. Sunlight gleamed off their sharp edges. "And chop down the hinges!"

The axes swung down, taking out more than just the hinges. Triangular, fist-size chunks fell out of the part of the door that had been *attached* to the hinges.

"Now move it! Angle it so we can get by," Lena said.

Ax handles hammered the wood, as loud and persistent as drumbeats. The door inched away from the frame, far enough to let us squeeze by.

"Back to the sack!" Lena cried. The axes swooped in obediently. "Maybe I should have done that from the beginning."

"You think?" Adelaide darted over the threshold and disappeared into the darkness beyond the door.

"Are you two coming?" she called from inside. "It's dark in here."

I reached into my carryall and groped around for the glass vial. Lena and I stepped inside.

A clap rang out, so loud it hurt my ears. Before I could even suck in a breath to whistle over Rapunzel's light, something else thunked into place, and something else, over and over until I lost count.

I couldn't even tell where it was coming from—the sound echoed too much, banging around us and then up and up.

Then I felt someone grab a fistful of my shirt. "The door," Lena whispered. From where I stood, it just looked like a gloomy patch only slightly brighter than the rest of the room, as if the vines had already closed in. "Rory, does it look smaller to you?"

Traps within traps, Rapunzel had said.

I whistled over the glass vial. Light spilled out of it, through my fingers, filling the inside of the tower.

Now we could see two piles of rectangular yellow stones sitting just beside the entrance. They shrank as blocks flew from the floor into neat rows, filling the door frame, walling us in.

But the real surprise was what *else* had been hiding in the dark.

The floor was packed with beasts. I would have never guessed that four dragons and a dozen ice griffins could fit into such a small space. I raised my sword and stepped in front of Lena automatically. Rapunzel's light swung in my hand, and shadows danced along the walls.

"They're *asleep*," Adelaide told me.

Curious, Lena squatted down beside the closest dragon. Its head was roughly the same size as a car tire, its eyes closed. "I'm guessing she sent them as soon as George, Ben, and Kyle went back to EAS. They were probably supposed to ambush us as soon as we got inside. The sleeping enchantment must be strong. Stronger than the Snow Queen thought. I mean, sometimes, the sleeping enchantment in this Tale knocks out a whole castle."

"Then why didn't it get George, Ben, and Kyle?" I asked.

"No, why aren't *we* sleeping?" Adelaide said shrilly.

"I'm not sure," Lena said, but in this excited way that meant she had some theories. "Spells are funny. It could have taken awhile for the enchantment to finish with Chase and start creeping to other living beings. Or maybe these beasts are more susceptible to spells than we are."

"So you don't think we'll be enchanted?" Adelaide said.

"No." Lena stood and dusted off her hands. "I think we got lucky."

I wish I could have believed her. "Does that mean that they'll all wake up when we break the spell over Chase?" The ice griffins could fly. They would find us at the top of the tower.

"We'll deal with that later," Adelaide said. "We need to find Chase." She started picking her way through the sleeping bodies.

"Oh, before I forget—" Lena pulled her M3 back out and called, "Melodie?"

No one answered. I didn't really expect a response. The Snow Queen must have set up a warding hex around the whole tower.

"Well, I was going to check on Kyle," Lena said, sticking her M3 in her back pocket, "but I guess we're on our own."

"You guys talk too much," Adelaide said.

Lena bristled. "Actually, we call it 'planning.' It's what experienced questers do so they don't die."

"Well, I found the staircase," Adelaide replied. "That's what questers do when they want to get to the top of the tower."

I'd been holding out a tiny hope that it was the kind of staircase with a railing between you and the drop, but no. We would have to climb steep spiral steps with nothing between us and a long fall onto a pile of dragons and ice griffins.

"This will be fun." Lena steered me around the beasts toward the base of the stone stairs. Hot, sulfur-smelling air hung above the dragons, but cold clung to the ice griffins.

Adelaide didn't wait for us. She started marching up. "Stop!" I said.

"Remember what Rapunzel said about booby traps!" Lena reminded her.

Adelaide froze. "Well, if you have so much quest experience, what do you suggest we do? Just walk up the steps *really* slowly?"

I sighed. If Ben were here, he would have repeated, "Same team." I didn't think I could get away with it. Adelaide hated me too much.

Lena plopped her carryall on the floor and pulled out a paste that glittered with dragon scales. "Melodie mentioned a spell for finding booby traps. Either we can cast it for every single step, or—" She finger-painted some green-and-gold dragon scale paste onto the mirror's surface. "We can adapt it. *This quest just gets stranger and stranger; do us a favor*," she said, switching to Fey. *"Light up when a stair means danger."*

The dragon-scale paste sank into the glass.

She was getting better at making up inventions on the go.

Adelaide was not impressed. "That can't possibly work."

In answer, Lena ran past her and stuck the mini mirror over the next stair, and the next. On the sixth try, white light flared across the M3's surface, so bright that all three of us had to look away.

Lena yanked her M3 back just in time. A hundred arrows flew out of the wall, straight at the mirror *and* the arm holding it out.

She squeaked and tucked her hands into her chest. Then she looked at them. Two long scratches marked her palm.

"You okay?" I asked.

"Still attached!" she said with so much forced cheer that she reminded me of my mother. "And now we have a booby-trap detector. I'll go first. Then Rory after me."

Adelaide was clearly about to go on another *I'm the girlfriend* rant. "Why am *I* last?"

Because Lena trusted me to bail her out of trouble more than Adelaide. Because Lena knew if I went last, I would lag behind and probably vomit as soon as vertigo hit.

You could practically hear Lena rolling her eyes. "Because Rory has the light."

I thrust Rapunzel's glass vial into the air and began to trudge up the steps. I wondered how old these traps were. I wondered if Solange was trying to protect her baby sister or trying to stop me when she had made them. I wondered if it mattered.

Lena was clearly in the lead for the Most Valuable Companion Award on this quest. Twelve more steps up, she found some stairs that only *looked* like reliable grey stone. If you laid a finger on them to check, you could feel that they were actually illusioned ice—cold and slick and more than ready to make you slip and fall to your death. Lena dug around her carryall until she found extra dragon scales. She cast the spell that we normally used when we fought ice griffins, and spikes sprouted out of the bottom of our sneakers.

Another two flights up, and three stairs in a row dropped on a hinge like a trap door. It would have dumped us onto the beasts below. Lena fixed those with a stasis spell a lot like the one General Searcaster had used to hold the city of Kiivinsh hostage.

I just focused on climbing, hugging the wall and placing one foot in front of the other.

You haven't met any winter today. The ice griffins are asleep. No winter, so no death, I reminded myself, but that wasn't what pushed me to take another step.

I pretended that Chase was awake. I pretended that he was watching and waiting, just like he had when we climbed up the beanstalk. Maybe my foot would slip, like it had back then. Maybe a stair would crumble, and I would go with it. Screaming, of course, because that was how I usually handled falling. And then the trap door would slam open, and Chase would swoop out from the top of the tower with a flash of orange wings and snatch my hand, just like he had when the troll bridge broke. And he'd say, extremely pleased with himself, *Can't I take a nap for three hours without you getting into trouble?*

It was a very stupid daydream.

But I let myself have it anyway. He would start explaining to Lena how the Fey of the Aspenwind clan have a natural resistance to sleeping enchantments; it just takes a while for it to kick in. I imagined him turning to me, grinning and saying, *You were worried about me, Rory? I'm touched. Especially considering how we aren't even friends.* I started to make up my apology, but I didn't get very far.

God, I couldn't cry. I needed to *see*.

I should have apologized before he went on that mission.

Either Adelaide heard me sniffle, or she sensed that I was having a conversation with her boyfriend in my head.

"Chase said *you* were the bravest?" Adelaide said.

My chest tightened.

This feeling had grown familiar. I'd felt it before at the Snow Queen's palace, watching the trolls pummel him, watching Solange lay her hands on his face. I'd felt it on my birthday, waiting for him to return from Atlantis, waiting to see if he'd come back at all. I was starting to think I would *always* feel this helpless terror that he may be hurt, and this desperation to stop it.

"You're completely overrated," Adelaide continued, stomping up behind me. "*You* might as well be under a sleeping spell. What good are you?"

"Stop it, Adelaide," said Lena.

"No!" She dashed up until she'd reached my step. She shoved her face close to mine, completely furious.

"It's *your* fault he's in danger, Rory." The accusation wouldn't have hurt me so much coming from anyone besides Adelaide. She was the only other person who worried about Chase the same way I did. "The Snow Queen never would have gone after him if you didn't care about him so much."

The stair cracked beneath us. Her mouth opened, but faster than she could scream, the pieces under our feet began to drop. Her fingers scraped across the wall, searching for a handhold.

My body took over, my mind barely involved, just like when I fought under my sword's magic. I grabbed her wrist, leapt up the stairs, and swung her up to safety above me.

Even without Rapunzel asking, I would have saved her. Saving her meant saving Chase.

"Oh my gumdrops," Lena whispered behind me. "How could I be so *stupid*? Another trap activates if more than one person stands on the same step. Two deaths using the same magic it takes to kill one."

Got it. Single file, I thought, but I didn't say it. I kept my mouth closed and concentrated on not throwing up.

"So you're not useless." Adelaide didn't look so impossibly pretty now. Her hair was plastered to her face, sticky with sweat. "But it's still your fault."

"I *know*, Adelaide," I said.

"Be quiet for a second." Lena sounded so breathless I glanced over to check on her. She was pointing upward. "Is that it?"

"Chase," Adelaide whispered. He was so close.

We could *see* the top of the tower, the landing where the stairs ended. A ladder stood on it, directly under a trap door.

My breath caught.

The wood of the door was black and cracked with age. Light from Rapunzel's vial gleamed across a silver doorknob. The shadows were too deep for me to see any symbols etched beneath it.

It looked like the door from my dreams. I'd been sure that I would find it in the Snow Queen's palace, but it could be here. I could believe that the fate of the world depended on Chase.

"That *has* to be it." Her jaw set and determined, Lena thrust the M3 over the next step—one of her quick swipes.

I kept waiting for another trap to spring, but Lena's mirror didn't glow with any more warnings.

Only three traps to protect Solange's sister? Only three traps to keep us from rescuing Chase?

We reached the landing. "That was easier than I thought," Lena said happily.

"Speak for yourself," Adelaide said.

I thrust Rapunzel's light toward the door.

It wasn't the one from my dream. I could see what was etched underneath the doorknob.

Not just an *S*. No, it had an *S* and an *R* entwined. I guess Rapunzel and Solange really *had* lived here.

Stupid of me. It couldn't have been *that* door. I couldn't go through it alone. The whole point was to get Adelaide in there.

The ladder was right in front of me. I started climbing. It was only ten feet tall. Barely a challenge at all, especially compared to the stairs.

"I should go first," Adelaide said, scurrying forward.

But I was already at the top. I couldn't help myself.

"Um, Rory—" Lena said, like she wanted to point out that she had a perfectly good booby-trap detector I wasn't using.

I reached for the knob. It turned easily, and the door creaked as I rammed my shoulder into the wood and shoved. It opened.

"I guess it's not locked?" But even Lena's worry didn't register.

The tower's only room was even smaller than I expected, maybe fifteen feet across. Child-size furniture was piled up against the wall.

Climbing in, I scraped my knee on the trap door's hinge and scrambled to my feet.

Chase was lying on a narrow cot. Its old-fashioned mattress might have once been very fluffy but now feathers spilled out of both sides, fluttering in the breeze coming from the open window.

He was curled up on his side, one arm flung out and the other hand curled toward his face. He must have been holding his weapon with that hand; the sword had slipped to the stone floor among the feathers.

His jawline was growing to be as rugged as his dad's, but he still looked so much like his mother. The summer had teased more gold out of his hair, and his long lashes cast dim shadows across his cheeks.

I hated seeing his face like this, empty of everything that made him Chase. He was *never* this still. I wanted to see him grin or scowl or laugh at me for worrying so much. I wanted him to tell me off for saying such terrible things.

I wished I hadn't dreamed anything about this day. I wished I was sure that Adelaide's kiss would work. I wished Chase had gotten any Tale but this one.

Adelaide entered the room, way more gracefully than I had. She didn't even glance my way. She sailed straight to the bed, took his hand, and whispered his name.

Well, I'd gotten her here. I didn't have to watch.

Lena poked her head through the trap door. "Rapunzel lived here? Not very long, though, right? It's so small."

I didn't answer. I was too busy trying not to hear Adelaide leaning on the bed, trying not to imagine her mouth lowering to Chase's. I offered Lena my hand. She took it and let me help her inside.

As soon as both of Lena's feet hit the room's floor, the wooden door rose, all by itself, and slammed shut.

This side didn't have a handle.

Traps within traps. Perfect.

I was almost relieved. It gave me something to focus on besides what was going on over there with Chase. "Maybe we can pry it open."

"We can try." Lena was too nice to point out that a magically sealed door probably couldn't be fixed by a crowbar. She moved closer to the furniture piled against the walls. She poked around, inspecting first a child-size table leg and then some very dusty drapes. "Ooo, I see the spinning wheels. There are two—a little one and a big one. Solange must have been teaching Rapunzel. But where are the spindles?"

"Or we could go out the window," I said, glancing at it. I hardly felt sick at all. From this height, the frost vines looked like fog. You could see the river from here too, its water glittering through the green-gold trees. It *was* a pretty view.

"I don't have any rope long enough," Lena said.

But any second, Chase would wake up. He would offer to fly us down. He would probably insist that we feed him first.

"We have bigger problems." Adelaide's voice broke over the last word. I turned to see her hugging herself, looking defeated. She actually stepped *away* from the bed.

And Chase still slept on.

11

"Try *again*," I said, furious at her for giving up so quickly.

She wouldn't meet my eyes. "I tried three times."

"Maybe you aren't kissing him right," I said frantically. "Maybe you need to kiss him for longer."

"I can't do it," Adelaide said through gritted teeth. "I can't save him."

Death isn't the only way you can lose someone. The Director had slept for a century.

A hundred years. A hundred *Chaseless* years. Even if I did survive the summer, even if I joined the Canon and lived long enough to see him wake up, it would never be the same. I would have lived a whole lifetime without him, and we would be strangers to each other.

I could have survived him being with Adelaide. I might have endured us growing apart, but I couldn't imagine him never teasing me again, never bossing me around, never telling me that I was better than I thought I was.

It wasn't like after losing Hansel. I didn't scream or sob, but tears cascaded down my face. I felt them drip off my chin, and when I tried to blink them back, they just fell faster.

Lena gave me a tiny, kind smile. "Rory, we'll get him back.

You're just going to have to kiss him, that's all."

I snorted—always a messy, snotty mistake when you're in the middle of crying. "And are you going to give it a try if that doesn't work?" We could create a portal in this room and march every single girl Character in here to attempt a kiss. It still wouldn't matter. I knew how this Tale worked—the girl who could wake up Chase might not have even been born yet.

"Are you *serious*?" Out of the corner of my eye, I saw Adelaide balk. I guess she'd seen my face. Ugh. The only thing worse than having a breakdown was doing it in front of *her*.

"Rory, sometimes, a kiss is just a kiss," Lena said. "Adelaide's kiss didn't mean anything. They've probably kissed tons of times."

I stared at her. That wasn't making me feel any better.

"It wasn't that many times," Adelaide mumbled, which actually did cheer me up a little.

Lena spoke slowly and calmly, like she always does when she doesn't want me to freak out. "It would be different if you kissed him." Her voice became tinny. She was reciting something. "'*A first kiss has its own magic. It is as powerful a change as the trans-formation into a sorcerer. Before a first kiss, a relationship was one thing. Afterward, it is irrevocably changed.*'"

"Don't you want to kiss him?" Adelaide asked bitterly.

That was a good question. It was easy to want to see my fam-ily and friends safely through the summer. It was easy to want to defeat the Snow Queen. It was only a tiny bit harder to want to live long enough to go to high school.

But with Chase . . .

I wanted to rewind our lives to the way things used to be between us, like I had pretended all summer. No, I wanted to rewind to the week between getting back from the Arctic Circle and finding out

Adelaide was Chase's girlfriend. I wanted to go back to the days when just seeing Chase made my stomach explode with happy butterflies and my face break into a goofy smile. If we'd just had a little more time before everything had gotten so complicated . . .

"Rory, you idiot, it has always been you." Adelaide's fists balled up. "When we're together, he's not even thinking about me. He's usually watching you on his M3."

"That's for those Itari lessons—" I protested.

"That's the excuse. He's watching *you*," Adelaide said. "He's been obsessed with you since you showed up in sixth grade."

Adelaide wouldn't lie to make me feel better. She wanted to save Chase as much as I did.

I turned to the bed. Sleeping, he looked so defenseless.

I knelt down beside him. I touched his cheek. His skin was chilled, like he'd been sitting in a refrigerator for hours.

This wasn't how I imagined my first kiss. With all this pressure and the terrible sinking fear that even this might not work.

But if a first kiss could save Chase, I would give it up gladly.

I took a deep breath and pressed my lips against his. They were cold too.

I hated that my mind was racing. I hated that Lena and Adelaide were watching. I hated that his eyes were still closed and his breaths were still even. It hadn't worked. It hadn't worked, and Chase was waiting for someone else, and he was lost to me.

Then a large hand encircled my wrist. The fingers were still half frozen, but his palm was warm.

"I'm pretty sure I've had a nightmare," said a voice, so weak that I barely recognized it. "They *suck*. How do humans deal with having them all the time?"

Chase sat up and looked at me drowsily, just like that time he'd overslept and I'd gone to wake him up before his group's session. He was even grinning.

Buckets of tears poured down my face. "I'm so sorry!"

Chase didn't draw back on that tiny cot. He didn't even shoot me a look that said he was too sleepy for this. He just yawned and said, "It's okay, Rory. I'm fine. I can't keep my eyes open, but I'm sure that'll wear off."

He thought I was apologizing for crying. "No, Chase. I'm sorry for what I *said*."

"You didn't mean it. It was stupid to corner you in front of everybody. Just—" He rubbed his eyes and managed to get both of them open. "Don't say it ever again, okay?"

He was looking at me like nothing had changed. He had no idea why he'd been asleep or why he'd woken up. If I had my way, I'd never tell him.

"Found them!" Across the room, Lena thrust two spindles into the air high above her head—an adult-size one and a kid-size one. Chase must have pricked himself on the smaller one. Blood had dried on the pointy end. "Okay, we can go home now."

Chase spotted what was in her hand—he looked from it to the long scratch on his arm and then to me. He started to look slightly green, but I didn't think nausea was a side effect of a sleeping enchantment.

He knew. He knew I'd kissed him, and the idea made him sick to his stomach.

"Please tell me that I didn't get my Tale," he said, strained.

"Okay. You didn't." I was too miserable to say anything else.

Chase gave me an exasperated look. Well, at least that much hadn't changed. "You usually lie better than that, Rory." He lurched to the window. Adelaide was standing there, staring at the drop like she was thinking about hurling herself out of the tower.

"Move," Chase said coldly. Hurt flashed across her face.

That wasn't fair. She'd been terrified for him too. She slunk back, her arms curled around her middle.

Chase surveyed the icy vines. Some sections were more translucent than the others, a silver-green strip cutting the misty white right down the middle. That must have been where Lena's axes had chopped a path. The vines had already grown back.

"They enchant you if they draw blood, don't they?" Chase said in a dead, faraway voice.

"They got Kyle," Lena said, obviously still a little worried about him. "He turned into—"

"Ice," Chase finished. I wondered how he knew. "We have to get back to EAS."

"No argument here," muttered Adelaide.

The Snow Queen had cast the warding hex on the tower, so we had to get outside for our rings to work. "Lena, do you think your axes could hack through the door?" I asked.

"Axes?" Chase repeated. "You have axes now? Are they Axes of Destruction? Because that just might cheer me up."

Lena eyed the trapdoor skeptically. "I do. They *might* be up to breaking us out."

Something roared far below. Something else shrieked a little closer. Yep, the dragons and ice griffins were awake.

"Looks like we're going out this way." Chase hoisted himself up on the windowsill. His wings fluttered into sight, an orange blur above his shoulders. Hovering just outside the tower, he extended a hand toward me. I took it, already dreading the flight. "I can only take one of you at a time. Rory first, obviously, and then—"

His wings blinked out of sight. Chase plummeted. My grip

tightened on reflex. His weight nearly tore my arm out of its socket. He banged against the stone below the window, but he didn't fall.

"Well, *that's* never happened before." Chase looked down. The surprise on his face turned very slowly to alarm. "Is this how people who can't fly feel all the time? The fear-of-heights thing makes sense now."

"Can you climb back inside?" I said through gritted teeth. Chase was heavier than I was, and I'd caught him with the hand that *didn't* wear the West Wind's ring.

"Hold on. My wings just let me down. I'm in *shock*. I'm wondering if I'll ever fly again." Chase had clearly woken up enough to be dramatic.

"It's temporary." Lena reached out the window and grabbed Chase's other hand. The strain in my shoulders eased. "It's just a side effect. The sleeping enchantment put your magic to sleep too, and it'll cut in and out for a while."

Together, we pulled him up. He threw a knee over the stone and sat on the windowsill.

"Lena, do you have a spell that can make rope longer or—" I started.

"Hey!" came a faint voice from the ground.

Lena pushed her head around Chase and looked down. "Kyle! Are you okay?"

He was *safe*. He'd even made it back to the quest. Another knot of tension eased.

Chase seemed worried, but not about Kyle. "What's happening at EAS?"

We couldn't really hear Kyle's response. Apparently, eight stories up was too far away to hold a conversation.

"What was that?" Chase said. To Lena, he added, "Think an M3 would work if we lean out the window like this?"

"Maybe." She stretched out as far from the tower window as possible. Her M3 flashed in the sun.

They were making me nervous. I grabbed a fistful of both of their T-shirts, ready to pull them back if either of them lost their balance.

From below, a few words drifted up. Either Kyle was shouting at the top of his lungs or he'd cast a voice-amplifying spell. "Rap . . . zel . . . long hair."

"All that effort for a joke? We don't have time for that crap," Chase said, furious. "Kyle, is everything all right at EAS?"

"Wait, what did he say?" Lena asked me.

"If I had to guess," I said, "'Rapunzel, Rapunzel, let down your long hair.'"

"Oh," Lena said. "Personally, I would take Rapunzel's magic carpet over her hair. She saw this, didn't she? Why couldn't she have sent it with us?"

"Maybe she needed it," I said absentmindedly.

I felt the change before I saw it.

The beads on the ends of Lena's braids brushed my hand. I looked down, and her hair kept growing. It fell past her waist.

"Um . . . ," I said.

Maybe Lena getting a second Tale should have seemed strange, but it didn't. Solange had already manipulated the conditions of "Sleeping Beauty." The magic that swirled around me had clearly decided to strike back with a Tale of its own. Besides, one Rapunzel was already important to me. It made sense that the same Tale would repeat in my best friend.

The extra weight must have hurt. Lena touched her head and

grimaced. Then the braids rippled past her fingers. She definitely noticed that. "Oh, my gumdrops."

Chase glanced at her, clearly wondering what her problem was. Then he did a double take. "Geez, Lena—just because I got *my* Tale doesn't mean *you* needed another one. It's not a competition."

Lena didn't think that was funny. She grabbed one of the strands and squinted at it, trying to see. "Rory—I can't tell—is it growing in braided?"

It was growing too fast for me to tell—a new foot every second. Dark loops curled on the floor, dotted with bright blue beads. "I *think* so."

"That's a first," Lena said slowly. I guess it was hard to think straight with new hair pouring out of your scalp. "Helpful, though."

"I'd say." Chase grabbed a handful of braids from the tower floor, but I tugged him back before he could jump.

"You'll yank the hair out of her head," I said. "Let it finish growing first."

"We're a little short on time," Chase told me, irritated.

"Why?" I said. I mean, we weren't stuck anymore. Lena's new braids were going to get us out. He could wait for the five minutes it took for her hair to grow.

"This is a trap," Chase said. "Every other time she laid a trap, she also sent someone to attack us. *Where are her fighters?*"

I had a sudden vision of General Searcaster arriving in Avalon, ripping off the roof of our tower, and plucking us out.

Lena's mouth trembled, so I knew she was thinking roughly the same thing. Another ten feet of braids coiled around our feet. Adelaide scooted away from the strands, trying not to look at any of us.

Then Lena's chin lifted. "This one's my Tale. So it's my

decision." She reached into her carryall and pulled out the small knife she used to chop spell ingredients. "Start at the other end. If you braid the braids, it'll be closer to real rope. I'll cut it when we have enough to reach the ground. *No one* goes out that window until then, you hear? We need everyone in fighting shape in case any giants show up."

"Yes, ma'am." I grabbed a handful of hair and tried to follow it to the end.

Chase watched me. "How do you braid again?"

"Um. Three strands." I found the ends and divided them. It had been a long time since I tried to do anyone else's hair. I wished Miriam, EAS's new expert on dwarvish braids, had come.

Adelaide rolled her eyes. "The mighty Triumvirate, defeated by hair. Get out of my way, and keep the ends from tangling."

I stepped back.

Chase edged away from her the second she grabbed Lena's hair. That had to kill her a little, but she didn't complain. She didn't even comment. A thick, tight, even, ropelike braid formed under Adelaide's quick fingers.

Finally, Lena sheared off her hair, close to her scalp. It kept growing for another minute, long enough for her to panic. But the braids just reached her calves and stopped. She handed me some string from her carryall and ordered me to wrap up her hair. "It doesn't have to be pretty," she told me. "I just don't want to step on it."

Chase finished separating the strands, and a few minutes later, Adelaide completed the rope.

Still no sign of our enemies, but nobody had told Chase that. He searched the room and hauled his carryall out from under the bed. He grabbed something inside and tossed it to me. I caught it—a jar filled with green-gold paint, labeled 2—WEAPONS CLOSET.

A temporary-transport spell. It wouldn't break through the warding hex. Besides, we had a way out. "Why—"

"Just hold on to it," he said. "And hope we don't need it."

Chase tied the end of the rope around the only thing nailed down in the room—an iron torch bracket attached to the stone wall about a foot above my head. He double-checked that his sword and sheath were secure. Then he scooped up an armful of rope and dumped it out the window. He jumped a second before Lena protested, "Wait! Let me check the knot!"

The rope went taut.

The knot held. Lena peeked outside again. "Okay, he's already three-quarters of the way—No, he's at the base. He's talking to Kyle. Your turn, Rory."

"We all know it'll take you the longest to get down," Adelaide said.

Just to spite her, I grabbed the rope, twirled a bit of it around my leg, anchored it with my other foot, and hopped out the window without even glancing down first. The hair rope *felt* weird—springy and too thin to bear my weight. I hoped the magic from our Tales was helping it hold together.

I closed my eyes and loosened my grip.

The rope ran out over my leg less than a minute later, way less time than I expected. There wasn't enough. I knew it. I should have checked. I—

Hands grasped my waist, steadying me.

"I get it. Your eyes are closed," Kyle said from a few feet away. "I thought you took that pretty fast, for you."

Kyle was manning three axes. He looked like he usually did when he offered to test Lena's inventions—amazed, nervous, and ready for anything.

He wasn't the one who caught me.

Holding my waist, Chase scowled up at the hair rope. His wings flickered in and out behind him, buzzing with agitation whenever his magic kicked in. It was the best thing I'd seen all day. All his Chaseness had come back.

"You can let go now, Rory," he said.

This was totally what I imagined would happen *after* my first kiss. "Right." I dropped the last few inches.

The second my feet thumped onto the grass, Chase grabbed the rope and held it steady for the next person. At the top of the tower, heart-stoppingly small, Adelaide was lowering herself out the window.

"Lena, don't wait for her!" Chase called, even though he knew perfectly well that she couldn't hear him up there.

Well, I didn't see any giants. The Snow Queen hadn't sent her forces. Yet.

That made the vines the scariest thing around, but Kyle had them under control. One of the icy tendrils sneaked into the clearing directly beside the tower. He pointed at it, and the ax on the right sailed forward and hacked it back.

I tugged my ring out of my pocket, ready to go. "Kyle, *was* everything okay at EAS?"

Kyle nodded slowly. "Rapunzel was there. She told me to say the long hair thing. I didn't think it would actually work, but she wanted me to promise. She'd just saved my life. It didn't seem polite to say no."

So, Rapunzel had known the Tale was coming, and she hadn't warned me *or* Lena. She hadn't even hinted. That wasn't like her.

Adelaide landed and backed away from Chase and the rope, without saying anything, without even looking at us. She took something out of her pocket. It flashed blue in the sun. Her ring of return.

"Don't even think about it, Adelaide," Chase said, and not in a very nice way. "We go back together."

She squeezed her eyes shut, wincing, but she curled her fingers around the ring and waited.

Chase wasn't telling us something. He was too freaked out. "Why?" I said.

He didn't answer right away.

Lena had made it halfway, but she was having trouble sliding down. The wind kept whipping the hair on her head around the rope. She stopped at least five times to unwrap one from the other. Chase's wings buzzed again, in and out. If she fell, he was ready to leap up as far as his malfunctioning magic would let him and catch her.

"Chase?" I said.

"Get your sword out," he said, without taking his eyes off Lena. "When we go back, we need to be armed."

That was it. He thought the Snow Queen had sent her fighters to EAS, the stronghold Solange had never even been able to find. His Tale was making him paranoid. "But, Chase," I said gently, "how would she get in? EAS is so well-protected."

"That is *exactly* what the Fey thought about their courts," Chase reminded me.

Anxiety churned my insides. That couldn't be true. We left EAS for the dangerous missions and quests, and when we got back, we were safe. That was how it *worked*.

Rapunzel would have told us if an attack was coming. I was almost sure.

"Okay." I drew my sword and dug my ring out of my pocket. Adelaide notched an arrow on her bowstring. Kyle called all but one ax back into the sack. Then he grabbed it in one hand and held his spear in the other.

"Any day now, Lena," Chase called.

This time, she was *definitely* close enough to hear him. "It's harder for me than it was for you guys! I don't think that this is how Rapunzels normally leave their tower." She'd gotten stuck again, just eight feet above us. "Forget it. I'll *jump* the rest of the way. See you at EAS."

Lena's ring flashed blue. Then she disappeared.

"She used hers," I said, Master of the Obvious.

"Crap." Chase unsheathed his sword. "NOW!"

I slipped my ring over my finger. I immediately stumbled over the EAS courtyard grass. Lena was crouched low, her eyes very wide and her arms shielding her head.

Smoke clogged the air. A cough scraped my throat. Just above us, the Tree of Hope was in flames. A *Draconus melodius* blew another stream of flame and blackened more leaves. Two squadrons of goblins cheered it on.

Chase was right. EAS, our last safe haven, was under attack.

The Snow Queen hadn't trapped us in that tower to kill us. She'd trapped us to keep us out of the way.

The air was full of screams and shouts. Ice griffins screeched. Another *Draconus melodius* sang its eerie three-note song much too close, but I barely heard.

George, Kenneth, and Miriam battled goblins less than twenty feet away. Beyond them, a tenth-grade squadron had taken on some wolves. Darcy riddled the furry heads with arrows, and her twin brother Bryan finished them off with his spear.

It didn't make sense. The Snow Queen's forces couldn't *be* here. They couldn't get in.

Lena shook me to snap me out of my stupor. Four green-gold dragons closed in, stinking of sulfur. They seemed so much bigger than the one Lena kept in the dungeon for its scales. Their yellow teeth glinted. They swatted at Kyle, and he went tumbling, his spear spinning out of his hands and rolling across the grass.

The nearest dragon dived toward us.

The runner's high flowed into me. I punched the underside of its chin. The gust of the West Wind's ring hit it, and the great scaly head jerked back. Stunned, the dragon stumbled to its knees. My sword thrust forward, piercing through the scaly hide into its heart. The dragon toppled, dead.

A bowstring twanged. The dragon to our right fell too, Adelaide's arrow sticking out of its eye.

The last two dragons reared, screaming their outrage. Chase jumped from the Tree of Hope's lowest branches. His sword flashed. The biggest dragon's head hit the ground, and Chase landed hard beside it. The last dragon blasted a fireball, but Chase had already moved. He ducked between its forepaws and stabbed it through the throat. Then he swung himself up into the Tree again with a grunt.

"This not-flying crap is getting old." Dragon blood had splattered across his face. He wiped at it with his T-shirt. "God, this stuff stings."

"Should you be in that tree if it's *burning*?" I said, feeling more like myself again. "We need a plan."

"First, we get away from the dragons." Lena pushed me away from the scaly bodies, her retractable spear tucked under her arm. "Because they're going to—yep!" Flames rippled over the dead dragons. "Combust."

Standing slowly, Kyle winced and pressed a hand to his ribs. Lena scooped up his spear and handed it back. "Thanks," he said. Then he threw it at the ice griffin swooping down at us from above. The spear nailed the beast right in its feather-covered heart. "There are so many of them."

"These are all the Snow Queen's forces," Chase said, completely ignoring the fire crackling on the other side of the Tree. "This is everything's she's got. They're clearing the way. She's keeping the pillars close to her, and she's planning to lead them in last."

He sounded so sure. He usually did, but I didn't see how he could sound so confident about this. "How do you know what she's planning? And how can a giant fit through a portal?"

"She'll shrink them," Chase said. I opened my mouth to ask

something else, but Chase cut me off. "Rory, *please*. I don't have time to explain. Just trust me."

Well, he had known about the vines.

"Is that shrinking thing even possible?" Kyle asked in an undertone.

Lena nodded reluctantly. "She had to transport the giants to your house somehow. Shrinking someone that huge would take a lot of power, but it's possible."

"We're going to make sure that doesn't happen. I'm looking for the portal. There! Over by the student apartments." He pointed, but all I saw were dozens of trolls in hockey masks. Three squadrons of spearmen had stopped them in their tracks. My *dad* held the line in the second-to-last row, wearing only a helmet for armor.

We had to end this quickly, before anyone got hurt. Hansel had been our general. He would have known what to do, but he was gone. I had to settle for someone who was supposed to be in charge. "Where's the Director?" I asked.

"I can see her. She's in front of her office, holding off some wolves," Chase said. He paused a second to deal with a swooping ice griffin, cutting off its head before it knocked him off his branch. "Defense first. The Snow Queen's forces are concentrating on getting into the library, the training courts, the dungeon, and the Director's office."

Now I knew why he'd given me the temporary-transport spell to the weapons closet. He wanted me at the training courts.

"She's after the Director?" Kyle asked.

"No. After the Water of Life," Chase said, "which the Director keeps in her office. Kyle, Adelaide, get as many kids from our grade as you can, and help her beat them back. Our numbers will take a blow if we can't heal ourselves."

"On it." Pressing a hand to his side, Kyle took off, picking up an abandoned spear. "Conner! Kevin! Paul!"

Adelaide was on his tail. Without breaking her stride, she squeezed off a shot at a wolf who'd turned her way. "Vicky! Daisy! *Candice!*"

"The dungeon is a no-brainer," Chase said. "The Snow Queen will want to free the prisoners we're keeping in there. I'll grab some spearmen and gather the Itari fighters. We'll rout them as fast as we can. Lena, do you remember the back way into the library?"

"Yes, but what does she want in there?" Then Lena's eyes widened. "Oh. Information."

The current volume of ongoing Tales. *My* Tale.

Chase squinted toward the library. "The trolls look like they're using a battering ram against the door, so someone probably locked it from the inside. It won't hold for long. Try to get the information *out* if you can. But if you can't, you've got something in your little bag of goodies to handle them, right?"

Lena hitched her carryall higher on her shoulder. "Right." She ran off, skirting around the trolls and disappearing down an avenue of brick houses.

I knew what was left. "What's going on in the training courts?"

"Not the training courts. The safe house." Chase jumped down with a thump.

Fear washed over me, icy even with the flames at our backs. The staff students. *Dani.* "That's where they put our families," I said, understanding. I sprinted along the courtyard wall. I could use any door to get in, but I wanted to look at what I was walking into first. Chase fell into step beside me.

"And the Unseelie king," he said. I *really* wished he would tell me how he could suddenly read the Snow Queen's mind. "Hansel thought the safe house would be easier to defend against an attack with just one entrance, but that backfired. The

Snow Queen's villains have bottled it up. The magic dummies can't get through."

"I'll break them out." I would make sure everyone in the training courts was safe too.

But he wasn't worried about the dummies. "You have to convince the Fey to fight. Tell them the Snow Queen expects them to. The Seelie and Unseelie heirs aren't in any danger from what the knights do in *this* battle."

"We need everyone we can get, don't we?" I said.

"We need more than we have," Chase admitted. Over his shoulder, I noticed a troll spot us and beckon to a couple of his buddies. They charged.

"Duck," I said, and Chase obliged.

With my left hand, I punched so hard I felt the troll's hockey mask shatter and my knuckles split. Chase slid his sword under the armor of the second one, and I smashed my hilt into the temple of the third. Then Chase shoved my head down. A fireball sailed above us, so close I smelled burnt hair and swatted at my ponytail.

Then Chase straightened and ran, tugging me around ranks of goblins. "You can't go alone. You're in the most danger. They have orders to mob *you* on sight. You need someone covering your back. Maybe George is around."

"How do you know?" I slipped through a side alley, and then I saw her. My mom, backed up against the wall of a brick house, where seven trolls had cornered her. Orange blood dripped off her blade. She must have gotten at least one.

"You're the mother," grunted the troll closest to her, the one wearing a full suit of armor. He had a spear. One jab, in the heart or throat, and I would lose her too.

I'd never seen that look on Mom's face, not in real life or in any of her movies. The fury in her eyes could peel paint off the walls. It could stop traffic on the highway. It would even make the Snow Queen take a step back.

"You won't *touch* my daughter," Mom snarled, and she swung, hard. The troll blocked. His spear's shaft broke under the blow.

"So *that's* where you get it," Chase muttered, but I was already running.

The head troll struck again, and broken spear or no, it was Mom's sword that fell to the ground.

"Be tame, human, and we won't hurt you." The troll smiled around his tusks and turned to the others. "Take her back to the portal. Put her in the dungeon. Her Majesty will reward us with feasting and with land, for a hostage such as—"

I leapt and punched. The head troll crashed to the ground. The rest recognized me. They stampeded forward, spears and swords raised.

"See? This is what I meant about them mobbing you," Chase said, coming up behind us. A troll swung at Chase, a beheading blow. Chase ducked. The blow landed on another troll's neck instead.

"Yeah, yeah, you told me so," I said. The head troll had scrambled to his feet. He peeled the helmet off his head and roared.

I couldn't waste such a great opportunity. I dashed forward, stepped into his guard, and smashed my hilt squarely between his eyes before he had a chance to close his mouth. He didn't get up that time.

Another troll stabbed toward my middle. I caught the shaft, just under the spearhead, and wrenched it out of his hand. I swung. The spear whistled through the air and shattered against two trolls' heads. They crumpled to the grass.

"Rory?" Mom said, breathless.

I whirled around. "Are you okay?"

Mom looked surprised. "I'm not the one who went on a quest this morning."

"Watch out!" Chase pointed to our left.

A trio of trolls were glancing between me, Mom, and Chase, and the alley between the houses, obviously trying to decide whether to attack or escape. Well, I wasn't going to let them go for reinforcements. "Got 'em."

I smashed one into the ground with so much ring-powered force that the dirt cracked around him. A second stabbed at me a few times, but after the Itari lessons, I dodged too well—he nabbed his ally in the heart instead of me. He cursed. I kicked him in the stomach. He doubled over, and a snap kick to the chin knocked him out.

All of Chase's opponents were down too. He knelt beside one of them, his sword stuck through the fallen troll's breast plate.

"We good?" I asked.

Chase yanked his sword free and popped up, grinning. "I'm *always* good."

I smiled. I had *really* missed him. "Well, don't use up all your awesome in one go. Save some for the dungeon. I'll go to the training—"

My gaze landed on my mom's sword, still on the ground. I picked it up. She wasn't a bad fighter, but besides the play sword-fighting skills she'd learned for a movie a few years ago, she'd only had a few days of training. She wasn't good enough yet, not for this battle—not with the Snow Queen putting a price on our heads.

So I pressed the hilt of *my* sword into her palm instead. "You want to protect me, right?"

"Of course I do," Mom said, obviously surprised I would even ask.

"Then focus on that feeling." I made a couple passes with Mom's blade, testing it. It was an inch or two shorter. The balance was slightly different, but it was a little lighter, too. I would be slightly faster. I could adjust. "That's what turns the magic on."

"An extra Itari fighter for the day," Chase said. "I like it."

Mom hesitated. "Won't you need it?"

"Rory hasn't needed it all year," Chase said, walking up behind us. "She needs you to watch her back when she goes to the training courts."

"Chase," I said, starting to tell him that he couldn't ask her to guard me—no one could send my mother into battle, not even him. Then I remembered: We were surrounded by enemies. Mom couldn't escape fighting. Plus, if I kept her close, I could keep her safer. So I told Mom what Rapunzel had told me, years ago. "Mom, you're probably the only person in the world who could turn the sword's magic completely on."

Mom wasn't sure whether to believe me or not. She looked both suspicious and pleased.

"I'll keep an eye on your dad," Chase said, and I understood why he'd decided to take some spearmen to defend the dungeons.

It was time to split up. We both had stuff to do.

I didn't want to leave him. I didn't want to let him out of my sight so soon after I'd almost lost him for a hundred years.

For a second, Chase's look softened, and I knew—for the first time ever—that he felt the same. He jogged backward. "When you're done, bring your forces to the portal. I'll meet you there, and we'll shut it down."

"Be careful," I said, hating how my voice cracked.

"Always," said the kid who had climbed a tree on fire less than five minutes before. Then he dashed down the alley.

I sighed. "This way, Mom." We ran past two dragons blasting flames at the library's locked door. It didn't seem like they were making a dent, but still, I wished I had time to check if Lena was okay. I hoped she'd gotten Rumpelstiltskin and the book out.

Mom was white-faced when I tugged her down a path between a row of mismatched condos, magically pasted together after Lena had transported them. "Just a second while I take a look. Afterward, we need to find a door for a temporary-transport spell," I told her. I peeked around the corner.

Villains had lined up outside the training courts. I expected them to seem seedier, scarier, but besides one guy in a mask and another guy with tusks who obviously had troll blood, they all looked like regular guys. Most of them were even wearing jeans. Only a few of them had put on armor.

I counted at least a dozen outside, but more were fighting in the hallway between the courtyard and the training courts. I watched long enough to see them change shifts. Four ugly guys, a severe-looking woman, and Torlauth stomped out, looking frustrated, sweaty, and sadly uninjured.

Well, Torlauth did have a new scar around his eye. *I* hadn't given that to him, but the Snow Queen might have punished him for losing his duel with me.

He wasn't in charge. The guy with the mask and short black hair was giving the orders, gesturing for six more fighters to enter the hall.

Eighteen or more. Probably more.

I eased back around the corner.

Mom was waiting, the blade in her hand, up and ready. "Did they see you?"

"No." Not yet.

"I found an unlocked door," she said, pointing to the one on our right.

"Great. Thanks." A few minutes with me, and I already had Mom breaking into other people's houses. I was a bad influence. "You be the lookout. I'll set up the spell."

I thought having Mom with me would make me more on guard, not less, but I didn't hear the goblins creep up on us. I was concentrating too hard on painting an unbroken line around the door frame. Then something crashed behind me.

I hurtled down the condo steps, but Mom didn't need me.

With the sword's magic, she moved like a stranger—fluid, graceful, and fearless. Fury blazed from her face. I don't know if the goblins recognized us, but they definitely underestimated her. One was still smirking when she slashed the blade across his chest. The other only managed to get in one good thrust before Mom parried and ran him through.

"Oh," she said in a tiny voice. She looked at what she'd done, at the bodies at her feet. Then she glanced at the sword. I knew that feeling. "I'm not sure I *like* that."

"It gets easier to control." I returned to the doorway and finished the last stripe. I set down the jar and the paintbrush and muttered the spell. I had only used temporary transports to escape. This was the first time I'd ever used one to *enter* a fight. "Let's go."

We stepped through the threshold. The weapons closet was dark and crammed with empty racks. All the staffs, spears, and bows were being used.

"Are you *sure* you don't need your sword?" Mom whispered. I couldn't tell if she was nervous about what we'd find in the training courts or about what the enchanted blade might make her do if she held on to it for much longer.

"Yes." Then I turned the doorknob and went out.

All the dummies were lined up near the entrance. Every once in a while, one of them would take a step forward, clunk against the metal statue in front of it, and then step back. Obviously, they were *trying* to get out and defend EAS, but their path was blocked. Four metal dragons were wedged into the doorway. Only a few dummies could fight the villains at a time, and a few weren't enough to overwhelm well-trained fighters.

The Fey knights had clustered in the back corner, standing shoulder-to-shoulder around their king. They didn't look as stoic as usual. They kept glancing to their right, toward the crowd of humans.

You could fit a lot of people in a tiny space if you really scrunched. I would have never guessed more than two hundred little kids, new moms, elderly, and wounded people were stuck back there.

Brie was easy to spot. She was on top of a stack of mats with Dani strapped to her back. Her bow was drawn.

Then I saw him. A slender man with a pointed face and a smile full of gold teeth. Ferdinand the Unfaithful, prowling along the edge of the people I'd come to save.

One of the villains had gotten *in*.

I ran, but halfway there, I realized they didn't need me any more than Mom had against the goblins.

The whole staff class had placed themselves right in front of Ferdinand, guarding the other humans in a formation as tight as the Fey knights' body shield. Every weapon was pointed at Ferdinand. Every jaw was set.

Mr. Swallow fluttered up and landed on my shoulder. "Rory!" said Sarah Thumb. "They said they had captured you."

Grinning, Kelly took one hand off her staff to wave at me. "I knew you hadn't been captured! I knew you would come!"

"Oh, good," Brie said, spotting me. "You're okay."

Mom stepped up close, determined to keep watching my back even though we weren't in any immediate danger. "You okay, Amy?" she called out.

"Spectacular," Amy said, standing beside Kelly. She didn't take her eyes off the villain.

"Rory Landon," Ferdinand spat. "I was hoping to see you. My teeth still need to be avenged."

Turning away from my students was a mistake. Priya swung hard at his elbow, just like I'd taught her. Ferdinand yelped and dropped his sword. He whirled around, so when Amy and the mom beside her swung at him, he got hit in the face with two staffs instead of on the side of the head.

He crumpled. Amy smacked him again to make sure he really was unconscious. "I think he lost a few more teeth," she said.

Maybe I shouldn't have grinned, but I couldn't help it. I was one proud teacher. "Well done," I said, and the whole class beamed back. "Is anyone badly hurt?"

"Only one," said Kelly.

One of the teenage students raised her hand. She had a bloody bandage tied around her thigh. "It was my fault. I stepped out of formation."

"They've taken out three villains so far." Sarah Thumb pointed to the wall. Two unconscious, greasy-haired men were slumped against the mirrors, all tied up. Three of the moms dragged Ferdinand over to them and looped rope around his wrists.

Hansel would have loved this.

"And what is the purpose of your arrival?" asked the Fey captain. His green armor had a new dent in the shoulder. "Now you are as trapped as we are."

The staff class turned to me eagerly, clearly waiting to hear my answer.

I had these students and my combs. The beginnings of a plan began to glimmer in my mind, but first, I needed to figure out what else I had to work with.

"Will you fight, Himorsal Liior?" I asked. I probably should have asked the Unseelie king first, but I didn't.

The Fey soldiers bristled at this.

"Do not taunt my knights." An old hand pushed one of them aside, and then King Mattanair stood in front of me. "You know my orders."

I did know. I felt for him. Solange had killed his daughter, and now she had his son. But I needed his men. "The Snow Queen expects them to join the battle. She didn't do anything to Prince Fael when they defended you at the Unseelie Court. Today's not any different."

The king sighed. He'd probably heard this argument already. "You can't know that for certain. No one can."

I knew he would refuse, but I'd spent years learning sneaky persuasion tactics from Chase. "Hey, Sarah Thumb. Can you check to see if Torlauth di Morgian is still in the corridor?"

At that name, every single Fey in the room tightened their grips on their weapons, and I knew I had them. Torlauth had tricked both Fey princes into raising Likon, the last pillar, and he was directly responsible for their capture. He was a traitor to both Fey courts.

Sarah Thumb and Mr. Swallow flapped up, above the dragon dummies crammed in the entrance. "Yes!"

"We will fight," said Himorsal Liior, his voice low and laced

225

with a dark hint of everything he'd like to do to Torlauth.

I didn't glance at the king. I didn't want to see him looking enraged or betrayed, and if I were him, I would have been both. "Wonderful, because I know how we're going to get them out of the hall." I pulled two combs out of my pocket and whispered, "We're going to let them in."

Sarah Thumb did the honors. She was the only one who *could* get us started. The dummies—including the metal dragons barricading the way in—were all spelled to follow her orders and *only* her orders.

The metal dragon statues moved away from the door. The villains didn't question why. They just ran in.

They paused for a second, confused. "Where did they go?" asked one.

I willed everyone to stand perfectly still. The Fey had glamoured us all to look like the metal dummies. Each knight could only handle a few students at once. The Fey king was the best at it. He'd glamoured all two hundred of the other humans to look like rows of metal wolf statues. Mom too—I'd asked her to guard him. We blended in with the ranks of the statue army, but only if no one sneezed or breathed too deeply.

"They couldn't have simply disappeared." The guy with the mask spotted what we'd set in the corner as bait—Ferdinand the Unfaithful and the two other villains my students had tied up. The captain walked straight toward them, and the rest of the villains followed. I hadn't been sure that they would even care about their fallen comrades. Villains weren't exactly known for being loyal to each other.

"Maybe they had those things," said a guy with a blond ponytail. He had bruises all over his face. I guess the metal dragons had done some damage after all. "Those paint things."

"The temporary-transport spells?" said the severe-looking woman. She had a Southern accent. "It's possible. They could have used the weapons closet there to get out."

That *would* have been a good plan. Oh well.

The villains were almost close enough. They didn't even look at the evil Fey dummies they were walking past. Good thing. The Unseelie knights' glamour looked exactly like their cranky usual selves, except covered in metal.

The guy in the masks *did* examine some witch statues, most of them smaller and prettier than real witches. The staff students were doing so well. They weren't even breathing.

I held my breath too.

I'd positioned myself right beside them, ready to jump in front and defend them if I needed to.

Torlauth prodded the bound villains with his foot. "The Unseelie have fled as well. The great King Mattanair, hiding under the protection of a child like a wolf with a tail between its—"

He broke off, frowning.

The glamour over two of my students had flickered—just long enough for a flash of pink and brown skin where the Fey had expected metal. One of the knights had lost his concentration.

Stupid Fey pride.

"They're still here!" The man with the blond ponytail sprang forward and slashed at the students whose glamour had flickered. The girls raised their staffs to block. They probably would have been fine, but I was faster. I caught the blow on my borrowed sword and snap-kicked as hard as I could. My sneaker connected with his jaw. He toppled back, and a couple other villains stumbled under his weight.

Wow, these guys really weren't used to fighting together.

"Now!" Himorsal Liior slashed at Torlauth's throat, but the traitor leapt into the air with one great beat of his red-and-cobalt wings.

Weapons raised, the villains barreled straight at my students, thinking they were the weaker targets. They weren't. In teams of two, my students picked an enemy and slammed the butts of their staffs into each respective chest. The villains gasped, the wind knocked out of them. They stumbled back into the corner just a few feet from where the guy in the mask stood, watching the skirmish. Priya gave hers an extra smack across the face.

"Rory Landon, I presume," said the guy in the mask. "It's pointless to—"

I tossed one of my combs between my students and our enemies. Bars zoomed out of the ground, a foot taller than every villain before they'd even recovered enough to take a step.

"Out! Now!" The guy with the mask pointed to the only side not blocked by a wall or by bars.

But the Fey knights had closed in. The lady with the accent sprinted past them. Brie shot her in the leg. She fell with a scream, and a yellow-winged knight shoved her back toward the other villains. One of the Unseelie dropped the comb I'd given him earlier. Bars raced up toward the ceiling, so quickly that the blond ponytailed guy ran into them.

The guy with the mask interrupted the duel between the Unseelie captain and the Fey traitor. "You must escape. You must tell Her Majesty—"

Torlauth tried to fly for the door. Himorsal Liior grabbed the Fey traitor's boots and swung him around in a circle. He let go. Torlauth slammed against the ceiling inside the comb cage before plummeting, arms and legs flopping, and knocking down half the villains inside. The last bars clanged against the stone, sealing all of them in.

The Unseelie captain landed lightly, smirking. King Mattanair dropped the glamour over the rest of the humans and swayed slightly, exhausted. Mom slowly started making her way back over to me, but it was hard with so many people celebrating. Brie was doing a happy dance with Dani.

Sarah Thumb cheered too. "Okay, statues. Get out into the courtyard and do your defending thing."

Metal feet marched. The training courts echoed with their ringing steps. Two lines streamed out the door, down the corridor, and into the sunshine. Sarah Thumb and Mr. Swallow sailed down the hallway after them.

The guy with the mask tried to rattle the bars, but the cage didn't budge. Most of his men were too shocked to move. I wasn't even sure Torlauth was *breathing*.

The staff students were looking a little stunned themselves. Amy in particular—I don't think she'd expected the plan to work. Mom still had her sword raised and her eyes narrowed, like she couldn't believe it was over.

"Beautifully executed," I told them.

At this, Torlauth snarled inside the cage. He was alive after all.

"Speak for yourself, human," said a Fey knight, pulling on his helmet. "I have never maintained a glamour for others before, and I have no desire to do it again. You say the Turnleaf has maintained such glamours often?"

"For hours," I said, trying not to sound as braggy as Chase. I looked at Himorsal Liior. The knights were watching him too. Some of them looked a little put out that they hadn't used their swords very much. The Fey captain had never given me a straight answer about whether or not he was joining the battle outside.

"I am sorry, my king," Himorsal Liior said heavily, like disobeying a royal order made him almost as big a traitor as Torlauth. "The invaders here are the very same forces who destroyed our home. I cannot fail to stand against them again. I cannot hide here."

King Mattanair nodded slowly. He didn't say it was okay, but he didn't condemn them either.

Himorsal Liior flicked a hand. The knights swooped out the door and over the marching statues to the courtyard. Only two flew over to their king to stand guard, and they looked very surly about being left out of the fight.

Quietly, almost to himself, the king said, "It is what Dyani would have wanted."

I sighed. Yep, I definitely felt bad, but I didn't regret it. I would just have to apologize when our lives *weren't* in danger.

I turned back to the staff class. "You'll do what we talked about, right?"

"We'll stay and defend the king." Priya still didn't sound happy about it.

"And everyone else," Amy said.

I grabbed her hand and dropped my second-to-last comb into it. "Can you stand guard at the door? If it looks like someone will get in again, throw this across the threshold. It'll trap you in here, but—"

"We'll be trapped but safe, like before," she said.

"Thanks, Amy." If I'd given the comb to Priya or Kelly, they might have let a few more bad guys in here, just to get a little more action.

Mom arrived beside us. "What now?"

I didn't ask her to stay here. I thought about it, but she would just say no. Besides, Chase was right about me needing backup. "We go out there and help," I said.

The statues were gone. The path back to the courtyard was clear.

We dashed down it and ducked out into the sunshine.

Four metal dragons had taken on a real one. Two had chunks melted off their backs, but the living *Draconus melodious* had a dozen bite marks up and down its flanks. Another metal dragon tried to close its jaws over the gold scales at its throat.

One lone figure had taken on two squadrons of trolls in hockey masks. He didn't move as fluidly as the Itari fighters, but he was just as brutal and efficient as he tore through their ranks. It was Jack, Champion of the Canon.

Farther along, the Fey knights had flown up to take on the ice griffins. From the look of it, even just a day of Itari practice had paid off. We passed metal wolves fighting some goblins and turned around the corner of a brick house.

Lena guarded the library door, retractable staff held at the ready, but she wasn't using it. Her Axes and Swords of Destruction flashed in the sun, keeping at least fifty goblins occupied.

"What happened to take the book and run?" I called.

The grim scowl on Lena's face faded. "Some goblins followed me to the back entrance," she said, clearly relieved to see me. "I had to improvise."

"Are you good here?" I said.

"Rumpelstiltskin is defending the back with the sabers." Lena waved me on. "We have this under control. Check on the prisons. It sounded like the witches got out."

My heart squeezed. *Chase.* He didn't have his wings. That cut his dodging abilities in half. I sprinted, cutting down an alley toward the dungeons. Mom kept up, for a little while. She started to lag and grabbed my elbow to make sure I didn't pull too far ahead. By then, we'd rounded the edge of the houses.

The prison entrance was in sight.

The witches of the Wolfsbane clan *had* escaped their cells, but they hadn't gotten past the exit. Some human spearmen had surrounded them. They'd flipped the Table of Never Ending Instant Refills on its side and turned it into a barricade. Dad was there. He didn't see us. The Wolfsbane witches were shooting off dozens of spells. Diving from above, Chase's mom snatched one of the witches from the doorway, ripped the wand from the flailing witch's hand, and flew up again, almost as high as the Tree of Hope. Then she dropped the witch.

While the Wolfsbane clan was distracted, the EAS Itari force inched closer to the entrance, hiding behind shields made out of iron bars.

"Lena finished making magical shields?" I said, surprised.

Maybe I shouldn't have spoken. The second the witches all spotted me, they let out that awful screech-caw sound. Istalina pointed her wand in our direction.

Mom knocked me to the ground just in time. A passing troll ten feet behind us turned to stone.

"Rufus found the shields and brought them to us." When I looked up, someone else was crouching right in front of us. Orange wings flickered in and out of view. Chase. He was okay. "Unfortunately, the shields can only take three or four hits. It would be great if we had some Water of Life in case any of us get enchanted."

I spat out a mouthful of grass.

"Is that a polite hint for me to go cover the Director's office instead?" I asked, slightly irritated. As much as I would have liked to fight with Chase, I could tell it was a terrible idea. Half of the witches were still screeching death threats at me.

Chase glanced back. "It wasn't that polite."

"It was for *you*." I spotted a swallow fluttering overhead. "Hey, Sarah. These guys could use some cover. Got any extra dragon dummies?"

Five metal wolves and two metal dragons galloped toward the dungeon door. The Wolfsbane clan spelled a few to stone, but the humans on the ground gained about fifteen yards in ten seconds.

"Great. Thanks." Without looking away from the witches, he helped me to my feet and passed the shield to me. "Now get out of here."

"Wait! You can't just walk back unprotected," I hissed.

"I won't." Instead, he flew, rolling midair to avoid whatever the witches blasted at him. His wings didn't cut out until he was ten feet from the Itari fighters. He let himself tumble the rest of the way and rolled back up next to Rufus. The elf passed him another shield.

"He shouldn't take risks like that," I said, furious, leading Mom to safety. A spell sizzled across the shield, and then another. A third one turned the iron bars to stone, but by then we'd reached Little Red Riding Hood's tiny bungalow at the edge of the courtyard. I dumped the shield and we kept running. "Sometimes I swear, I could just—"

"We'll get you some chocolate cake to throw at him later," Mom said, not quite smiling. "Which way to the Director's office?"

We jogged again, my calves protesting with every step. We *did* need to end this soon. I couldn't be the only one tired.

When we reached the office, the triplets were dragging the Director outside the amethyst door.

"You don't understand!" The Director tried to free her arms from Kevin and Conner's grip. "She mustn't get her hands on the Water of Life."

"She won't," Kyle told her. An ice griffin reared in the doorway and slashed with its sharp talons. He slayed it swiftly, jabbing his spear into its heart. "The stepsisters said they would grab it."

But then the stepsisters stumbled out. Tina had gotten an ice griffin blast directly to the face. Her skin was white and waxy, her eyes squeezed shut, her lashes laced with icicles.

"It's all right," said Vicky, who didn't look all right. Talons had sliced open the shoulder of her T-shirt. Blood soaked the torn edges. Paul kept glancing at the wound anxiously, but he had his hands full, half-carrying Tina. I ran over to her other side and wrapped her arm over my shoulders, helping her walk to the others.

"Where is it?" the Director asked. "Where is the Water?"

"We had to get out. It's too small to fight in there," said Vicky. "Is it worth saving the Water of Life if we die trying to get it?"

"Do you recall how much damage she caused with just two bottles of Water?" the Director asked. "Can you imagine what she'll do with all of it?"

"Calm down, Mildred. We'll get it back." Gretel emerged, leaning hard on Daisy. I couldn't see where she was hurt, but her dress was spotted with blood. Mom hurried over to help her. "We've blocked off the back exit. They'll have to come through here to reach the portal."

Adelaide stumbled outside and turned back to fire off three quick shots through the doorway. Something shrieked. The rest of the archers in our grade darted out. "That's all of us and all the ice griffins, too."

"That leaves the wolves," Kyle told me.

Wolves didn't always use a portal to get home. "Do they have those cuff things?" I said, helping Tina to sit in the grass. Her lashes were melting. One eye was half-open.

"I disabled them," said Gretel. "It took all the sorcery I possess."

I waved my last comb at them. "I say we seal them in, and then we take care of their exit over there." I pointed toward the student apartments, where Chase had said the portal was. They all glanced that way.

The Director went as white as Tina. "No," she breathed. "Not here."

I didn't recognize Likon at first. I'd never seen an ice giant shrunken down to a mere seven feet. He leered at me, and I wondered why Solange was so attached to blue-skinned villains with bad dental problems.

Someone else glided through the portal after him. Her long pale blond hair was braided into a coronet under an icicle crown. Her first step onto the EAS courtyard frosted the grass white in a twenty-foot circle around her. My heart stopped.

The Snow Queen.

13

I blinked and Likon rocketed up five feet. In another breath, he was as tall as the wall behind him. By the time Adelaide spotted him and screamed, he was his usual height—huge and blue and coming straight at us.

A one-eyed wolf loped in behind the Snow Queen, his sides matted with dried blood. Ripper. Then an old green-skinned woman with a metal cane and an eye patch, followed by a green-skinned man who was just as ugly as she was. The Searcasters, who immediately started to expand to their usual giant selves.

A lumpy figure flew through on wings the color of concrete. He grew as he soared toward the prisons. Ori'an.

My body felt the fear that showed on the Director's face, and Adelaide's and Gretel's. I was too petrified to even scream.

We were out of time. The pillars would reach full size in a few seconds. We were *really* outmatched now. We needed to get the Water of Life back, and we needed to get it back now.

The Snow Queen had raised a hand toward a pack of our metal dragon dummies, and a sheet of ice grew around them, trapping the moving statues mid-snarl. That wouldn't keep her busy for long.

"How many wolves are left in there?" I said.

Gretel recovered the fastest. "Ten to fifteen."

I could take that many. I'd taken a hundred once. "Okay, here's what I want us to do—"

"Aurora, it's all over." The Director couldn't drag her gaze off the Snow Queen. "You don't know what she's like. The second she entered this place, the battle was lost."

Screams rippled through the courtyard as the Searcasters grew two stories tall, then four. Ripper bounded through metal wolf statues, scattering more as he got bigger. This *was* bad. But we didn't need our grown-ups to give up. We needed them to be brave. Courage was catching as much as fear was.

They were all looking at me, the kids in my grade. If *I* freaked, the way the Director was freaking . . . "The battle isn't as important as the war," I said, as evenly as I could. "We need the Water—"

A huge blue leg bigger than the Tree of Hope's trunk sprouted four feet from us, so close that Daisy screamed. Likon could have stepped on any of us in that instant, and we couldn't have done anything about it.

He stooped in the doorway of the Director's office. "Shut up, you beasts. I'm not Ripper. I can't understand you when you speak over each other," he told the wolves in a surprisingly soft voice. "Now, where is the Water Her Majesty wants?"

We had all taken the same giant-slaying seminar. I turned to the triplets. "Knees," I reminded them. "Archers, go for the eyes."

The stepsisters nodded and notched arrows on their bowstrings. Adelaide's hands shook as she reached for her quiver.

I would go for the Achilles tendon. Likon couldn't take the Water back to his mistress if he couldn't walk. I was pretty sure.

"You're not going to—" Mom said, her voice faltering.

I didn't meet her eyes. If I did, she would know that this was the most dangerous thing we'd done all day. "Mom, I need you to take the Director back to the safe house. We can't protect you and do this, too."

This time Mom didn't argue with me.

"No. *No*. You must flee," said the Director, as Mom and Gretel led her away.

Likon thrust his arm into the Director's office, but he could only fit it in partway. His elbow got stuck in the door frame. He couldn't reach any farther, no matter how much he pushed, no matter how many cracks appeared in the wall around his arm.

Someone was going to die again. I couldn't stop it. I'd spend my whole life—what was left of it—remembering this moment and wondering what I could have done differently.

But I couldn't think of another plan. The Director had been right. The Water could save so many lives.

"Enough of this." Likon withdrew his arm and gripped the edge of the roof. With a grunt, he yanked. Bits of stone and plaster rained down as the roof ripped free. The blue giant held it aloft while he shoved his head inside the Director's office, like a normal-size person might peer into a heavy chest.

It was time. The Snow Queen was still distracted. She'd finished freezing the metal dragons, and she'd turned her attention to a flock of ice griffin statues. Both of Likon's hands were occupied. If we hit now, his grip would slip. The roof could do way more damage than we ever could. "N—" I started.

"Stop!" shouted a light, musical voice that didn't have any business on the battlefield. "Rory, no!"

I hadn't expected to find Rapunzel in the air, flying on her purple carpet. Her long silver hair fluttered out behind her, the braid unraveling in the wind, as long as a banner. "It's not worth your lives," she said.

It was easy to change my mind. I'd practically been begging someone to stop us. "Get clear," I told the kids in my grade. If we were letting Likon have the Water of Life, we might as well move out of the pillar's reach.

The Searcasters pushed forward. The burning Tree of Hope was in General Searcaster's way so she tore it out, totally unfazed by the flames licking up its branches. The pop I heard when the roots gave wasn't natural. *Magic*, I thought in a distant way, watching her toss it aside. It bounced off the roof of a Tudor and landed on the brick house besides Lena's, cutting the top story nearly in half.

Likon reached inside the Director's office. He pulled out a crate that rattled with glass bottles, and he cradled it in his humungous blue hand.

It had to be all right, if Rapunzel said so. It had to.

The blue giant dropped the roof. It crunched back into place. Splinters drizzled over our heads.

Rapunzel swooped down. The carpet circled me, so close that its fringe brushed my arm, but she didn't land. "There wasn't time to gather them all. I was forced to choose. I hope I chose right."

I stared at her. Either she wasn't making sense because I was still in shock over the whole giant-kills-tree episode, or she was telling me the kind of thing that only makes sense afterward.

"There you are," said a cold voice, as musical as Rapunzel's. I turned and met glacier-blue eyes. The Snow Queen had noticed me—*No, not me*, I thought, following her gaze. She'd spotted her sister, and she approached with a swift, deliberate tread. Fifteen feet away, ten. "Likon," said Solange.

Whatever vision Rapunzel might have seen about today, I'm

sure getting swatted out of the air by a giant hadn't been part of it. Her eyes widened. She leaned back, and her carpet launched into the sky. But Likon's reach was too long. He caught her in his fist.

Rapunzel didn't look afraid, not at first. Only confused. "Rory, it doesn't happen like this," she said, like that was supposed to be comforting.

But it *had* happened just like this. George Searcaster had trapped Hansel in exactly the same way, and I'd been helpless to save him, too.

I'd never worried about Rapunzel dying. Stupid of me, I know. Solange had cared about her *once*, long ago. That didn't make Rapunzel safe.

The Snow Queen's smile was tiny but growing slowly, like I was the person she'd most hoped to see. She took one final step and stopped, and the grass under my sneakers crackled with frost, bleached white. My next shaky breath came out in a white plume.

"Do you know why I have come, Aurora Landon?" she asked.

I did know. I understood intimidation. The Director had learned it from someone, after all.

"Do you know why I waited until this precise moment—when you felt sure that the tables had turned?" said Solange. "Because the message must be made clear to you in particular, Aurora Landon. No matter how close you believe you are to defeating my forces and foiling my plans, victory will always belong to me."

I forced myself not to check how far my mother had gotten with the Director and Gretel. I couldn't risk reminding Solange that my family was here.

Somewhere to our left, Genevieve Searcaster laughed. "Girl, you *are* a fool." The four-story-tall general touched her throat. Then Lena's voice poured out of Searcaster's green lips, high and girlish and just plain wrong. It said, "Up, axes! Chop!"

It was the Bats of Destruction all over again.

Lena screamed, the *real* Lena. I knew what she sounded like when she was just scared and what she sounded like she was hurt, and this was definitely the second.

I couldn't see. Too many stupid houses stood between me and the library.

Then something exploded.

I started to run, forgetting who stood beside me. The Snow Queen flicked a finger. I jumped back, arms up to protect my heart, like *that* would do anything if she decided to put an icicle through me. But she'd only raised a waist-high wall of ice to block my path. "I am not done with you yet." Solange swirled a finger, and two smooth bands of ice clamped around my shoulders.

I was completely trapped. This could count as winter. It could be despair too, but it felt more like panic.

The Snow Queen smiled at me. "Witness how futile your efforts are."

Goblins ran toward us. The same ones who had been fighting Lena's axes outside the library. One of them limped, his pant leg soaked with blood, but he carried a huge book bound with blue leather, the edges smeared with soot.

Behind him stumbled another goblin, bleeding from a dozen cuts and struggling to roll up a long, wide piece of paper. I caught a glimpse of a section marked SOUTH CAROLINA. I didn't want to imagine why the Snow Queen needed a map of human lands.

With squawks and caws, the Wolfsbane clan thundered down the middle of the grassy street. The witches tossed out spells at a few passersby, but mostly they were focused on the portal.

Istalina stopped beside the Snow Queen. She gave a sort of

curtsy, except instead of sweeping out her skirts, she swept out her wand, and bowed her head. "We are in your debt, Your Majesty. You have our loyalty now."

The Wolfsbane clan hadn't really liked the Snow Queen any more than the other witches. Istalina and her clan mates had only allied with Solange because she could give them a chance to kill me and revenge Istalina's mother. Being rescued by the Snow Queen had changed their minds.

It probably wouldn't stop at the witches, either.

Attacking the Fey courts had earned back all Solange's usual allies, but EAS was a more impressive target. It would earn her more than allies. It would inspire *allegiances*.

Maybe *this* was despair.

The Snow Queen inclined her head "Then I welcome you back with open arms. Please return. We will speak soon."

"Shall we kill the human child?" said Istalina. It took me a while to realize she meant me.

Displeasure entered Solange's voice. "Does it seem that I require help in this matter?"

Istalina stepped away, straight into the ranks of the other witches. "As you wish, Your Majesty," she said, sounding only the slightest bit disappointed. She passed through the portal after the goblins.

The Snow Queen turned back to me, her eyes narrowing. Probably deciding how to kill me.

"Not like this." Rapunzel could barely croak the words out. Likon must have been holding her too tight.

The Snow Queen brightened. "Yes, sister. I believe you're correct. I could kill you now, Aurora Landon—" She flicked a few fingers. The bands of ice around me contracted, pinching me so hard

I gasped. "But I'll wait. You are not worth the small magic it would take to kill you. You are not worthy of *me*. Besides . . ." She leaned in and lowered her voice, like she was sharing a delicious secret. "This isn't enough despair for my taste," she explained. "I would like to see your face when you lose someone irreplaceable."

She might as well have pricked my heart with one of her ice daggers. She knew Mom was here.

But my mother wasn't the "someone" Solange had in mind.

"Likon. Here, please." The Snow Queen pointed at the ground directly between us.

The ice giant set Rapunzel down so fast that she stumbled to one knee. Solange grabbed Rapunzel's elbow, steadying her sister.

I wondered when they had seen each other last. The end of the last war? The day Solange threw Rapunzel, bleeding, from her tower?

They really did look alike. They had the same slender build and pointed chin. Their eyes were different colors, but they both tilted up at the corners. What really set them apart were their expressions. Rapunzel looked as defiant as she did when the Director bossed her around.

Solange smiled again. This one was smaller and surprisingly sweet. She dropped her hand on her little sister's head. "You've done well, Rapunzel. You have gotten us here. You can come home now."

Rapunzel reeled back like Solange had hit her. "No," she breathed. She glanced sideways, where the archers had their arrows trained on the Snow Queen. Now Adelaide was shaking so badly that she couldn't keep hers on the bowstring.

I didn't believe it. The Snow Queen thought it was fun to smear her sister's name. I could see the lie in her suppressed glee.

But apparently not everyone could spot it.

"I knew it!" the Director said triumphantly, somewhere behind me. So much for getting her to safety. I hope Mom had managed to hide. "All of these years, I *knew* it."

The last of the goblins were retreating through the portal. Ripper chewed the charm off his cuff, and his whole wolf army vanished. Jimmy Searcaster stamped hard on the portal. Silver and purple sparks fizzled out of it, the spell destroyed. Then Jimmy pulled a ring as wide as a hula hoop out of his pocket. He slipped it on and left footprints the size of cars in his wake.

Everyone was gone except Solange and her giant blue bodyguard.

"I will never return to you," Rapunzel told her sister. "Even if I am welcome nowhere but among your followers, I will not come to you."

"Pity," said the Snow Queen, one eyebrow raised in a way that clearly said, *I'll believe it when I see it*. Then she turned to me. "Until we meet again."

She thrust two hands in the air. A cloud gathered, low and gray, and showered us with tiny glittery flakes. I flinched, sure that she had saved her most destructive magic for last, but it was only snow.

I looked again. Solange was gone. So was Likon.

They'd left the dragons and ice griffins behind for us to clean up.

A fine white powder collected on the battlefield. It fell onto my eyelashes and down the back of my shirt, making me shiver. It must have been enchanted to not melt. Some snow even began to collect on the embers of the dead *Draconus melodius*.

"I see," Rapunzel said, staring up at the sky. Then her eyes cut to me. "Winter."

This definitely counted. Cold coated my insides, too. Death came after the winter in the beginning of my Tale. Chase would never have let the witches walk out of the prison; he could be hurt. Dad had been with him. The way Lena had *screamed*. I needed to check on them. I strained against the bands of ice around my middle. "Get me out of this!"

"Rory, I'm here," said Mom, not hurt, just pale. One person safe. She smashed her hilt against the ice until it cracked.

I burst free and bolted. I didn't even pause when the Director pointed at Rapunzel and said, "Arrest her." We could sort that out later. Nobody here was in immediate danger.

The prisons were closer. The doorway had been reduced to rubble, now dusted with white flakes. Jimmy had clearly done a smash-and-grab.

I found Dad first. His shirt was streaked with soot, and an angry burn shone red on his arm. His face was grim but he was okay.

"Chase?" I gasped out, my heart plummeting down to my stomach, my toes, to the snow beginning to cover the frozen grass.

"He's fine," Dad said. "Well, the giant broke his arm. I got distracted for a second. He went that way with some others." He pointed toward the library.

Chase must have heard Lena too.

I didn't even feel my legs, sprinting down a side street, slipping on the snow, ducking through a skirmish between ten seventh graders and a leftover ice griffin. I could hear someone crying—big, wrenching wails. It sounded like Jenny.

Around the next corner, ax heads were buried in the library door. A clump of people had gathered beside it. Chase was with the triplets, his back to me. Mrs. LaMarelle was sitting on the ground, her head bent. I couldn't see Lena.

My feet crunched over the snow. Chase turned. His broken arm must have been hurting him, but that wasn't the kind of misery on his face. Something terrible must have happened, something we couldn't fix. He threw out his good hand. "Wait. Let them put a cloth down first. You don't need to see the damage."

I slowed to a walk. I shouldered through the others.

A yellow sheet covered Lena from chest to knees. Her face twisted with pain, her skin shining with sweat. Red bloomed on the fabric, soaking through in two places. She was losing too much blood.

Jenny knelt at her sister's side, crying. She held a short bit of rope out, but Lena squirmed away from it.

Their grandmother stroked Lena's forehead, brushing away the too-long braids so gently, but her voice was firm. "You have to let Jenny apply the tourniquet."

"I don't want it," Lena said, her voice shaking.

I didn't see what they needed a tourniquet for, and then, all of a sudden, I did. There, peeking out of the cloth near Lena's foot, was my friend's small palm and slender fingers, too far from her arm.

General Searcaster's voice. Her laugh. Lena's scream. The axes had been so sharp.

"I can be your hands." I hadn't noticed Melodie, held by the metal Fey dummy chauffeur. Golden tears slid down her nose. "I can be your hands, like the statue is my legs."

"Lena . . . ," I breathed.

Jenny looked up. She spotted me. "We need the Water of Life. *Now*."

But I'd given it up. I'd let Likon carry it off to the Arctic Circle. Rapunzel had told me to.

"No, *please*," Lena murmured. I wasn't sure she'd noticed how many people had gathered around us. "I should have guessed Searcaster would come. I threw the self-destruct switch, but it was too late. It was my fault—"

Mrs. LaMarelle turned away. She pressed a hand over her mouth.

Lena's lips were bleached and cracked, her eyes sunken, scared. She was dying. We couldn't save her.

"Rory, snap out of it," Jenny said. "The *Water*."

I shook my head.

Chase guessed the truth first. "It's gone. The Snow Queen got it."

No one spoke for a moment, and the silence stretched out. Even the sounds of the final skirmishes seemed to grow quieter.

Then Jenny said, not sounding very sure, "Then we tie the tourniquet. We get her to the hospital."

Mrs. LaMarelle shook her head. "Too much blood. Not enough time."

"We have to try *something*," Jenny told her grandmother. "We can't just let this happen."

A dozen metallic clatters disturbed the silence behind us. Rapunzel soared over the house where the Tree of Hope had fallen, riding her purple magic carpet through the smoke. It had a new rip down its middle. Trailing them were a dozen evil Fey dummies, looking like one of the giants had stepped on them. They lurched along with crushed feet, twisted knees, flattened heads, bent wings, and missing shoulders. Behind them, jogging to catch up, were the human Itari warriors.

"George!" Chase said. "Get over here!"

"Can't! The Director's orders!" George called back, irritated. He had no idea.

"It's Lena!" Chase said. Then George's jog turned into a sprint.

Rapunzel's carpet pulled up beside me. She stepped onto the ground. "I could not find Gretel. Someone needs to tell her to search under her bed for that which was lost."

I couldn't believe she thought any of us would leave Lena now. "I'll go later." My voice gave out on the last word. I didn't mean *later*. I meant *after*.

"Not you, and not later." Rapunzel turned to the triplets and pointed at Kevin and Conner. "You. Tell her those with the most dire wounds are beside the doors to Baltimore, the kitchen, and Atlantis."

Kevin and Conner looked at Chase, who nodded. They took off.

For once, I wasn't the one who understood her first. Hope blazed across Jenny's face. "The Water?"

"I only had time for one," Rapunzel said again. "I hope I made the right choice."

"You switched them," I said, understanding. "You let Solange think she had the Water."

Rapunzel nodded. "She would not leave unless she had what she sought."

Mrs. LaMarelle wasn't comforted. "Jenny, it won't come in time."

The blood had soaked through most of the sheet, and still, it spread, creeping out in a circle around Lena, dying the snow crimson.

Lena saw it. She squeezed her eyes shut. "I've read about this. You *do* get cold."

The crowd parted. George barreled through, so fast he would have fallen on his sister if Chase and Kyle hadn't steadied him. "Lena," he whispered. "God, no. *Lena*."

"Come and say good-bye." Mrs. LaMarelle's voice seemed to come from a different person, someone not losing her grand-daughter. Her face was so serene. "Saying good-bye is a gift. Not many people get it."

But I didn't *want* to say good-bye. Neither did George and Jenny. We wanted something in this big, complicated magical world to turn up and save her.

Rapunzel dropped her hand over my head. She waited until my eyes met hers.

"Rory, this was always my ending, and I have always known it. You did not fail to save us. This is my choice." I was taller than she was, but on her tiptoes, she still managed to kiss my forehead.

I was barely listening. Lena filled the corners of my mind, and nothing else processed. "I have to say good-bye."

"No. You need her more than you need me, and I can give her back to you." Rapunzel turned to the LaMarelles. They'd gathered around her so tightly they crowded everyone else out. "Excuse me. I must speak with Lena."

Jenny and George glared up at Rapunzel. Mrs. LaMarelle didn't bother to lift her head.

George started to push Rapunzel back, but Kyle dragged him away. Rapunzel knelt in the space he'd left behind, blood staining her skirt. She held something hidden in her hands.

"Lena's the new Rapunzel," Kyle told George, and then I understood.

The Canon's golden apple had saved Rapunzel's life once. Two hundred years later, she was passing on the favor.

"Lena, I can pin this token upon your person, but the spell will only transfer if we make a verbal agreement," Rapunzel said. "Do you take this gift and this burden?"

Lena struggled to swallow. "You're making me part of the Canon?"

"I am asking," Rapunzel said.

"Yes," Lena croaked.

As calm as you please, Rapunzel reached under the sodden cloth. Her fingers moved, sliding the golden apple onto Lena's clothes. But what she was giving away had kept her alive for hundreds of years, longer than her natural life span. When she let go, she would be gone. Forever gone, and her prophecies would go with her, and her advice, and her kindness.

"But—" I had to say something. At this point, words were all I had left. "I need you both."

Rapunzel looked up, and the smile she gave me was real and warm. "No. I needed you. We cannot choose our family in this life, but if I could have chosen myself a sister, it would have been you."

And before I could answer, she let go. In a heartbeat, she turned translucent—a soft pretty gray pearly dust, exactly the same shade her hair had been. For an instant, it still held Rapunzel's shape.

A dry sob ripped out of my throat.

Then the dust began to blow away, swirling across the courtyard in a stream of silver, mixing with the falling snow.

Lena kicked the sheet away, not even looking at the blood. Her lips were pink again, her eyes bright. She sat up. She looked at her hands. Gold covered the left one up to the wrist and the right one halfway to the elbow, like a pair of mismatched metallic gloves.

"Just like Madame Benne," whispered Melodie, awed.

Mrs. LaMarelle grabbed one of the new hands, and Lena promptly burst into tears.

14

y eyes burned, but I didn't cry.

A second grief doesn't cancel out the first. It just scoops a bigger chunk from your insides. Losing Hansel had hallowed out a vast cavern, echoing and empty. Losing Rapunzel cut even farther, piercing the heart of my world, a hole so deep and so dark I couldn't imagine that it had an end.

But Lena was okay. I clung to that thought. It was the only thing keeping me from falling apart completely.

Rumpelstiltskin ran toward us, his plaid blazer singed. He carried an enormous book over his shoulder, and it knocked into people as he shoved through the crowd.

He didn't stop until he saw Lena and her golden hands. Then his whole body sagged with relief. His favorite student was safe. "So it's true, then. You have one of the double Tales." He opened the blue book and read, straining to hold it up without a table supporting its weight. "'The Rapunzel Without Hands.'"

Wow, I thought leadenly. The magic around me was working overtime today.

"That's creepy," said George. Jenny smacked his arm.

Lena stared at her golden palms. "And the apple still let me into the Canon? Even though my Tale is contaminated?"

"Not *contaminated*, just combined," Rumpelstiltskin said. "'The Maiden Without Hands' is another Grimm Tale. Two other Tales fused this spring—'The Pied Piper' and 'The Snow Queen.' You can see it here in the book."

At first I thought the library had just automatically started a new volume of tales when the other one was stolen. But this book was bound in blue leather, the edges of its paper gilded, almost identical to the one I'd seen the goblin carrying through the portal. My voice was hoarse, like I'd actually been screaming instead of just wishing that I could. "You switched the current volume for one of the older ones."

Melodie nodded. "Lena and I held them off while Rumpel hid it."

"I didn't even think about the maps." Lena wiped her tear-streaked face on her shoulder, like she was trying not to use her new hands.

"She got the *maps*?" Chase said.

"The maps and the volume of Tales from Summer 1990 are gone forever, I fear," Rumpelstiltskin said mournfully.

But keeping the current volume was good news. It should have made me glad, like Lena being alive should have, but that got smothered by the unfathomable emptiness. Rapunzel was gone.

"Where is Rapunzel?" cried a voice so cold that I was sure for a second that Solange had come back, but it was the Director. Sarah Thumb flew up behind her. Mr. Swallow was missing a few tail feathers. His clumsy flight was zigzaggy, but he still managed to land on the Director's shoulder. "Where is the traitor?"

I couldn't even muster up the energy to argue. I'd said it all before. The Director never listened to me anyway.

But this time, it wasn't me who piped up.

"She's dead," said Jenny.

Rapunzel would have loved to see the Director's face then. Shocked, then baffled, then hastily stern as she backtracked. "It does not clear her. Someone gave the Snow Queen the means to enter this place. Our fortress held for the entirety of the last war. Someone must have aided the invasion. What Rapunzel did—"

"Was save my grandbaby," interrupted Mrs. LaMarelle, like her word was final.

"They had to get in *somehow*," the Director insisted.

"There's an easy way to figure it out." Lena climbed to her feet and swayed, still woozy. Her grandmother clamped her hands on Lena's shoulders, holding her up. "A simple scrying spell could find the item the Snow Queen used to make the portal. All you have to do is—"

The wreckage around the portal shuddered. We all jumped. Chase and a few others drew their swords again.

But something else zoomed out of the rubble. Glinting, it whistled through the air and landed on Lena's outstretched palm with a clink. A coin, tarnished on one side and as gold as Lena's new hands on the other.

"Oh my gumdrops." Horrified, Lena looked at me, but I didn't know how magic could happen without anyone casting a spell.

Melodie did. "You're a sorcerer now!"

"Gretel has never cast a scrying spell just by thinking it before," said Sarah Thumb.

"You must be more powerful," Melodie told her mistress.

Miriam frowned at the object resting in Lena's hand. "Isn't that a wishing coin?"

I'd forgotten about those. The day after we'd returned from the Snow Queen's palace, the elves had confirmed the coins were embedded with recharge capabilities that tapped directly into the

Snow Queen's own magic. So much had happened since then.

"Didn't the elves gather all those and toss them to the bottom of the ocean?" asked Chase.

They obviously missed one.

"If you wished on this coin enough, if it kept recharging, the link between it and the Snow Queen would get stronger," Lena said slowly. "It could turn into the receiving end of a portal, just like the letter in Matilda Searcaster's desk during my Tale up the beanstalk."

"I am uninterested in how the magic was performed," said the Director. "I am only interested in who planted this coin here. Create a scrying spell for that."

Trust the Director to start commanding Lena to use a new power we'd just found out about two minutes ago.

Lena straightened up and opened her mouth, already distressed, but Melodie raised her hand, obviously eager to help her mistress any way she could. "I can! Well, as long as nobody has destroyed the scrying spell ingredients from the workshop."

"Hold on. We need to get this out of here." Chase pointed at the coin in Lena's hand, careful not to touch it. "It's still *active*. The Snow Queen is still listening."

A hush fell over the crowd.

Solange knew her sister was dead. She knew Lena was alive. She knew Lena was a *sorceress*. Had she gotten anything else?

"I'll take it." Golden face grim, Melodie picked up the coin and gestured to the workshop. Her metal fairy chauffeur lumbered off, clumsier than usual. Some enemy blade had chopped off half its foot.

So much damage. I'd fought as hard as I could, and nobody had come out of this intact.

Once the door to the workshop closed safely behind Melodie,

the hush broke. The Director did what she did best. She issued orders. "Send Jack to inspect the dungeons. We'll need somewhere to hold the villains in the training courts, and the traitor as well."

We needed to *find* the traitor first, but my mind couldn't hold on to that thought. One spy didn't feel as important as Rapunzel's death and the Snow Queen getting what she'd wanted.

Chase thought so too. "All that is just cleanup," he told the Director impatiently. "You can do it later. We need to figure out a plan. The Snow Queen got the maps."

He made it sound like it was a huge catastrophe, but considering all the destruction around us, lost maps seemed pretty minor.

But Lena acted as nervous as Chase. "What would the Snow Queen want with . . . ?"

"Think about it," Chase said. "What was *on* those maps?"

"Just the locations of all the known portals between the human world and the Arctic Circle," Lena said. "But it wouldn't help her kill Characters. We all live here now. It wouldn't help her unless she planned to—"

"—invade the human world," Chase finished.

Of course. What had happened here could happen everywhere.

"I can see why you waited until the wishing coin was gone before mentioning this to us," the Director said, arms crossed. "Solange would laugh to hear such a ludicrous theory."

"It's not a theory," Chase said. "She always said she would take back the lands the humans stole and return them to their rightful owners. After tonight, she'll be even stronger than before. When she has her army together, her forces will march on DC, Ottawa, and Mexico City, but she has assigned a task force to every major city on those maps. Getting the witches back was part of the Snow Queen's plan too. She has a spell that can stop all human machinery in a mile radius. Guns, tanks, fighter jets—it doesn't matter. They're useless with this enchantment, and now she has the witches to cast it for her. After she controls this continent, she'll go after the rest. The humans won't know what hit them."

So this was what would happen if I didn't stop the Snow Queen. Forget the fate of magic. The fate of the world depended on whether or not I failed my Tale.

"It's a possibility," the Director admitted, "but you can't *know*—"

"He can," I said. Chase had known about the invasion as soon as he woke up. He'd known exactly what Solange was after. He'd been right about all of it, and now he had time to explain how. "What haven't you told us, Chase?"

"Did you dream when you were under the Sleeping Beauty curse?" Chase asked the Director.

She frowned. "Did you?"

"I dreamed I was in the Snow Queen's war council," Chase said. "I dreamed I was hovering right over the room, listening to all their plans, and the last thing I heard before the questers woke me up was the Snow Queen telling General Searcaster to begin the invasion of EAS's North American chapter."

This time, they believed him.

"The sleeping enchantment backfired," Lena told Chase, her voice barely a whisper. "It was only meant for human Characters, and you're half Fey."

"Nice to go behind enemy lines when you're having a nightmare," Chase said bitterly.

"We need to contact the other chapters," Sarah Thumb said, panicked. "We need to convince them that they're next if they don't help. Oh my God. Should we even be talking about this here? We still don't know who planted that coin. They could be listening right now, waiting to report everything—"

"No," Chase said in his *Do you think I'm an idiot?* voice. "The Snow Queen called it a sweetened deal—she said she got the end of the portal and a way to hurt the Triumvirate, all in one clueless little idiot. Whoever had that coin had no idea."

"It . . . ," came a choked voice near the back.

The crowd shuffled to the side so we could see our accidental traitor.

Adelaide's cheeks were sticky with tears. Her blond hair had matted to them. "It was me," she said, and hiccuped.

She looked so pale and stricken. She really hadn't known.

"We *took* your coin," Sarah Thumb said, scowling at Adelaide. "I processed the paperwork myself."

"The coin I gave you wasn't real." Adelaide hiccuped again. "I mean, it might have been, but it wasn't the one Chase gave me. When the elves came for it, I wished I didn't have to give it back. A second coin appeared. It looked exactly the same as the first. That's what I gave you."

"What did you *wish* for?" Chase said coldly.

Adelaide choked back a sob. "I'm so sorry. I really am."

I was missing something.

"You just forgot about me when you started hanging out with Rory," Adelaide told Chase. "I thought if we just spent more time together, if we dated, you might—" She sobbed for real, and Chase recoiled, disgust all over his face.

"Oh my gumdrops," Lena whispered, glancing at me.

Chase turned my way too. His stare was so hard and furious that it pierced through my numbness. "I *told* you something was wrong with me."

Oh no. Chase never remembered asking her out. He didn't

know how he'd gotten to dinner with her parents. He'd said she had power over him.

Adelaide had wished Chase was her boyfriend. She wished that he would come with her on whatever stupid outing she thought up. She'd wished it over and over again. None of this had been Chase's fault.

My mouth fell open, but nothing came out. "Sorry" didn't seem to cover it. He had come to me for help, and I had been too angry to even listen to him.

"Take her away," said the Director quietly. "Her apartment will be fine until her parents come for her."

Mangled metal dummies stepped up alongside Adelaide now. She didn't put up a fight. She walked away between them, still weeping.

Such a stupid thing to cause the fall of Ever After School—one stupid crush from one stupid, lonely girl.

The Director turned to Chase. "Come to my office. We need to go over everything you may have heard in your dream."

"Sure, let's chat. It's not like I need the sleep," Chase said.

A few smirks flickered on our friends' faces.

But they didn't know Chase the way I did. They didn't notice the disappointment that shuttered his face. They didn't realize what it cost him—to wish for so long for a Tale, and to finally get this one.

He didn't even glance at me when the Director led him away. Lena was right. A first kiss could change everything, but not always for the better. Chase might not have minded having one in his Tale, but he'd definitely wanted to be the one doing the kissing. He'd wanted to be the one who'd pulled off the daring rescue.

The crowd thinned. Everyone else was leaving too.

"We need scouts at the portals," Sarah Thumb said, flying after the Director. "We'll need to know when she moves again, so we can sound the alarm."

Rumpelstiltskin followed them, carrying away the current volume. "But do we remember where the portals are?"

Jenny and George helped Lena step forward. "I know where the portals are," Lena said, sounding woozy. "I have to tell Rumpel. I saw all the maps when I was searching for the one to the Arctic Circle."

Her photographic memory. It saved us again.

But her grandmother didn't want to hear about it. "Shh, we'll take care of it. Let's just get you home first."

Limping toward her house, Lena didn't look back, and I couldn't speak.

It was so much worse that the last attack on EAS, when the Snow Queen had poisoned the Fey fudge pies at the feast. We had all pulled together then. We hadn't left each other until we figured out a solution.

This time, we just melted into our homes and tended to our own wounds. If the Snow Queen struck again, if she attacked the human world right *then*, I didn't think we could organize ourselves enough to fight. That was exactly what Solange wanted.

"Rory?" I felt a hand on my shoulder. Mom's worry was plastered all over her face. Beyond her were Amy and, all in a cluster, Dad, Brie, and Dani. Their expressions matched Mom's.

"It'll be okay, sweetie," Mom said, hugging me, but I didn't see how.

Mom sent me to bed early that evening. I didn't think I could sleep with the threat of another invasion looming over us, but I'd underestimated how exhausted I was.

When I fell asleep, the door flooded my dreams again, all the details in place. The ancient black wood, the grain etched with frost. The Snow Queen's symbol—a swirl of silver—over the doorknob. My breath hanging in the air, a tiny white cloud, deep within the bowels of Solange's palace.

This time, though, it wasn't the cold that bothered me, or the mystery of what was on the other side of the door, or even the burden of the world's fate on my shoulders.

It was knowing I had to face the end of my Tale, and I had to face it alone. No one would help me. The Snow Queen had taken everyone from me.

I woke up, shouting. Panic throbbed in my chest.

I needed to find that door. We were running out of time. But the Snow Queen was waiting for me by now. I could die trying to get through it, and I still had no idea what was on the other side.

Mom must have heard me yell. She came in, sat on my bed, and put her arms around me.

I curled into her. My whole body was shaking, and my tongue felt clumsy. "I don't know what to do. I don't know how to fix it."

She didn't say I was too young to be putting so much pressure on myself. She didn't tell me I should let the grown-ups handle it. She knew better now.

The only grown-up who might have known what to do was gone. She couldn't help me anymore.

"No one knows how to fix everything," Mom whispered. "We can only keep moving in the right direction. You just need to figure out what the next step is."

I had to figure out what was behind that door. That was the next step.

Amy woke me up the next morning. "You have a visitor." She was in her pajamas, so whoever had come to the door had woken her up too.

It all came to me in a flash. The portals. The Snow Queen. I rolled out of bed and barreled out of my bedroom, snatching up the sword and belt hanging from my doorknob. Mom must have returned it the night before without me noticing.

But it wasn't an emergency. Adelaide sat on our couch in a pretty yellow dress, her long hair hanging in a perfectly smooth blond curtain. Her eyes were as huge as Lena's and very puffy, like she'd cried most of the night.

"Um," I said, wondering if I was still dreaming. An evil fairy dummy and a witch dummy waited beside the door. Her guards.

"I'm leaving," she said. "This morning, before everyone's up. I'm not allowed to come back."

I glanced at Mom and Amy, who were standing in the kitchen. They looked confused too. "Okay . . . ," I said.

"I know I got off easy. My parents made a deal with the Canon," Adelaide said in a rush, like she expected me to interrupt her. "I'll be traveling to the other chapters and telling them what happened here. That was my idea. I want to tell them how they could be next. I want to convince them to fight for us. It would be nice to do something that's actually helpful," she added with her usual sarcasm.

"Adelaide, why are you *here*?" I said.

For the first time, she looked lost. "None of the others would listen to me, and you're the only one Chase listens to."

I had every right to throw her out. Even if I set aside everything she'd done this summer, she'd never been nice to me. I didn't owe her anything.

"Where are your *parents*?" Mom said, like she couldn't believe Adelaide was alone.

"They're waiting for me at the European Chapter of Ever After School," Adelaide said dismissively, but the corners of her mouth turned down. They hadn't come for her, and she'd wanted them to.

No wonder she'd always liked Chase. They had so much in common.

I pitied her. She'd convinced me to kiss Chase and break his enchantment as soon as she realized she couldn't. She was one of the last pieces of Rapunzel left in the world. So I sat down. I waited for whatever she'd come to say.

Adelaide clasped her hands tightly in front of her, trying hard to hide her trembling. Before yesterday, I hadn't realized she did that too. "I knew it was wrong to use the coin on Chase, but I thought it would be okay in the end." I bet she had thought if they were together for a while, Chase would eventually start to like her back. "I wanted him to like me so much. I didn't care how it happened. I didn't think too hard about the coin. But he got hurt. So many people got hurt." She wasn't crying, but she was close. "I'm so sorry. I won't ever stop being sorry, for the rest of my life."

This was what made the Snow Queen so terrible. She found out what you wanted most, and she used it against you.

Adelaide did care about Chase. That had never been the problem. It was that she wanted to be with him more than anything else, even more than she wanted Chase to be happy. That was probably how the Snow Queen had cared for Rapunzel, too. Maybe it ran in the family.

The bells clanged. We were pretty far from the courtyard, so someone had to be ringing them as hard as they could. And they just kept ringing.

The alarm. The second invasion.

"It wasn't me this time, I swear!" Adelaide said, but I didn't waste any more time on her.

The Snow Queen was coming for the human world. She would attack while we were still reeling from the last battle, before we could figure out how to stop her. That must have been her plan all along.

I didn't bother putting on real clothes. Or even shoes. I just grabbed my sword again, threw open the door, and burst out of the apartment. I flew down the hall, dodging the few people brave enough to venture out of their homes.

The courtyard was still dark. I stumbled in the snow, which had definitely not melted overnight. My toes immediately ached with cold. I searched the courtyard for the problem. The men on duty had thrust their spears in the faces of the intruders—a bunch of short, stout men with huge beards—but they weren't attacking. Their arms were crossed over their chests, with their hands clapped on their own shoulders. Their lances and axes lay at their feet. They didn't look too pleased with the welcome wagon, either. At least they were dressed for the snow. They all wore skins.

The two shortest ones had capes of white fur. Like the skin of a polar bear.

Oh.

"It's okay! Stand down," I told the guards quickly. I hurried through the snow, which clung to my pajama bottoms, and I swept a curtsy, trying not to wobble. "Welcome, Prince Ignatius and Princess Imelda of the Living Stone Dwarves."

"They would probably feel more welcome if you didn't use their full names." Forrel smiled at me from the back of the group. He had a beard now, with gray threaded through it. He looked like he hadn't slept a day since April.

"Yes, and no bowing, please. We're past that, I think," said Princess Ima, sounding a lot like her big sister. Her brother hastily straightened out of *his* bow.

"Hopefully, we aren't past explanations," said the Director, emerging from the orange door. She hadn't stopped long enough for full armor either. Just her rose-engraved shield.

"Do we need one?" asked Princess Ima.

"The Frog Prince sent us word. If we extend our alliance, the bearer of the Unwritten Tale will help us reclaim our homeland," said Iggy, and every dwarf head swiveled to me.

That Canon meeting had been *ages* ago. "I can only *help*. I can't guarantee anything." I couldn't even be sure I would live through the next few days.

"We do not need guarantees," said the prince. "Help is more than the dwarves have ever had from the Canon."

Ima rolled her eyes. "What he really means is we've been itching for an excuse to join you Characters, and the message Forrel got helped us convince our father."

"Does the offer still stand?" Forrel asked the Director.

"Of course it stands," said the Director. "However, I would like to speak with Henry myself and find out why he didn't mention he could send a message to you. He told me he didn't know where you were."

"I would like to meet the Frog Prince," said Forrel. "He knew my father."

Everyone's attention was on the Director and the dwarves. No one else noticed the blond girl walking between two metal dummies toward the cobalt blue door. Before she stepped into the European chapter of EAS, she turned back to look at me.

Her face didn't say *sorry*. It was too fierce. It said, *You better take care of him, Rory.*

I nodded once, very slowly. Adelaide nodded back and let the guards escort her through the door.

The sun rose and failed to melt the snow. The emptiness Hansel and Rapunzel's deaths had caused yawned even wider. I tried not to let myself get angry, like I had the day before. Instead, work kept me numb.

The entire morning was full of new allies. I ran home to put on some boots and armor, and then helped them settle in. The dwarf twins ducked back into Muirland to tell their dad the alliance was on, and by the time they got back—with practically a whole city of dwarves for us to house—King Oberon had also arrived with his knights. The Seelie still couldn't fight, but they promised to join the second their prince and queen were freed. More and more Fey trickled in through the Atlantis and Avalon doors. A small convoy from the Gnomes of Shining Waters showed up, asking if we would promise to help them resettle secretly in their lost lands just like we were helping the Dwarves of Living Stone. Then some red caps came with the same request.

Eventually, the courtyard bustled with other Characters trying to pitch in wherever they could. Every time I emerged from the apartments to guide more allies to their rooms, I ran into someone with news.

Hurrying toward the infirmary with more bandages, Jenny told me Gretel had found the Water of Life under her bed, at her home in Cleveland. It was in huge jugs, with a note from Rapunzel, explaining how she had switched them. "Rapunzel saved a lot of lives last night," she added softly.

When I was helping a gnome as old and gnarled as the mother of the four Winds with her pack, Sarah Thumb flew by. "It took us a while to get past Mrs. Lamarelle, but Lena helped Rumpel redraw the maps last night. We have an eleventh grader and a twelfth grader posted at every major portal. We'll know the second the Snow Queen decides to strike."

Ellie couldn't bear to tell me her news. She just let me read the list of the deceased before she took it to the Director. Besides Rapunzel, we lost one Fey knight, two elves, a dozen adult Characters, a dozen and a half parents, and five kid Characters. One of them was Kenneth. He got flamed protecting some fourth graders from three dragons. The chasm inside me grew a little wider.

My voice came out steady, but it didn't sound like mine. It was too flat. "Anything else?"

I expected Ellie to tell me about a few more grisly injuries, but what she said was even worse. "The Seelie Fey told the Director that the other witch clans joined the Snow Queen. Rescuing the Wolfsbane clan won them over. According to Chase, the Snow Queen ordered them to cast the technology-stopping spell *and* this one." She pointed at the snow crunching under foot.

Ugh. The spell that turned summer into winter. She *loved* that spell. "Thanks, Ellie."

She nodded grimly and swerved around a squadron of dwarves, and I went to look for Chase. I'd seen him around, helping out, but we hadn't spoken. Even after this summer, it was weird hearing what he thought from other people, instead of hearing from Chase himself.

I spotted him beside the brick house where General Searcaster had dropped the Tree of Hope. He was speaking to the Director and some Fey refugees, a bedraggled family with two very young children still in diapers. He spoke to most of the Fey, even though only the knights who wanted to learn Itari sought him out. I could tell even from far away that something was wrong with him. It wasn't the injury. Gretel had spared some of the Water to heal his broken arm. The Director had wanted him in fighting shape. This went deeper than the wishing coin's enchantment, and at first, I couldn't figure it out. He was totally polite and courteous. The Fey family never bristled at him. The Director never yelled at him. That wasn't normal, but that wasn't the worst of it either. His face was completely blank when he spoke, just as still and controlled as it had been during the quest through Atlantis.

I kept watching him, even after the Fey and the Director left.

He looked *empty*, but not the grief-hollowed kind. All his Chaseness was gone, as if he'd never really woken up from the sleeping spell. He was just going through the motions, acting like the perfect little Fey-human ambassador and unwilling spy the Director wanted him to be. It hurt me to watch him be less than he was.

He could have handled one of them. I was sure of that. If he'd *just* been enchanted by Adelaide's wishing coin, or he'd *just* gotten a disappointing wait-to-be-rescued Tale, or if he'd actually managed to turn the battle around, he would have shrugged it off and kept going. But all three at once was too much.

I started toward him. I didn't know what I'd say, but I needed to talk to him.

He noticed me walking across the courtyard. He stared at me with that terrible, empty face. Then he turned and walked in the opposite direction.

I didn't follow.

That afternoon, a small crowd gathered near the Tree of Hope. Last time I had seen the Tree, it had still been on the roof of that brick house. If it was back in the ground, someone must have moved it. They must have also reattached the roots, because it stood as straight and tall as it had before the invasion.

I didn't see why everyone seemed so pleased about it. The Tree looked awful. Soot blackened its trunk. Very few branches still snaked down to the ground and then back to the sky. Most of them had fallen off. Many had been charred. Only two limbs had any green leaves left on them, and even those drooped, wilted and unhealthy.

I skimmed the area for anyone who might have answers, and I spotted two elves standing beside a clump of excited sixth graders. I threaded my way through the crowd.

Rufus was clearly thrilled about the poor broken Tree, and a few steps later, I could hear what he was saying. ". . . already impressive as a magician. But to lose her hands . . ." He whistled. "Once she learns how to control all that magic, she'll be unstoppable. She's probably almost as powerful as the Snow Queen."

"But there's no time for her to learn control," said Kefmin mournfully. "Gretel asked Lena to *move* the Tree, not put it back where it was. Do you think the Triumvirate has any chance—"

They noticed me. Kefmin gawked, clearly shocked that he'd been caught talking about us.

But I couldn't care less. I was too focused on the other thing he'd said. "*Lena* did this?"

Rufus nodded. "The Director wanted to get it off the roof. She asked us"—he pointed to himself and Kefmin—"to start chopping it up and hauling it away. She said she wanted the reminder of last night out of the courtyard."

That sounded like the Director. "And she thought she should put a new sorceress to work right away?" I said, a little ticked off.

"We cleared the area," said Kefmin, mildly offended. "In case Lena lost control and dropped it on someone."

Control and aim weren't the problem. Lena has always liked to challenge herself.

"Lena didn't even need Gretel to teach her," said Rufus proudly. "She knows all these spells. She has been a magician for years. She said, 'Up, Tree' and the Tree sailed up."

"And that's where it landed," said Kefmin, a lot less excited. "She passed out approximately six seconds after that."

"She's fine. She just used too much magic," Rufus explained, seeing my face and the panic that must have blazed across it. "The Director sent her back to bed to sleep it off."

I was already backing away. The Tree forgotten, refugees suddenly unimportant, I sprinted over to her house and up her steps, throwing myself at the knocker.

Mrs. LaMarelle answered the door with a smile. She wouldn't have been so cheerful if Lena wasn't okay. A little bit of my panic eased. "You too? Nothing like a fainting spell after a close call to bring friends running. Don't wear her out, you hear me? Ten minutes is all you get. Otherwise I'll need to steal some more Water to revive Lena."

I recognized Chase's voice from all the way down the stairs, and I heard Kyle's when I reached the second floor.

I couldn't hear what they were saying, but I didn't need to. The second I opened the door, they all went quiet. For one split second, Lena looked as trapped and terrified as she had when we'd gotten stuck in the Searcasters' bread box during her Tale. Kyle's face clearly said, *How much did she overhear?*

Chase didn't even turn my way.

They'd been talking about me.

"Hey," I said. A solid opener.

"I'm really feeling much better," Lena said. She was in bed, her new hands resting on top of the covers.

Maybe I should have just scuttled back out and let them finish their conversation. Maybe I should have—

But Chase pushed himself off the wall. "Kyle, we gotta go take care of that thing." Wow. He didn't even want me to know what he was working on. He slipped out the door, staring over my head, sending the *I need my space* signals loud and clear.

Kyle loped after him, obviously feeling as awkward as I was. He paused in the doorway just long enough to smile at Lena. "See ya."

"Have you talked to him yet?" Lena said the second we heard the front door open. I didn't answer. I wasn't sure I had to. Chase clearly didn't want to speak with me. "You *have* to talk to each other."

"It's you I came to see," I said lightly. I couldn't force him to do anything. That was what Adelaide had done.

"It's what the Snow Queen wanted. She wanted to weaken the Triumvirate—she wanted . . ." Lena stared down at her lap, at her golden fingers.

The Snow Queen and General Searcaster had wanted to kill her.

"Did you get your letter yet?" Lena suddenly asked. I stared at her, wondering why she wanted to talk about random mail at a time like this.

"From Rapunzel," Lena added.

"Rapunzel left *letters*?" I said.

If she'd left me one, it would tell me what I needed to do to defeat the Snow Queen. It would tell me what was behind the door in my dreams.

"Melodie found mine when she went back to the workshop for supplies." Lena nodded at her nightstand. An envelope rested there, and Lena's name curled across its front. Rapunzel's handwriting was old-fashioned, full of loops and whirls and flourishes no one bothered with anymore. When she'd learned to write, alone in her tower, she'd had a lot of extra time to kill. "Chase and Sarah Thumb found theirs shoved under their front doors. Henry found his tied to his cane with a silver ribbon. The Director's was actually in the pocket of the dress she put on this morning. Apparently, that upset her, but I think it's kind of funny." She looked at me expectantly.

"I didn't find one." I wondered *why*. The other letters had been easily discovered.

"You can read mine if you want. She says the tower belongs to me now," Lena explained, before I even asked. "She says I can use it as my very own workshop. She . . . she said she knows how difficult the choice was—whether to become the new Rapunzel or to let yourself die." Lena's voice quivered a little. Without thinking, I reached out and touched the back of her hand. The metal was as warm as her skin used to be. "She said it might be even harder for me, because I have to deal with becoming a sorceress, too. She said she at least had a little warning. . . ."

I was suddenly desperate to cheer her up. I would do anything.

Lena added, "She said you would probably lend me the light she gave you. Examining it might make a good distraction."

I had it with me. Actually, I had my entire carryall. I wanted to be prepared whenever the Snow Queen struck. I unzipped the front pocket, slid the glass vial out, and wrapped Lena's hand around it.

When I let go, she only barely managed to snag its chain before it crashed to the floor. "Thanks. Sorry," she added. "These hands take some getting used to." She set the glass vial on the table with extra concentration.

We were quiet for a moment. I was wondering if it would be totally insensitive for me to tell her about Adelaide's visit, considering everything she'd just been through, but then she said, "Kyle kissed me."

I had *not* been expecting that. "What? Just now?"

"Before Chase came in." Lena's eyes filled with tears. I hadn't expected *that* reaction either. "He came to see me, and he took my hand, and he told me how awful it was, to see me like that, so hurt, and to not be able to do anything about it. Then he kissed me."

It was her first kiss too. Hers was so simple, so nice, so free of wishing-coin girlfriends and sleeping enchantments and the Snow Queen's traps. I'd seen the look Kyle had given her from the doorway. She knew where she stood with him.

Lena lifted her hands from the covers. Her golden palms caught the sunlight through her window. For a second they seemed to glow. "And the whole time, I kept thinking about how I'll never feel him holding my hand."

"Oh, *Lena*," I breathed. It was such a minor detail in *The Livves & Tymes of Sorcerers & Sorceresses*. I'd completely forgotten it. When magic regrew a limb, it didn't usually grow back the nerve endings.

"I'm happy to be alive. I can't ever repay Rapunzel for saving me." Tears spilled down her cheeks. "But you never realize how much you feel around for stuff until you *can't* anymore. I almost broke my glasses this morning, searching my nightstand for them. And being part of the Canon? Well, I never thought I would get stuck looking fourteen for the rest of my life. I already look a little young for my age. I'm going to be such a freak."

I didn't take her hand—I knew she wouldn't feel it. I squeezed her shoulder.

So much for a simple kiss. Sometimes I was a terrible friend.

"Plus, solid-gold hands are *heavy*. My arms are so sore, and it's not like I can put them down for a rest." Lena sat up and wiped her face on her shoulder. "I really don't want to go to tonight's Canon meeting." I resisted the urge to ask if she was serious. A meeting with all its boring reports and all the Director's sniping seemed like the last thing EAS needed. "They want me to swear a Binding Oath. The Director is going to order me to make stuff, more and more and more, and I'll never ever leave the workshop, and I'll know everything I create is out there, destroying—"

"Whoa. Hold on," I said before she picked up steam again. "You don't have to let the Director boss you around. The last Rapunzel—" A lump clogged my throat. I swallowed it. "Well, she wasn't super obedient. She ignored the Director and did her own thing all the time. Change the Binding Oath. Say that you'll do what is in the best interest of the Characters the Canon serves."

Lena pressed her lips together. "I'm sorry about Rapunzel, Rory," she said, and in my chest, in the great hole Hansel and Rapunzel's death had left, I felt how much she meant it.

I couldn't talk about Rapunzel yet, even with Lena. We couldn't both break down. "I'm glad you're okay."

Footsteps thumped on the stairs. Lena's grandmother was coming to tell me my ten minutes were up.

I stood. "Lena, you're the best magical inventor the world has seen in centuries. Melodie thinks you could be even better than Madame Benne. If *anyone* can figure out a way to replace those golden hands with real ones, it's you."

Lena looked at me before her gran opened the door and her face was better than the Tree of Hope returned to its usual spot. Her inventing spark was back.

I went back to my apartment and searched everywhere for my letter. I dumped out my carryall and every drawer in my room and every cabinet in our tiny apartment. I checked under beds and mattresses, beneath plates and between books. I even checked all of my pockets.

I couldn't find it.

"Maybe you're not *meant* to find it yet," said Amy, watching me throw my clothes against the wall in frustration. She didn't say anything about the mess I was making, but I knew my sympathy pass would run out soon.

"Maybe she didn't write me one," I said, trying not to sound resentful. "Maybe she told me everything she needed to say in person. She did talk to me the most, at the end."

But I didn't believe that. It had to be *somewhere*, and in it, Rapunzel would tell me how to stop the Snow Queen.

"I'll help you look until Maggie and I have to go," Amy said, feeling under the sofa cushions for the letter. "There's a sort of town hall thing happening before the Canon meets."

Wow, it was like Ever After School had completely forgotten an invasion could hit the human world any minute. "Well, that is a colossal waste of time."

Amy shot me a sharp glance over the couch. "You better hope not. Half the families are thinking about leaving. It's obviously not safe here, like we thought. Your parents are going to try to talk them out of it."

"Oh," I said in a small voice. I'd been so busy worrying about the dwarves and the gnomes this morning, I'd never thought about how the humans might feel.

Mom glided out of her bedroom. On her, armor looked like just another costume. Parents weren't supposed to join the actual battle again, but after yesterday, she wasn't taking any chances.

"Your father and I decided that you'll babysit Danica while we're in the meeting," she told me cheerfully.

The phrase "your father and I decided" kind of threw me. I couldn't remember the last time I'd heard her say it. Then I realized what she'd said. "No *way*. I won't do anything while you're gone, but I have to find this letter."

"You can take the baby with you for that," Mom said, smiling in that steely way that meant she refused to argue about this.

"But what if the *invasion* starts?" I said. "I can't take my baby sister into battle."

"Exactly," Amy said, tossing a few more throw pillows on the floor. "Rory, you say you won't do anything dangerous while we're gone, but the only way we'll know for *sure* is if we put you in charge of someone tiny and helpless. You wouldn't leave Dani."

Mom scowled at Amy. So it was true. I didn't know if I should be pleased my parents were working together or upset that they were ganging up on me.

"What?" Amy said, suddenly awkward. "Was I not supposed to tell her? She was just going to keep arguing."

"No, I'm glad you said something. Arguing really would have

been a waste of time," I said, and Amy laughed, even though I hadn't meant for it to be funny.

I showed up at Dad and Brie's apartment five minutes before the meeting.

"Good! You're here!" Brie plunked Dani in my arms before I even stepped inside. Then she walked back into the apartment and opened the hall closet. I stared from her to the baby, almost afraid to move. I'd never held Dani without someone watching us before. I wanted a chaperone who could swoop in if it looked like I might drop her. I tucked her against my shoulder, one hand over her head and one over her diaper, like I'd seen Brie and Dad do a thousand times.

Then the baby sucked in a huge breath and let it whoosh out, sleepy and content. The fear fizzled out.

Actually, for the first time all day, I didn't feel empty. Or even terrible.

This was probably what they meant by "heartwarming." Maybe the Snow Queen should try this.

I immediately sobered. Maybe she had. Maybe that was why she had kidnapped Rapunzel.

"Are you *sure* this is okay?" I asked my stepmother.

Brie didn't bother looking up. She just kept digging through her closet. "You're her big sister! That's the best kind of babysitter there is."

"Free?" I said.

"Family. You love her just as much as we love her. You won't let anything happen to her," Brie said. "Diaper bag is beside your dad's desk. You should be all set. If you have any trouble, call us on our M3's. I'll come right away."

Diapers. I'd *never* changed one. I edged away from the designer bag, covered in a print of rubber duckies, hoping I wouldn't need it.

"The harp lady dropped that off earlier. Looks kind of important." Brie pointed to the table. Rapunzel's glass vial stood there, and I was surprised at how happy I was to see it again. I drifted over and glanced at the note sitting under it.

Sorry I couldn't drop it off myself! Gran wouldn't let me do "unnecessary errands." She says it's pretty, though. She's strongly hinting that she would like a chandelier of these vials for her birthday. I'll make sure it's from both of us.—Lena

Brie stuffed one arm in the sleeve of her hoodie. "Oh my God— is that really the time? ERIC! We're supposed to be there in three minutes!"

Dani heard her mother shouting. Her eyes opened and swiveled up to mine in a way that clearly said, *Should I be worried?* I stroked her back.

"Brie, did you say something?" my dad called. "Can't hear you with the shower running."

My stepmother sighed and headed for the bathroom. "I love your father to pieces, I really do, but he has a very creative understanding of the term 'on time.' And the man *loves* his long showers."

Then she poked her head inside the bathroom and started talking to Dad. I kept my eyes averted.

I hadn't been sure about it at first, but I loved Brie too. I loved the way she was honest. I loved the way she talked about things— how she always had a way of sounding cheery and goofy instead of scared or bitter. I hadn't figured out if she worked hard at it the same way Chase did—hiding what she was really thinking—or if she was just born that way.

She laughed at something Dad said. Then she blew him a kiss

and shut the door. "Okay, he's gonna meet me there. You make sure he gets his butt out of this apartment, okay?" She crossed the room, gathering her second shoe and her purse along the way. "You know what my mom said to me after I broke up with my first boyfriend? 'Someday, you'll find a keeper. He'll still drive you crazy, but you'll look forward to him driving you crazy for the rest of your life.' Kind of annoying that she was right."

She kissed my forehead and then Dani's. "Love you both. Remember: You'll do great. Sister bonding time! And, Rory, don't forget to open your gift. It's on your dad's desk." Then she grabbed her keys and was gone.

The Snow Queen could invade the human world any minute, and my stepmother was worried about me getting my belated birthday present.

It was hard to tear the wrapping off with the baby dozing on my shoulder, but I managed.

Inside the gift box was a stack of typed pages—Dad's screenplay—with a Post-it attached: *I know you're busy, but after things settle down, could you read this for me and tell me what you think?* I obviously wasn't the only person he'd asked. The margins of the first page were crammed with handwritten comments.

I spotted Brie's messy scrawl, but Amy's tidy cursive surprised me.

She'd circled some dialogue and written, *Rory would never say this. Listen to her more, and you'll get a better idea of how kids talk.*

Then I read that circled dialogue.

                    RACHEL
        You don't scare me, Ice Witch, but
        your armies . . . well, I don't like
        them very much.

Amy was right. I would never say that. Who *did* like armies?

I skimmed the rest of the page. A girl, talking to this Ice Witch. Her friend held captive by the witch's trolls. Agreeing to fight this fairy guy. Swearing to free them.

Oh.

The door to the bathroom cracked open, and Dad strolled out in jeans and a T-shirt that was damp at the neck, rubbing his hair with a towel. "Brie asked you to make sure I didn't take too long, didn't she? I'm sure they don't care if I'm a little late—" Then he spotted the wrapping paper on the floor.

"It's about *me*," I said. "And my friends. Did I *tell* you about fighting Torlauth in the Snow Queen's entrance hall?" I thought I'd left out that detail when I told him, Mom, and Amy the story in April.

"Miriam did," Dad admitted. "She let me pick her brain."

He hadn't been hanging out with me just because Brie had told him to. He'd been investigating me behind the scenes. He cared about me just as much as he cared about Dani.

Dad made a face. "Are you mad? I was afraid you'd be mad."

I shook my head. I was almost happy. "I'll try to read it before I go back to school."

We didn't mention that I might not get a chance to be a freshman, but I saw a muscle twitching in Dad's jaw, like he was trying hard not to get emotional right before he went to a meeting. "You're going to look for that letter, aren't you?"

I nodded. He *had* been paying attention.

He tossed the wet towel over the back of the leather couch, which would probably drive Brie crazy again. He picked up the carrier that usually kept Dani strapped to his chest. "Let's get you in this thing. It'll keep your hands free."

He had to tighten it a lot, but it fit. Dani was so used to it that she kept snoozing. For a second, Dad kept one hand on my shoulder and one hand on the baby's head. He stroked her hair with his thumb. "You know what I think about? I missed so much with you. I can't get it back, but I won't make the same mistake with Dani."

I had it so much better than Solange. My dad never abandoned me for another family. He had just made ours bigger.

I was misty-eyed. Dad kind of was too. We were a mess, but the good kind.

"You're ten minutes late now," I reminded him. "If you don't show up soon, I'll be in trouble with Brie."

"Better go, then." Dad hugged me and Dani both, careful not to squeeze too tight and wake her up. "If you want to, I completely encourage you to crash the meeting. I wouldn't mind getting rescued by my girls."

I rolled my eyes. He grinned. Then he left, and I was alone with the baby.

Dani slept long enough for her drool to soak through my T-shirt. She woke up on the way to the courtyard, but she didn't cry. She stared at Rapunzel's glass vial swinging from my hand, fascinated.

The only other person I saw outside was the Director. She sat in front of the ruins that used to be her office. Someone had salvaged one of the big rose-carved armchairs. Stuffing was coming out of the back, but the Director was still sitting in it.

Rapunzel wouldn't leave me to figure it all out on my own.

The Director might, though. My letter could have been waiting under our door, just like Chase's and Sarah Thumb's. She could have sent someone to steal it. She might be keeping it from me. She had a habit of withholding information.

You might say that confronting someone a lot older and more powerful than you while your baby sister was strapped to your chest would be a bad idea. You might be right, but I marched over to her anyway. "Do you have my letter?"

"Hello, Aurora," the Director said. Standing above her, I could see the dark circles under her eyes. "What makes you believe I would take your letter?"

"You have a history," I reminded her. Dani spat out her pacifier. I stooped to pick it up.

Yes, I was *really* intimidating.

"What a mild way of putting it." The Director rubbed the back of her neck, wincing like she had a crick in it. "The Canon is probably accusing me of worse crimes at the moment."

Oh right. The meeting.

"It didn't occur to you, did it?" said the Director. "Why I am not there? I can tell you: The only reason they don't invite someone to a Canon meeting is if they're discussing that person, especially if that person is the head. First, the Tale representatives will vote to see if the families living here will get a vote. Then they'll vote on whether or not I can keep my position."

I didn't know they could fire her. I couldn't imagine EAS without her leading it. "You still didn't answer my question."

"I did not take your letter, Rory," the Director said with a deep, weary sigh. I wasn't sure if I believed her or not. Her gaze fell on the glass vial Dani was playing with. "Rapunzel's sister gave her that. Did she tell you?"

I shook my head. I slowly tugged it out of the baby's hands. It didn't seem so harmless anymore. Dani started to fuss. I put a fresh pacifier in her mouth.

"We were traveling to steal the Pounce Pot," said the Director. "We passed an elven market. Solange bought it when she saw how the vial lit up when she whistled. She said she was going to give it to her little sister, who was afraid of the dark. Sebastian and I were surprised—she hadn't told us she'd found her father and his new family. That came later."

Time, for me, is messy. And timing delicate, Rapunzel had said.

Something clicked into place. "She stole her sister *before* the end of her Tale?"

"We went with Solange to the tower to deliver the present," said the Director softly. "Rapunzel's hair was brown then. She was afraid of us at first. She hid behind the metal dummy enchanted to be her nurse, but Solange coaxed her out—she used the new light to make shadow puppets on the wall. She made up voices for each of them."

I didn't want to know how much Solange had cared about Rapunzel. The memory of their last conversation in the courtyard was too fresh. It would make me angry, and Rapunzel wouldn't want that.

"It is hard to explain the horror of recognizing what my closest friend had done," the Director whispered. "To steal a child from her parents, to shut her in a tower, to plan to harm her after she'd grown. Solange was shocked when we didn't immediately exclaim over how clever she was. To be fair, we usually did. During the rest of the quest, she told us the way she had rescued her sister from her peasant mother's hovel; how happy Rapunzel was; how happy they would be forever after they both joined the Canon; how they would take care of each other always. She'd half-convinced us by the end. Three weeks later, I was asleep."

I wondered what I would do if Lena or Chase told me something like that. But that was the thing—they never would.

"Rapunzel was perhaps four then. I was certain she didn't remember. I thought if she knew, she would resent me for failing to rescue her," the Director continued. "But that is what her letter addresses. She said she never blamed me for the past. She said Solange would not have listened to me. I didn't expect that kindness."

"Rapunzel *was* kind," I said, angry after all. I hoped the Director felt guilty for suspecting Rapunzel of betraying EAS so often.

Mr. Swallow soared between the houses. "Mildred, they're ready for you," Sarah Thumb called before she and her mount circled back.

The Director stood and smoothed her violet skirt. "You are thinking the wrong way about the letter, Rory. When I met her, Rapunzel was fascinated by my dress. I showed her the pockets. She liked them so much that Solange promised her a dress with pockets of her own."

Then the Director walked to the Canon building, gloved hands folded in front of her.

I stared after her. Pockets. Rapunzel had left a letter to the Director in the Director's pocket, a place that reminded Mildred of the first time they'd met. Maybe she'd done the same for me.

I'd first seen Rapunzel at the Table of Never Ending Instant Refills. It had been turned to stone when the spearman had used it as a barricade the day before, but it still worked.

I found nothing under any of the plates or trays or bowls. I squatted down and checked under the table. No letter taped down there either.

Well, it had been a long shot. The Table got too much traffic to be a good hiding place.

It's pretty awkward to stand up when you have a baby strapped to you. Dani didn't like it either. She curled her fists in my T-shirt, hanging on. Then she reached for Rapunzel's light again. I didn't let her touch it.

I'd always assumed Solange had stolen her sister after she had already lost Sebastian and Mildred. I'd thought being lonely had driven her a little nuts.

But she'd been my age when she'd stolen Rapunzel—or maybe even younger. She had already started to play the witch in Rapunzel's Tale.

I curled my hand around Dani's back. I walked along the doors that lined the courtyard, thinking.

The idea of someone hurting my sister terrified me. I couldn't imagine planning to do it myself. I couldn't even imagine keeping her in a tower for that long. I wanted Dani to grow up and have adventures and make friends like I had.

Maybe that is what Rapunzel meant when she said I was nothing like Solange.

Maybe wasn't good enough. The world couldn't survive another Snow Queen, and even if I stopped her, who would stop me if I became just as—

My eyes landed on the ruby red door. I halted so fast Dani grabbed my T-shirt again.

The first time I'd seen Rapunzel had been at the Table. The first time we'd *talked* had been in the hallway between that door and the outside world. She'd been chiseling something. I hadn't been back to that corridor since the day before the Wolfsbane witches attacked us in San Francisco.

The door wasn't locked. I stepped into the hallway. It was dark, but then it had always been dark in there. I whistled over Rapunzel's light, held it up, and gasped.

I'd seen her carving, but I'd never seen the finished product. The walls showed four scenes.

In the first, a young woman—maybe Rapunzel—buried her face in her hands in front of a table. Spread across it was a candle, a knife, and a stack of paper. Rapunzel had even carved writing on it, upside down. French, I think, or Latin. I couldn't read it unless I put in my gumdrop translator, but I didn't think it was my letter. Too short. It looked more like a list.

The second panel was the one I'd seen Rapunzel carving. I recognized the woman's profile now. Rapunzel had captured the Snow Queen's icicle crown perfectly, but not the frosty smile she usually wore. Solange just looked confused.

The third scene was the Snow Queen's palace, the massive doors flung open, thousands of tiny figures marching in neat lines. The only ones big enough to recognize were the pillars. I couldn't tell if her allies were marching in or out.

The last was the strangest. It showed a tower and two figures on its roof. The Snow Queen's arm was outstretched to defend herself, but her eyes were wide with fear.

The other figure was me. I was pretty sure. That looked like my messy ponytail. The Rory figure had something cupped in her hands, and she was sprinting at Solange, cradling whatever it was against her collarbone.

"Well, I guess this means I find something the Snow Queen is afraid of," I told Dani, feeling a little calmer now that I had some clues to work with. I stepped closer, trying to get a better look, but paper crinkled under my sneaker.

I looked down.

An envelope, covered with my name and all the fancy curlicues Rapunzel could fit on it.

16

 sat down and ripped the letter open. My hands shook a tiny bit.

> *Dear Rory,*
>
> *If I had your courage, I would tell you this face-to-face. It is all but too late for that now. I must make a confession: I turned my sister into what she is.*
>
> *She came to me, after the former Rapunzel had given me her place in the Canon. I was great with child, very near the birth of my twins. The scar on my neck, made by my sister's shears, still pained me, but Solange was full of smiles.*
>
> *Her plan had succeeded. She, of all Characters, had successfully manipulated a Tale. She had given me an endless, unaging life. She believed she had given herself a Companion for the centuries ahead. She spoke of raising my babes in the self-same tower she had thrown me from.*
>
> *She did not understand the reason for my anger. She did not believe me at first when I told her I would never live with her again, when I said I would never allow her near*

*my children. Then I threatened to stand before the Canon
and to reveal the identity of the witch in my Tale if she
dared to speak to any of us.*

I told her we were no longer sisters, and she looked so hurt.

*She left then and disappeared for decades. She did not
return to the Canon until she had already kidnapped Kai
and begun calling herself the Snow Queen.*

*I knew what she had planned. I had seen her books. I
had read her notes. She was fully aware she could die in
the attempt. I recognized that I was her only hesitation. I
knew what she would do if she lost me, and I did not care.*

*My sister has always had two great desires—one for
power and one for affection. Her mother was long dead.
Her father had abandoned her for my family. Her other
relatives had passed her among themselves, neglectful
and distant. Sebastian was stone. Mildred was asleep. I
was her last link to a different sort of life. I shunned her. I
pushed her toward power.*

*I believed she would die in the attempt, and still I did
not care.*

Now she is heartless.

I tried to imagine forcing that choice on Dani: stay and try
to stop me from becoming a great villain, or leave and live her
whole life overshadowed by the destruction I caused.

I wished Rapunzel were still alive. I wished I could tell her that Solange had made her own decisions.

> *With this letter and these carvings, you have all the*
> *pieces you need to do what must be done. The first panel*
> *happened the day I told my sister we would not share our*
> *lives with each other. This last panel is a vision which will*
> *not come to pass within my lifetime. I have seen this final*
> *confrontation, but not the outcome.*
>
> *Knowing you, I can guess it.*
>
> *Living will carve you open. You can't choose what wounds*
> *you. You can only choose what seals the scar. You will*
> *never choose power as my sister did.*
>
> *You are willing to sacrifice too. You would die to keep safe*
> *your loved ones and the world they inhabit. But consider too,*
> *my dear Rory: There is more than one way to give your life.*
>
> *Solange only speaks of uniting magical peoples and giving*
> *them aid. You have already begun acting on what she has*
> *long promised.*
>
> *You have a way of looking past traditional mistrust and*
> *forging bonds previously held to be impossible. As you*
> *read this, the Living Stone Dwarves live at Ever After*
> *School. Seelie and Unseelie Fey alike flock here.*
>
> *These are only the changes you have wrought in two and a*
> *half years. Think of the good you can do within a lifetime.*

I gave my immortality to Lena, not simply to allow her to
reach adulthood, but for you to grow together. I want this
world to be transformed by Rory Landon. I want you to live.

Rapunzel

Only Rapunzel would completely fail to tell me how Solange
had turned into the Snow Queen. Only Rapunzel would try to tell
me who I was instead.

I was crying by then. Rapunzel wasn't here to comfort me, and
that thought made me sob even harder.

This didn't bother Dani as much as I thought it would. She
just stared at me and then at the tears landing on her baby carrier. She'd probably never seen someone so big cry before. She
must have thought it was only something she did.

My sister patted my cheek with her little hand. I used my T-shirt
to rub her fingers dry. Then I wiped my face on my sleeve. Took a
deep breath. Examined the wall.

Rapunzel said I had all the pieces. Maybe it would have been
easier if she'd just *told* me, but I had to trust her. I had to believe I
could solve the puzzle she'd left me.

The last panel showed me taking something to the Snow
Queen, something small enough for me to cover with my hands.
That was a pretty solid clue.

It had to be the key to the power she'd gotten after Rapunzel
left her. The magic Solange had almost died to gain.

I raised Rapunzel's light over the first carving. I looked at
Solange's hands over her eyes. I would be devastated too, if Dani
decided she didn't want anything to do with me, but I liked to
think I would understand why.

Grief is a messy thing though. It could make you reckless.

I focused on what was on the table in the panel.

A knife. It could be the same one she cut her sister with— No, Rapunzel said Solange had used shears. The knife could be for anything.

But the list . . . I dug my gumdrop translator out of my back pocket again and stuck it in my ear. The writing was upside down, but the translator slowly recognized the carving had words. The letters melted into something I could read:

Limbs (all 4)

Eyes

Heart

Head

A list of body parts. Great. In the early days of my research, I'd kept a list of body parts too. Reading *The Lyvves & Tymes of Sorcerers & Sorceresses*, I'd jotted down which limbs regular people lost to gain their magic. I'd stopped, because they repeated so often— hands and feet and sometimes eyes.

So, we had that, a knife, and a very upset Solange who wanted more power—

I gasped and stared at the list again.

Genevieve Searcaster cut out her own eye to become the first sorceress-giant ever. Solange had helped her. What if that hadn't been the first time the Snow Queen had tried that experiment? What if she'd done that to herself, but not with her eye?

Now she is heartless. Rapunzel had told us. She'd been telling us all along.

Solange had cut out her own heart. The magic that flared up around the bearer of the Unwritten Tale had flowed into the spot where her heart should be.

What would you do if power flowed through your veins instead of blood? Rapunzel had asked. I hadn't realized she was being so literal then, either.

No wonder Solange was so powerful. No wonder Rapunzel had kept saying her sister was dead. No wonder nothing had happened when she'd given up the Canon's golden apple. The Snow Queen wasn't really human anymore.

Her heart must be what was hidden behind that ancient cracked door from my dreams. I had to bring it to her. It was the only way to stop her.

Parents were pouring out of the Canon building when I got there. The town hall portion of the program must have been over. I couldn't tell how it had gone.

Through the crowd, Mom spotted me first. "We convinced the other families to stay. Are you all right?"

"Fine. I just—" I didn't want to talk about it with all these worried-looking families around me. Dad started loosening the straps of the baby carrier. "I have to speak to the Canon."

Brie plucked Dani from my arms and swung the diaper bag from my shoulder to hers. Then she kissed my cheek and whispered, "Either you *really* want to get out of babysitting, or you're onto something."

"Thanks." I burst through the doors to the Canon's building and shouted, "I know why the Snow Queen's immortal!"

The Director stared at me from her huge thronelike chair, carved all over with roses. She didn't look like she'd been fired. She looked annoyed at the interruption. The thrones of the Canon members were arranged behind her.

"Really?" Lena stood in front. They must have been swearing her in.

"Rory, you weren't invited," the Director reminded me.

Maybe I should have thought things through before I crashed the meeting. But this was huge news. "Didn't you hear me before? *I figured out how to stop the Snow Queen.*"

I expected shock. I expected gasps and relief.

Instead, the Director sighed. "Rory, this entire meeting is about how to stop the Snow Queen and her forces. If you believe you have new information to share, you can wait your turn."

"But—" She couldn't be serious.

"*Sit.*" The Director stabbed a finger at the student representative section, completely unoccupied except for Chase. The Director must have wanted to ask him stuff. He was the only person in the room not staring at me.

Sarah Thumb shot me a look that said, *She'll kick you out if you don't do what she says.*

I picked a spot a couple feet from Chase.

His gaze was on his dad, who was pointedly looking at the floor, at the other Canon members, everywhere but at his son. I wondered if Jack had been like that since Chase had come home from his Tale. Maybe that was why Chase's face was so blank. Maybe it was armor against a father who was too embarrassed to acknowledge him.

The Director turned back to Lena. "Tell me again, how many of those flying swords and axes can you make before the battle?"

"None." Lena squeezed her hands together so hard it would've hurt her if she could feel them. "I'm busy making spell shields. Now that the other witch clans have joined the Snow Queen, we're going to need them."

The Director frowned at Lena. "Our numbers are paltry beside the Snow Queen's. We need any means you have of allowing one individual to fight many."

Lena glanced at me. I tried to smile encouragingly. Then she spoke a little louder. "If you're really worried about numbers, you should focus on stuff that will keep us alive, not stuff that'll kill us if it falls into the wrong hands."

The Director's voice softened, full of fake understanding. "We have full confidence that you'll find a method which ensures more safety for the wielder."

Lena wasn't having it. Her chin lifted the way it does when she feels stubborn. "I've tried to do that and failed twice. I'm not risking it again."

"You'll do this," the Director said, "even if we have to forcibly remove you to your workshop and keep you there until you finish."

I would have defended Lena, but I didn't need to.

Lena raised both her golden hands. I think she was just trying to make a point, but she didn't have great control yet. The air crackled, like it was full of static electricity. The Canon representatives shifted nervously. Jack leaned back so far that his throne actually squeaked. *This* was the girl whose magic had lifted the Tree of Hope, and no one was really sure what she was capable of. "I have a new rule. I won't make anything I would hate my enemies to use against us. I'll make the shields. If you don't like it, lock me in my workshop. Let's see how long I stay there."

No one argued with her.

Lena walked over to the extra-tall throne and threw herself into it. Then she looked at me with an *Oh gumdrops, what have I done?* expression.

I was ridiculously proud of her.

The Director turned my way, furious. I'm sure she blamed me, but Lena made her own choices. "Well?" Aurora asked.

"The Snow Queen doesn't have a heart," I said. "She cut it

out herself after Rapunzel left her. Magic rushed in—the magic that surrounds the bearer of an Unwritten Tale. Power flows in Solange's veins instead of blood, just like Rapunzel said."

"That's impossible," said Rumpelstiltskin.

But Lena had pressed her golden hands over her own heart like she was making sure it was still there. Even Chase had looked up.

Sarah Thumb's whole face brightened. "Solange has done lots of stuff Ever Afters always thought were impossible."

"We need to get the heart," I said.

"The heart's gone," Gretel said, confused. "After a sorcerer is made, they don't keep the body part they lost. The magic replaces it. That's the whole point."

"Not necessarily true," Lena said. "I mean, yeah, I didn't keep my hands, but losing a limb isn't the same as losing a heart. You *need* a heart. Something has to pump a current through your body—whether it's magic or oxygen."

"Koshei the Deathless," said Sarah Thumb, understanding. I sensed a magical theory discussion coming on.

"Exactly," said Lena. "The procedure itself has been done before."

"Koshei the Deathless didn't have the power the Snow Queen has, and he stored his soul in an egg," said Rumpelstiltskin, "not his heart."

"No, some texts say that it's his heart," said Lena firmly.

"Koshei didn't have the same amount of magic surrounding him that Solange and Rory do," Sarah Thumb said.

I wasn't following any of this conversation, and I didn't really care. "Look, we can work out how Solange did it later. But I need that heart. It's the key to stopping her."

"No." The Director didn't even *pretend* to think about it. "A battle is coming. You are required here."

"It's the quest in my Tale." I glanced at Lena, then Chase. He *was* looking at me now, so intently that my heart skidded. I turned quickly back to the Director. "You can't stop me and my Companions from going."

"This is merely a theory," the Director said. "We don't even know where she would keep such an item, *if* it exists."

"Her palace, of course—" I started, getting ready to tell her about my dream.

The Director cut me off. "Too far. You can go on the quest, but not now. The invasion could start any minute. You carry the combs that stopped the Snow Queen during the last war. We need you on the front lines. We've already decided."

The only reason they don't invite someone to a Canon meeting is if they're discussing that person, the Director had said. So the Canon had talked about her first, then me.

Sarah Thumb's smile was full of sympathy. "Thank you for sharing this new development, Rory. The Canon will discuss it further, and we'll get back to you soon."

"You children may go," said the Director.

Lena had that blazing look she sometimes gets when she's inventing something new. She had an idea, but she hadn't gotten up yet . . .

"She's not leaving," Chase reminded me. I hated the blankness on his face. I couldn't read him when he was this way. "Lena has to stay. She's part of the Canon now."

"Oh." That would take some getting used to. We walked out together, and I felt the Canon's stares like needles in my back. I hadn't been this close to Chase since I'd kissed him in the tower, and I wasn't completely sure what to do with my arms. They felt awkward just swinging at my sides.

His hands shoved deep in his pockets, he glanced over his

shoulder. Jack was still examining the floor, but the Director was looking right at us, watching us go, her mouth a very thin line.

It didn't matter. She couldn't read my thoughts just by looking at me. She couldn't guess at the plan forming in my head. I needed to get the heart, so we could *win* the battle. It was the first thing I'd felt sure about in a very long time.

We stepped outside. Half the parents had stayed in the courtyard to discuss the meeting. I didn't see mine, but I spotted plenty of people glancing our way.

The doors closed behind us. Chase didn't leave me like I thought he would.

I knew he was sort of not talking to me, but this quest was important enough for me to stop worrying about respecting his boundaries. I lowered my voice. "Chase—"

"Not here," he said, even though he couldn't know what I was going to say.

Someone called his name, and we both turned to see who it was.

Mr. Zipes caught up to us and clapped Chase on the shoulder. "Thanks for speaking in there. I feel a lot better knowing what we'll be facing."

So he'd spoken at the town hall, too.

Chase's expression didn't change. "Well, you know, if I have to be lame, I like to at least be helpful."

"Don't say that," I said.

"Why? It's funny," Chase said. I'd never heard him sound so bitter before. "If I have to be a Sleeping Beauty, I better have a sense of humor about it."

He knew I'd laughed when I'd found out what his Tale was. I wondered who told him. Kenneth, maybe? No, I remembered with a pang: Kenneth was dead. "Chase, I'm *sorry*."

"You have no reason to be sorry." His voice was clipped and cold.

Mr. Zipes moved away. Even the triplets' dad could feel a fight brewing.

"I do," I said fiercely. "I should have listened when you said something was wrong with you."

"Things turned out okay." Chase shrugged. "If Adelaide hadn't done her thing, then maybe the Snow Queen wouldn't have lured me to that tower and I wouldn't have been gotten the chance to be the very first half-human spy camera—"

"I said, *stop it*. Stop talking about yourself like that."

He was staring at the ground, just like his dad. "I'm just telling the truth."

"You aren't a half-human spy camera." I hear my voice rising. I could sense more and more people turning to look, but I couldn't stop myself. "You're the best fighter in our grade, in all of Ever After School."

"Not anymore," Chase said, pointing at me.

"You *threw* that fight," I said, not caring whether or not it was true. "You're the first Turnleaf the Fey have had in more than a century."

That got Chase to glance at me. And scowl. "Historically, not something to brag about."

"You can hold a glamour over multiple people for *days*." I was complimenting Chase, and he was *arguing* with me about it?

He rolled his eyes. "I have a tenth the amount of magic the average Fey has. Like a hundredth of what Lena has. Probably less."

"During the battle, you knew exactly what to do."

"Rory, the Snow Queen won anyway. She won as soon as she showed up."

"Do you think we could have saved the people trapped in the training courts if you hadn't gotten us organized? Do you think Rapunzel would have had time to hide the Water?"

Chase didn't respond to this. He just stood there with his arms folded, back to glaring at the ground.

I grabbed his shoulders, hard. That made him look at me again. "When the Snow Queen attacked the Unseelie Court, you went in and rescued her primary target. You got King Mattanair and your mother here safe and sound. You knew exactly what to say to convince the Snow Queen's allies to turn against her last spring. You singlehandedly brought back Itari, which is so old even the Fey had forgotten it, and you taught it to like thirty people in less than three months. You are *Chase Turnleaf*, and you don't need a Tale to be awesome. You never have."

The dead mask cracked. His mouth twitched. He met my gaze steadily, and for a second, all of his Chaseness was back.

"I need you," I said. "I can't get that heart without you."

He shot me an exasperated frown and glanced over my head. I remembered how many people were watching.

"No," he said. "You can't get the heart, period. The Director's right. The battle's more important now."

My hands fell from his shoulders. He couldn't have seriously said that the Director was *right*. He knew this quest needed to happen.

He sighed. His voice changed again. "I've seen the Snow Queen's plans, Rory. You haven't. We're going to need all the help we can get." He never sounded this patronizing, even with the *third graders* he helped in the training courts.

"We can stop all her forces if we just stop her," I said. "If she falls, her armies won't keep going. No one can take her place."

"Searcaster could. I heard them talking about it," Chase said.

He was just determined not to listen to me, the same way I hadn't listened to him. I couldn't believe he would be so petty. This was bigger than us. "Chase, we're still the Triumvirate. We're still the ones who are supposed to take her down."

"Technically," he said, "that's *your* job."

He didn't believe that. He couldn't. He'd promised to help me. Things couldn't have gotten this messed up. "You're still mad at me."

"I'm not." But he said it too quickly.

"Do you want me to apologize again?" I said. "Because I'm not sorry for breaking the enchantment."

Chase's jaw set. "I wouldn't have been under an enchantment at all if it hadn't been for you."

That wasn't fair. "Are you *still* under an enchantment? Because you're kind of acting like it."

"Don't be stupid," Chase said, furious. If we didn't have important things to do, I might have been relieved he'd broken out of whatever fog he'd been in since Adelaide confessed.

"Then how can I make this better?" I asked. "What do you *want* from me?"

"I wanted you to fight for me!" Chase said. "I would have fought for you. God, dating Adelaide sucked, but at least I got to be around someone who knew *exactly* how she felt, for once."

That last bit hurt more than the rest of the conversation put together. It hurt almost like watching Rapunzel turn to dust. This was a kind of death too.

I refused to cry here. I could *feel* all those people looking at us.

Even Chase looked kind of stricken. Shocked, like he hadn't planned to give up the moral high ground so fast.

But he'd meant what he said.

Enchantments aren't exactly subtle. Chase hadn't mentioned that something was wrong with him until the day after my birthday. He'd spent months under the wishing coin's enchantment without noticing it, and maybe this was why. Maybe a part of Chase didn't mind letting Adelaide make being his girlfriend the biggest and most important thing in her life.

First-kiss magic or not, I was never going to be like that with him.

I didn't have that in me. I couldn't help who I was.

"All right," I said. "Good-bye, Chase."

Then I walked away, sailing past the crowd without even

looking at them, feeling my insides splintering.

Everyone probably thought I was going to my apartment to cry after arguing with Chase.

That was what I wanted them to think. It was what I wanted the Director to think.

Technically, taking down the Snow Queen *was* my job.

I could still go alone.

First stop was the storerooms. I stole two big sacks of dragon scales and threw them in my carryall. I wouldn't risk running out again, especially if I was going to the Arctic Circle by myself.

I'd decided not to hold up the quest for Lena. Waiting for the Canon meeting to end meant waiting for the Director to come out and check on what I was doing. I had just pretty much shouted my plans to go without permission to the whole courtyard. If *I* got caught, then no one would retrieve the heart, and the Snow Queen really would win. Maybe not this invasion, but eventually.

The one-key safe was my second stop.

Sebastian's statue was still there, and I wasted a few seconds examining his face, searching his expression. He'd been shielding Solange when Arica had turned him to stone. Mildred said she never confronted Solange about Rapunzel, but maybe Sebastian did. Maybe they'd fought the day she lost him.

At least he had still gone with her. I didn't want Chase to turn to stone for me, but I didn't think questing together was too much to ask.

I reached for the Pounce Pot only to realize that I didn't have paper or anything to write with, but Rapunzel had thought of everything. Some square stationery and a pen rested on top of the pedestal, right beside the dented saltshaker. I scrawled:

- *The Snow Queen/Solange de Chateies*
- *General Genevieve Searcaster*
- *The pillars*
- *Anyone from the Snow Queen's forces who might stop me*

I kind of wanted to add the names of everyone in the Canon, but I'd already put a lot of people down. Too many diluted the magic. Oh well. Once I finished up here and locked myself in my room, even the Director really couldn't do anything to stop me.

I wrote down the secret I needed kept: *Rory Landon knows about the Snow Queen's heart, and she's going on a quest to get it.*

It looked so small on paper.

No wonder the Canon hadn't made a big deal over it. *How* the Snow Queen had gotten so much power wasn't nearly as scary as what she could do with it. After hearing her plans, it was easy to see why they thought I was wrong.

I grabbed the Pounce Pot and froze.

A scrap of paper had been hidden underneath it, filled with tiny writing: *I wished for Chase to be my boyfriend, and I ~~still have~~ am still using the wishing coin.* Around the edges of the paper, like a tidy little border, were the names of everyone in our grade. *Rory* was underlined three times.

Adelaide had found the Pounce Pot before Rapunzel put it inside the one-key safe.

No wonder Chase had had such a hard time explaining what was wrong with him. No wonder I hadn't been able to focus on the traitor until Adelaide had confessed and broken the spell. The Pounce Pot had protected her all summer.

Rapunzel had moved it here on purpose. She must have known. The Pounce Pot wouldn't have let her tell me. It wouldn't have let her show me this slip of paper, but she could have told the Canon. She could have stopped it.

Time, for me, is messy, and timing delicate, Rapunzel had told me, dozens of times.

Just once, she'd said, *Family is the one part of my life I haven't made my peace with*.

It didn't matter now. I grabbed the Pounce Pot again. I ignored the buzz of magic that rattled my teeth. I sprinkled ground unicorn horn over the square stationery I'd written on.

Finding Adelaide's secret made one thing clear: The Pounce Pot still worked.

I walked back home. Alone in the apartment, Mom was waiting on the couch.

"I heard a rumor you want to go find that Snow Queen's heart," she said slowly, her arms crossed. "Were you going to leave without telling me?"

"I don't know." I didn't want to admit this, but I hadn't even thought about my family since deciding to go. I'd been too focused on the heart, on making sure the Director didn't catch me. "I was going to use the closet doorway to create a temporary-transport spell."

"So, you weren't going to say good-bye?" Mom said, clearly hurt.

"Well, 'good-bye' with you usually turns into 'don't go.'" I didn't want her to tell me that now. I didn't want to argue with her, not when I was leaving to do something so dangerous. "And I *have* to go. This time, especially."

Mom sighed. "I know." She walked into my room, picked her way around the mess on my floor, and sat on my bed, looking mournfully at the closet door.

I followed her, expecting a trick and kind of hating myself for it. "You're really not going to try to stop me?"

"Not this time." Mom's smile was tiny, but it had so much love in it. "I want so badly to keep you safe, Rory. You have to understand that. But your dad is right. That's not what you need from us now."

"Dad was right?" Definitely a trick. Mom would never say that.

Mom knew what I was thinking. "Amy said it too."

I didn't bother to hide my disbelief. "Since when?"

"Since she saw you fight for real," Mom said.

Maybe I could believe her. If Chase could really decide not to come with me, maybe Mom could really be okay with me leaving. My face started twisting in that horrible way it does when I want to cry but won't let myself.

"Oh, sweetie." Mom scooted off the bed, wrapped her arms around me, and kissed my hair. It was her usual *I'm the mother* routine, but I didn't mind this time. I dropped my head onto her shoulder. It was a little uncomfortable. I was taller than she was now.

"Who's my favorite daughter?" Mom whispered.

I laughed, in spite of myself. "I'm your *only* daughter."

She pulled back a little. Her stare was intent. "That's why you have to come back. You're the most important person in the world to me."

Don't go had turned into *Don't die*.

I hugged her again. She didn't ask for any promises. She knew I couldn't make any.

I waited in a quiet, abandoned spot to meet up with my ride to the Snow Queen's palace.

I'd let Mom pick from the unlabeled vials of leftover dirt that had been collecting in the bottom of my carryall. I'd collected a lot since Lena invented temporary-transport spells in seventh grade. I'd lost track of where they all came from. This way, Mom could honestly tell anyone who asked that she didn't know where I had gone, and being unpredictable cut way down on the possibility that the Snow Queen had set a trap for me.

After we'd painted the doorway and chanted the spell, after I'd slung on my carryall and buckled my sword belt, I'd stepped through, and I'd known exactly where I was. Atlantis. The same spot where Fael had taken us prisoner.

No one would look for me here—no one except the Wind who owed me a boon and would come when I called.

"Just you?" said a voice above me. I glanced up from the boulder I was sitting on.

I didn't recognize the West Wind at first. He wore a dark, well-made suit, but he was bulky with muscles, his head shaved, his fingers thick and strong. One shoulder bulged bigger than the other, like he carried a weapon there. He reminded me of the private security guys one of my mom's actress friends had hired back in L.A. When he flew up, he was nearly as humungous as Jimmy Searcaster, but he shrank down to human size so that he could talk to me.

"Are you supposed to be a bodyguard?" I asked, gesturing to his new personification. "Was that for me, or are you just getting ready for the battle?"

His gaze swept across the beach in front of us, scanning the area for threats, but we were alone. The tall trees behind us were far away. Anyone trying to ambush us from there would have to cross the beach to get to us. Only the waves were keeping us company.

"My personifications have all been fighters this week. Just you?" he repeated.

I sighed. I didn't need the reminder. "Just me. Can you please take me to the Snow Queen's palace?"

"She'll see us coming," he said. "She will knock us out of the sky before we get anywhere near it."

"Not today. Ever heard of the Pounce Pot?" I asked.

"Mildred Grubb would never let you use it."

"She wouldn't *let* me, but she couldn't *stop* me either." Rapunzel had made sure of that.

West didn't ask me what I was going to do there. Either he'd already heard about what I'd said at the Canon meeting, or he didn't want to know.

He only regarded me silently. He hadn't been so serious with me since he'd first given me the ring. I wondered if this was how he really was, all the time—an ancient being whose strength could snap me in half.

So old and so powerful, and *he* was afraid of the Snow Queen.

I wasn't scared, exactly. I felt the way I had when I'd pulled Chase off the beanstalk. Determination had crowded out all the fear—determination and a weird sort of certainty that this was the right thing to do, no matter how dangerous it seemed.

West grew to his full size again. "All right, but it'll take half a day to reach her from here."

I slung my carryall on. "Good. I can't risk going into the palace until the Snow Queen marches her forces out toward the portals."

The West Wind lifted me up and set me on his shoulder. I didn't look at the drop. When we rose off the beach, I barely felt a twinge of nausea. I just grabbed a handful of West's collar and held on.

He raced across the water. The speed made my eyes sting. "You are terrifying sometimes," he said, so close that his voice was a deep rumble. "Just like her."

I'm not sure how long it took for West to reach the Arctic Circle. Long enough for me to fall asleep. It was one of those supremely unrestful naps, where you close your eyes and it feels like a normal blink but, when you open them, the whole landscape has changed. The ocean that had stretched out ahead of us was gone. Instead, we sailed over a glacier, capped with a roof of stars. Great canyons ran through the ice, carved with meltwater, and they forked and merged like dark veins running underneath too-pale skin.

I was really glad I'd cast one of the heating spells hours ago. The wind chill over the ocean had been fierce.

I hadn't dreamed. I would probably never dream of the door again. I would reach it before I slept.

Suddenly West said, "Her army *has* marched."

So it was starting. The scouts must have spread the word. Back at Ever After School, the Director was probably assigning squadrons to portals. They'd probably noticed I was gone by now. Some probably wished I hadn't left. Some of them probably hoped I *already* had the heart.

"Let's see if you were right about the Pounce Pot," said West.

He swooped upward, vaulting over an extra-high rocky ridge streaked with ice. Over the next plain, the Snow Queen's army stepped in ranks, dark lines against the snow.

The West Wind didn't try to strain the Pounce Pot's magic. He slid down into a meltwater canyon and morphed into someone more slender, a tall and lean athlete, wiry under his spandex. Out of sight, we twisted along the canyon's shadows, moving north below the ice's surface.

But the army's image was seared into my mind anyway, as if I had Lena's photographic memory. It had spread across a field that would have taken a reindeer hours to cross. Huge herds of ice griffins and *Draconus melodius* had come first. The goblins and the witches followed them, and near the back were the Snow Queen's private forces, her pillars, and her villains. The only one I'd recognized from this far off was the East Wind, West's brother, who looked like an aging football player stuffed in a suit.

I hadn't seen the Snow Queen herself, but it was easy to guess where she was. The five giants in the back had to be protecting her.

I could see why the Director didn't want me to go. Even if—when—I managed to get the heart, I would have to fight my way through thousands of her allies to reach her.

But this army would have heavy casualties, too. The Snow Queen had enough fighters to populate a small city, but very few magical peoples were left these days. Many of them would die in this battle, and in the battles afterward. It was such a waste of life.

"How much farther?" I asked West.

"If we emerged from this canyon, we would be able to see her palace," he said. "And any allies left behind to stand guard would be able to see *us*."

It seemed impossible that Solange could have more fighters stashed away in her fortress, but West was probably right. Hopefully, the Pounce Pot could keep them from contacting the Snow Queen.

West whipped around another curve. "I'll get you as close as I can."

That turned out to be roughly a hundred feet from the door. He swooped out of the canyon, slowed to a stop, and set me down. His breath gusted out of him. West seemed . . . well, *winded*, but only Ben would have actually said so. "I haven't flown that far with a passenger in a long, long time," he said.

"Thank you." I was officially out of boons, but it was worth it.

The palace walls loomed above us like a huge crown of ice, ghostly gray in the night, blocking out the stars. The doors—twice as tall as General Searcaster—were shut. No way could I open them on my own, but maybe West could, before he left. It looked deserted. "No guards?"

West straightened up. "Someone's here."

I looked again. An ice column, nearly four stories tall, stood beside the entrance, too lumpy to be decorative. An illusion, then. Only a few of the Snow Queen's allies were that big. Only one hadn't been marching toward the portals.

"Matilda." The illusion of the ice column began to tremble. She definitely heard me. "Is that you?"

The overgrown icicle stepped away from the wall. Then it dropped something, and the illusion vanished. Matilda held two huge mittens high in the air. She was standing fine, like I'd never broken her ankle at the Zipes' ranch. Someone must have healed her. "I don't want to fight."

"Are you the only guard?" asked West. That didn't seem very likely.

She nodded. "Outside. I don't know exactly what the Snow Queen set up in there." She jerked her head at the doors. "She called it 'reinforcements.' She left last, and she took her time."

Sure. Matilda could have backup out here disguised as more overgrown icicles. They could be sneaking up on us right now.

Only one way to check. Bad-guy radar. I fished around the front pocket of my carryall, where I usually kept my M3. But that pocket was empty.

My stomach flipped.

I knew exactly where my M3 was: on my bedroom floor. Looking for Rapunzel's letter, I'd dumped out my entire bag. I hadn't finished repacking before I'd gone to babysit Dani.

I hadn't brought the mirror with me.

I couldn't call for help, even if I wanted to.

The cold had begun to sink into my bones. I needed to recast my heating enchantment. I couldn't waste more time here. "What am I going to do with Matilda?" I asked West. I still didn't want to kill her.

"Let me help you," said the giantess.

I narrowed my eyes. "In my experience, the Searcasters aren't very helpful people."

Matilda still hadn't lowered her hands. "Just think back for a second. Your enemies have been Jimmy and Genevieve, not me."

"Except for that time a couple weeks ago, when you tried to kill me," I said.

"You tried to kill me too," Matilda said. That was a really good point. "And I tried to get Jimmy home before he killed Hansel. You saw that."

A wave of emptiness washed over me. I wished she hadn't brought that up.

"It is hard to believe that the wife of a pillar and the daughter-in-law of the Snow Queen's sorceress-general would switch sides," said West.

Matilda was quiet for a moment, gathering her thoughts, just like Rapunzel used to do. Then she said, "The Snow Queen will always want more and more. We'll always be fighting. It's not the life I want for my baby."

Oh. She really was pregnant. Well, *if* she was telling the truth.

"It's been a while since Texas. A lot of other people made it to EAS today. Why wait till now?"

"The Canon isn't always fair, but you are, Rory." Matilda sighed. "If you tell them not to punish me for Jimmy and Genevieve's crimes, they'll listen."

"I'm not a Tale representative," I reminded her. "I have no power over Characters."

"You have influence," West said thoughtfully.

You have a way of looking past traditional mistrust and forging bonds previously held to be impossible, Rapunzel had said in her letter. This was probably what she meant. I already knew I was going to vouch for Matilda, if I could.

"I can't do anything for Jimmy. Not when he's a pillar." I figured she already knew that I wouldn't be sticking up for General Searcaster in a million years.

Matilda's voice turned as hard and sharp as a blade. "I know."

I'd kind of gotten the impression that the Searcasters had an unhappy marriage, but it must have become a *lot* worse if she was willing to betray her husband. "Matilda, I might not leave this battlefield."

The giantess lowered her mittens, very slowly, so West and I knew she wasn't trying anything sneaky. "That's what I mean about you being fair. We can swear a Binding Oath, if the West Wind is willing."

I glanced at West. "Can you?" He nodded. "Would you mind?" I didn't have any more boons, so he didn't owe me anything.

"It would be my privilege. I don't think I could face Lena if I just left you here. And I wouldn't mind it if *you* owed me a favor," West said, which kind of explained why he'd been hanging back for so long.

So West performed the Binding Oath. Matilda swore not to

Shelby Bach

deliver me to my enemies, and she swore to help me in any way she was able. I swore to do everything I could to persuade the Canon to treat her fairly, and I swore to help protect her from the Characters' punishment if at all possible.

I wondered how a giantess and one of the four Winds had sort of become Companions on my Tale, instead of the rest of the Triumvirate.

Chase would have done the Binding Oath if he were here. He would have given me a thumbs-up behind Matilda Searcaster's back. Lena would ask if sorceresses could perform Binding Oaths. My chest ached with cold and with missing them.

If Solange had felt this way all the time, I couldn't blame her for cutting out her heart.

When he was finished, West turned to me. "I'll go back now. When the battle begins, I must meet my brothers and keep them from entering the human lands." He rose into the air and sailed back south, not bothering to hide this time.

I wished I'd waited for Lena. She would probably know if a personification could die.

The giantess and I watched as he shrank to the size of a normal human, to the size of an elf, then a pixie, and then disappeared altogether.

"He's friendlier than East is," said Matilda.

I forced myself to focus on the quest. Solange didn't know I was coming *today*, but she would never have left her heart in a palace guarded only by a pregnant giantess with questionable loyalties. "What can you tell me about the traps the Snow Queen has set up inside?"

"She said not to open the doors until she gave the signal," said Matilda. "Her reinforcements are in the entrance hall, waiting.

They're supposed to rush to her side as soon as she gains control of the portals. I was planning to ignore the signal. Maybe pretend I fell asleep. I'm still in the first trimester. That does happen."

"Reinforcements, huh?" So her army *was* bigger than what I'd seen on that glacier. Perfect.

"Yes." Matilda hesitated. "I don't think they're people, exactly. Genevieve gave me very strict instructions to keep the door shut until the right time. Like the reinforcements couldn't think for themselves."

Knowing General Searcaster, "strict instructions" probably meant "threatened." "Is there another way in?" I asked.

"No." Then she added, "Well, you could blast your way through the palace walls, but unless you know where you're going, you'll probably still end up in the entrance hall. It takes up most of the first floor."

I thought for a second and finally decided that it would be easier to keep the reinforcements bottled up if I didn't create extra exits for them. "This will be fine," I said. "Close the doors once I'm through."

"You don't want me to fight with you?" Matilda said, sounding a little surprised. She *was* big enough to do some damage, but I'd seen her fight before. I hadn't been super impressed.

"Let me see what I'm up against, and then I'll tell you." I wondered if Solange had felt this calm on the day she had infiltrated King Navaire's palace to take him down.

Matilda turned the handle and pulled it open. The bottom of the door—as wide as my arm and longer than our apartment—scraped against the frozen ground. We both peeked inside.

The Snow Queen's reinforcements were made of ice. As alive as the metal dummies we used to practice on, but way more bloodthirsty. The whole horde rushed for the open exit—ice dragons, ice goblins, ice wolves, and at least five ice *giants*.

No wonder the witches were supposed to cast a spell to turn summer into winter. Solange wanted to make sure her reinforcements didn't melt when they reached the human world.

As they pounded toward us, I knew how to keep them from rushing out, and I knew how I was going to get past them to the door that led down to the prisons.

I should have been afraid of the fight that was coming, but I wasn't. Instead, I was afraid of *not* being scared. I was afraid of who I might become after I'd done this.

 stepped over the threshold, pulled out one of my combs, and tossed it over my shoulder.

"Did you want—" Matilda stopped asking when bars sprouted up across the doorway, each as thick around as the Tree of Hope's trunk, and raced to the top of the door frame. "Oh. So . . . no."

A squadron of ice trolls struck the barrier so hard that hairline cracks filled their translucent frames. Not so smart, then. One of them took a step toward me. His spear was made of wood and sharp metal.

But I was still safe. Just that step was enough to widen all the tiny fractures in the troll's ice body. It broke into a bunch of chunks that looked disturbingly like the crushed ice that comes out of a fridge.

The reinforcements couldn't take a hit like real fighters could. I could work with that.

"Behind you!" Matilda said.

Sadly, the ice army had noticed that the exit was blocked again. It would have been nice if they'd all run at the bars and broken themselves into itty-bitty pieces.

They'd also noticed *me*, and it seemed like the Snow Queen had enchanted them to kill any intruders.

An ice dragon reached me first. The Snow Queen had formed it slightly larger than a real, adult *Draconus melodius*. For teeth, she'd frozen metal spearheads in its jaws, two rows deep, like a shark.

It didn't matter. I was faster. I dashed between its legs and smashed two of its knees. It toppled and fell, right onto a horde of ice goblins who'd been racing my way.

Okay, I thought, facing down the rows of ice soldiers between me and the door under the balcony, the one that led down to the prisons. It was too dark to see faces, only shadowy shapes. Twenty down, and a few thousand more to go.

"Are you *sure* you don't want help?" said Matilda. "Not even you can fight them all."

I didn't plan to.

Two of the giants in the back—twin translucent Likons—ran at me. I threw down another comb like a gauntlet. Bars shot toward the ceiling. They caught the faster Likon through the torso. He shattered instantly, and his pieces crushed at least fifty ice wolves. The second Likon crashed into the bars and cracked his elbow. He pounded on the barrier, and his damaged arm fell off.

The second comb cut the room *and* the number of my opponents in half.

I was safe along the wall of bars. I started running.

Some ice trolls swarmed me, but they didn't last long—all it took was a solid hilt-smash or a punch to bring them down. I even beheaded an ice dragon with a simple snap kick.

Only the giants made me nervous. I steered clear when an ice Ori'an came my way, but I underestimated the frozen General Searcaster. I wove in between some slow-moving goblin statues, thinking the giants wouldn't smash them up to get to me. Not my smartest idea.

A huge see-through foot swept through the ranks and struck me so hard I went flying. The ice goblins caught in the kick cracked to pieces around me before we even touched down.

I smacked into one of the bars. My right side flared white-hot. I gasped with pain and choked on blood.

The Searcaster statue stretched her hand toward me. She moved way slower than the real thing.

She's just big, I reminded myself. *She's not as smart. She doesn't have any magic.*

I groped inside my carryall. I threw the third comb, rolled to my feet, and ran, only half as fast as before. I didn't think anything was broken. My right side just felt off, barely there, like it had been flattened when I'd fallen on it and it hadn't reinflated yet.

"She made it past that comb, Rory!" Matilda warned me. "She's coming!"

Scratch what I said about not being afraid.

It was even darker in the back of the Snow Queen's entrance hall. I could barely see. A dragon reared up out of the gloom. Next, two goblins. Then a hand of ice—larger than my entire bedroom at EAS—slammed down in front of me.

I couldn't stop. The ground was too slippery. So I curled my left hand into a fist and punched.

It didn't work. Her fingers closed around me, blocking out the little light I had left. They slapped me against her palm, and pain exploded against my temple.

My arms flew up to protect my face. My left knuckles banged into the thick thumb joint, and that did it. The ice hand fell off along the wrist. The fingers and I went tumbling like logs, and I rolled to my feet again.

Two hits. That was what it took to break a giant-size ice statue.

Losing a hand didn't seem to bother the Searcaster statue at all. She just started reaching down with the other one. I wasn't going to let her grab me again.

I broke into a sprint. Away from the door under the balcony. *Toward* the giantess statue.

I slid through her legs and skidded to a stop behind her. My left fist slammed into her ankle, just like I'd done with Matilda. I felt my knuckle split against the ice. I winced, and then I struck again in exactly the same place. Completely unbalanced, the Searcaster statue began to topple backward.

She would crash to the floor. She might even break into pieces, but she would definitely crush anyone underneath her when she landed.

As Lena might say, I ran like hiccups. I ran like *Lena*.

A dozen ice trolls tripped on each other in their rush to ambush me. Chase would have been proud of the way I vaulted over them, the way I slashed through a swarm of tiny gremlin-looking things.

The shadows deepened. Searcaster's ice statue was still falling.

The door rose up, just ahead, a square solid shape slightly darker than the gloom.

The ice giantess's head cracked against the balcony.

I threw open the door and dove through.

The balcony shattered. Shards of ice rained down, sharp as the darts the Snow Queen had sent through Hadriane's heart.

Still, the ice statues were following me. White shapes streamed around the fallen ice giantess.

One comb left. I pulled it out. I only had an instant to decide.

I could chant the retrieval spell, call the combs back, and toss one comb down afterward to make sure none of them followed me. But then the way would be clear. The ice army could leave through the front door as soon as the Snow Queen called them, and she would have her reinforcements. Matilda couldn't stop them all.

Or I could drop the last one and leave behind all four combs—the only cage ever proven to catch the Snow Queen.

I tossed the comb I was holding. Bars grew between me and the army, sealing them in.

I turned and began to hobble down the hall. My ribs hurt.

It really was up to me now—me and the heart.

Light doesn't travel too well through ice. The gloom deepened to black. Luckily, the combs weren't the only things Rapunzel had given me.

I fished out the glass vial and whistled. Light bloomed over my fingers and spilled down the hall. Blood was smeared over my forearm.

I couldn't close my hand without gasping. Green clouds had gathered under the skin around my knuckles, the beginnings of some very serious bruises. Plus my scalp was tender with goose eggs, my hair sticky with blood, my mouth swollen. If this was how I felt *before* confronting the Snow Queen, maybe it would be a mercy to put me out of my misery now.

I didn't really mean that. Well, maybe just a tiny bit.

I limped onward. My right leg was beginning to hurt more than my ribs.

The icy hallway sloped and narrowed. I paused. I couldn't remember if it had done that before. I didn't think so. The white fox had led us straight back, and then we'd gone through a door to the Treasury, where we'd taken a secret staircase down to the dungeons.

Solange must have done some remodeling since I was here last. Of course she had. She knew I might come.

Ugh. I needed a plan.

I leaned against the wall. I'd just wanted to take some of the weight off my leg, but then I kept leaning. Despite the heating spell I'd cast, the ice felt good. It numbed the ache in my ribs and my leg.

The soles of my sneakers squeaked against the floor and slid an inch toward the middle of the hallway. I hadn't moved, not even a muscle. I was sure.

Then with another squeak, my shoes slid two more inches.

I stepped back.

The corridor wasn't getting narrower. The wall was *moving*. The Snow Queen had clearly included booby traps in her remodel.

I took off down the hall. I didn't run, not quite. The wall wasn't moving quick enough to crush me, so a fast walk would—

Triumphant squawk-shrieks echoed down the corridor. Fear knifed me through the chest. *Witches*.

"Took you long enough to notice, Aurora Landon," said a silky voice.

Three green-skinned witches blocked the hall twenty meters ahead. A taller witch stood a little bit ahead of the others, her back straight, her hair woven with moonstones. It was Istalina and two more Wolfsbane witches, their wands raised.

They weren't like Matilda and the Living Stone Dwarves. There would be no last-minute alliance here.

It was officially time for make a break for it. I opened my stride, ignoring the pain lancing my knee.

"Not so fast." Istalina flicked her wand at the right wall.

It leapt forward, like it was spring-loaded. I shoved back with my left hand, hoping that West's ring could hold it.

The impact nearly shattered the bones in my arm. It probably would have if wind hadn't built up around my elbow and blasted it, so hard that it carved a divot out of the ice under my palm. The gust grew stronger. It ricocheted off the ceiling, blowing my hair into my mouth and swirling down the hall.

The wall stopped, but I wasn't sure how long the wind—even if it was laced with magic—could last against solid ice.

My shoes squeaked again. The wall gained another inch. Not long, I guessed.

"Quick thinking," said one of Istalina's clan mates.

"Thinking isn't enough," said the other.

"You'll need power," said the first.

"More power than you have," added Istalina, but she didn't sound as happy about it as the others did. She was probably thinking of her mother.

Apologizing wouldn't begin to make it better, not when their hate was so *personal*. Even telling them I knew would probably just set them off.

The ring had grown as thin as a strand of cooked spaghetti. I could almost *see* it shrinking.

"You'll be dead in a minute or two," said the first witch. "All we have to do is watch."

I glared at her. I'd just taken out an entire army of ice statues. I refused to be defeated by a *wall*.

The trap didn't extend the whole length of the corridor. The witches were in a safe section. All I had to do was cross the forty feet or so between us, and I would be out of danger.

Well, from being crushed.

I took one step toward the witches.

The wall gained at least four more inches. West's ring carved a fresh divot in the wall, about two feet from the last, and three craters opened up in the ceiling directly above me.

"Warning shots," Istalina said. "Try to move again, and we'll aim for your legs. The wall will crush you all the quicker then."

"You're supposed to die by the trap," said the first witch, clearly sad about it. "Orders from Her Majesty."

You are not worthy of me, the Snow Queen had said in the courtyard.

All this time, Solange had wanted her palace to finish me off. She would get all the credit, and tell her followers I wasn't anything special. *In the end*, she might say, with that cold, triumphant smile, *all it took to kill Aurora Landon was one small enchantment*.

No wonder the door below the balcony hadn't been locked.

The witches cackled.

The wind rippling up from my left hand seemed to falter. The ring had shrunk to the width of paperclip wire.

My head throbbed. I was so tired.

Not like this. Not killed by the Snow Queen's stupid *house*. If I had to die, I wanted to bring that heart back to her. I wanted her to kill me herself.

A crash echoed in the hall behind the witches.

Istalina raised her wand. "They've gotten through," she hissed.

It took a second for me to catch on. Someone *else* had come.

The witches lashed the air with their wands. Spells sizzled down the corridor and, at the end, a familiar voice gave an order. "Shields! Good. Now arrows!"

No way. It was another trick. The Snow Queen was trying to confuse me, to get me to lower my guard—

But arrows *did* thud into the witches. One struck the second witch in the chest, and she fell back into the path of the wall. Another pierced Istalina's shoulder. She ripped it out and stabbed her wand at the wound. Smoke puffed up, and before the gusting wind could blow it away, she squeezed off another shot. "Don't let them get any closer!"

"She doesn't have much time!" said another voice down the hall. Lena. My heart leapt with hope. "Here! I'll make sure it holds!"

"Cover me." Orange wings, so huge that they brushed the ceiling, flapped down the hall and toward the frantic Wolfsbane witches. Another flap and I could see the rest of him, the wooden cylinder in one hand, a shield in the other, and his mouth a grim twist.

Chase.

"No!" Istalina raised her wand, but right above her, Chase folded his wings. Both of his sneakers landed on her face. She crumpled to the ground.

Then Chase ran my way.

I couldn't believe he'd followed me. It should have been impossible. I'd sealed the entrance hall.

The first witch, bleeding from her hip, flicked her wand. "Duck!" I shouted.

He did. The spell missed and hit the ceiling instead. Still running, he shouted over his shoulder, "Geez, what part of 'cover me' did you not understand? There are only two witches left."

"And we only have *one archer* left!" came Lena's voice.

Both of them came, and one of the archers, too.

Chase slid to a stop. Holding his shield in front of us, he fumbled with the ends of Lena's retractable spear. "How do you—"

"You twist it," I said. "But I don't think that'll hold this wall."

"Lena promised it would. Besides, we're out of time." Chase nodded at my ring. It was finer than a hair, just a tiny shine of metal. He twisted the staff-stump. The shaft zoomed open. Both ends stopped just a few inches from either side of the corridor.

The gust around my arm petered out. The ring was gone, all used up.

The wall shot forward. Chase's arm reached back and kind of scooped me behind him. Sweet, but it wouldn't stop us from getting crushed.

With a crack, the staff hit and held. Fractures crackled across both walls.

As rescues go, this one had some room for improvement. My worries about cave-ins tripled. "That still might not hold."

"Better go before we're squished." Chase pointed down the hall. "Lena's casting a strengthening spell on it from over there. Her control is still kind of spotty. Can you walk? If the answer's no, it's piggyback ride time."

"I can walk." I didn't want to be carried. Last time Chase had tried, he'd told me how heavy I was. "Maybe not far, though."

"No, not far," he said softly. He hadn't turned around yet. I think he was afraid to take his eyes off the two remaining witches. The archer was keeping them busy, firing off so many arrows that the witches couldn't use their wands for anything more than blasting the missiles out of the air. "What do you say we tackle those two while we're at it?" He started forward.

I followed, just a step behind. "What do you say we keep the shield in place in case they're bluffing?" I said, not ready to take any more risks. My left arm ached as much as my right leg.

"Your Tale. Your call," Chase said, sounding vaguely disappointed, and my chest swelled, suddenly full to bursting. He'd *come*. He was talking to me.

We had cleared most of the hall. I tested my sword arm. It was okay. I could handle a brief surprise attack. I put a hand on his shoulder and whispered in his ear, "I'll take the one on the left."

Chase nodded. "Now!"

The witches hadn't realized we'd gotten so close. When I pounced, Istalina shriek-squawked and stuck her wand in my face. My hilt struck her temple before she could cast anything.

The one on the right slumped against the floor, bleeding from her hip and her shoulder, and her wand rolled out from between her fingers. Chase didn't spare her a second glance. He turned down the hall and spoke to the shadows that Rapunzel's light couldn't reach. "We're good, Lena."

The booby trap wall slammed against the other side, and then the corridor *did* cave in. Ice chips rained down. Cold bits invaded my collar. Chase shielded me, his arm around my shoulders again.

"Oh, thank gumdrops," Lena called. Footsteps padded down the hall, fast.

When I looked up, Chase was glaring down at the witches, sword raised like he expected one to jump up and start casting at any second. He didn't seem to notice that slivers of ice had melted in his hair. Or that his arm was still around me. Or that I was leaning half my weight against him.

"What are you *doing* here?" I didn't mean to say it like an accusation.

Chase looked genuinely surprised. "You said you needed me."

It's totally possible for a person to be overjoyed and completely exasperated at the same time. After so many years of knowing Chase, I was pretty familiar with the feeling.

He leaned in, examining my face. His fingers grazed my cheek. "Rory, what happened to you?"

I probably looked horrible. I shouldn't have cared about that, especially when he was pretty banged up too. His lip was swollen, and his chin had a huge bruise. "What happened to *you*?"

"Jailbreak. Our target was the Fey royalty, but while we were there, we went ahead and let out everybody." He tried to play it cool. That only lasted two seconds. His grin took up half his face, fat lip and all. "It happened to us. So, I thought to myself, why can't it happen to the Snow Queen too?"

"Since *when*?" I said.

A small, wiry body slammed into me. When she wrapped her arms around my waist, I felt her metal hands. "Lena? How did you even get inside?" I whispered, ignoring the pain that flared in my ribs. I hugged her back.

"I told you, Chase," Lena said fiercely. "She didn't know you were trying to trick the Canon. She's not *that* good at lying."

I sheathed my sword. My head was still throbbing, so I was having trouble keeping up with this conversation. "You were trying to trick the Canon?"

"Weren't you?" Chase said. "Everybody was watching us when we left the meeting, and then you shouted that we were planning on leaving. We had to throw them off. A big, ugly fight in the middle of the courtyard was a genius . . ." He drifted off. "Lena's right. You didn't know. You were serious."

And Chase hadn't been. He had lied so well that he managed to fool me. It had been a long time since that happened. We really *had* drifted apart this summer.

"Told you!" Lena knelt next to Istalina and pocketed her wand. "So, they're all still alive. I'll go ahead and send them back to the dungeons." Lena pulled a brassy-green ring out of her pocket. She slid it on Istalina's finger. The witch vanished, and Lena moved toward the other two. "I enchanted these to send them straight there. They'll be a little cramped, their whole clan in one cell."

"Poor cramped killer witches. I'm all torn up over it." Gently, Chase grabbed my chin and tilted my face to examine the side that had hit the comb bar.

"What?" I said, wondering if Rapunzel's glass vial was bright enough for my blush to be visible.

Chase took my hand, the one with the light swinging from it, and he held it close to my face. I jerked away, grimacing in pain. "Sorry," he said, and it sounded like he actually meant it. "I had to check. Lena, I think Rory has a concussion."

Lena gasped. We were alone in the hallway. She'd already gotten rid of the other witches without me noticing. Well, a concussion was one explanation for being so disoriented.

Chase grabbed my right arm, the one that hurt less, and secured it around his shoulders. He helped me down the hall. The glass vial bobbed and weaved, making shadows dance down the corridor. The path curved up ahead. "We brought some Water of Life."

Wow. The Director's rationing didn't count for much. EAS had used a ton of it during the week. We would be lucky if we still had some left over by the end of the day.

"You stole the Water from the Director?" I said, determined to prove that I wasn't as dumb as I'd been acting. It did not help that my stomach was doing somersaults. Either my head really was spinning, or being pressed up against Chase was having a very embarrassing effect on me.

"Didn't have to," Chase said gleefully.

"Rapunzel left us some in my workshop," Lena said apologetically. "I kind of didn't mention it to the Director."

"Or to me," I pointed out.

"She was *supposed* to tell you," Chase said.

"I was going to!" Lena said. "But first I had to tell her about the letter, and then we got to talking about other things, and then Gran came in . . ."

Another figure stepped around the corner. Kyle. He didn't have a scratch on him, but blood stained his shirt collar, like he'd had a very close call earlier. "What kind of other things?" he said, like he knew exactly what we'd been talking about in Lena's room.

She launched herself at him, threw her arms around his neck, and started talking so fast that my poor, bruised brain couldn't make out any words.

"The rest of the Wolfsbane clan was guarding the prisons," Chase said conversationally. "He got turned to stone."

"Ice. Stone. Kyle, you've been enchanted a lot this week," I said, happy he was okay.

"Only for like five minutes." Kyle passed a bottle to Lena, with strange metal symbols trapped in the glass. It was even smaller than the little jars she used to make temporary-transport spells, and through it, you could see an eyedropper attached to the lid. The Water of Life. Rapunzel hadn't given them much, but the fight in the dungeons must have been intense. It would take dozens of wounds and enchantments to go through that bottle one drop at a time. "And the witches only got me once. Paul got turned to stone at least three times tonight."

Lena unscrewed the bottle and turned to me. Liquid sloshed around the bottom, only a few drops left. I hesitated. I *wanted* to get healed. Apparently, now that I actually did have Companions on my Tale, *all* the adrenaline was leaking out of my system. It left me with lots of pain. But the quest wasn't over yet. "You can't give that to me."

"That's what it's *for*," Lena said.

"We'd better save it. In case someone gets seriously hurt again," I said. Chase's back muscles tensed under my arm. Maybe he hadn't planned on half-carrying me through the Snow Queen's basement. "Is that okay with you?"

Chase gave me a look. "If you get any worse, we're overriding that order—Tale bearer or no."

I decided not to protest. "Deal."

Lena's gaze slid from me to Chase and back again. "We'll start checking to see if the Snow Queen has laid any more traps for us. You guys need to talk." She looped her arm through Kyle's and marched out.

After a second, Chase and I started after her. Much slower than before.

I broke the silence. "You're mad at me." Again.

"I'm not," said Chase, obviously mad. His face was even turning red. Oh great. If I could see *that*, then he definitely had noticed my blushing earlier. "I'm just going back over everything you said in the courtyard, now that I know you meant it."

"It was a fight," I said flatly. We reached a staircase, one of those awful twisting ones.

Chase let my arm go and switched sides, so that I could hold on to the wall to steady myself. "Not to me! I didn't mean any of it. Everything I said was for the Director's benefit."

I looked him right in the eye. "Not everything. Not the part about it being nice knowing Adelaide liked you. You *meant* that."

He didn't argue. He stepped in front of me and walked ahead, ready to catch me if I fell. We took the stairs *really* slow.

"Do you know what Iron Hans said about you?" Chase said finally.

"When did you see Iron Hans?" I said, confused.

"I called him on the M3 earlier," Chase said. "We needed a fast ride from the Portland portal to here. Lena thinks she has almost figured out how he can send the Dapplegrim from Atlantis to here and back."

"I thought they refused to go in the snow," I said.

"Lena adapted the heating spell for humans." Chase shot me a scowl, like I was changing the subject on purpose. "Iron Hans says you constantly underestimate me."

"I meant what I said at the beginning of our fight too. The part about you being awesome." Because I was annoyed, I almost added that I was considering taking it back now, but it wouldn't have been true.

"No, you underestimate the way I care about *you*," Chase said, "and it's getting old."

I limped down another step. If my legs had worked a little better, I might have tried to outrun this conversation. "We never talked about it," I said in a small voice.

Chase's eyes blazed. "*You didn't want to*. Geez, Rory, it's like you think I'm the same kid you met in sixth grade."

"I do not." I didn't think the Chase I'd met back then ever really existed.

"But you treat me the same sometimes." Now he sounded more upset than angry. Something twisted in my chest, hearing how much I'd hurt him. "That's not okay."

"It's not okay. And I *am* sorry." Apologizing sounded so feeble. If I hadn't doubted him, then I might have noticed something was wrong sooner. We could have told someone outside the Pounce Pot's influence, someone who *could* figure it out. He wouldn't have spent the whole summer enchanted. "But you can't just assume I *know* stuff, Chase. I can't read your mind."

He snorted. "Seems like it sometimes."

I almost didn't tell him the next part. I didn't want to bring her up again. "You know, Adelaide was using the Pounce Pot."

"Not shocked," Chase grumbled, but I knew he kind of was.

I wanted to tell him that he'd seemed like a stranger lately. He'd only say it was the enchantment, but that wasn't it. Something new was opening up between us, and it was like Chase had a map and I didn't. I never recognized any of the landmarks like he seemed to. I hadn't even realized that there *were* landmarks until we went on Miriam's Tale.

"Wanna hear the other thing Iron Hans says about us?" Chase asked after a few more stairs.

"Can it wait? I'm still processing the first one," I said.

"You'll like this one better," he said, almost smiling. "He said that the biggest difference between us is that you assume that if you screw up enough, we won't even be friends anymore, and *I* assume that no matter how much I screw up, we'll be all right in the end."

I peeked at him. "The end" as in the end of the Snow Queen's reign, or the end of the summer, or the end of us going to EAS, or the end of something even bigger?

"Are you guys coming?" someone called up the stairwell. Vicky, I think. "We can see Rory's light. We know how close you two are."

"There *is* a war on, you know," said Kevin.

Chase rolled his eyes. "We're going to talk about this more later, but are we good for now? At least until we make sure we don't die?"

I nodded. We were definitely good. Better than we'd been in months.

We made our way down the last few steps.

The prison door had been busted off its hinges. A breeze whistled through it, and once Chase and I reached the floor, I spotted why. A hole gaped in the middle of the prison hall, as big as Amy's car. Wow. I guess I knew how our fighters had gotten inside.

The others were waiting.

Nine in all. The triplets. The stepsisters. Paul Stockton. Daisy. Plus Chase and Lena. No one else had ever had nine Companions on their quest before. They had taken the time to dress for the cold. Every single one had on a coat, unlike me.

Lena held up a jacket, a regular gray one that was kind of worn. "Remember the spell the dwarves put on Hadriane's polar bear cloak? I borrowed it. This should keep you warm."

I shrugged on the jacket, thrilled to see everyone, practically giddy. "Hey."

They didn't look so excited to see me. Mostly, they just stared.

I definitely looked as horrible as I felt then.

Chase cleared his throat. "How did the rest of the jailbreak go?"

Conner ripped his gaze off me and turned to Chase. "The prison's empty."

Tina couldn't keep the shock out of her voice. "What did that to you, Rory?"

"The Snow Queen was keeping an army of ice statues in her entrance hall," I explained. "That was the way I came in."

Chase's whole torso had begun shaking. I wasn't sure if I should worry or not.

"And what? They all tackled you?" asked Kevin.

"One of them was the same shape as Genevieve Searcaster," I said, trying to see Chase's face and figure out what his deal was. "Same size, too."

"*She* tackled you?" whispered Lena. "I mean, attacked you?"

I nodded. "Don't worry. I used the combs to lock them all in. They won't be bothering us."

Chase was *laughing*. "And you didn't think to mention this until now?"

"Concussion," I reminded him, and now I was laughing too.

Laughing with *Chase*. The world was slowly pulling itself back together again.

"Rory, you have to stop being so competitive," Chase said, grinning. "Just because I organized a jailbreak doesn't mean you have to neutralize an entire army."

I decided not to answer that. "So, where's that door? The pale one?"

"This way." Lena led the charge down the dim hallway. Chase was still helping me, but I felt steadier now.

"I'm thinking that Rory is winning this one, though," Vicky said. "I mean, she took out that army *single-handed*."

"Hey, I personally gave the Seelie and Unseelie royals rings of return and sent them back to EAS. That means I single-handedly mobilized the entire Fey army," Chase pointed out. "I'd say Rory and I are even."

I smiled. EAS's odds had gotten a lot better since we'd reached the palace.

"Here it is." Lena had managed to open the door made of pale wood. Beyond it was another dark corridor. Everybody else went ahead, their weapons drawn, their M3's held high, with their flashlight functions shining all the way into the corners.

"All clear?" Chase asked.

"Clear," Paul called back.

"Yeah, I don't sense any spells," Lena added. It was news to me that she could do that now.

With the kids in our grade parading down the hall and the lights from our magic mirrors bobbing up ahead, the corridor grew almost cheerful. It didn't even really feel like a quest. More like just another field trip.

Chase helped me forward, but I almost didn't need him to. Not anymore.

The fear had left me. I was practically floating.

"You know, mood swings are a symptom of a concussion," Chase said, "but usually people get bummed, not happy."

So maybe I shouldn't have been grinning. Something worse than the Wolfsbane clan could ambush us back here, and we still didn't know what exactly we would find behind that door.

But I'd been alone, and now I wasn't. After this awful summer, it was enough to make anyone happy.

"Found another door!" Lena called from the front. "Rory, is this the one?"

The other kids cleared a path so I could see.

It was chestnut brown, and the doorknob and hinges were black instead of silver. "No."

Shoulders slumped and weapon stances drooped. No one said anything, but they were probably thinking that the Director could be right. This could be a decoy, made by the Snow Queen to keep us out of her way during the invasion.

It was nice of them not to say it.

"Well, it's locked." Lena looked pointedly at Chase.

"If the Snow Queen is really trying to keep us out, a simple unlocking spell isn't going to open it." But Chase pressed a hand on the door and whispered in Fey anyway.

It clicked under his palm. He twisted the knob. The door swung open.

Not a corridor this time. A windowless square room, barely big enough for all ten of us to fit inside. Cut into the white wall directly opposite us was a door of ancient black wood, fitted with silver hinges.

"*That's* it." I had expected my heart to stop with fear when I saw the door in person, but it didn't. Instead, it sang with excitement, drumming a jig against my ribs.

"Okay," Chase said. "Like we talked about. Front guard enters first, then me and Rory and Lena, then rear guard."

The others started moving into position. Maybe everyone *else* had talked about it, but I had no clue what he meant.

Then it hit me. "No, I have to go in alone."

Everyone paused and looked at me.

"Five minutes," Tina told Vicky. "That's how long they lasted without arguing. Pay up."

"We're *not* arguing about this," Chase said, scowling. "Because Rory can't expect us to just wait out here while she walks into another trap with a concussion."

"Not even 'walks.'" Even Kyle was frowning. *"Limps."*

They thought I had a choice. "Look, I would love to have you with me for this part, but you won't make it through the door."

Chase just folded his arms and shot me a look that clearly said, *I'd like to see you try and stop me.*

"No, really." I pointed. "Look again. Around the frame and under the doorknob. It's a one-key safe."

"Ooooh," Lena said, going over to look at it. "I've never seen one in person before."

Paul leaned closer to Vicky. "Should I know what that is?"

"Basically, it's a door that only lets one person pass through," said Kyle. "They're really complicated to set up."

"Not just that," Lena said. "It takes thirty-seven months to create one. It's been less than a year and a half since the Snow Queen got out of prison. She hasn't had time to make a new one."

"Oh." I hadn't known that. "Well, Rapunzel made me one at EAS. To keep the Pounce Pot safe."

"Rory, if it's a one-key safe, it must be enchanted to only let the Snow Queen in," Chase pointed out. "What makes you think you can open it?"

"I think because the key for this one is having an Unwritten Tale," I said. Rapunzel hadn't picked that quality when she made my one-key safe, but when Solange had made this one, she'd probably assumed she would always be the only bearer of an Unwritten Tale.

"The one-key safe uses the most unusual thing about you to identify you," Lena explained to the others, catching on fast. "The safe must identify the Snow Queen by her magic—the same magic that has been hanging around her since her Unwritten Tale. The magic around Rory is nearly identical. I'm sure the Snow Queen would have made a new, more specific one if she'd had more time."

"And you don't think the Snow Queen just moved it?" asked Daisy sarcastically.

That hadn't occurred to me. It should have.

"No," Kyle said slowly. "Think about it. If you had a safe only one other person could open, would you move it someplace where *anyone* could get at it?"

"Rory's right," Lena said. "She can fool the safe."

For the first time ever, being like the Snow Queen felt like a good thing.

Chase still didn't like the idea, but he was considering it now. "Can you break the enchantment, Lena?"

She examined the door. You could practically see the wheels turning in her head. "Rory, did you swipe EAS's extra supply of dragon scales before you left?" I nodded, shrugging off my carryall and passing over the two sacks. "Then I can. It would take some time though."

"We don't *have* time," Daisy said. "The invasion could begin like, any minute."

Chase cursed in Fey, and I knew he'd given in.

"Come on, Chase. Even Maerwynne, Rikard, and Madame Benne weren't together all the time." I unsheathed my sword and crossed the room, trying to hide my limp as much as possible. "They were united in purpose even when their paths diverged."

"Rory, I can tell when you're just repeating something Rapunzel said," Chase told me.

"Well, it makes *me* feel better." I stopped in front of the door. It seemed smaller in person. Under Rapunzel's light, the tiny frost crystals on the dark wood sparkled just as brightly as the enchantment around the door frame.

"Wait." Chase came over. His fingertips traced my jaw, tilting my face up again and checking my concussion. Ugh, not again. "All the rest of you, turn around. Lena, you too."

Well, that was a ridiculous order. I thought some of them would protest, but they did it, smirking.

I didn't blame him for being worried, but he couldn't convince me to take the rest of the Water. "I'll be fine. Just let me do this. We *are* on a time crunch."

"Rory," Chase whispered. "Please stop talking. I'm trying to do this right."

Then he lowered his head and pressed his lips against mine.

They were a little cold, like they'd been in the tower, and suddenly, they weren't. All the places where he touched me thawed, and the warmth spread, chasing away the chill. The whole room soared, like we were weightless, on top of the world. It was like flying without being afraid I would fall.

He drew back, so careful not to brush any of my bruises. "*That* was our first one. The thing in the tower didn't count."

I laughed a little. I didn't realize how close I was to crying until I heard how shaky I sounded. "Of course it counted. It woke you up."

"We clearly have a different definition of 'counting.'" He had that smile on—the one that I rarely saw, the one that was almost shy.

"For me, it can't count unless both people are conscious."

I wanted to stand here and tease him until we both laughed. I wanted to savor this. I didn't want to feel like time was running out. I didn't want to feel like this might be our last kiss.

"I told you," Vicky muttered to Tina. I jumped. I'd totally forgotten other people were in the room. "I knew it would happen before the end of her Tale. You pay up."

"Shhh," Lena hissed.

So the kids in our grade took bets about me and Chase fighting *and* kissing. Great. I wondered if they had bets on whether or not we would die, too.

"You're not going to die, Rory." And Chase thought *I* read minds sometimes.

"You don't know that." He was afraid too. You don't make a point of kissing someone who's about to walk into a trap, unless you think they might not come back. "I have to go."

He nodded. He stepped away, but he didn't drop my hand. I reached for the knob with my sword arm. It turned easily. The door creaked open. Cold air spilled out.

"See you in a bit," I told Chase, and before I could lose my nerve, I pulled my hand out of his and slipped through the doorway.

No giant ice statues. No crushing walls. Not even an enchantment to freeze me where I stood.

It was a plain white chamber, identical to the one I'd just left, except that this room only had one person in it.

She wasn't the Snow Queen. She was taller and not as slender. Her hair hung in perfect brown waves all the way down her back, streaked with lighter honey strands. Her hazel eyes had a piercing gaze under arched eyebrows. Her dress flowed to the floor in a cascade of dark gray silk. She was beautiful in that chilly, distant way that the Snow Queen was—like her beauty was a prelude to some sort of catastrophe.

She also didn't look armed. That was the part that really mattered. "So . . . who are you?"

The girl laughed. "Isn't it obvious?" she said, with *my* voice.

No. Walking into a one-key safe couldn't split one person into two. Even the Snow Queen couldn't manage that, right?

"I got all your best traits," said the other Rory. "None of the indecision that holds *you* back, none of your fears, none of your failings."

Well, if she had all my best traits, she was missing my stubbornness. I had a job to do, and I was going to do it—weird other Rory or no. I circled her once to make sure she hadn't tucked any weapons under her skirt. Then I turned away. I inspected the walls, looking for some hidden compartment where the Snow Queen might have stored her heart. I even risked sheathing my sword so that I could run both hands over the ice, feeling for cracks too small to see.

Nothing. I should have at least felt the doorway, but that blended in too. No handles or keyholes either. I probably should have left it ajar when I walked in.

Oh well. I would deal with that problem *after* I got the heart.

The other Rory didn't try to stop me. She didn't even move closer. "If I was the one out there, your father wouldn't need another family. Your mother wouldn't be in danger."

I squatted down to inspect the floor, barely listening. I didn't see anything there either. My head throbbed.

"If I was the one out there, the Snow Queen would have been dead ages ago. Lena would not need Melodie. Chase would never have been ensnared by someone else." Geez, for someone who was supposed to be me, she sure talked a lot like Mia. Like the Snow Queen, when she was trying to stop me.

I turned back to the other Rory, suddenly interested. "You're a doll, aren't you? Solange, are you in there?"

The girl didn't speak. Maybe the Snow Queen didn't trust herself to answer. Maybe she regretted trying to use the same trick twice. Maybe she was starting to feel fear.

I drew my sword slowly.

If I had figured out her identity, she should have attacked. Even Mia had poisoned knives for fingers. Solange wouldn't leave the last guardian of her heart completely defenseless.

Well, unless attacking me would risk the heart she was protecting.

It was stupid of the Snow Queen to make the doll look like me.

If it had resembled Chase or Lena, I would have hesitated longer.

I leapt and stabbed. My sword slid into the other Rory's torso easily, like her skin was made of papier-mâché. No bones got in my blade's way. No wood like the Mia puppet, no metal screws to hold it together.

The doll's illusion didn't even flicker. Something wet—a red so dark it was only a shade away from black—oozed down my sword.

Eww. I might have rethought my strategy if I'd known *that* was going to happen. I twisted the blade, and its edge scraped something solid and hollow—something big enough to hold a heart. Well, if I had to cut it out of her, I would.

The other Rory glanced down at my weapon. The fake blood had trickled across the metal and covered up all the ancient Fey symbols on the blade.

Her chin tilted up. Her lips curled slowly. Solange's smile was on *my* face.

"Very clever, Rory. You've figured out how to kill me." Her voice was her own again. A small relief. "Pity you'll die here."

Traps within traps, Rapunzel had said. It had been too easy. The Snow Queen was planning something else.

An explosion blasted me off my feet. Shrapnel—as long as my hand, as sharp as scalpels—thudded into my chest, into my stomach, into my hips and shoulders. I crashed into the wall. My head cracked against the ice.

At least I passed out before I could feel the pain.

"Rory?" Lena's voice was trembling. A warm metal fingertip brushed hair away from my forehead. "Rory, *please* wake up."

"'M okay," I mumbled. Then I managed to open my eyes. Lena let out an *I'm happy but too scared to believe it* gasp.

The room was splattered with that awful dark-red ooze. Splashed up against the white walls like that, it made the room look way too similar to the crime scenes in Mom and Dad's movies, the ones they still said I was too young to watch. The red had left craters wherever it landed.

"Concentrated dragon blood." Lena's voice got stronger when it took on that familiar tinny reciting tone. *"In this form, it acts like—"*

"—an acid. I remember." I sat up. Beside us, a bean-shaped pool of scarlet had eaten through at least three inches of ice. "It burned me, didn't it?"

Lena nodded. "And your sword." She pointed to my other side, at a pile of sharp metal slivers. That couldn't be my weapon. They looked like misshapen silver spikes, tipped with a much brighter red than what was on the walls. "That was what caused the explosion. The spell was forged into the actual blade, and the acid ate away at the metal. The enchantment unraveled. All the magic spilled out at once, and then—"

"Boom," I finished. The Snow Queen had expected me to cut into the doll. Maybe she knew about the Itari curse Lady Aspenwind had warned me about. I looked from the shrapnel to Lena. "You pulled those out of me, didn't you?"

She nodded again. "I was on the other side, and you screamed," Lena said. I didn't remember doing that. "I tricked the one-key safe. I used my sorcery to rip all the magic out of the dragon scales and kind of hold it around me, and the door wouldn't budge, but then it did. I heard the others try to follow me, but they couldn't, and there you were, lying on the floor . . ." She swallowed hard. "It took the rest of the Water to bring you back."

All of it? We'd had enough to last us through a few more

wounds and enchantments, so I must have been really bad off. Maybe near death.

Well, at least all my banged-up places had stopped aching. "Lena, I'm so sorry."

She shot me an exasperated look. "It's not your fault the Snow Queen tried to kill you."

But it was me who had brought her here, where she had to fish sword shards out of her best friend.

I stood. Doll pieces were strewn around the room, which kind of added to the crime-scene vibe, but since most of the dragon blood acid had leaked out, it was *slightly* less horrifying than it could have been. I searched for a container big enough to put a heart in.

A small chest had fallen against the wall. It was covered in symbols just like the ones on the bottles we used to hold the Water. With those symbols, the chest could contain magic, or maybe stop a magical acid from eating away at the heart it protected.

I knelt beside it. The dragon blood had gotten into the cracks, tracing all the symbols. It wasn't safe to touch. My T-shirt was full of holes. It was easy to rip off a section from the hem.

"Be careful!" Lena said, way more worried now that we didn't have any Water to heal us. "Are you sure that this isn't just another trap?"

I wasn't, but we had to risk it. "Lena, she thinks I'm dead. Besides, she would want to have a way inside the chest too."

"It's bound to be locked . . . ," Lena said.

"It is." I pointed to the faint gleam all around the rim of the lid. "It's another one-key safe."

Lena squinted at it. "I didn't know you could make one so small." Her expression shifted from concern to interest. I flipped the lid open.

Light spilled out, so bright that I was sure for one terrible second that I'd been wrong, that a second blast was waiting for us. Then my eyes adjusted.

"It's definitely still connected to her," Lena said. "Look. It's still beating."

A heart. Larger than I expected. It was mostly red, but cobalt streaks curled all around its lumps and chambers. Silver light leaked from its center, shifting as the heart moved—swelling and squeezing, then swelling and squeezing again.

Gross. I hadn't expected it to look so . . . anatomically correct. "Do you think she'll feel it if I pick it up?"

I'd asked the Pounce Pot to keep the Snow Queen from finding out about my quest for the heart. The enchantment was probably broken, considering the Snow Queen and I had talked through the doll. The Pounce Pot wouldn't stop her from discovering that I was alive and that I was bringing the heart to her.

"I don't know!" Lena said, clearly freaked. "The Snow Queen is the only Character who has ever tried this!"

"Yeah, but you're probably the only Character alive who could figure out exactly how she did it." I dropped the rag I'd used to open the chest. It had a few dragon blood spots, and I didn't want it near whatever enchantments Solange had cast around the heart. The last thing we needed was another explosion. "What's your opinion?"

Lena thought about it. "Fifty-fifty chance. I mean, she and the heart share some sort of psychic link that transcends temporal space, so she might know. But the nerve endings aren't attached."

Much better odds than I was expecting. "Lena, I think everything's going to be okay. I have this feeling."

"That doesn't mean much, considering I just had to dig pieces of your sword out of you, Rory," Lena said. "I'm not worried about defeating the Snow Queen. You'll handle it like you always do. I'm worried about *you*."

I didn't tell her not to worry. I knew better. "I'm glad you're my best friend," I said, just in case I never got a chance to say it afterward.

Then I reached both hands into the box.

My fingertips tingled as I slid my palms underneath the heart and lifted it out. Vibrations buzzed all the way up my arm, but the only other change in the heart was the light. His color grew warmer, more amber than silver, so bright you could barely make out the heart's outline. It was like touching pure magic.

"Wow," Lena whispered. "Do you feel that?"

"Um. I'm *holding* it." Of course I felt it.

My pulse thudded in perfect time with the thumping heart in my hands. I wondered whose heartbeat was setting the pace.

"No, I mean the *heat*." She pointed down at the floor. A new puddle had formed under my knees. The water reflected my face. My temple was covered with dried blood, but the wound underneath it had healed.

"That puddle has gotten bigger since I've been staring at it." Lena glanced up. The ceiling glistened with a wet sheen, and a few drops plunked into the water below. "Okay, if it's hot enough to melt the ceiling, then we *really* need to get out of here."

"Okay." It was awkward to get up when I was holding something in both hands. I glanced at what was left of my sword. It felt weird to go into a fight without it, but I forced myself to look away. "Do you remember which way you came in?"

Lena pointed at the wall behind me. "The door vanished when it shut. I'm sorry. I didn't even think about keeping it open."

"I did the same thing. Besides, you were distracted by the horror-movie scene." I stepped close to the door and held the blazing heart up, hoping that the extra bright light would bring out the cracks.

Lena tied a chain to my wrist. Rapunzel's glass vial dangled from it, no longer glowing now that something else was giving us light. "For luck," she said. "Look! Well, that solves one problem!"

The heat was melting the wall. Water cascaded down it, and in the place where the ice was thinnest, we could see the outline of a figure. Chase.

He elbowed through the wall's weak spot, and then he stuck his face through the opening. He spotted the scarlet craters everywhere, the other Rory in pieces. His mouth opened, but no sound came out. Oh no. He thought she was me.

"It's just a doll, Chase," I said, quickly stepping into his line of sight. "We got the heart."

Chase's mouth closed, but he took in the bloodstains on my shirt and Lena's pinched face. "Good call on saving the Water." He made it sound like a joke, but his face was still too pale. "Hold on. Let me make a bigger hole."

He hammered at the ice with his sword hilt. Big chunks fell at his feet. Lena squeezed through easily, and then I splashed after her. The heart had already created a puddle of melted ice water around the door.

Chase squinted at what was in my hands. "The battle started fifteen minutes ago. Just so you know. Ben said he'll call me if any of the Snow Queen's forces actually reach the human world."

I wondered how long I'd been unconscious. It had to be a while if the invasion had already started, if people were already dying. It was time to end this.

Something cracked above us. Chase was ready for it. He yanked me and Lena forward a few feet, a second before a huge slab of glistening ice crashed down onto the spot where we'd been standing.

"I was afraid of that," Lena said.

"The heart's a portable furnace." Chase led us to the exit. "Maybe you shouldn't stand too long in one place while we're in a building *made of ice*." He opened the brown wooden door for me.

The other kids in our grade hung back. Lena's golden skin flashed as she waved them forward. "Go on. The Snow Queen's heart doesn't bite. Just melts."

I glanced back, wondering if we should wait. Chase took my elbow and hurried me on ahead. "Rory, it's *your* Tale. Your Companions are supposed to keep up with you, not the other way around." We reached the next door. He opened it too. I should keep my hands full more often. It made him as gentlemanly as Ben.

The heat was taking the place out *fast*. Something crashed behind us. I almost turned back.

"We're okay!" Lena called. "Keep going!"

"Come on. The heart's making it worse."

Chase dragged me through the busted doors. The prisons looked like I remembered them, empty and huge, too pale except for the horrible stains frozen to the floor.

Those stains were starting to look kind of wet now. The melting floor was *very* slippery.

Chase grabbed my arm just before I face-planted. "Lena, we could use that shoe spike spell."

Lena hurried into the prisons, chanting in Fey. When the spell took hold, she ran forward.

"Thanks, Lena." The heart wasn't buzzing gently anymore. It was vibrating hard enough to make my voice shake.

Behind us came Conner's voice. "I don't get it. All she has to do is stab the heart. That would kill the Snow Queen, wouldn't it? Then this would all be over."

That should have occurred to me. It hadn't. I had been so focused on getting the heart and bringing it to the Snow Queen. I hadn't considered that there might be another option.

But stabbing the heart would work. It was pumping magic through her veins instead of blood. Destroying it would end that flow, and considering she was over two hundred years old, magic was the only thing keeping her alive.

We'd reached the hole in the main corridor. They'd blasted through five feet of solid ice. I wondered what Lena had used on it.

"Step on the chunks." Lena pointed out a path up the huge blocks of ice that had fallen out of the wall.

The others ran down the corridor toward us. "It could all be *over*," Conner told his brothers again.

"What do you think?" I asked Chase before our grade could catch up with us.

"I think it's your Tale. It's your decision." Chase was saying that a lot tonight. It would only last until he *really* disagreed with me.

I stepped onto the first ice block. It melted underfoot, and I almost slipped on my second step.

Stabbing the heart wasn't the right way to stop Solange. I glanced back. "I need to bring it to the Snow Queen. That's what Rapunzel saw in her vision."

That didn't seem to be a good enough reason for Conner. Or Kevin, Paul, Vicky, Tina, and especially not for Daisy. I wondered if I should tell them the heart would probably explode if we put a knife through it. Returning it still wouldn't be a natural death, but it was as close as we would be able to get under the circumstances. Maybe that would minimize the blast.

"It wouldn't end the war," Chase said, climbing out right behind me. "The Snow Queen would die, sure, but then General Searcaster would lead the army. The invasion would still happen."

Something else cracked. Everyone looked up, horrified, but forty feet up, the ceiling was smooth, still frozen.

"Wall," Kyle said, pointing to what we had heard. Another huge crack, and the wall began to topple. The others scattered, out of its way.

Chase took matters into his own hands and decided to get the heart out of the palace before it could destroy anything else. He unfurled his wings, scooped me up, and flew out of the hole. A second later we landed on the snow.

"You okay?" Chase asked. I nodded, counting the others as they climbed out. All nine of them came out, uninjured.

Then an enormous shadow fell over us.

Chase drew his sword. "Giant!"

21

atilda threw up her hands. It was very strange to see a four-story-tall woman cowering in front of a kid who had only cleared six feet this summer.

"Rory!" she said in a tone that clearly meant *Help me*.

"Don't move!" Vicky said, drawing back her bowstring. "Rory already got what she came here for. And if you think that we'll let you stop her now—"

"Whoa!" I stepped between them before anyone could do any damage. "Matilda's on our side! She opened the front door for me."

The triplets lowered their spears. They were staring at me again. Well, squinting actually. The heart glowed even brighter outside.

Chase hadn't sheathed his sword. "There was an *army* in there. She might not have thought she was doing you a favor when she opened the door."

"She swore a Binding Oath," I said. "West helped us."

Chase eased out of his battle stance. The others followed him.

The heart had melted another puddle around me, and I sloshed through it, toward a very unnerved-looking Matilda. "Do you think you could give us a ride?"

They were bound to see us coming. A four-story-tall pregnant giantess was hard to ignore. Add me and Lena on one shoulder, three archers on the other, and our spearmen in her pockets, plus Chase winging his way along beside her, and no one could miss us.

But the real giveaway was the heart. It wasn't content with just blazing now that we were getting closer to the Snow Queen. It had decided to put on a show. Yellow light spilled into the air above us, rippling with flame-red streaks. Green ribbons unfurled across the sky.

The Snow Queen knew by now that I had her heart. She had to.

Matilda climbed a ridge. She walked quickly, carefully. The way was steep. Melted water made it slick. Her neck glistened with sweat, but then again, so did Lena's face. I didn't feel the heart's heat, but its vibrations definitely got worse. My teeth chattered inside my mouth.

The giantess paused at the top of the rise. The Snow Queen had chosen to make her stand right next to Ivinhoor's Bay. The Ever Afters and their allies had arrived. Both armies were spread out across the valley beside the shore. We were still half a mile away, and from this distance they all looked the same, like a rolling sea of people, with a few giants thrown in like boulders sticking out in the water.

Thousands upon thousands.

Well, the people brawling far over the bay did kind of stand out. West had found his brothers, and between the three Winds, they'd created a cyclone twisting horizontally over the ocean. I really hoped West didn't need backup, because I wasn't sure anyone could help him.

"How close can you get us?" Chase asked.

"Where are you trying to go?" Matilda replied.

The fighting clustered around four or five spots on the ice, a swirl and ebb of bodies, like eddies in the tide.

Lena pointed one out to me, which seemed to disappear into a small white ridge, scattered with black rock. "That's where we came out, hours ago. The Portland portal. It was easier this time. The Seelie moved Queen Titania's pavilion. Miriam and Philip's grades are defending it."

The pillars were just behind the portal. Jimmy Searcaster was stomping on people. Likon was picking fighters up and playing with them. Ripper barked orders to his wolf army. Ori'an flew laps around the sorceress-giant, patrolling against any Fey who might try to get close, and General Searcaster . . .

She was bent close to the ground, listening to someone.

"That way," I said.

Chase scanned the battlefield, taking in the troops that blanketed the valley. He pointed with his sword. "No. Right there. Between the trolls and the goblins."

"How are we supposed to get through?" Daisy asked. "There's no opening."

"We'll make one." Chase's confidence shut everyone up. Hopefully that meant he had a plan.

Matilda picked her way down the rise and kept walking. Up close, I could see the separate forces—the goblins to the right fighting the Living Stone Dwarves on the left. One skirmish was raging right on the shore. Heads would pop out of the waves, just long enough for a spear or a trident to come sailing out at some really ugly people with wands. More witches, but not from the Wolfsbane clan. Spells couldn't travel through water. The mermaids were the natural choice to fight them, but I still hoped Chatty was safe, and Ben too. He was probably fighting with her.

The Snow Queen had to have noticed us by now. But when Matilda stopped a hundred feet from the fighting, she didn't throw everything she had at us.

Instead, the goblins turned away from the dwarves. They *ran*, their spears and swords raised high, out of the way of their pounding legs.

"Um. What are they doing?" I asked.

"Deserting, looks like." Matilda's voice was smug, like she was pleased that she wasn't the only one who had turned against Solange. She fished our spearmen out of her pockets and set them down. The triplets staggered, trying to get their bearings. Matilda set Lena and me down next, and then the archers on her other shoulder. "They know you've reached the battlefield, so now they think the Snow Queen will lose."

That was hard to believe. Nobody else was running.

The witches continued to sling spells at the merpeople, who ducked under the surface to avoid them and then popped back up to throw more spears. Trolls in hockey masks fought against Characters I'd never seen before. They must have come from EAS's other chapters. Adelaide had convinced them after all.

Instead of holding the line with the other Characters, Jack tore through the trolls' ranks, slashing and stabbing and mowing down his enemies in droves.

A little further away, some of the Itari fighters had taken on a flock of ice griffins—less than a dozen against hundreds.

The griffins fell and fell and fell. Bodies lay in a mound in front of George.

I hadn't noticed the dwarves coming closer until one of them pulled a helmet off. Forrel leaned on his spear and glanced up at Chase, breathing hard. "Would you like us to pursue the goblins?"

"No," Chase said. "Engage the ice griffins. We'll need to borrow the Itari fighters."

Chase was in charge? Since when?

The dwarf nodded. Then he shoved the helmet back over his sweaty hair and started shouting orders at his men. They formed ranks and attacked the ice griffins' flank.

My grip tightened on the heart nestled in my hands. It trembled so hard that my arm bones rattled.

When I looked up again, determined to ask Chase what he was up to, he was gone. He'd swooped over the battlefield, found his students, and was talking to them.

Lena yanked the stack of dragon scales out of the front pocket of her carryall, saying, "Okay, guys. Shields out. I need to recharge them. The mermaids are keeping the witches busy, but when we go in, they might change tactics."

I hadn't even known that the shields *could* be recharged. I had been so focused on taking the heart to Solange. But this battle was so much bigger than me and her—with all these troops, and all their intricate strategies, and just a tiny chance that I could stop her.

Chase was back. He landed among the other kids in our grade. "All right. The Itari fighters will go first, cutting a path to the Snow Queen. We'll do cleanup right behind them, making sure nobody gets to Rory. Got it?"

"We get it," said Vicky. "We've got bodyguard duty."

"We did go over this plan back at EAS, you know," Kyle said. "In detail."

Then I understood. I didn't need to worry about how we were going to fight through the Snow Queen's forces. I had the best friends in the history of Characters.

The magic around me stirred. Orange diffused through the light spilling from the heart.

I turned to Matilda. "I would stay back. We can't protect you from the Searcasters. They'll know you brought us."

"I'm not worried. Jimmy and Genevieve will have to fight their way through all of you to reach me." Matilda's chin was raised, just like Lena when she was being stubborn. "Besides, I want them to see me. I want them to know what I have done. They always thought I was useless anyway."

Wow. Someday I wanted to find out what they'd done to make Matilda *want* to betray them.

"Rory!" Chase said.

I ran over to him. The heart melted the ice ahead of me.

I stopped right between Chase and Lena. In front of us, the kids in our grade and the Itari fighters pushed forward through the griffins and attacked the next section of the Snow Queen's army: the dragons.

Their usual creepy song echoed around us, but most of them only got out two notes, cut down before they got to the long hissing part. The Itari squadron cut through the herd, opening up a path for the rest of us.

"Do I even want to know what the plan is?" I asked my friends.

"Nope. You would probably freak." Chase's face didn't have even a hint of a smile, but that might have been because one of the dragons had gotten past the Itari fighters' line.

"Or possibly not believe us," Lena said, sounding like she was pretty close to freaking herself. "I barely do."

I trusted them. We'd gotten this far.

Vicky and Tina blinded the dragon with two well-aimed arrows in its eyes. Conner finished it off with a spear through the heart.

The dragon fell. We jogged past it before it combusted, right on the Itari fighters' heels.

We'd caught up with the goblins. They'd *slain* dozens of the singing serpents in the area. No wonder we were making such good time. The goblins were taking out half our enemies for us. "Now what are they doing?" I said.

"Don't know," Chase said, and he clearly didn't care. "Maybe the *Draconus melodious* call got creepy even for them."

"*Or* maybe they switched sides!" Lena said excitedly. "Like Matilda!"

The witches noticed us finally. They raised their wands, and my fellow questers raised their shields. But the witches only managed to squeeze off a couple shots before newcomers swooped in on colorful wings and took on the magic-casters.

"For Princess Dyani!" cried Himorsal Liior, soaring at the head of a Fey squadron. "For Prince Callion!"

I expected Chase to react to his brother's name, but he didn't. "Finally. Fael was always slow for a Fey." He led us forward.

Ripper's wolf army tried to cut us off. A big Arctic white sprang first, and our Aladdin fell under his paws. The wolf's jaws closed over Aladdin's throat, and in the next instant, Keon's sword beheaded the white-furred wolf. Both deaths were that quick.

George took the lead in Aladdin's place. Four small red-brown wolves leapt at him. George spun, his sword flashing gold in the light coming from the heart. The wolves fell.

Then Lena's brother looked back at us, his blade wet. "Chase, looks like you're up."

The ice shook underneath us.

Jimmy Searcaster was coming, and Likon stalked up along the ridge to make sure he didn't step on any of his own allies. Ori'an had dropped the Fey he'd been pounding into the ice and taken flight. Ripper bounded over the ranks of his wolves.

All four pillars, closing in.

Chase watched them. "Yep, that's my cue."

Fear sliced through me. Chase couldn't fight the pillars, especially not all four of them at once. They couldn't be killed except by another pillar, and none of *them* were going to desert the Snow Queen.

"No," I said. "It's my Tale, and I say no."

"You're overruled," Chase said. "We shifted from quest mode to battle mode about a half hour ago. Besides, what was it Rapunzel said? 'United in purpose even when their paths diverged'?"

I opened my mouth, ticked that he would throw that back in my face, but Lena said, quickly and sternly, "*No bickering right now.* Save it for after."

"We're not bickering." We were saying good-bye.

"Rory, you're not going to die," Chase said, "and *I'm* going to live to be an old man and die in my sleep."

Ripper howled, only about a hundred feet away. He would reach us first.

"You can't *know* that," I said. Sounding confident wouldn't help, not with this. I knew him too well. I knew how often it covered up what he really thought.

"I do." Then Chase's hand cupped my face. I thought for sure that he was going to kiss me again, but he just tilted my head so he could speak into my ear. "Do you remember my dream? About my birthday party?"

"Of course. Grandpa Chase." *He* might live, then. His dreams about the Snow Queen had turned out to be true.

"There's the cake with all the candles, and all these people.

And then . . ." He paused, like he always did when he was thinking about chickening out. "You make a really beautiful old lady."

My own heart gave a great, walloping thump. I didn't expect to feel hope. Gold and scarlet ribbons pierced through the light pouring out of my hands.

Chase stepped back. His gaze was steady. "Gotta go. Lena will get you the rest of the way."

He leapt up. His vivid orange wings spread out, so bright under the heart's blaze that he looked like he was trailing fire. Seeing a warrior coming for him, Ripper stopped in his tracks. His jaw split in a wolfish grin.

"Wait!" Lena told the others. "Let Chase draw them off first."

Chase swooped down at the Big Bad Wolf. Panic replaced my hope.

Ripper's jaw snapped hard. I heard the teeth even from twenty-five feet away, but Chase *was* a good flier. He dipped lower, missing the fangs by a few inches, and delivered a long slash along Ripper's underside, slitting him from throat to tail.

I knew from experience that a wound like that wouldn't kill a pillar, no matter how much blood he lost, but it would definitely hurt. It would make even the Big Bad Wolf sloppy.

Ripper whirled around, spraying blood, but he didn't seem to notice. He pounded after Chase, who was soaring straight for Likon, the second-closest pillar.

"Okay. They're far enough away." Lena stepped behind me, planted her hands on my shoulders, and guided me forward. "Come on, Rory."

I went, but still I didn't take my eyes off Chase.

He'd drawn even with Likon, but Ripper had caught up to him as well. Two at once.

359

Then Chase doubled back, so swiftly he was just an orange streak across the sky. He dove at Ripper's face again. The wolf stood his ground, expecting another feint, but this time, Chase landed a slice across Ripper's good eye.

A howl of pain split the air around us. Chase had blinded the Big Bad Wolf.

He flew over to Ripper again, so close that the rusty black fur rippled. Then he pricked the wolf's ear.

Ripper pounced on the spot where Chase had been last, claws and teeth tearing with everything he had. He couldn't see Chase fly away. He couldn't see Likon coming to help him. The Big Bad Wolf landed on the blue giant's throat, killing him as swiftly as the white wolf had killed our Aladdin.

This was why Chase had taught himself Itari. He'd been planning to take out the pillars himself.

Likon didn't get up. Ripper didn't even stop to sniff his comrade and see what he'd done. Chase jabbed Ripper's flank, and the wolf tore after him without realizing that Chase was leading him straight to the next closest giant, Jimmy Searcaster.

It was almost enough to make me stop worrying about Chase. *Almost*.

"Stop, everyone! Rory, down!" Lena shouted, leaping in front of me. I ducked, hunching over to protect the heart. I felt a hint of the heat the others had complained about. I watched the heart sear a hole right through my jacket collar.

Then the spell Lena had sensed struck with the force of a two-ton boulder, but *something* deflected it. Ice cracked into a ten-foot-wide crater ahead of us.

The sorceress-giant limped forward on her basilisk cane.

Up front, George glanced back at his sister. "Did she *miss*?"

"Searcaster doesn't miss." Lena spread both of her golden hands, and the hair stood up on my arms. "I cast the same protection spell as in your shields. Just with more power."

"And more focus. You're learning quickly, baby sorceress." Searcaster raised her cane again. I felt something drag across my skin, like the sea sucking itself back, seconds before a huge wave hit. Another blast was coming.

"Genevieve, no!" Solange emerged from behind the giantess. Her dress glittered with crystal and ice. It even had a lacy train patterned with delicate snowflakes. She looked the part of a conquering queen, not like someone expecting a fight. She must not have thought we'd get this far. "Think of what she's carrying!"

She meant the heart. I had never heard the Snow Queen sound afraid.

So, what I carried kept us safe from General Searcaster's magic. I stepped forward. I could be another kind of shield.

The sorceress-giant lifted an eyebrow. "Don't worry, Your Majesty. I'll capture her."

If she did, I couldn't get the heart to Solange. I was *so close*.

"You won't *touch* Rory," Lena said. "Your fight is with me."

Searcaster smiled. Her yellow teeth looked terrifyingly pointy. "Come on, then, baby sorceress. What have you brought for me to play with today?"

Lena's chin jutted out.

I should have seen this coming. Chase had picked the pillars, but Searcaster had made this duel *personal*.

"As your big brother, I heartily disapprove," George said.

Lena stepped ahead of him, putting herself between us and Searcaster. "I'll make sure to tell Gran when we get back."

"Wait!" I called after her. Her golden hands were empty. She'd lost her spear in the fight with the Wolfsbane witches. "You don't even have a weapon."

"Rory," Lena said, in the slow, calm voice she only used when she didn't want me to freak out, "I *am* the weapon. *Up, ice!*" A frozen slab as big as a door rose up from beside her. It glistened in the light leaking from the heart, already beginning to melt. *"Beat!"* The ice launched itself at Searcaster's face.

The sorceress-giant ducked before it crashed into her nose.

It was official. Chase wasn't the only one of my friends who scared me sometimes.

"Be safe," Kyle said.

Lena didn't turn away from Searcaster. She reached a hand into her unzipped carryall. "Get Rory to the Snow Queen."

I didn't want to leave her. I wanted to stay and watch her back. But we both had a job to do.

The Itari fighters took off, fanning out ahead of me and the kids in our grade. This close to the Snow Queen, the heart shook so hard it nearly slipped out of my grasp. The sorceress-giant took a step toward us, but Lena launched five more chunks of ice. General Searcaster smashed them all—three with her basilisk cane and two with magic, but they distracted her long enough for us to get past her. We chased after Solange.

Out of nowhere, at least two hundred ice statues rose up ahead of us. Trolls in hockey masks, translucent and glistening.

"What the—" George's sprint faltered.

I was the only one who had fought Solange's magical reinforcements before. "They're strong, but they're *brittle*. They'll bash each other to pieces if you give them the opportunity," I told him.

"If you say so." George pulled ahead, whirling and ducking through the first line. The rest of the Itari fighters followed his lead, swords raised high, hollering a war cry. The two forces clashed, and within seconds, a dozen trolls were in pieces.

The Itari fighters were going to win. The trolls were only slowing them down. Not for long, but long enough for the Snow Queen to get away. Along the shore, she *ran*, her skirt bunched up in her hands. Right in front of all her armies and her allies.

She could have a portal waiting. I couldn't let her reach it.

I darted around George, ducked under the arms of three ice trolls, and sprinted after her.

"You're supposed to wait for us!" George called after me.

My feet dug grooves into the slush the heart was creating. A few times I nearly slipped, but I was gaining on the Snow Queen. Solange hadn't had a lot of reasons to run in the past few years. I was in way better shape. Only twenty feet behind. No, fifteen.

Solange glanced back. She raised her hands, ready to blast me with a spell.

The ice beneath her cracked and broke away from the shore. Her own private island.

A defensive spell, then. That made more sense, considering it was *her* heart I was holding. Attacking me would be suicide.

I didn't stop. I couldn't jump as far as Chase, but I could still jump pretty far for someone without wings.

She noticed. The ice under her shot up. Not just her private island—a private *iceberg*, and I knew she wouldn't stop feeding it with magic until it had grown as tall as the tower where she'd trapped Chase and her little sister.

I leapt.

I cleared the distance, but the ice had grown too fast. I landed on my elbows instead of my feet, hard enough to bruise, but I barely felt the pain. By the time I threw a knee up over the ledge, the new iceberg was already slick with melting water. Still, it grew.

"How are you feeling, Rory?" The Snow Queen's gaze was pinned on the heart in my hands. I wondered if she'd ever taken it out of its symbol-covered box, especially considering she got a light show every time she got close. We traveled upward fast. The ice troll–Itari fighter battle shrank to the size of dolls, of mice, of *ants*. "This isn't making you nervous?"

I just looked at her. A little sick to my stomach, definitely. But not nervous. I'd been chasing *her*. I knew which one of us was more scared.

We were very high now. Light unfurled across the sky. Golds and reds threaded through a delicate silver green. The bay water mirrored the colors. The land was dark, the armies just shadowy silhouettes. General Searcaster slammed a spell down with her basilisk cane, then another. Jimmy Searcaster had fallen, and Ripper bounded over his fellow pillar, jaws snapping at a figure I couldn't see.

I shouldn't have taken my eyes off Solange. Something whistled through the air toward me.

The ice darts flew, aimed at my head, no danger at all to the heart I held at my chest. I didn't have enough time to dodge, but it didn't matter.

Inches from my face, they vanished in a puff of steam.

The heart was *very* hot. It hadn't just melted a puddle around us—it was practically a pool. The water had reached our shins.

I took a step toward her.

The Snow Queen thrust her hands into the water. It froze, and ice stretched toward me but never reached my legs. The water on my side of the pool stayed liquid no matter how hard Solange strained.

All she managed to do was create a breeze, her cold swirling around my heat. Rapunzel's glass vial banged against my hip, whipping along its silver chain. Solange spotted it.

"Is that all you have left to help you?" she snarled. "Where are your combs and your ring? Where is your magic sword? You've given up *everything* that made you a threat."

Liar. I had *her heart*. I didn't need those other things.

I took another step. The heart was getting harder to hold. Its shuddering sent ripples through the water.

"Your friends will lose! They'll lose unless you help them!" Solange sounded desperate. I risked another glance at the battle below. Ori'an swooped down and plucked Ripper off Jimmy, trying to save one pillar from the other. He carried the Big Bad Wolf upward, trying to reason with him, but Ripper must have nipped him or something. Ori'an dropped him. It was too dark for me to see him land, but I heard the cracking boom when he hit.

Mistake. I couldn't believe I fell for that again. Something silver flashed out of the corner of my vision, much too close to my eye.

I whirled back to the Snow Queen.

Her skin had dulled to the color of slush, and her hands bristled with snowflake-shaped throwing stars, probably all poisoned. Heat weakened her magic. So she'd brought out some weapons way harder to melt than ice darts.

I took another step. The heart shook so violently that it almost lurched out of my hands. Steam rose from the water, blocking the view of the battlefield. All I could see now was her.

She launched another barbed snowflake. I splashed to the side, barely fast enough. The throwing star whizzed past my cheek, shearing off a lock of hair growing at my temple. I felt it brush my ear and fly away.

Too close. Solange had adjusted her aim to compensate for the wind. She was good. Throwing stars had probably been her weapon before she'd become the Snow Queen. No wonder they'd become her trademark.

Fine. My dodging skills weren't half-bad either.

Another step, and another throwing star. I ducked to avoid it.

She hurled two more at my knees. I splashed to my left out of their path, moving much slower in the water. The Snow Queen noticed and changed tactics.

She launched four of her weapons, rapid shots to each leg. I had to jump back to keep from getting hit.

"Is it vengeance you're after, Rory?" Solange said scornfully. "Vengeance for Rapunzel and all the others?" She reached into her pockets for another round of snowflakes, and while her hands were busy, I slogged forward, the pool sloshing around us.

Solange raised her arm, but before she could throw, I shifted the heart a little lower, shielding my legs. The Snow Queen whirled a throwing star at my unprotected throat instead. I leaned out of its way and splashed right up to her.

Only three feet remained between us. The heart leapt forward, like it was reaching for its former owner. The light made the steam around us glow.

Eyes wide, she threw again, but I was ready. I jumped aside and aimed a snap kick at her left hand, the one holding the rest of her ammo. My sneaker connected with a wet smack. The Snow Queen cried out, caught by surprise. The barbed snowflakes plunked into the pool and sank out of sight.

She stared at me, defenseless now and furious about it.

"SAY SOMETHING!" she shrieked. She had realized she couldn't stop me. She couldn't even make me talk. "YOUR SILENCE IS THE SAME AS HERS!"

Maybe Solange had cut out her own heart to stop her loneliness, but it hadn't stopped her from wanting Rapunzel. She'd followed her little sister from Europe to North America just to stay close to her. I'd never thought about it like that before.

The Snow Queen had woken up missing Rapunzel like I had. We didn't miss her the same way. Solange wanted her sister like a possession she could keep locked in a tower, but the absence still ached in her, too. Even with all her power, all her clever schemes, Solange was still just a broken person.

"Rapunzel saw this, you know," I said. "She even saw the iceberg."

Resignation crept into the Snow Queen's face, reminding me of Rapunzel every time the Director had accused her of something.

Solange looked so much like her sister. When she was gone, another part of Rapunzel would be gone too.

"What are you going to do?" she whispered. "Do you even know?"

Rapunzel hadn't told me what to do with the heart after I'd brought it to the Snow Queen, but yeah, I still knew what to do with it.

The thought occurred to Solange at exactly the same second.

She lashed out and grabbed my wrists. She twisted them, her grip so tight I felt her fingernails digging into my tendons, trying to force me to drop the heart. She was strong, but I was stronger. I shoved hard.

The heart slid into her chest, easier than sliding a sword through flesh. She screamed, but when she sucked in another breath, it sounded more like a sob.

The light winked out and the wind died when the heart vanished. All grew dark and still. My palms tingled with the aftermath of strong magic. My arms felt rubbery after fighting the heart's vibrations for so long.

Solange didn't burst into silver dust like her sister had.

Even in the starlight, I could see her coloring change—the strawlike hair grew a darker shade of blond, ivory skin grew rosy with a very human flush. She held her hands out, staring at her body. Red and yellow ribbons seared burning lines under her skin, as if the light show that had once covered the sky was now trapped inside her veins.

The hairs on my arms began to stand up, and not because of the cold.

The returned heart was forcing out the magic that had turned Solange into a sorceress. I felt a current sweep across my skin, its power swelling and swelling just like it had with the sorceress-giant, but if Searcaster's spell was a wave, this would be a monstrous tsunami of power, huge enough to drown whole towns, to destroy beaches, to recarve the shore into an unrecognizable landscape.

Solange looked up, green and gold lines curling across her cheeks. Except for that, except for the length of her face and the color of her eyes, she could have been Rapunzel. Her gaze met mine with the same sorrow. The magic inside her was seconds away from bursting free, and she had lost control over it.

Her lips parted, like she was going to say something, the last words I would probably ever hear.

Instead, her hand shot out. Her palm struck right above my collarbone, and I flew back. I didn't realize how close we had gotten to the edge of the iceberg until I toppled over the side.

I fell toward the dark sea, my face inches from the pale ice. Hitting the water would kill me if I didn't crash into the side of the Snow Queen's frozen tower first.

Above me, the power trapped inside Solange clawed its way out. Reds and oranges licked the sky like flames, more violent than before, and waves of color cascaded down the ice. A ribbon of yellow whipped toward me. I twisted away as best as I could, but the raw magic still wrapped around my shoe and ripped it to pieces. It would have torn apart my foot, too, if I hadn't pulled my knees up and out of its reach.

Solange was gone. All of that magic must have shredded her as it ripped free of her veins, and it looked like her magic wanted me, too.

Maybe it was for the best. With both bearers of Unwritten Tales gone, no one like the Snow Queen could ever exist again.

There is more than one way to give your life, Rapunzel had said. My hand closed over the glass light she'd given me.

Stupid. Deciding I wanted to live right then.

The sound of shattering attacked my eardrums, echoing across the bay like the Glass Mountain itself had been smashed. Frozen chunks exploded outward.

I curled my arms around my head, but a huge piece slammed into my body, knocking me to the side, away from the raw magic spilling into the sea. Around me, light pulsed brighter and redder.

Then something small struck my temple, and black conquered everything.

Ice chilled my back, and my legs felt like they were covered in icicles. I started shivering before I even opened my eyes.

A hand burned against my cheek. Chase sounded impatient. "Come *on*, Rory."

I looked up. His face was inches from mine. "It is so cold," I said, my teeth chattering.

Of course it was. I was wearing a coat with a hole seared through it. I'd lost a shoe, and the breeze was ripping through my ragged sock. My jeans—thanks to all the water the heart had melted— were now frozen up to the knee. The Snow Queen and the magic that poured out of her had failed to kill me, so the Arctic Circle was giving it its best shot.

Chase's arms slid around me, deliciously warm. *His* jacket's spell was still working. I snuggled into his chest, greedy for the heat, cradling Rapunzel's light between us. Soon my shivering eased.

Then I noticed Chase was trembling.

"Hey." I wrapped my arms around his shoulders. He didn't stop shaking, and he didn't answer. "Chase? Are you hurt?"

"I have never been so scared in my entire life." His whole torso had curled over mine.

"You told *me* that I wasn't going to die." He was a good liar. What he had said about his dream could have been completely made up. It had worked, though.

"Well, I didn't think so," Chase said. "But I didn't know if the plan was going to work. Rapunzel said you were in danger. She put it in her letter: *The ice will rise. Rory will fall. Chase can catch her, but in the explosion, you'll need to find her. Put Lena in charge of the light.* So Lena reworked Rapunzel's vial. She said she was pretty sure it would glow when she blew into her whistle, but she didn't have time to test it before she gave it back to you."

"Lena made Rapunzel's light glow red? So you could find me and catch me?" I said, slowly starting to understand. Three of my favorite people had worked together to save me. "But Rapunzel said she hadn't seen the final outcome—"

"You were unconscious when I grabbed you—" His voice broke.

I decided to stop asking him questions. "Chase, I'm okay. I promise."

His forehead rested against my shoulder. Something wet soaked through the hole in my coat. If anybody asked, I would have lied and said it was snow.

"Rory!" Our favorite inventor ran along the shore, so fast it was like she wasn't even tired, but the rest of the kids in our grade sure were. They jogged doggedly behind her.

"Chase, Lena will reach us in less than a minute." I kissed his cheek, stood up, and stepped in front of him, shivering again. The wet sock on my shoeless foot instantly turned to ice under my heel. If we were lucky, all the focus would be on me. No one would have any reason to notice Chase's red eyes.

The only problem with this plan was Chase himself. His arm snaked around my shoulders, and I was pretty sure he'd thrown a glamour over his face. "You'll freeze on your own."

My trembling stopped. Smiling, I leaned into him. "How did Lena take down Searcaster?"

"Sleeping enchantment," he said, as we watched our friends speed toward us. "She supercharged the leftover spindle from my Tale and stabbed Searcaster in the foot with it."

"Wow," I said, trying to get him to smile again. "My friends' jobs were way more impressive than mine. Technically, all I really did was carry something."

"Yeah, right. You thought we were famous before, but after this . . ." Chase grinned, just like I'd hoped he would. "We'll go down in *history*."

Yep. He sounded more like himself.

"It's over!" Lena was closer now. She was practically skipping with joy. "They don't even have a leader with the Snow Queen and Searcaster gone, but they're all surrendering! If I had any magic left over, I would figure out how to cast fireworks!"

The kids in our grade and the human Itari fighters joined us before we trudged back to the portal.

The rest of the news came in fits and starts.

"I didn't want to kill Searcaster," Lena told me. "I mean, we already knew the Snow Queen's death would create a huge blast. The second spindle still had a sleeping enchantment. Pricking her forced the enchantment past her defenses. She was guarding just against magical attacks, so a physical one took her by surprise. She almost squished George when she fell. He'd been coming to help me."

When I asked Chase if all the pillars were dead, he said, "Everybody but Jimmy. He aimed for me and accidentally beheaded Ori'an. Jimmy will probably bleed out soon, though. Ripper really tore him up."

I wondered how Matilda had taken her husband's defeat. I didn't see her anywhere on the battlefield, but I was sure we'd see her again.

Lena handed me a dragon scale, and I chanted the heating spell. Chase didn't move his arm from around my shoulders, though. A huge smile grew on my face and didn't budge.

Light—good, old-fashioned sunlight—revealed the mess in the valley. All the snow was churned up, most of it bloody.

We'd been up all night. Fatigue hit me, and then I really was glad Chase's arm was keeping me steady.

Jenny pounced on George and Lena, telling them how dangerous that was, and how proud she was of them, and how they needed to get their behinds through the portal back to EAS. Jenny, Gretel, and the elves would sweep the area for the wounded. Anyone who could walk was not a priority.

We all happily let her boss us around. We joined the line waiting to enter the portal.

Forrel and the twins were ahead of us. The soldier had a gash on his arm. Ima reminded him anxiously to keep pressure on the wound, and a smile flickered around Forrel's mouth, like he'd suffered much worse but he kind of enjoyed getting fussed over. Ben told us that we'd missed a real treat, seeing the mermaids fight. Chatty was "poetry in motion," according to him. When the twelfth graders stepped into the line near the back, George excused himself to go to Miriam. He dipped her backward and kissed her so intensely that people whistled and cheered. Lena was louder than everyone else.

Chase watched them like he was taking notes. I pretended not to notice.

When it was our turn, we stepped through the portal into the EAS courtyard. The elves had hacked a few burnt branches off the Tree of Hope, but no one had taken them away. People were sitting on them.

"Rory!" Dad yelled when he spotted me.

Chase removed his arm. I missed it instantly—not the warmth anymore, but his solidness. I glanced at him before I turned to my family. He was looking right back at me.

Mom nearly bowled me over with the force of her hug. Then she kissed my face all over, like she'd done when I was small. Maybe that should have embarrassed me, but I just smiled.

Mrs. LaMarelle squeezed Lena so hard that it looked like she couldn't breathe. Lady Aspenwind had arrived too, trying hard not to cry and failing miserably. Dad fished a tissue out of his pocket and passed it over. Lady Aspenwind didn't realize what it was for, so Chase had to take it, nodding his thanks and explaining to his mom in rapid Fey.

Then Dad was hugging me too. "I think we should just all pile on," Brie said, and then I felt her arm circle around us from Dad's side, and then Amy's from Mom's end. Dani contributed to the group hug with a spit bubble.

I laughed. My sister could grow up safe now. Solange was gone. The worry had been so constant for the past few years that I'd gotten used to the pressure, the tight feeling of suppressed panic. Now it had evaporated. I felt . . . new. I felt *joy*.

Then my nose started prickling, right under the bridge. I blinked hard. I refused to cry just because I was finally happy, and Hansel and Rapunzel weren't around to see it.

"I'm supposed to bring you before the Canon for a meeting." Sarah Thumb and Mr. Swallow had landed on the branch right above our heads. It didn't look particularly safe, with half its wood charred black. "But I'll pretend I didn't see you if you want to go clean up and tend to your wounds first."

"You can just tell the Director to wait." I was done following the Canon's orders for a while. "I'm taking the day off. She can yell at me later."

"Mildred's dead, Rory," Sarah Thumb said gently. "The tenth and eleventh graders were having a hard time defending their portal. The Director was bringing some students as reinforcements. The Snow Queen had just sent a fresh slew of wolves. They went straight for the spearmen, who weren't in position yet, and the Director threw herself between them."

That was it, then. The previous Triumvirate was gone, all of them.

I hadn't liked the Director. She was petty sometimes and controlling *most* of the time, but in her way, she had tried to protect us as fiercely as Hansel had. Ever After School wouldn't be the same without her.

"So who's in charge?" Lena said, in a tone that really meant, *Who is going to yell at us in the Canon meeting?*

"You?" Chase asked Sarah.

She snorted. "Hardly. The Canon still needs to vote on a new Director. I was Mildred's deputy, which only means I get none of the authority and *all* the paperwork."

"Whatever this meeting is about, it can wait," said Lena's grandmother, her hands on her hips. "Look at these children. They're dead on their feet. They need breakfast, a shower, and a nap—in that order."

Sarah Thumb raised both hands in surrender. "I *just* said I would look the other way if they wanted to tend to their wounds."

"No, I'll come." As awesome as sleep sounded, I wanted everything to be over, and I meant *everything*. I didn't want this meeting hanging over my head. "Besides, I'm not hurt."

Everyone paused, like they didn't know how to break it to me.

Then Amy said, "Rory, you have blood matted in your hair and a red handprint on your chest."

I looked down and across my collarbone was the imprint of five long fingers. I hoped that was the kind of red mark that turned into an ugly bruise, not the magical kind that tended to have side effects. "Well, I *feel* fine. I had some Water of Life."

"*Did* you?" Sarah Thumb said. "Because it's still under strict rationing."

Lena's voice was hard. "Trust me. She needed it."

Sarah backed off. "Well," she said, "then it's up to you."

"I say we go. Just like this." Somehow, Chase made that response seem like a threat. "Hard to punish someone when they look like they've already been punished enough."

Mr. Swallow took flight. "You kids are so pessimistic," Sarah Thumb said, shaking her head. "We're grown-ups, not monsters."

They didn't want to punish us. When I heard their request, I just stared at Sarah Thumb and all the serious faces of the strangers sitting on the thrones.

"You want me to join the Canon?" I repeated, just to be sure I'd heard them right.

Lena squeaked from her extra-tall chair. An extremely happy squeak.

"Both of you, actually," Sarah Thumb said. "The Snow Queen is dead. Your Tale is over. Rumpelstiltskin confirmed it. He would have brought the book and told you himself, but he took an arrow in the shoulder. Gretel's fixing him up."

Chase's eyes cut to Mildred Grubb's old chair, covered with carved roses and conspicuously empty. I guess they did have an opening now. "Pass," he said flatly.

"No, not as 'Sleeping Beauty,'" said Sarah Thumb. "As 'Jack the Giant Killer.' Your fight with the pillars earned you a second Tale."

"No way," Chase said, but it was the kind of "no way" that begged to be proved wrong.

"It's in the current volume," Sarah Thumb said. "Your dad offered to share his position."

"I don't need to represent both Jacks," said the Champion of the Canon. Proud again, like he should have been proud of his son all along.

Chase *was* glad. Not as overjoyed as I thought he would be, though. He'd talked for years about getting a good Tale, but I guess that wasn't why he'd taken on the pillars. Finding out he was a "Giant Killer" was just a bonus.

"Well?" Sarah Thumb asked us. Lena tipped forward in her seat like she thought I couldn't see her, nodding as hard as she could.

Chase glanced at me. He wasn't going to choose first.

"I want to know something before I decide," I said. "Did my Tale explain about me holding the fate of magic?"

"You don't think carrying the heart was enough?" Chase said, only half joking.

I really didn't. "That was just the fate of the Snow Queen."

Sarah Thumb's eyes gleamed. We were about to get a dose of magical theory, and I probably wouldn't understand it. "If you had just stabbed the heart, all of the magic inside the Snow Queen would have been destroyed too. But you returned the heart first. That forced the magic back out into the world before the Snow Queen died in the explosion. If that magic had disappeared completely, it would have caused a ripple effect and started the decline of magic all around the globe—"

"Never mind the ripple effect. Who do you think had cast the heating enchantment over her whole army?" Lena burst out. "It must have been Solange. She was holding her forces hostage just like the city of Kiivinsh. Imagine what would have happened if Rory *had* stabbed the heart, and all of the Snow Queen's magic—all her *spells*—had winked out. Thousands of people would have been stranded in the middle of the Arctic."

"We wouldn't have let them escape through the portals," Sarah said, stunned. "They would have frozen to death first."

The goblins had gone specifically for the dragons. They'd been after the *scales*.

"So, basically, what you're saying is that most of the people on that battlefield—like maybe half the population of all the hidden continents—owe Rory their lives?" Chase said.

"Well. Not the witches," Lena said. "They could handle their own heating spells."

I was glad that I hadn't listened to Conner.

"Do they even realize?" What Chase really meant was: *Can we tell them?*

"They're going to know," said Sarah Thumb, delighted that she'd just gained another bargaining chip in the magical world. The Director had definitely trained her.

I scowled. That wasn't why I took the heart to Solange.

Sarah Thumb didn't notice. "So, do you accept the responsibility and privilege of joining the Canon? Usually people don't take so long to decide."

Some members didn't really get to decide, I thought, looking at Lena. Her face beamed with excitement, her body brimming with hope. She didn't want to be the only one of us stuck in the Canon.

Chase didn't want to join at all. He just wanted to grow up. But he hadn't refused yet. If Lena and I were Tale representatives, then he wasn't about to be left out.

So it was up to me.

If I was honest with myself, getting the whole Triumvirate into the Canon made sense. Between the three of us, we would be able to change some of their decision-making processes.

But I didn't want the Canon to take credit for what I'd done. They would guilt the goblins and the trolls into doing what they wanted. They'd done it before.

I didn't want the Canon to feel like they were in charge of me.

But the real problem would be immortality. Sure, Solange had done wrong by her sister before her Tale had even ended, but the *really* bad stuff had happened after she had lived longer than a normal human. I wasn't Solange, but I would still make my own mistakes. As a regular Character, I would only have a limited number of decades to screw stuff up. That was comforting.

I looked at Lena again. The hope had drained out of her. Then she nodded, understanding.

"No," I said.

The grown-ups weren't expecting that. A bunch of shocked faces jerked toward me.

"Are you *sure*?" Jack must have known that Chase wouldn't join unless I did.

"Maybe you should ask me again in a few years," I said. "Maybe you should wait and see what kind of person I turn out to be before you invite another bearer of an Unwritten Tale to live forever."

That shut everyone up. Well, everyone except Chase.

"Same," he said, grinning.

Maybe someday, when I was a little older, I might ask if they needed another weapons instructor. Maybe Chase would try to get a job too. That would keep us in the loop, and we would get stuck in almost as many Canon meetings as Lena.

For now, I had a Binding Oath to keep. "While I'm here, I need to talk to you all about Matilda Searcaster."

Nothing had been decided. Sarah Thumb said that they would have to vote on any and all punishments. For now, our top priority would be finding Matilda before the Snow Queen's followers did. Some of them might blame her. She *had* been my ride to the battle. But when the meeting was adjourned, Lena told us that she was pretty sure that Matilda would be okay. "She definitely helped us, and they know it. Plus, she's a *giant*. Kind of hard for her to stay in hiding, especially considering she's going to have a huge green baby soon. Do you think we're free to go sleep now? I'm beat."

Chase yawned. "Yeah. We can tell by the way you're barely talking."

Lena ignored him. "Gran's right. Food, shower, sleep. That's what we need."

And that was exactly what I did. I sleepwalked home to our EAS apartment and sat at the kitchen table, where Mom had fixed my favorite, apple-cinnamon oatmeal. I almost skipped the shower to be honest, but Amy put her foot down. "Rory, your mom needs to *see* that that blood isn't coming from a serious wound. Also, I don't want to have to wash the sheets after your nap."

Hours later, when I woke up again, I almost regretted sleeping. I shouldn't have left Mom and Amy unsupervised for that long.

I stumbled out of my room, rubbing my eyes, and Mom said, "We're throwing you a party."

"What?" I wondered if I should be rubbing my ears instead. There was no way I could have heard her right.

"Just roll with it," Amy said. "It's too late to stop her. Lena came an hour ago, and your mom put her and that harp thing to work inviting everybody. By the way, does Lena always have that much energy? Or is it a sorceress thing?"

"A *party*?" I repeated, still not processing the idea.

"Well, we missed your birthday party this year," Mom said regretfully, like we'd just gotten busy and forgotten. "So, it's more of an end-of-your-tale celebration."

"We don't have those at EAS," I said.

"Well, maybe you should," Mom said. "Your Tale has been going on for years, hasn't it? It's kind of like a graduation."

Amy leaned in closer to me. "Actually, it's more of a *Yay, I'm still alive!* celebration."

"Amy," Mom said. Too soon to joke about it then.

"They don't have those either," I said, trying not to smile. "Come on, Mom—it's not the right time to celebrate. The Director's dead." Rapunzel and Hansel too, but I didn't think I could say their names without getting emotional. "The wounded haven't healed. We haven't started rebuilding from the attack a few days ago . . ."

Mom interrupted me. "Rory, there will *always* be more reasons not to have a party than to have a party, but you've got to let me do it. We can call it whatever you want. It can be a *Welcome to high school* party. It can be a *Your mom is proud of you* party, but it's happening."

I should have listened to Amy. There *was* no talking Mom out of it. "So what time does it start?"

Mom smiled. "You've got an hour."

Amy plunked a couple boxes on the table, wrapped with paper patterned with balloons. "You can change into these."

I stared at them. "The Snow Queen is gone, and the first thing you decide to do in the new safe world outside is . . . go shopping?"

"Don't be silly," Mom said. "These are birthday presents."

"You didn't get a chance to open them on your actual birthday," Amy said. "Then your mom was afraid that you might wear them during a mission. You're *hard* on your clothes, Rory. I don't know if you ever noticed, but you will. In high school, you're going to start doing your own laundry."

We might have been discussing math homework. It was just so ridiculous and so nice, talking to my family about being a Character. All the tension was gone. It was part of *my* life, so they had made it part of theirs.

I should have known that it would turn into a mini makeover some-how. The gifts turned out to be a pretty green blouse embroidered with ferns or feathers or something, plus some shorts nicer than any of the others I owned.

I almost protested when I saw the green flats that Mom was determined to lend me. They *always* fell off when I had to go slay dragons or battle trolls. Then I remembered I was done fighting for the day. I might even be done fighting for the whole month. No one was trying to kill me. I took the shoes and slipped them on. I only added one thing to the outfit—Rapunzel's light. It was too big to wear as a necklace, so I looped its chain around my belt, like I'd seen Rapunzel do a couple times. It rested where my sword used to be, and the weight was kind of reassuring.

"*Now* you look like you're going into high school," Amy said. "Well, except for that glass thing."

I rolled my eyes. "I won't wear it to school." I would put the vial in my carryall. I just didn't want to leave it for a while. It had saved my life that morning.

"Hopefully your face will heal before then too." Mom gasped. "It's only three and a half weeks away! We still need to enroll you someplace."

"I've already looked up a few places in San Fran," Amy said.

"Do we want to stay in San Fran?" Mom replied.

"Well," I said, deciding to go for broke on the hint-dropping front, "if we're living here, then I can really go to school *anywhere*."

Amy shot me a look that clearly said, *Please be joking.*

Mom just looked thoughtful. "Maybe. This place has grown on me, but if we stay, we're getting a real house and moving it into the courtyard. This apartment is way too small."

"If we *stay*?" repeated Amy, horrified.

"Your dad's moving back to L.A. tomorrow morning," Mom said, which probably explained why she was even *considering* moving here. It didn't matter. Now that my family knew about the Door Trek system, I could visit him, Dani, and Brie whenever I wanted. "He wants to shorten his commute. Apparently, some studios are showing interest in his screenplay."

Mom gave me a list of invitees who hadn't confirmed yet, and she practically pushed me out the door in a way that screamed, *I need to prepare a surprise*. I bet it was cake. I sincerely hoped it was coming from the Table of Never Ending Instant Refills, not from Mom's oven.

As soon as I left, I pocketed the list. It could wait. I needed to check on something.

The library door was locked, and I was trying to decide whether or not to track down a dragon scale and try Chase's unlocking spell when the bolt slid back.

Busted. I'd been hoping Rumpelstiltskin was still in the infirmary.

But Chase opened the door. He grinned. "I thought it was you. Great minds. Come on in. I hear you're having a party."

"My *mom* is having a party. I'm just one of the people she invited." I stepped inside. "How did you get in?"

"You'll never guess." Chase headed back to the only table in the room. The current volume was open on top of it.

"Um. Back door? Fey unlocking spell?"

"Not even close." Chase lifted up a key. "Sarah Thumb made Rumpelstiltskin give it to me. She said being deputy Director didn't have many perks, but letting Characters read their own Tales was one of them."

The illustration on the open page showed Ripper tearing after a winged fighter, but it was Chase's face in the picture that trapped my attention. He didn't look smug or even afraid. He looked calculating and determined—he'd always been that way, but very few people noticed. "You wanted to read yours?" I asked.

"I thought Dad had convinced them to pretend I was a 'Giant-Killer' after finding out about the pillars," Chase admitted. "Having a Sleeping Beauty for a son has been kind of embarrassing for him."

I remembered the meeting when Jack had stared anywhere but at Chase. "Jerk," I said pointedly.

"Yeah, yeah, I know." Chase's eyes dropped to my collarbone. During my nap, the mark from the Snow Queen's hand had darkened to purple, and the outlines of her fingertips peeked out above the neckline of my blouse. "The Snow Queen's good-bye gift. She had to try to kill you one more time."

I remembered Solange's face the second before she pushed me.

"Maybe. But if she hadn't pushed me, I would have been right there when the magic ripped her apart." No matter what she'd been trying to do, I owed my life to Solange. That was a weird thought.

I wasn't sorry she was dead. I was sorry she had lived like she had—first lonely, then with so much cruelty.

We were silent for a moment. I toyed with the glass vial. Chase folded and unfolded his arms. He felt awkward, being alone with me. For some reason, that made me feel less nervous.

He nodded at the book. "Yours is the one after mine."

I flipped the pages, and there it was: "The Tale of Rory Landon." I turned to the end.

I read:

> She returned to her home with a vaguely unfinished feeling.
> Other Characters were lucky. They ended their quests with
> their happily-ever-afters outlined in neat terms, backed up by
> dozens of similar Tales that had come before. She had a life she
> hadn't expected to keep. Making the most of it seemed like an

*overwhelming responsibility. She had gone from having too few
choices to having too many.*

Then she remembered what a friend had once told her: So
much of a Character's life is unknown. One's Tale only sheds
light on one small part.

Perhaps everyone experienced this unfinished feeling.

Perhaps she wasn't alone in it.

Well, of *course* I didn't know what to do now. No one was here to
tell me what I should focus on next.

"Do you want my opinion?" Chase asked when he was sure I had
finished reading. "Or should I pretend I haven't read it?"

"I *miss* Rapunzel," I said. I missed Hansel too, but not like I missed
her. She'd told me I could do good things with my life. Unfortunately,
Solange thought she was doing good things too.

"I know you do." Chase did know. He missed Cal as much as I
missed Rapunzel. That almost made it worse, because suddenly, I
realized I would miss her forever like Chase would miss Cal forever.
The giant chasm her death had carved out of me would never seal
up, not completely.

"I don't know who I am now that my Tale is over," I whispered.
"Solange must have felt the same way, and what *she* decided to do
was become the Snow Queen." My voice rose. I hadn't told anyone else, not even Rapunzel. But she'd known. She put it in her letter. "I want some of the same things she wanted. I want to make a
difference. I want to help people like Matilda and the Living Stone
Dwarves. I don't want them to be stuck in the forgotten corners of
the world either."

"Rory, let's tone down the freak-out for a second," Chase said,
sounding way more calm than he had any right to be. I'd basically
told him I was turning into a villain. "What you're saying is that you

have some stuff in common with the Snow Queen—the stuff that people actually *liked* about her. That doesn't mean you'll become her. Lena and I wouldn't let that happen."

That was true. Solange had lost her Triumvirate. I still had Chase and Lena. We could be more like Maerwynne, Rikard, and Madame Benne. We could change things together.

"You have to stop me if I become more like her," I told Chase fiercely. "You have to *promise*."

"I'll swear a Binding Oath," Chase said, and my panic subsided. He'd taken down the pillars. He could stop me too, if I became terrible enough. "But not right now. We'll fight over the wording for hours, and we have a party to go to in a few minutes."

Oh right. The party.

Slowly, I started to feel better.

I had so much more than Solange had ever had. I had so many more people who cared about me. Maybe it was enough to change history.

"You know," Chase said, studying me, "I think I like your new outfit."

My cheeks betrayed me. They blushed so red that I was sure my face was stuck that way.

"What? I can't tell you you're pretty?" Chase said.

I couldn't exactly *help* what my face did. "I just wasn't expecting it!"

Chase groaned. "Look we don't have to, like, date or anything right away if you don't want to."

"Date." Our first kiss woke him up from a sleeping enchantment that was supposed to last a hundred years, and he wanted to *date*?

"Yeah. Go to see a movie and other human stuff," Chase said. "I've always wanted to try that."

"Do I get to pick the movie or do you?" I asked.

"There's more than one?" Chase said. Oh wow, he really *was* clueless. "But don't change the subject. We have to get a few things straight."

"Uh-oh," I said, and Chase looked pleased that I was joking around again. "I sense some oversharing in my near future."

"Yep. Unavoidable. First . . ." He held up one finger. "If I *ever* say a last-minute quest is too dangerous, assume that I'm lying."

"Got it." This wasn't so bad.

"If I ever say the Director is—was—right, assume that I'm lying."

It was still hard to believe that she was gone. "No problem."

Chase sucked in a big breath, leaning against the table, his arms folded. "And if I ever start acting like I prefer another girl over you, assume that I'm under an enchantment, and *figure out a way to break it*."

I froze.

I was not brave the way Chase was brave. My own feelings scared me sometimes. I was afraid to even acknowledge them, let alone talk about them.

"Rory?" Chase said, terribly resigned, like he expected me to run from the room or something.

But for him, I would learn.

"Okay," I said, and he looked relieved. If I were a tiny bit braver, I would have added, *Same here*, but I wasn't quite there yet. "Was it a lie? What you told me about your dream?"

Chase's shoulders hunched, defensive. "We need to get that straight too. Top of the list of stuff I don't ever lie about? My dreams."

He would tell me the rest of it if I asked him. I knew he would, but I didn't.

I hadn't always noticed how handsome he was, but I did now. His hair had been bleached blonder by the sun, his eyebrows startlingly pale on his tan face, his eyes green and magnetic. He was even hand-some when he was scowling at me.

I wanted to step closer, stand on tiptoe, and kiss him. Maybe after-ward, I would say, *There. I claim number three.* Chase would argue with me. He would say it was just the second one, and we would probably bicker for a while about it. Then Chase would offer to fix it. *I'll make it three*, he might say, an instant before he kissed me again.

Just imagining made me *giddy*.

Too bad I was a coward.

I thought we had so much time, Chase had said during our duel in the training courts, and now we actually did.

It would be a shame to waste more time waiting, though. "How about tomorrow? We'll see if we can agree on a movie we both like." He would need to figure out how they worked anyway, if a studio *did* pick up Dad's screenplay.

Then it finally showed up—the happiness I'd thought his Tale would give him.

Chase's smile blazed brighter than the Snow Queen's heart. I could get used to putting it there.

A little while later, we went to the party. I never did get around to finding the people on Mom's list, but once we stepped out of the library's front door, they were all in the courtyard anyway.

For a moment, they didn't notice us, and I could see them all.

The spearmen in our grade looked like they were reenacting Chase's fight with the pillars for the others. Conner played Chase, directing his brothers and Paul around. He wouldn't make a half-bad Itari fighter if he ever decided to take up the sword. Kelly and Priya had front-row seats. Darcy and Bryan looked on with identically skeptical expressions, like they didn't believe a word of it. Melodie glanced between them and the workshop door, like she was worry-ing about an experiment-in-progress. Ben was barely watching. He kept glancing at the girl beside him. She hopped with excitement, and her crazy braids bounced around her shoulders.

"Whoa," Chase said. "Chatty made it. Lena must have figured out how to give her legs."

The dwarves had come too. Forrel, Ima, and Iggy watched, smiling lost, distracted smiles. They must have been thinking of Hadriane.

Sarah Thumb circled around the Tree's trunk, like she was hoping someone would invite her to stay. Amy's eyes followed her, and I could tell she was debating about whether or not to take pity on the Thumbelina character. Dad and Brie sat on a blanket, Dani between them, kicking her feet and squealing in the way she did when she was excited. Mom was holding the cake that was supposed to be a surprise. The layers were a little lopsided, definitely homemade, but at least she hadn't written any embarrassing messages in the icing.

We started across the grass. Chase and I were holding hands. I wasn't sure which one of us had grabbed the other, but I wasn't letting go and neither was he.

The others would spot us in a second.

"Whatever you do," I said, grasping Rapunzel's vial to keep it from banging against my knee, "don't eat Mom's cake."

"Don't worry. Lena warned me already."

"You can't tell her, though. She'll just get embarrassed and say she was distracted. Oh, and she's trying to figure out what high school she's going to send me to."

"That's a good question. What high school *are* we going to, Rory?"

I was used to my heart pounding when I was scared. I wasn't used to it thumping so hard when I was happy. It knocked against my ribs like it wanted to fly out and visit the people I loved most in the world. "So you're coming too?"

Chase pretended to be hurt that I'd even asked. "Just make sure they have nice long breaks. King Mattanair has invited me back to the Unseelie court to give more Itari lessons. I'm supposed to teach Fael," he added gleefully. "I'm thinking about making them run laps during the workshops *without using their wings.*"

Wow. As my teacher, Chase had gone pretty easy on me.

At least one Fey hadn't gone back to Atlantis yet. Lady Aspenwind knelt at the base of the Tree, her head bent close to a girl with extra-long braids. "What's your mom doing with Lena?"

"Teaching her Fey magic, looks like," Chase said. "Humans can't replicate it, though—not even sorceresses . . ."

Lena was the first to spot us. "Rory! Look!"

She placed her golden hands on the Tree's scorched trunk. The tree shuddered, its leaves rustling, and then a few more blackened branches dropped off and rolled through the grass. Partygoers sprinted away to avoid them. Brie snatched Dani up and hollered that they should watch out for the baby, even though the branches hadn't fallen anywhere near them.

Lena wasn't done. New limbs sprouted out from the trunk, dipping low to the ground and then up to the sky, like the Tree was stretching out its arms. Leaves unfurled and red flowers bloomed between them, even though I'd never seen anything but green grow on the Tree before.

"The flowers were my idea!" Lena said. Lady Aspenwind clapped her hands, delighted, and that got the rest of the partygoers cheering.

"I guess she figured it out," Chase said, sounding impressed. "God, a Character who can do Fey magic. What's next?"

I didn't know. I didn't need to. Whatever came next, we would figure it out, and we would do it together.

ACKNOWLEDGMENTS

While I was drafting this manuscript, I dubbed it a "beast" and referred to it like that often during the revision process—sometimes affectionately, usually with fatigue-driven despair. Fortunately, with the help of wonderfully supportive people, the beast was tamed and turned into an actual book.

Julia Maguire, you proved yourself to be the most patient editor in the world. I'm sorry that I missed so many deadlines, and thank you for letting me take the time I needed to mesh all the story threads into a coherent plot. Catherine Laudone, you are a rock star for stepping in at the eleventh hour to see this book to completion. You went above and beyond the editorial line of duty; thank you for helping me make *Of Enemies and Endings* as perfect as it could possibly be. Chloë and Cory, this cover is MY FAVORITE! Thank you both, and thank you to everyone at S&S BFYR for putting this series into the world.

Jo—oh agent, my agent—you were my captain through the whole Ever Afters journey, and your vision, enthusiasm, and savvy have guided me since the day you first called me to tell me how much you'd loved EAS. You are the actual best, and I'm so happy to work with you. Jaida, master scheduler, keen proofreader, and marketing idea machine: This was the first time I ever had to promote one book while still working on the next one, and I literally could *not* have managed it without you keeping me on track. Danielle, Kathleen, Jess, Jackie, Suzie, Pouya, Dave, and Mackenzie, your support of the Ever Afters means the world to me—I love being part of the marvelous New Leaf gang.

Certain people in my life became the guardians of my sanity: Mom, you have given me unconditional support and encouragement through this project and many others (you are definitely NOT like Rory's mom). Dad, you always help me look past the deadline and gain career perspective. I love you guys. Angela, you always remind me that I have a life as well as a dream, and when I was stressing madly, all the puppygrams from you and Hunny lifted my spirits. Megan, you're the best roommate for a writer under deadline: you make sure I'm fed and you make sure I remember how many other times I've managed to finish a revision.

I'm also deeply grateful to individuals who have shared the Ever Afters with others: Amanda, supreme Wordbender, your unbridled enthusiasm and epic vlogs have helped me more than you know. Brenda, lady of Log Cabin Literary, you have a sixth sense for reaching out when I'm feeling down. Special thanks also go to Kevin of Middle Grade Mafia, Sherri of Park Road Books, Jenny and Earl of Green Bean Books, Mel of University Book Store, Katie of the Book Bin, and Jill of Fiction Addiction as well as the people behind Middle Grade Mafioso, From the Mixed up Files, and Green Bean Teen Queen.

Most of all though, I need to thank the readers. (I wish I could name every person who reached out to me, but sadly, the book is running out of pages!) On my website, many of you listed incredible guesses about Book 4's title, and I have to especially thank Rachel of Random Rants by Rcubed, who coined "Of Enemies and Endings." It makes me really happy that you named the book,

Rachel, and it makes me even happier that so many of you pitched in to help me brainstorm. It gives me an excuse to brag about how awesome you are. The transition from being a private writer to a public author can sometimes be difficult, but you guys make it worth all the long hours. By far, my favorite part of the past few years has been getting to know such passionate, funny, clever, and nurturing readers. Thank you guys for being amazing. I couldn't have finished this series without you.